A TEXT BOOK OF

ADVANCED DATA STRUCTURES

FOR

SEMESTER – II

SECOND YEAR DEGREE COURSE IN COMPUTER ENGINEERING

Strictly According to New Revised Credit System Syllabus
of Savitribai Phule Pune University
(w.e.f June 2016)

NITIN N. SAKHARE

M. E. (Comp. Networks)
Assistant Professor,
Computer Engineering Deptt.,
Vishwakarma Institute of Inform. Technology
Kondhwa (Bk.), PUNE

SWATI D. SHIRKE

M.E. (Computer)
Assistant Professor,
Computer Engineering Deptt.,
NBN Sinhgad School of Engineering
Ambegoan, PUNE

ABHIJEET P. TIKAR

M. E. (IT)
Assistant Professor,
Computer Engineering Deptt.,
Sinhgad Tech. Edu. Society's
NBN Sinhgad School of Engineering
Ambegaon., PUNE

SHITAL M. AHER

M.E. (Computer)
Assistant Professor,
Computer Engineering Deptt.,
AJMVPS's Shri. Chhatrapati Shivaji Maharaj
College of Engineering
Nepti, AHMEDNAGER.

NIRALI PRAKASHAN
ADVANCEMENT OF KNOWLEDGE

N3578

ADVANCED DATA STRUCTURES (SE COMPUTER)　　ISBN 978-93-86353-22-1

First Edition　　　:　　January 2017

©　　　　　　　:　　Authors

Published By :　　　　　　　Polyplate

NIRALI PRAKASHAN

Abhyudaya Pragati, 1312, Shivaji Nagar,
Off J.M. Road, Pune – 411005
Tel - (020) 25512336/37/39, Fax - (020) 25511379
Email : niralipune@pragationline.com

☞ **DISTRIBUTION CENTRES**

PUNE

Nirali Prakashan　　: 119, Budhwar Peth, Jogeshwari Mandir Lane, Pune 411002, Maharashtra
Tel : (020) 2445 2044, 66022708, Fax : (020) 2445 1538
Email : bookorder@pragationline.com, niralilocal@pragationline.com

Nirali Prakashan　　: S. No. 28/27, Dhyari, Near Pari Company, Pune 411041
Tel : (020) 24690204 Fax : (020) 24690316
Email : dhyari@pragationline.com, bookorder@pragationline.com

MUMBAI

Nirali Prakashan　　: 385, S.V.P. Road, Rasdhara Co-op. Hsg. Society Ltd.,
Girgaum, Mumbai 400004, Maharashtra
Tel : (022) 2385 6339 / 2386 9976, Fax : (022) 2386 9976
Email : niralimumbai@pragationline.com

☞ **DISTRIBUTION BRANCHES**

JALGAON

Nirali Prakashan　　: 34, V. V. Golani Market, Navi Peth, Jalgaon 425001,
Maharashtra, Tel : (0257) 222 0395, Mob : 94234 91860

KOLHAPUR

Nirali Prakashan　　: New Mahadvar Road, Kedar Plaza, 1st Floor Opp. IDBI Bank
Kolhapur 416 012, Maharashtra. Mob : 9850046155

NAGPUR

Pratibha Book Distributors : Above Maratha Mandir, Shop No. 3, First Floor,
Rani Jhanshi Square, Sitabuldi, Nagpur 440012, Maharashtra
Tel : (0712) 254 7129

DELHI

Nirali Prakashan　　: 4593/21, Basement, Aggarwal Lane 15, Ansari Road, Daryaganj
Near Times of India Building, New Delhi 110002
Mob : 08505972553

BENGALURU

Pragati Book House　　: House No. 1, Sanjeevappa Lane, Avenue Road Cross,
Opp. Rice Church, Bengaluru – 560002.
Tel : (080) 64513344, 64513355,Mob : 9880582331, 9845021552
Email:bharatsavla@yahoo.com

CHENNAI

Pragati Books　　: 9/1, Montieth Road, Behind Taas Mahal, Egmore,
Chennai 600008 Tamil Nadu, Tel : (044) 6518 3535,
Mob : 94440 01782 / 98450 21552 / 98805 82331,
Email : bharatsavla@yahoo.com

niralipune@pragationline.com | www.pragationline.com

Also find us on 🅕 www.facebook.com/niralibooks

Dedicated to…

" Our Beloved Parents"

…Authors

PREFACE

It gives us great pleasure in publishing this text book on "**Advanced Data Structures**" for the students of Second Year Degree Course in Computer Engineering. This book is strictly written according to **New Revised Credit System Syllabus** of Savitribai Phule Pune University (2015 Pattern).

As per the policy of the University, Engineering Syllabi is revised every five years. Last revision was in the year 2012. New revision is coming little earlier, as university has introduced **Online System of Examination** from year 2012.

As per the **New Credit System**, the **Online Examinations** Phase-I will be conducted based on First & Second Units and Phase II on Third & Fourth Units. The **Online** examinations will have objective types of questions with multiple choices. End Sem. Theory Examination will be based on all the six units and that will be conducted in traditional way and the Theory Course will have 4 credits.

It is our objective to keep the presentation systematic, consistent, intensive and clear presentation of concept through explanatory notes and figures. So we are sure that this book will cater for all your needs for this subject.

Main feature of this book is, **Complete Coverage** of the New Credit System Syllabus with large number of **Worked (Solved) Programs, Examples and Exercises.**

We have given Separate Book of Multiple Choice Questions (MCQ's) which will be very useful to the students especially for Online Examinations.

We take this opportunity to express our sincere thanks to Shri. Dineshbhai Furia, Shri. Jignesh Furia, Mrs. Nirali Verma and Shri. M. P. Munde and entire team of Nirali Prakashan namely Mrs. Deepali Lachake (Co-ordinator), who really have taken keen interest and untiring efforts in publishing this text.

The advice and suggestions of our esteemed readers to improve the text are most welcomed, and will be highly appreciated.

Pune   **Authors**

SYLLABUS

Unit I Trees   **(09 Hrs)**

Tree- basic terminology, General tree and its representation, representation using sequential and linked organization, Binary tree- properties, converting tree to binary tree, **Binary Tree Traversals-** inorder, preorder, post order, level wise -depth first and breadth first, Operations on binary tree. Binary Search Tree (BST), BST operations, Threaded binary tree- concepts, threading, insertion and deletion of nodes in in-order threaded binary tree, in order traversal of in-order threaded binary tree.

Case Study- Use of binary tree in expression tree-evaluation and Huffman's coding

Unit II Graphs   **(09 Hrs)**

Basic Concepts, Storage representation, Adjacency matrix, adjacency list, adjacency multi list, inverse adjacency list. Traversals-depth first and breadth first, Introduction to Greedy Strategy, Minimum spanning Tree, Greedy algorithms for computing minimum spanning tree- Prims and Kruskal Algorithms, Dikjtra's Single source shortest path, Topological ordering.

Case Study- Data structure used in Webgraph and Google map.

Unit III Hashing   **(09 Hrs)**

Hash Table- Concepts-hash table, hash function, bucket, collision, probe, synonym, overflow, open hashing, closed hashing, perfect hash function, load density, full table, load factor, rehashing, issues in hashing, hash functions- properties of good hash function, division, multiplication, extraction, mid-square, folding and universal, Collision resolution strategies- open addressing and chaining, Hash table overflow- open addressing and chaining, extendible hashing.

Dictionary- Dictionary as ADT, ordered dictionaries.

Skip List- representation, searching and operations- insertion, removal.

Unit IV Search Trees   **(09 Hrs)**

Symbol Table-Representation of Symbol Tables- Static tree table and Dynamic tree table, Introduction to Dynamic Programming, Weight balanced tree, Optimal Binary Search Tree (OBST), OBST as an example of Dynamic Programming, Height Balanced Tree- AVL tree.

Unit V Indexing and Multiway Trees   **(09 Hrs)**

Indexing and Multiway Trees- Indexing, indexing techniques, Types of search tree- Multiway search tree, B-Tree, B+Tree, Trie Tree, Splay Tree, Red-Black Tree, K-dimensional tree, AA tree. **Set-** Set ADT, realization of Set and operations.

Heap-Basic concepts, realization of heap and operations, Heap as a priority queue, heap sort

Unit VI File Organization   **(09 Hrs)**

Sequential file organization- concept and primitive operations, Direct Access

File- Concepts and Primitive operations, Indexed sequential file organization-concept, types of indices, structure of index sequential file, **Linked Organization-** multi list files, coral rings, inverted files and cellular partitions.

External Sort- Consequential processing and merging two lists, multiday merging- a k way merge algorithm.

CONTENTS

TREES

1.1 INTRODUCTION

Till now we have seen data structures such as arrays, linked lists, stacks, queues, etc. All these are linear data structures. The data is stored in sequential locations. In order to retrieve data, we have to traverse in sequence. For large amount of data this kind of access is not efficient because, time complexity of retrieval in such data structures will be poor, i.e. O(n).

If we arrange the data in hierarchical manner, we can have more than one successor of a data element as shown in Fig. 1.1.

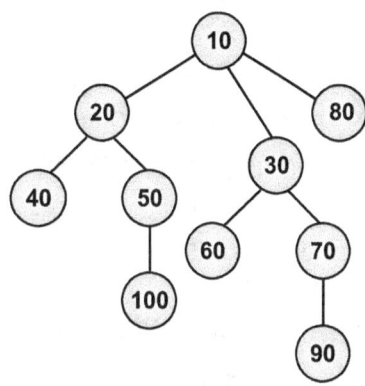

Fig. 1.1 : Tree

Such a structure is called tree. There are number of applications in computer science where we can use this data structure. A tree can be defined in several ways.

Definition 1 :

A tree (T) is a set of nodes. The set can be empty. If its nonempty set, consists of a specially designated node called root node and zero or more (sub) trees T_1, T_2, T_3, ..., T_n, each of whose roots are connected by a directed edge from the root of T.

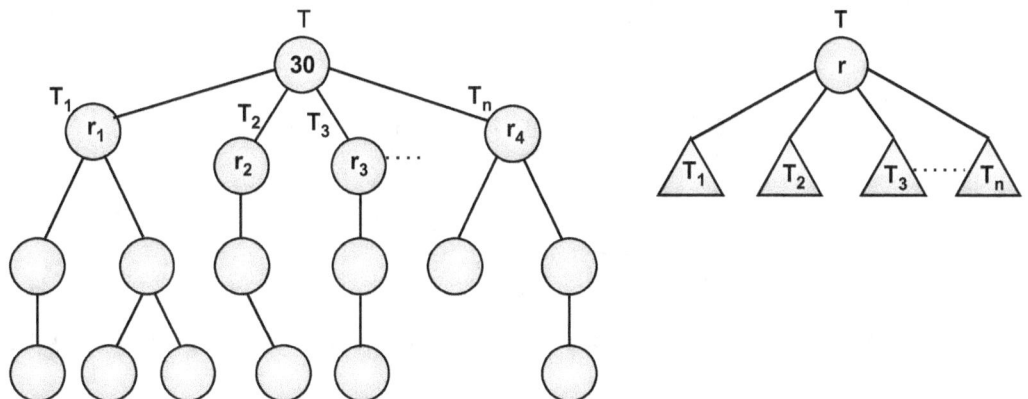

Fig. 1.2 : Tree definition

Definition 2 :

A tree consists of finite set of elements called nodes and a finite set of directed lines called branch edges that connect the nodes.

1.2 BASIC TERMINOLOGY

There are number of terms used with tree. Let us see the definition of each of them.

1. **Node :** It stands for item of information plus the branches to other items.
2. **Degree :** The total number of edges associated with a node is called degree of that node.
3. **Indegree :** The total number of edges converging a node is called indegree of the node. Root node will have indegree 0.
4. **Outdegree :** The total number of edges diverging from a node is called outdegree of the node.
5. **Leaf Node or Terminal Node :** The nodes that have outdegree zero are called leaf node or terminal node.
6. **Non-Terminals :** The nodes which have nonzero outdegree are called nonterminals.
7. **Children :** The root nodes of the sub-tree of a node are called children of that node, i.e., they are immediate successors of node.
8. **Parent Node :** If A is child of B then B is the parent node of A, i.e., it is immediate predecessor of a node.
9. **Siblings :** Children of the same parent are called siblings.
10. **Degree of a Tree :** It is maximum degree of a node in the tree.

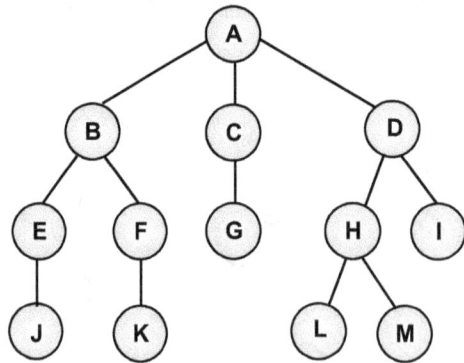

Fig. 1.3 : Tree

11. **Ancestor Nodes :** Ancestors of a node are all the nodes along the path from the root to that node.

12. Level of a Node : Root node of a tree is said to be at level 1. Its children will be at level 2. In general, the node at level l will have its children at level $l + 1$.

13. Height or Depth of Tree : It is the maximum level of any node in the tree.

14. Forest : It is a set of disjoint trees, i.e., these trees will not have common node amongst them. Let us draw a tree and represent these terms.

Observation :

1. Total degree of A $\Rightarrow$ 3

2. Indegree of H $\Rightarrow$ 1

3. Out-degree of H $\Rightarrow$ 2

4. Leaf nodes $\Rightarrow$ J, K, G, L, M, I

5. Non-terminal $\Rightarrow$ A, B, C, D, E, F, H

6. Children of B $\Rightarrow$ E, F

7. Parent node of J $\Rightarrow$ E

8. Siblings $\Rightarrow$ {B, C,D}, {E, F}, {H, I} {L, M}

9. Ancestors of J $\Rightarrow$ E, B, A

10. Degree of Tree $\Rightarrow$ 3

11. Level of H $\Rightarrow$ 3

12. Height of Tree $\Rightarrow$ 4

13. Forest : if we remove root A of the tree we get set of three trees which is a forest.

The tree can be represented in a linked list format, where each node in the tree will be as :

For a general tree there are no restrictions on the number of sub-trees. The data field will store the information. The link fields will store the addresses of children of the node. Now the question is how many link fields should be defined? It is going to depend on maximum number of branches a node can have. Hence, it is very difficult to create a general tree. Binary trees are used in most of the applications where the number of branches will be fixed to 2. Hence, we will restrict our study to binary trees.

1.3 GENERAL TREE

A general tree T is a finite set of one or more nodes such that there is one designated node r, called the root of T, and the remaining nodes are partitioned into $n \geq 0$ disjoint subsets $T_1, T_2, ..., T_n$, each of which is a tree, and whose roots $r_1, r_2, ..., r_n$, respectively, are children of r.

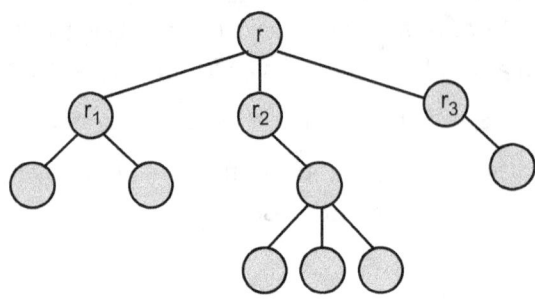

Fig. 1.4 : General tree

In general tree, parent node may have any number of children which are not there in case of binary tree. In binary tree every parent may have maximum two children. Refer the above diagram, where one parent node has three children associated with it.

Difference between Tree and Binary Search Tree :   **[May 10]**

Sr. No.	Tree	Binary Search Tree
1.	Parent node can have multiple Childs.	Parent can have maximum two Childs.
2.	Right and left child may have any value.	Child to the left of parent is having less value than parent while child to the right of parent is having greater value than the parent node.
3.	Can not used for sorting.	Used in sorting. Also it takes less time for it.
4.	Not used for storing data.	Used for storing data.
5.	Complex to implement.	Easy to implement.

Conversion of General Tree into Binary Tree   **[May 05]**

- In case of general tree each node can have outgoing degree n, where n>=0. While in case of binary tree maximum degree of any node is two.

- We are going to convert general tree into binary tree because representation of binary tree is easier than that of general tree.

Steps for converting general tree into binary :

Connect each node to its right siblings by drawing a line between them.

Disconnect each node from all except the leftmost child.

SOLVED EXAMPLES

Example 1.1 : Consider the following general tree and convert it into binary tree.

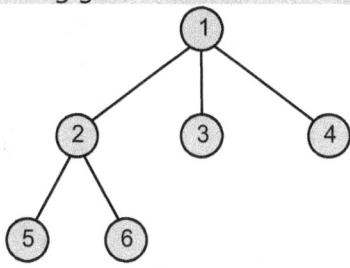

Fig. 1.5 (a)

Solution :

According to step 1, connect each node to its right sibling by drawing a line.

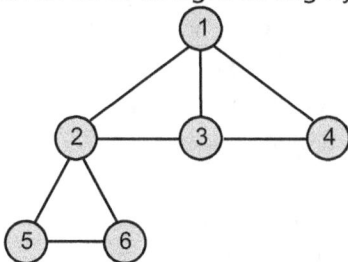

1.5 (b)

According to step 2, disconnect each node from all except the leftmost child.

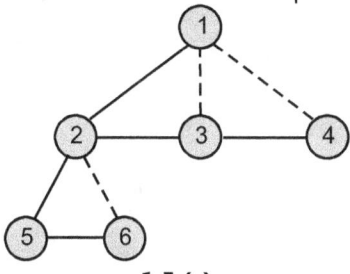

1.5 (c)

Remove the dotted lines and redraw the tree that will give us binary tree.

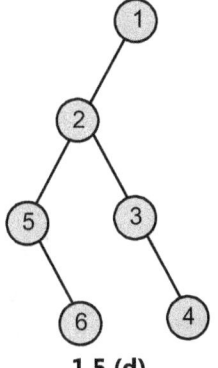

1.5 (d)

Example 1.2 : Consider the following general tree and convert it into binary tree.

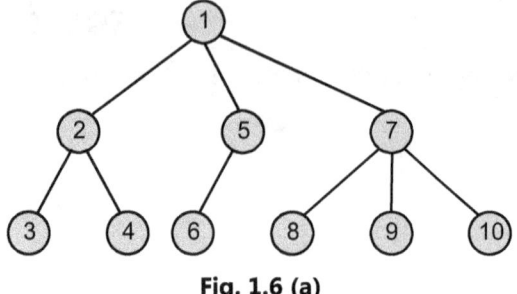

Fig. 1.6 (a)

Solution :

In the above tree, the leftmost child of 2 is 3 and the next right sibling of 3 is 4. The binary tree corresponding to this tree is obtained by connecting together all siblings of each node and deleting all links from a node to its children except for the link to its leftmost child. The binary tree obtained is drawn :

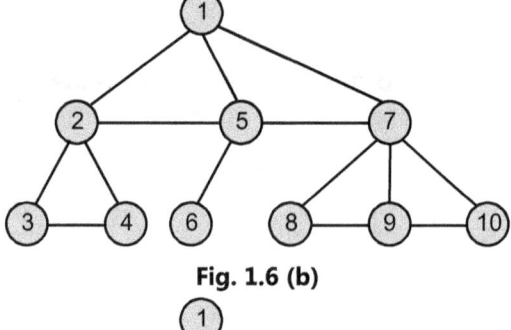

Fig. 1.6 (b)

Disconnect each node from all except the leftmost child, which is shown by dotted lines.

The resultant binary tree will be as follows :

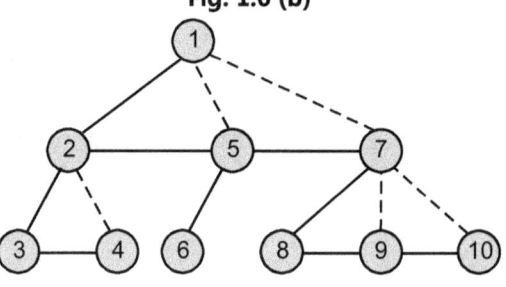

Fig. 1.6 (c)

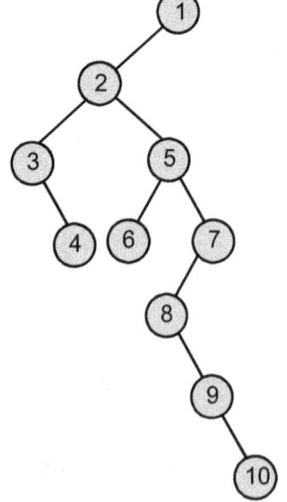

Fig. 1.6 (d)

Example 1.3 : Let us consider following tree :

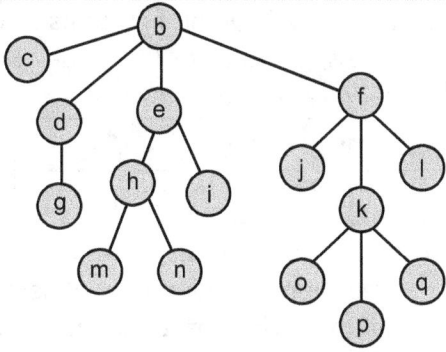

Fig. 1.7

The binary tree representation of above tree is drawn below :

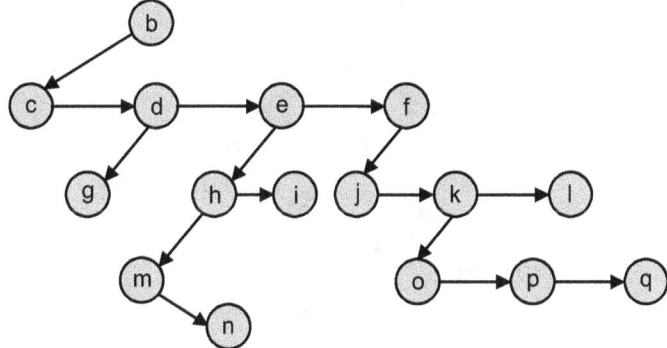

Fig. 1.8 (a)

The Fig. 1.8 (a) binary tree can be drawn in more familiar format as below :

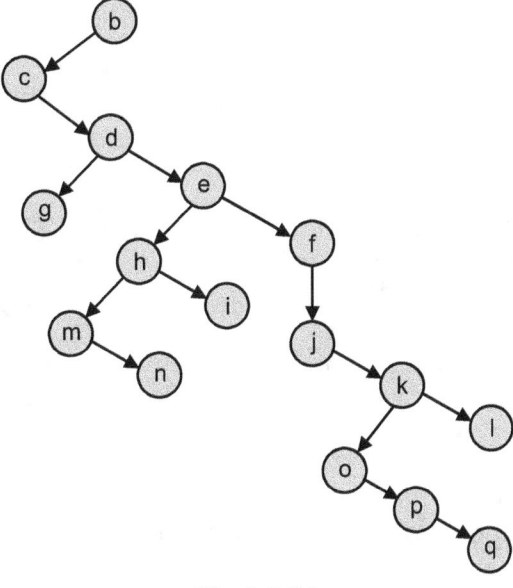

Fig. 1.8 (b)

Note that, if the order of children in a tree is not important (unordered tree), any of the children of a node could be its leftmost child and any of its siblings could be its next right siblings. For the sake of definiteness, we choose the nodes based upon how the tree is drawn. The node structure for binary tree can be shown as,

Data	
Child	Sibling

Also notice that the transformation from resultant binary tree to original n-ary tree is reversible. That is, given binary tree representation of a general tree, we can re-create the general tree. A left node is the leftmost child of its parent. A right node is a sibling of its parent. Do verify the same for following tree.

Example 1.4 : Convert the following tree into a binary tree.

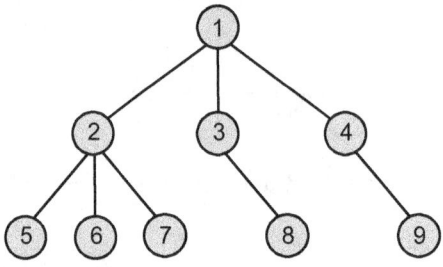

Fig. 1.9

Solution : Connect the siblings and drop all the pointers from the parent to the children except to the first child as in following Fig. 1.10.

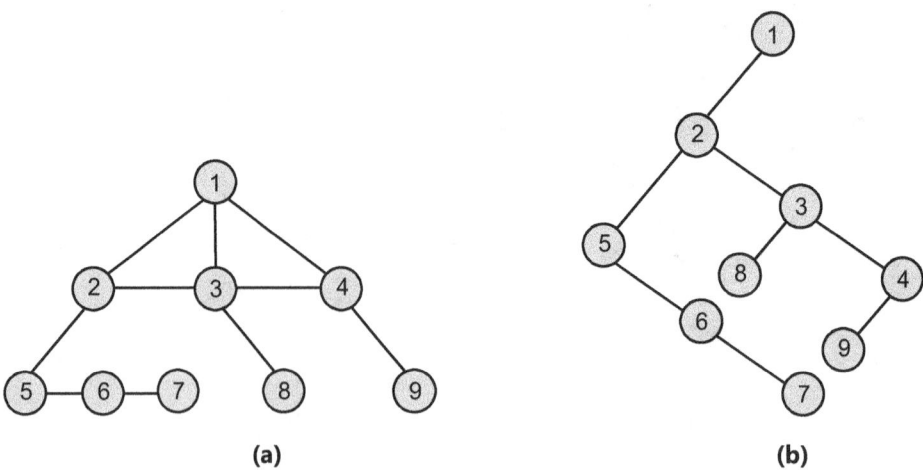

(a)   (b)

Fig. 1.10

While converting it child goes to left and sibling goes to right, so that the given tree is converted to the following tree.

Example 1.5 : Convert the Following tree to binary tree step by step.   **[Dec. 10]**

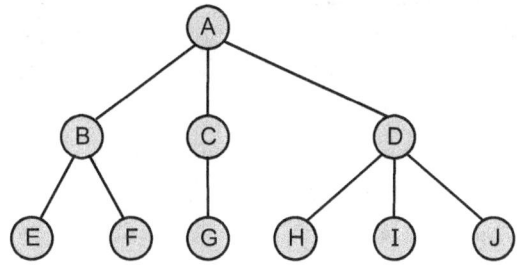

Fig. 1.11

Solution : Conversion into Binary tree :

Step 1 :

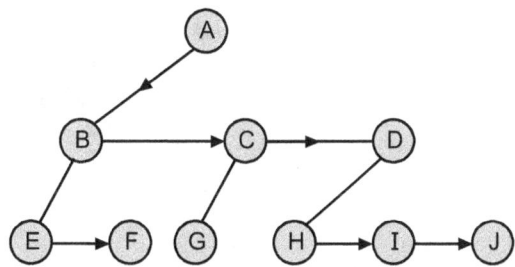

Fig. 1.12 (a) : Leftmost child right sibling representation of tree

Step 2 : Rotating Fig. 1.12 (a) by 45 degree.

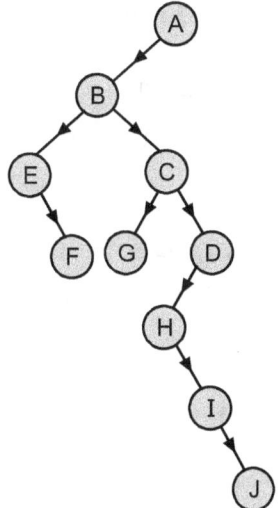

Fig. 1.12 (b) : Tree in Fig. 1.12 (a) is redrawn after rotating it by 45°

So, final binary tree is shown in Fig. 1.12 (b).

1.4 BINARY TREE

A binary tree is a tree in which no node has more than two sub-trees. It means any node can have at most two branches. i.e., there is no node with degree greater than two.

Definition :

A binary tree is a finite set of nodes which is either empty or consists of root and two disjoint binary trees called left sub-tree and right sub-tree.

Following are examples of binary trees.

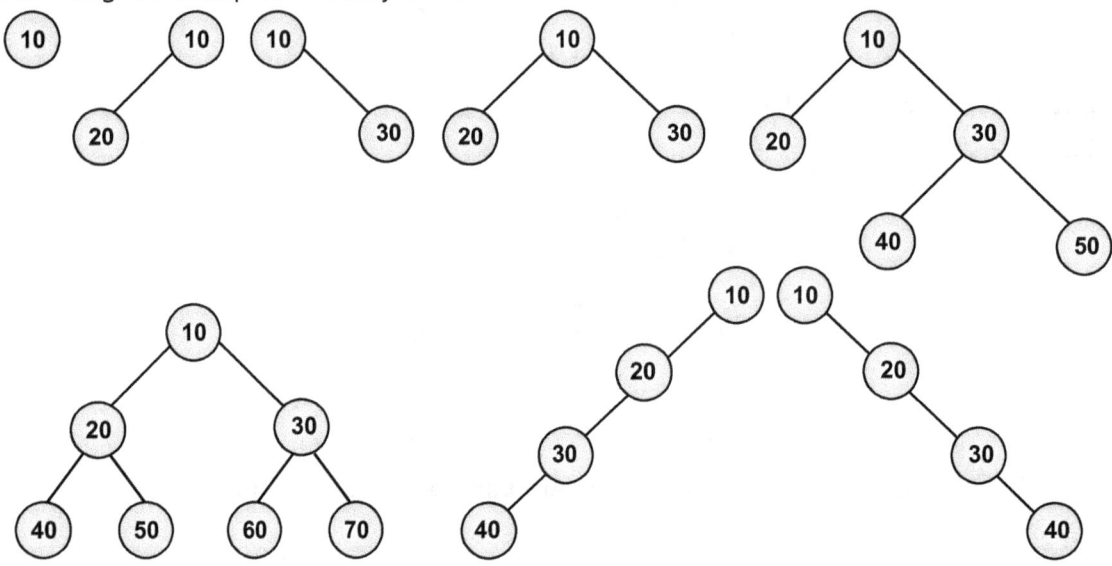

Fig. 1.13 : Binary trees

The maximum number of nodes in a binary tree will be 2^h-1 where h is height of the tree. The number of leaf nodes in the binary tree will be 2^{h-1}.

Depending on how the nodes are placed in the binary, we can have following types of binary tree.

1. Complete Binary Tree :

If the height of binary tree is h and there are 2^{h-1} node at least level, then it is complete binary tree. Following are examples of complete binary tree. It is also called full binary tree.

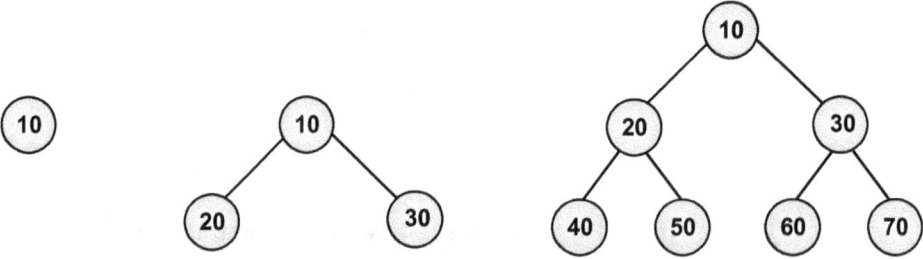

Fig. 1.14 : Complete binary tree

2. Almost Complete Binary Tree :

If the height of binary tree is h, then the binary tree is said to be almost complete if

- The leaf nodes are at level h or h − 1.
- There is no leaf node at level h − 2 i.e., at h − 2 level every node has two children.
- At level h the leaf nodes are as far to the left as possible.

Following are examples of almost complete binary tree.

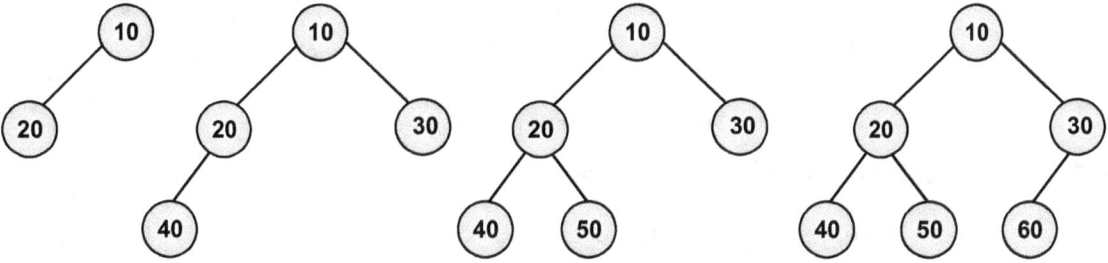

Fig. 1.15 : Almost complete binary tree

3. Left Skewed Binary Tree :

If the nodes in a binary tree have only left child it is called left skewed binary tree.

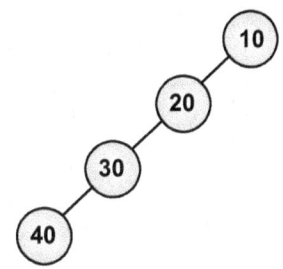

Fig. 1.16 : Left skewed binary tree

4. Right Skewed Binary Tree :

If the nodes in a binary tree have only right child it is called right skewed binary tree.

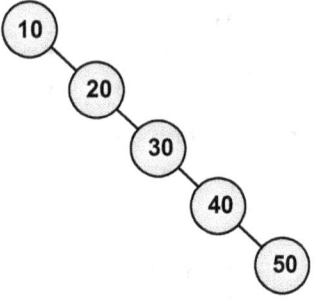

Fig. 1.17 : Right skewed binary tree

5. Strictly Binary Tree :

It is a binary tree in which each node will have either two children or no child. Examples of strictly binary tree are shown in Fig. 1.18.

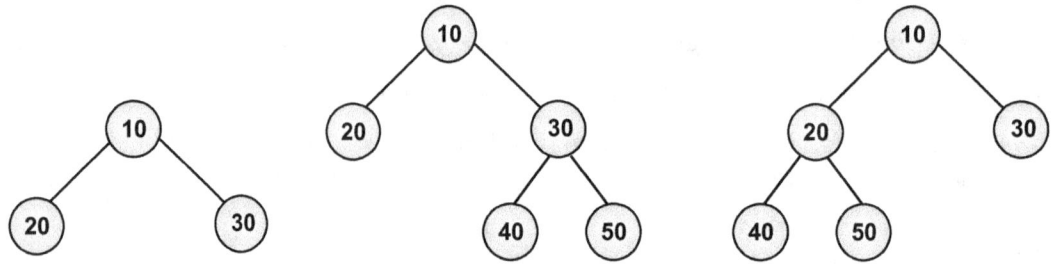

Fig. 1.18 : Strictly binary tree

1.4.1 Representation of Binary Tree

A binary tree can be represented using arrays or linked lists.

The array representation of binary tree is very simple for implementations where each node in binary tree will be stored in the array sequentially. Consider a complete binary tree as shown in Fig. 1.19.

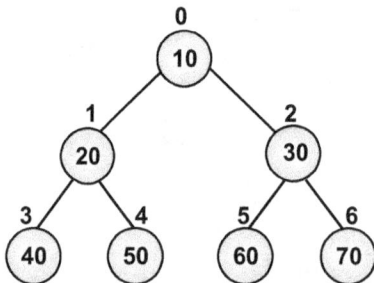

Fig. 1.19 : Binary tree

The nodes are designated by numbers which can be used as location number of the element in the array for example, the element 30 will be stored a[2]. The array representation of above binary tree is shown in Fig. 1.20.

a[0]	a[1]	a[2]	a[3]	a[4]	a[5]	a[6]
10	20	30	40	50	60	70

Fig. 1.20 : Array representation of binary tree in Fig. 1.19

Observe that if an element is at i^{th} location, its left child will be at $(2i+1)^{th}$ location and right child will be at $(2i+2)^{th}$ location.

But, if we have binary tree which is not complete binary tree or almost complete binary tree most of the space in the array will be unutilized. For example, if we have a binary tree as shown in Fig. 1.21.

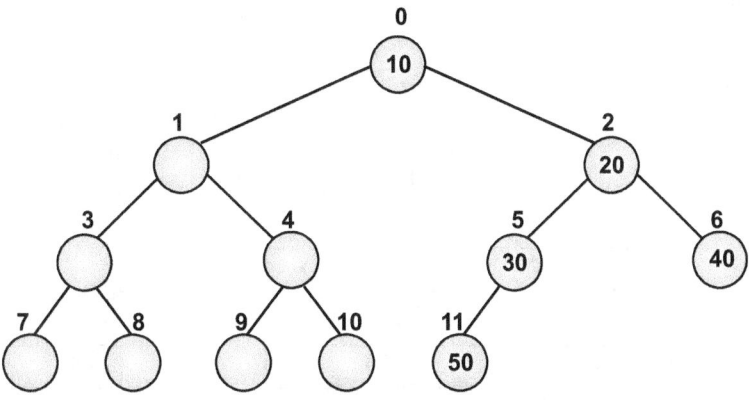

Fig. 1.21 : Binary tree

Its array representation will be

a[0]	a[1]	a[2]	a[3]	a[4]	a[5]	a[6]	a[7]	a[8]	a[9]	a[10]	a[2]	a[12]
10	–	20	–	–	30	40	–	–	–	–	50	–

Fig. 1.22 : Array representation of binary tree in Fig. 1.21

It is not only wastage of space, the insertion or deletion of node is also going to cause lot of movements. These problems can be eliminated using linked representation.

In linked representation, each node will be having three fields viz., data, lchild and rchild. The data field is information to be stored. It can be int, float, char, array or records. The two field's lchild and rchild will be pointers storing the addresses of left sub-tree and right sub-tree.

The node structure can be defined as

```
    typedef struct node
    {
        int data;
        struct node *lchild, *rchild;
    }   NODE;
```

The node will be as shown in Fig. 1.23.

Fig. 1.23 : Node in a binary tree

The binary tree in node structure will be as shown in Fig. 1.24.

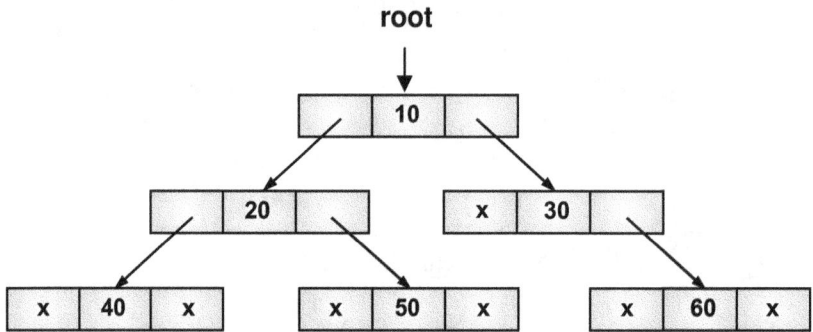

Fig. 1.24 : Linked list representation of binary tree

1.5 BINARY TREE TRAVERSAL (DFS)

- Traversing a binary tree is a process of visiting every node of a tree exactly once.
- The tree traversals can be done recursively as well as non recursively.
- Three main techniques are used for traversing the binary tree
  - ➢ Preorder (Root, Left, Right)
  - ➢ Inorder (Left, Root, Right)
  - ➢ Postorder (Left, Right, Root)

We will now discuss the various traversals of binary tree. Traversing the tree means visiting each node exactly once. Basically there are six ways to traverse a tree. For these traversals we will use some notations as follows :

L means move to the Left child.

R means move to the Right child.

D means the root/parent node.

Now, with this L, R, D one can have six different combinations of L, R, D nodes.

Such as LDR, LRD, DLR, DRL, RLD, RDL. But from computing point of view we will have three different ways of traversing a tree. Those three combinations will be LDR, DLR, LRD. Those are called Inorder, Preorder and Postorder traversals.

1. Inorder Traversal :

C-B-A-D-E is the inorder traversal i.e. first we go towards the leftmost node Le C so print that node C. Then go back to the node B and print B. Then root node A then move towards the right sub-tree print D and finally E. Thus we are following the tracing sequence of LDR. This type of traversal is called inorder traversal. The basic principal is to traverse left sub-tree then root and then the right sub-tree.

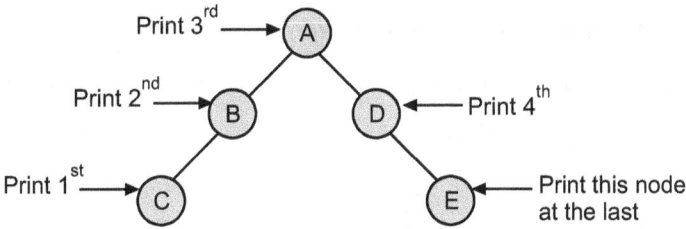

Fig. 1.25 (a) : Inorder traversal

2. Preorder Traversal :

A-B-C-D-E is the preorder traversal of the Fig. 1.25 (b). We are following DLR path. i.e. data at the root node will be printed first then we move on the left sub-tree and go on printing the data till we reach to the leftmost node. Print the data at that node and then move to the right subtree. Follow the same DLR principle at each sub-tree and go on printing the data accordingly.

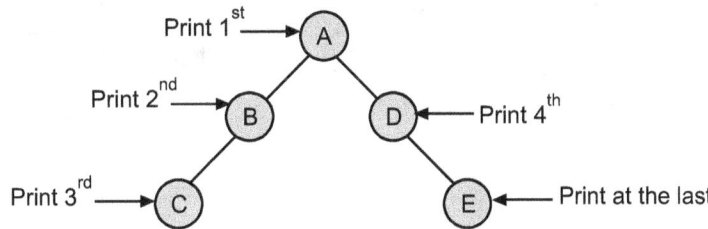

Fig. 1.25 (b) : Preorder traversal

3. Postorder Traversal :

From Fig. 1.25 (c) the postorder sequence is C-D-B-E-A. In the postorder traversal we are following the LRD principle i.e. move to the leftmost node check if right sub-tree is there or not if not then print the leftmost node, if right subtree is there move towards the rightmost node. The key idea here is thatat each sub-tree we are following the LRD principle and print the data accordingly.

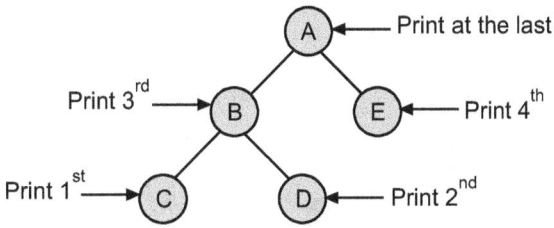

Fig. 1.25 (c) : Postorder traversal

1.5.1 Inorder Traversal (Non-Recursive)

Example 1.6 : Consider the following binary tree. It's inorder traversal is shown below.

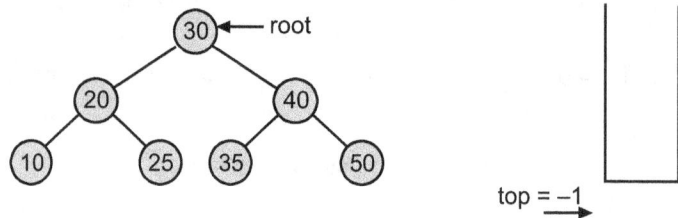

Fig. 1.26

*   move trav to extreme left and push the elements on the stack.

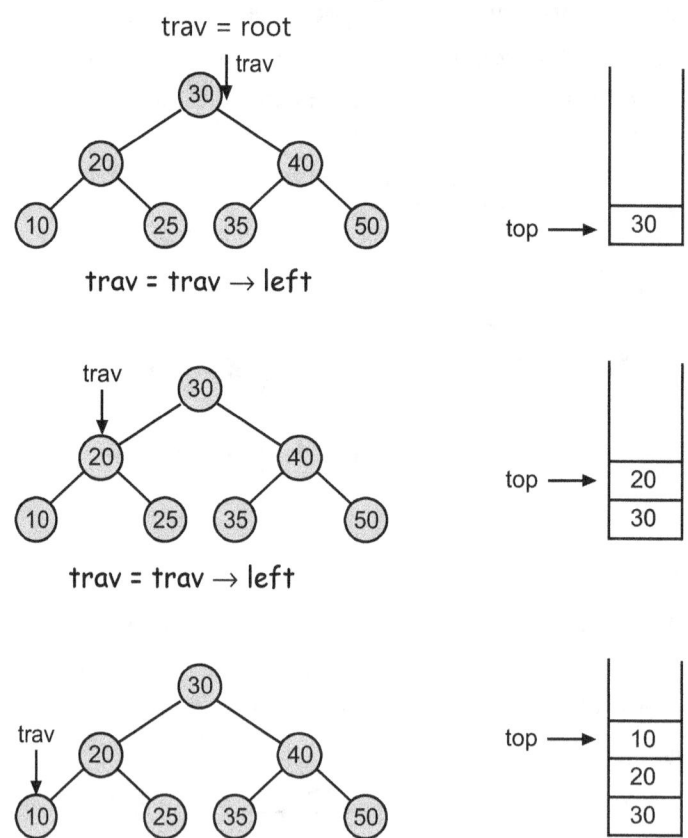

Now **trav → left==NULL**. So pop the element from the stack and print it.

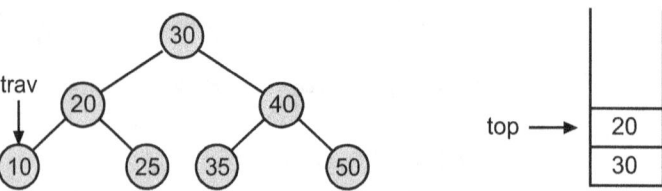

Output : 10

Now check for trav → right, if it is not NULL then move trav to right.

Here trav → right==NULL so pop one more element from the stack, print its data and move trav to its right.

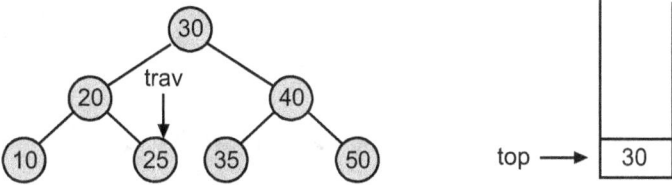

Output : 10, 20

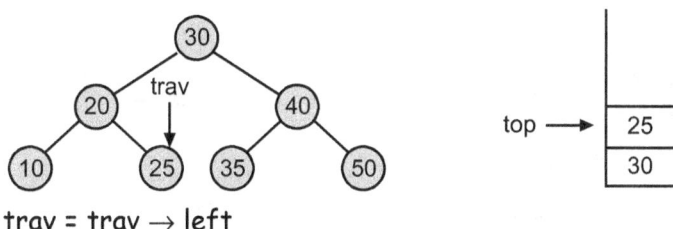

trav = trav → left

Output : 10, 20

As trav = NULL, pop the element from the stack top and print it.

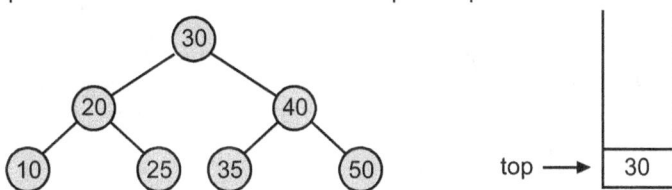

Output : 10, 20, 25

As there is no right child to 25, pop next element from the stack- top and print it.

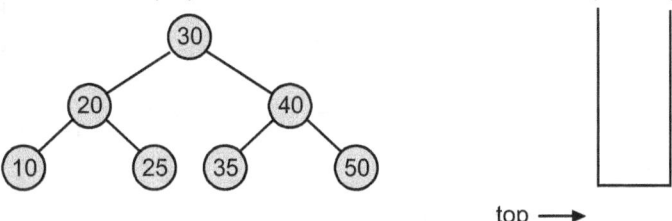

Output : 10, 20, 25, 30

Move trav to its right hand side. i.e. trav = trav → right and push 40 on stack.

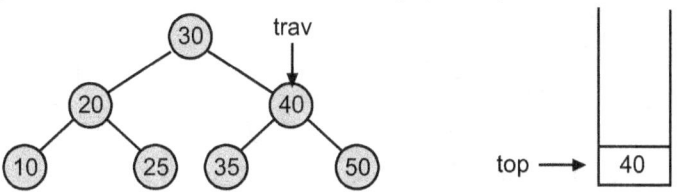

Move to left of trav (i.e. trav = trav → left).

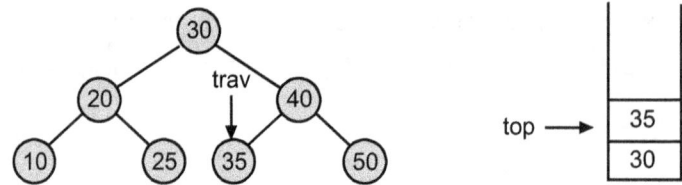

Output : 10, 20, 25, 30

Now trav → left==NULL. So pop the element from the stack top and print it.

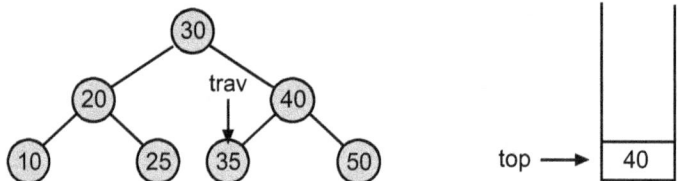

Output : 10, 20, 25, 30, 35

As trav → right==NULL so pop one more element from stack.

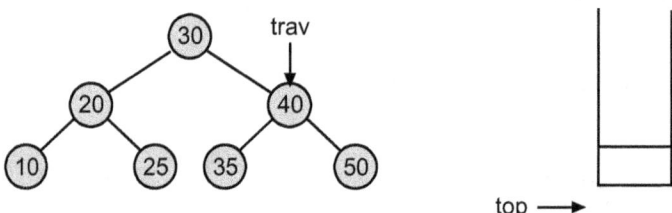

Output : 10, 20, 25, 30, 35, 40

Move trav to right i.e. trav=trav→right

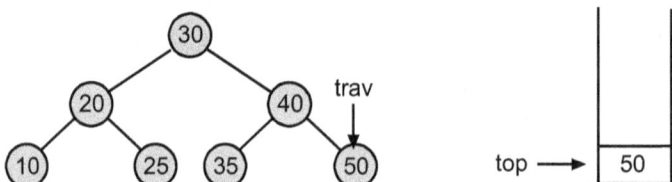

Output : 10, 20, 25, 30, 35, 40

Now there is no left child to 50 so pop it.

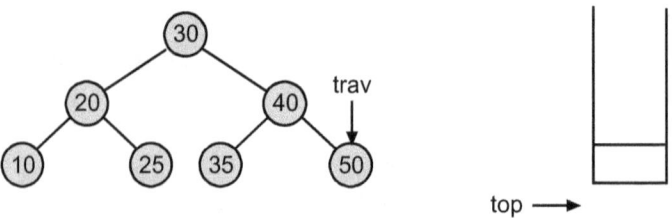

As there is no right child to 50, print it.

Output : 10, 20, 25, 30, 35, 40, 50

Now **stack is EMPTY** so **stop**.

Algorithm :

1) initially trav = root

2) if(trav==NULL&&top==-1) break; else goto step (3)

3) while(trav!=NULL)

   {

      push trav on the stack

      move trav to its left

   }

4) if(top!=-1)

   {

      pop the content from the stack.

      Assign the poped node to trav

      print trav → data

   }

5) if(trav→right!=NULL)

   {

      move trav to its right side

   }

   else

   {

      if (top!=-1)

      {

            pop the content from the stack & assign it to trav

            print trav → data

      }

            move trav to its right side

   }

      go to step (2)

}

Function for Inorder Traversal of Binary Tree :

```
void tree : :inorder(tree*root)
{
    tree*trav;
    tree*stack[20];
    int top=-1;
    trav=root;
    while(1)
    {
        if(trav==NULL&&top==-1)
        break;
        while(trav!=NULL)
        {
            top++;
            stack[top]=trav;
            trav=trav->left;
        }
        if(top!=-1)
        {
            trav=stack[top];
            top--;
            cout<<" "<<trav->data;
        }

        if(trav->right!=NULL)
        {
            trav=trav->right;
        }
        else
        {
```

```
        if(top!=-1)
        {
            trav=stack[top];
            top--;
            cout<<" "<<trav->data;
        }
            trav=trav->right;
    }
  }
}
```

Inorder Traversal (Recursive)

```
void inorder (node *root)
{
........... if (root!=NULL)
........... {
.................. inorder (root → left);
.................. cut << root → data;
.................. inorder (root → right);
........... }
}
```

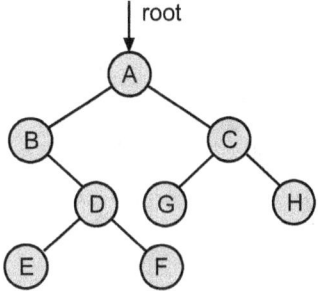

Fig. 1.27 : Binary tree

Working of Inorder Traversal :

Line No. :	Code	Root	T/F	Stack (Compiler)	Output
1	void inorder (node *root)	A	-	A	
3	if(root!=NULL)	A	T	A	
5	inorder (root → left)	A	-	A	
1	void inorder (node *root)	B	-	BA	
3	if(root!=NULL)	B	T	BA	
5	inorder (root → left)	B	-	BA	
1	void inorder (node *root)	NULL	-	NULL BA	

3	if (root!=NULL)	NULL	F	NULL BA	
8	}	NULL	F	NULL BA	
6	cout<<root → data	B	-	BA	B
7	inorder (root → right)	B	-	BA	B
1	void inorder (node *root)	D	-	DBA	B
3	if(root!=NULL)	D	T	DBA	B
5	inorder (root → left)	D	-	DBA	B
1	void inorder (node *root)	E	-	EDBA	B
3	if(root!=NULL)	E	-	EDBA	B
5	inorder(root → left)	E	-	EDBA	B
1	void inorder (node *root)	NULL	-	NULL EDBA	B
3	if (root!=NULL)	NULL	F	NULL EDBA	B
8	}	NULL	-	NULL EDBA	
6	cout << root → data	E	-	EDBA	BE
7	inorder (root → right)	E	-	EDBA	BE
1	void inorder (node *root)	NULL	-	NULL EDBA	BE
3	if (root!=NULL)	NULL	F	NULL EDBA	BE
8	}	NULL	-	NULL EDBA	BE
8	}	E	-	EDBA	BE
6	cout << root → data	D	-	DBA	BED
7	inorder (root → right)	D	-	DBA	BED
1	void inorder (node *root)	F	-	FDBA	BED
3	if (root!=NULL)	F	T	FDBA	BED
5	inorder (root → left)	F	-	FDBA	BED
1	void inorder (node *root)	NULL	-	NULL FDBA	BED
3	if (root!=NULL)	NULL	F	NULL FDBA	BED
8	}	NULL	F	NULL FDBA	BED
6	cout << root → data	F	-	FDBA	BEDF
7	inorder (root → right)	F	-	FDBA	BEDF

1	void inorder (node *root)	NULL	-	NULL FDBA	BEDF
3	if(root!=NULL)	NULL	F	NULL FDBA	BEDF
8	}	NULL	F	NULL FDBA	BEDF
8	}	F	-	FDBA	BEDF
8	}	D	-	DBA	BEDF
8	}	B	-	BA	BEDF
6	cout<<root→data	A	-	A	BEDFA
7	inorder (root → right)	A	-	A	BEDFA
1	void inorder (node *root)	C	-	CA	BEDFA
3	if (root!=NULL)	C	T	CA	BEDFA
5	inorder (root → left)	C	-	CA	BEDFA
1	void inorder (node *root)	G	-	GCA	BEDFA
3	if (root!=NULL)	G	T	GCA	BEDFA
5	inorder (root → left)	G	-	GCA	BEDFA
1	void inorder (node *root)	NULL	-	NULL GCA	BEDFA
3	if (root!=NULL)	NULL	F	NULL GCA	BEDFA
8	}	NULL	-	NULL GCA	BEDFA
6	cout <<root → data	G	-	GCA	BEDFAG
7	inorder (root → right)	G	-	GCA	BEDFAG
1	void inorder (node *root)	NULL	-	NULL GCA	BEDFAG
3	if (root!=NULL)	NULL	F	NULL GCA	BEDFAG
8	}	NULL	F	NULL GCA	BEDFAG
8	}	G	-	GCA	BEDFAG
6	cout << root → data	C	-	CA	BEDFAGC
7	inorder (root → right)	C	-	CA	BEDFAGC
1	void inorder (node *root)	H	-	HCA	BEDFAGC
3	if(root!=NULL)	H	T	HCA	BEDFAGC
5	inorder (root → left)	H	-	HCA	BEDFAGC
1	void inorder (node *root)	NULL	-	NULL HCA	BEDFAGC

3	if (root!=NULL)	NULL	F	NULL HCA	BEDFAGC
8	}	NULL	-	NULL HCA	BEDFAGC
6	cout<<root→data	H	-	HCA	BEDFAGCH
7	inorder (root→right)	H	-	HCA	BEDFAGCH
1	void inorder (node *root)	NULL	-	NULL HCA	BEDFAGCH
3	if(root!=NULL)	NULL	F	NULL HCA	BEDFAGCH
8	}	NULL	-	NULL HCA	BEDFAGCH
8	}	H	-	HCA	BEDFAGCH
8	}	C	-	CA	BEDFAGCH
8	}	A	-	A	BEDFAGCH
9	}	A	-	empty	BEDFAGCH

1.5.2 Preorder Traversal (Non Recursive)

Example 1.7 : Consider the following tree and give its preorder traversal.

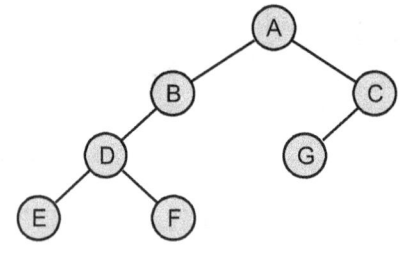

Fig. 1.28

Expected Output :

A B   D   E   F   C   G

1. Initially trav = root

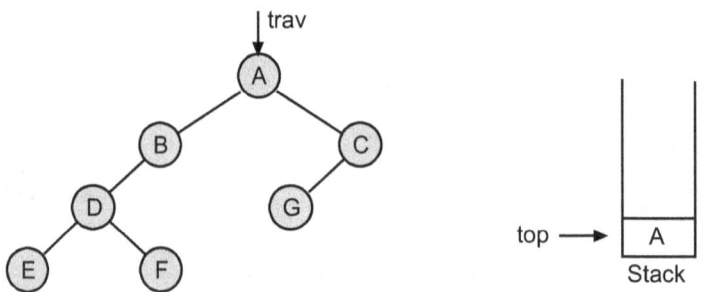

Output : A

2.

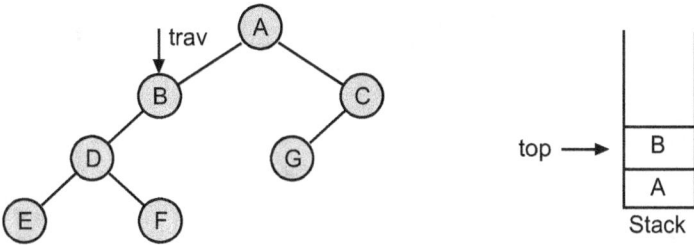

Output : A B

3.

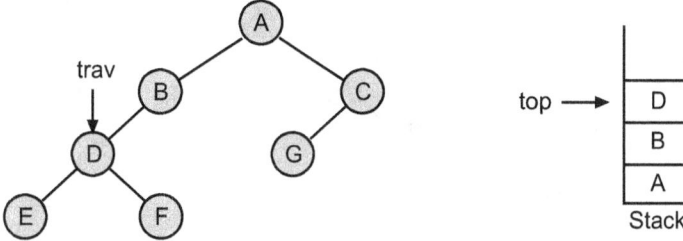

Output : A B D

4.

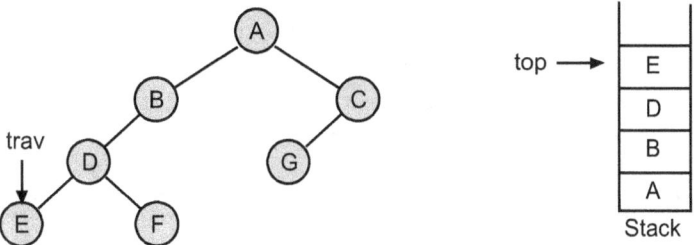

Output : A B D E

5.

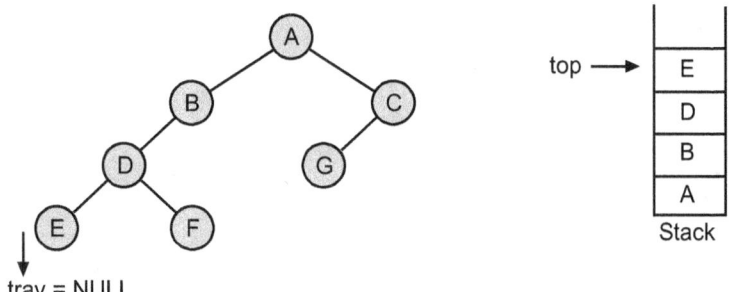

Output : A B D E

6. Pop the content from stack top

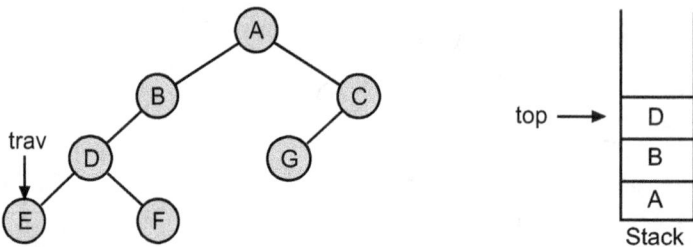

Output : A B D E

7. Move trav to right side

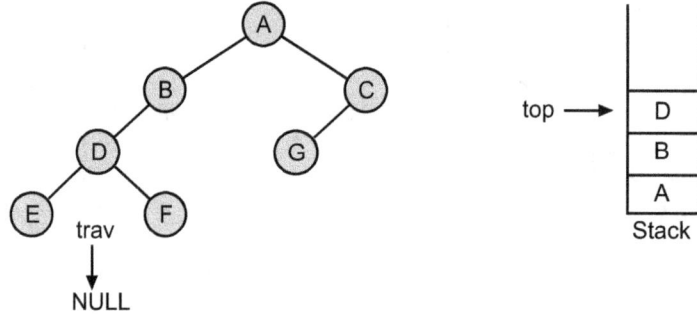

Output : A B D E

8. Pop the content from stack. Trav will point to D.

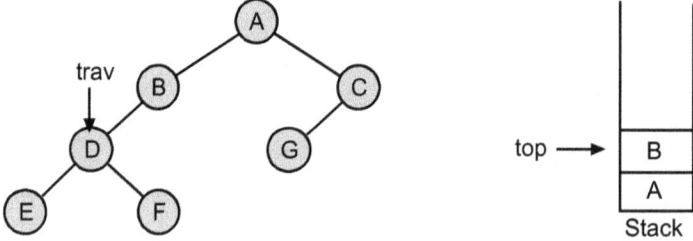

Output : A B D E

9. Move trav to its right side

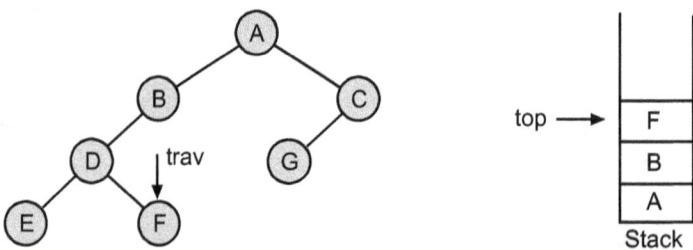

Output : A B D E F

10. Move trav to its left side

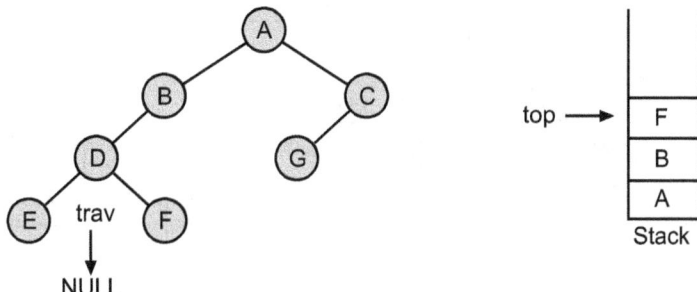

Output : A B D E F

11. Pop the content from stack top. So trav will point to F.

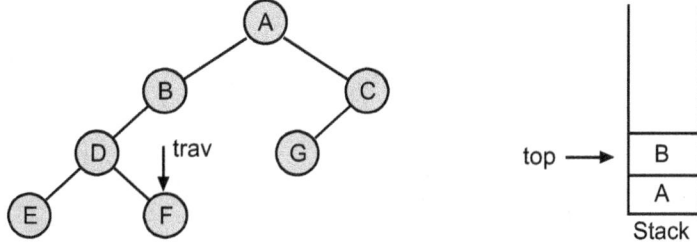

Output : A B D E F

12. Move trav to its right side.

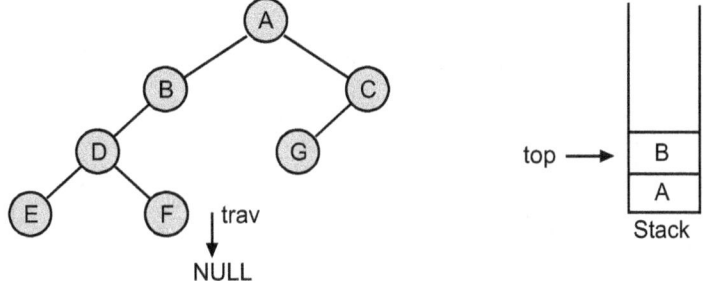

Output : A B D E F

13. Pop the content from stack. So trav will point to B.

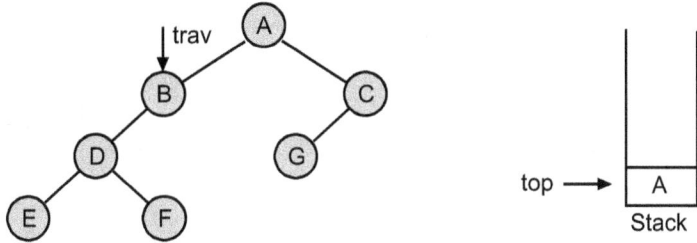

Output : A B D E F

14. Move trav to its right side

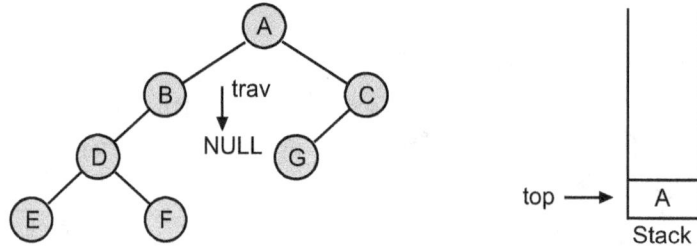

Output : A B D E F

15. Pop the content from stack. Trav will point to A.

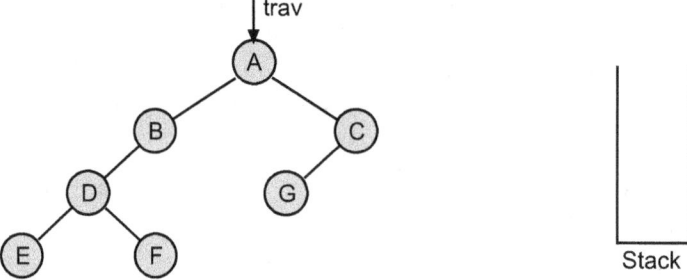

Output : A B D E F

16. Move trav to its right side

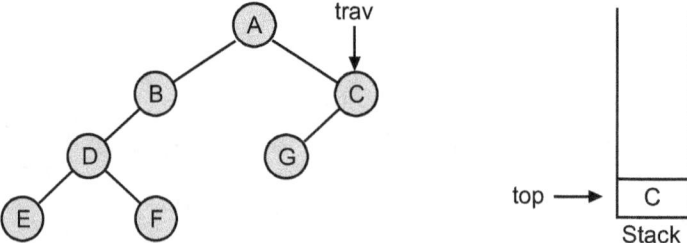

Output : A B D E F C

17. Move trav to its left side.

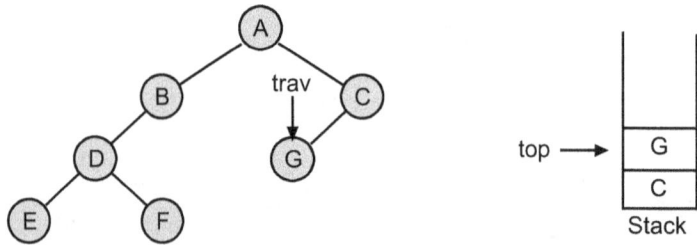

Output : A B D E F C G

18. Move trav to its left side

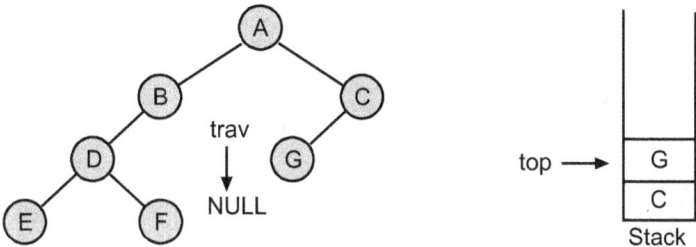

Output : A B D E F C G

19. Pop the content from the stack. Now trav will point to G.

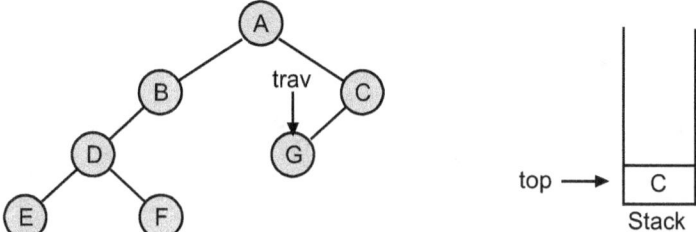

Output : A B D E F C G

20. Move to right side of trav.

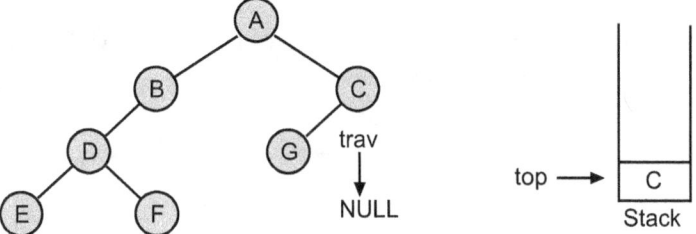

Output : A B D E F C G

21. Pop the content from the stack. Now trav will point to C.

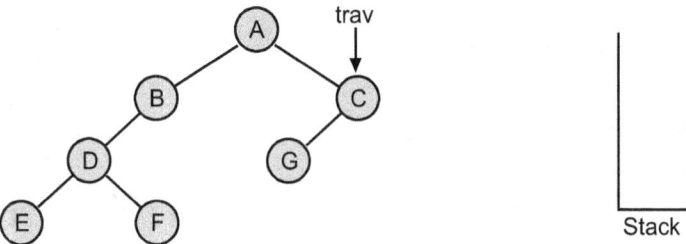

Output : A B D E F C G

22. Move to right side of trav

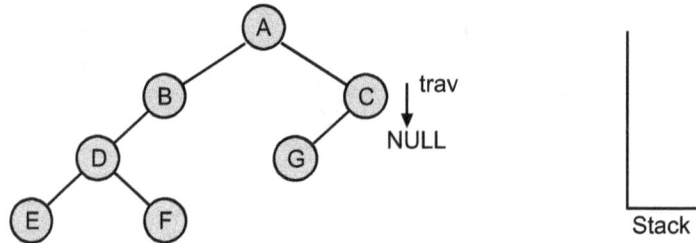

Output : A B D E F C G

23. Pop the content from the stack. Here stack is empty.

   So stop.

Algorithm :

1. trav=root;
2. while(trav!=NULL)

   {

        print trav → data

        push trav on stock top

        go to left hand side of trav

   }

   Above while loop moves trav pointer to its left side till it becomes NULL. While moving trav to left side, it is printing the data of trav and also pushing the trav on the stack top.

3. if(top==-1)

   {

        break;

   }

   if top==-1, then come out of the loop

4. while (top!=-1)

   {

        pop the content from the stack. Assign the poped content to trav, move trav to its right side.

        while(trav!=NULL)

```
        {
            print data of trav
            push trav on stack top
            move trav to its left side
        }
    }
    go to step (2)
```

Function for Preorder Traversal of Binary Tree :

```
void tree : :preorder(tree*root)
{
    int top=-1;
    tree*stack[40],*trav;

    trav=root;

    while(1)
    {
        while(trav!=NULL)
        {
            cout<<" "<<trav->data;
            top++;
            stack[top]=trav;
            trav=trav->left;
        }
        while(top!=-1)
        {
            trav=stack[top];
            top--;
            trav=trav->right;
```

```
        while(trav!=NULL)
        {
            cout<<" "<<trav->data;
            top++;
            stack[top]=trav;
            trav=trav->left;
        }
    }
    if(top==-1)
    {
        break;
    }
    }
}
```

Preorder Traversal (Recursive) :

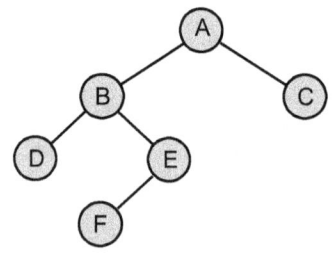

Fig. 1.29

Expected Output : A B D E F C

Algorithm/Source Code

```
    void preorder (tree *root)
    {
        if(root!=NULL)
        {
            cout << "\n" <<root→data;   /* visit the root node */
            preorder (root→left);  /* preorder traversal of left subtree */
            preorder(root→right);  /* preorder traversal of right subtree */
        }
    }
```

Working of Preorder Traversal :

Line No :	Input to Function	Code	Compilers Stack	Output
1	root = A	preorder (note *root)	A	
3	root = A	if(root!=NULL) ⟹ True	A	
5	root = A	cout<<root→data	A	A
6	root = A	preorder(root→left)	B A	A
1	root = B	preorder (note *root)	B A	A
3	root = B	if(root!=NULL) ⟹ True	B A	A
5	root = B	cout<<root→data	B A	A B
6	root = B	preorder(root→left)	D B A	A B
1	root = D	preorder (note *root)	D B A	A B
3	root = D	if(root!=NULL) ⟹ True	D B A	A B
5	root = D	cout<<root→data	D B A	A B D
6	root = D	preorder(root→left)	NULL D B A	A B D
1	root = NULL	preorder (note *root)	NULL D B A	A B D
3	root = NULL	if(root!=NULL) ⟹ False	D B A	A B D
7	root = D	preorder(root→right)	NULL D B A	A B D
1	root = NULL	preorder (note *root)	NULL D B A	A B D
3	root = NULL	if(root!=NULL) ⟹ False	D B A	A B D
7	root = B	preorder(root→right)	E B A	A B D
1	root = E	preorder (node *root)	E B A	A B D
3	root = E	if(root!=NULL) ⟹ True	E B A	A B D
5	root = E	cout<<root→data	E B A	A B D E
6	root = E	preorder(root→left)	F E B A	A B D E

1	root = F	preorder (node *root)	F E B A	A B D E
3	root = F	if(root!=NULL) ⇒ True	F E B A	A B D E
5	root = F	cout<<root→data	F E B A	A B D E F
6	root = F	preorder(root→left)	NULL F E B A	A B D E F
1	root = NULL	preorder (node *root)	NULL F E B A	A B D E F
3	root = NULL	if(root!=NULL) ⇒ False	F E B A	A B D E F
7	root = F	preorder(root→right)	NULL F E B A	A B D E F
1	root = NULL	preorder (node *root)	NULL F E B A	A B D E F
3	root = NULL	if(root!=NULL) ⇒ False	F E B A	A B D E F
7	root = E	preorder(root→right)	NULL E B A	A B D E F
1	root = NULL	preorder (node *root)	NULL E B A	A B D E F
3	root = NULL	if(root!=NULL) ⇒ False	E B A	A B D E F
7	root = A	preorder(root→right)	C A	A B D E F
1	root = C	preorder (node *root)	C A	A B D E F
3	root = C	if(root!=NULL) ⇒ True	C A	A B D E F
5	root = C	cout<<root→data	C A	A B D E F C
6	root = C	preorder(root→left)	NULL C A	A B D E F C
1	root = NULL	preorder (node *root)	NULL C A	A B D E F C
3	root = NULL	if(root!=NULL) ⇒ False	C A	A B D E F C
7	root = C	preorder(root→right)	NULL C A	A B D E F C
1	root = NULL	preorder (node *root)	NULL C A	A B D E F C
3	root = NULL	if(root!=NULL) ⇒ False	C A	A B D E F C
8	root = A		A	A B D E F C
9	-		empty	A B D E F C

1.5.3 Postorder Traversal (Non recursive)

Postorder Traversal :

Example 1.8 : Consider the following binary tree. It's postorder traversal is shown below :

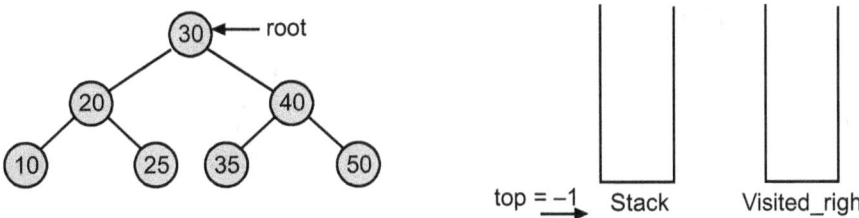

Fig. 1.30

1.   trav = root

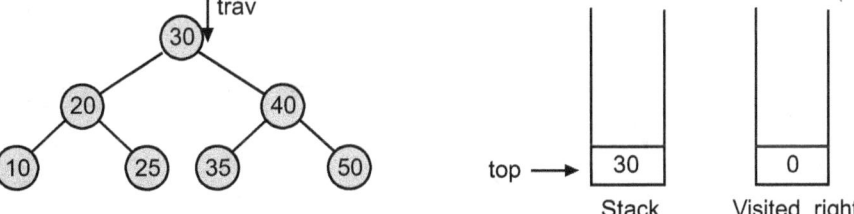

trav = trav → left

2.

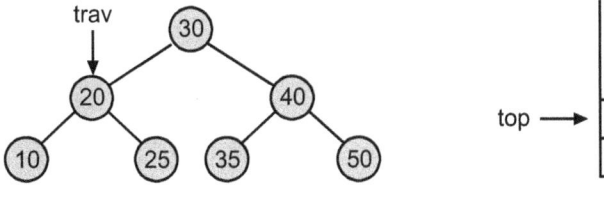

trav = trav → left

3.

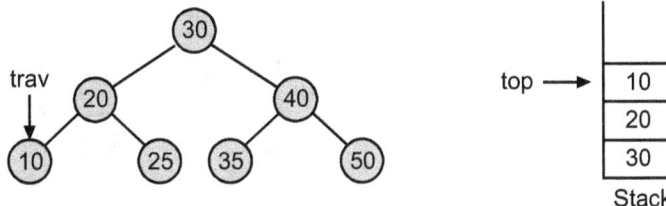

trav = trav → left

4. Now trav will be NULL

So, trav = stack [top];

flag = visited_right [top];

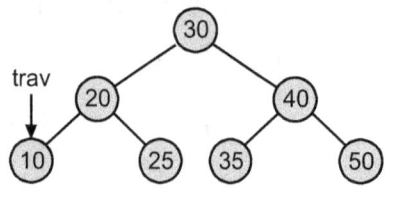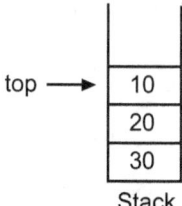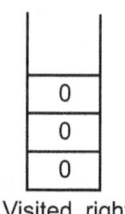

∴ flag = 0

5. Move trav to its right as flag ==0.

Here trav will be NULL, while moving trav to its right side make the corresponding visited_right flag as 1.

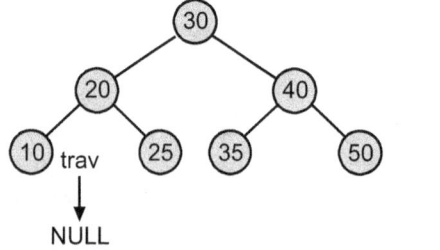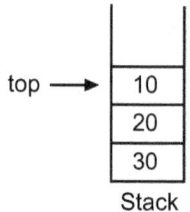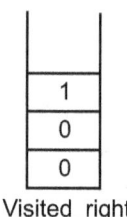

6. As trav == NULL pop the content from stack and visited_right.

trav = stack [top];

flag = visited_right [top];

Here flag = 1

∴ print the content of trav as flag is 1.

∴ Output = 10

Say top --; pop the content from stack.

i.e. trav = stack [top] and flag = visited_right [top]

7.

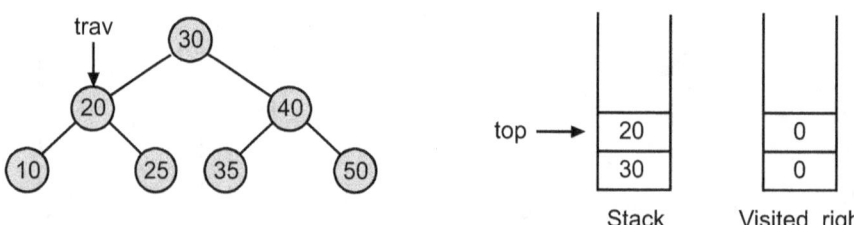

Here flag is equal to 0.

So make visited_right [top] = 1 and move trave to its right side.

8.

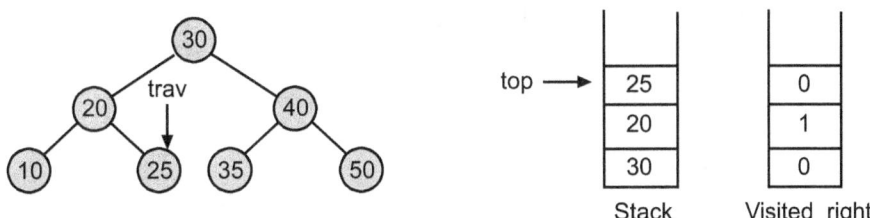

9. Move trav to its left. (trav = trav → left)

Now trav will become NULL.

As trav becomes NULL, say

trav = stack [top];

flag = visited_right [top];

So trav will point to 25 and flag will become 0.

as flag == 0, make visited_right [top] = 1 and move trav to it's right.

Here trav will become NULL.

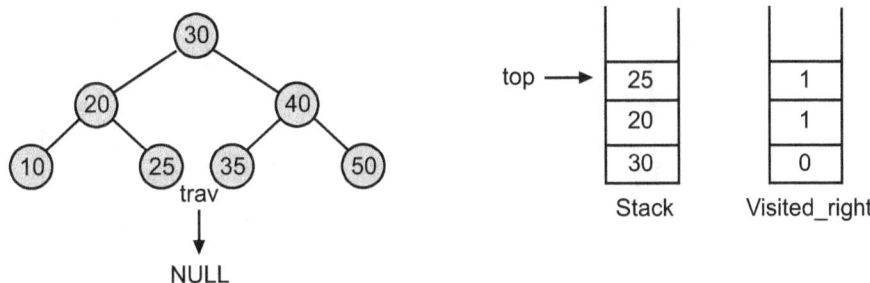

NULL

10. As trav is NULL, say trav = stack [top] and flag = visited_right [top].

Here flag becomes equal to 1. So print the value of trav.

∴   Output = 10, 25

top = top – 1;

trav = stack [top];

∴   Now trav will point to 20.

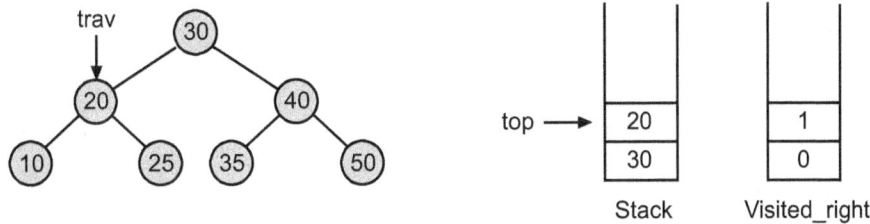

11. Flag = visited_right [top];
    so flag becomes 1. print the content of trav
    ∴   Output = 10, 25, 20
        top = top – 1;
        trav = stack [top];
        so trav will point to 30.
        flag = visited_right [top]
        so flag will become 0.
        As flag == 0, make visited_right [top]=1 and move trav to its right side.

12.

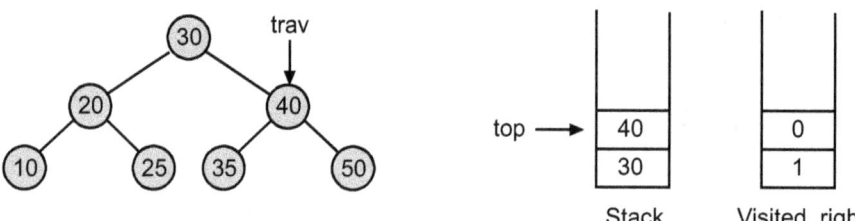

13. Now move trav to its left side till it becomes NULL. push the content on the stack [top]
    and make visited_right [top] as 0.

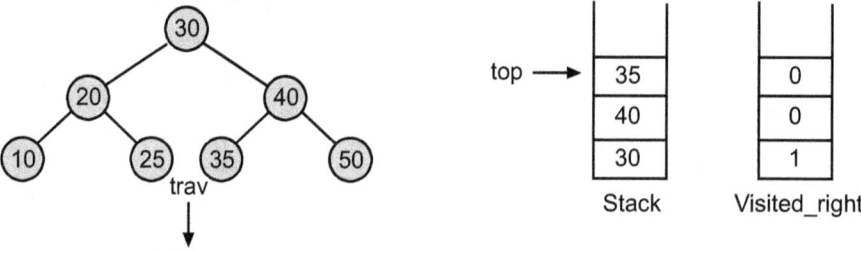

14. As trav becomes NULL,
    make trav = stack [top]; and
    flag = visited_right [top];
    Now trav will point to 35 and flag will be 0. As flag is 0, make visited_right [top] = 1 and
    move trav to its right side (right side of 35).

15.

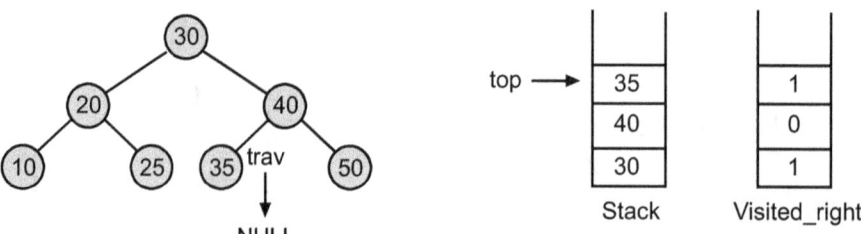

    Now trav is NULL.

16. Trav = stack [top];

    flag = visited_right [top];

    so trav will point to 35 and flag will be 1. print 35 as flag is 1.

    ∴ Output : 10, 25, 20, 35

    top = top – 1;

17. Trav = stack [top];

    flag = visited_right [top];

    Here trav will point to 40 and flag will be 0.

18. Move trav to its right and make its corresponding visited_right flag as 1.

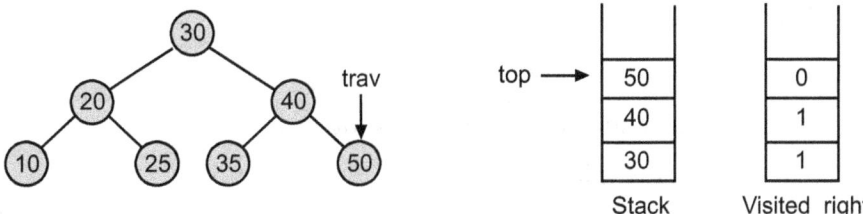

19. Move trav to its left side. It will become NULL.

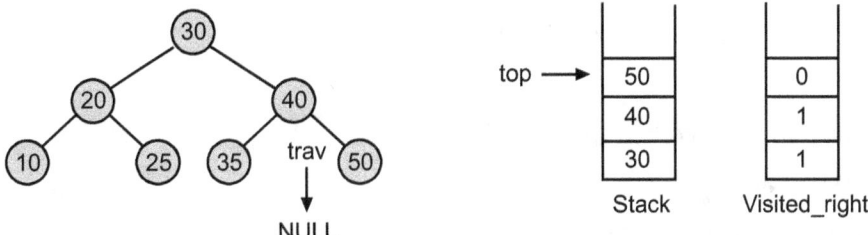

20. Trav = stack [top]

    flag = visited_right [top]

    trav will point to 50 and flag will be 0.

    As flag is 0, make visited_rigth [top] = 1 and move trav to its right side.

21. As trav is NULL

    trav = stack [top];

    flag = visited_right [top];

    Now trav will point to 50 and flag will be 1. So print value of trav

    Output : 10, 25, 20, 35, 50

    top = top-1;

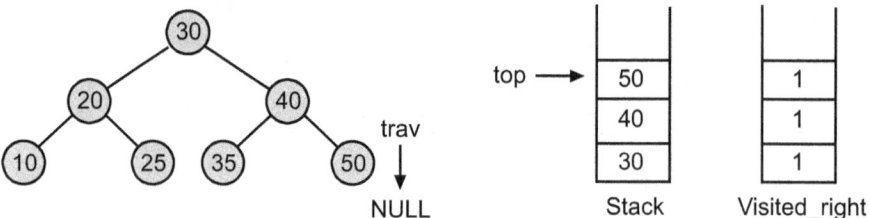

22. trav = stack [top];

flag = visited_right [top];

Now trav will point to 40 and flag will be 1. So print value of trav

Output : 10, 25, 20, 35, 50, 40

top = top – 1;

23. Trav = stack [top];

flag = visited_right [top];

Now trav will point to 30 and flag will be 1. So print value of trav.

Output : 10, 25, 20, 35, 50, 40, 30

top = top -1;

Now top will become -1. So stop.

Final Output : 10, 25, 20, 35, 50, 40, 30

Algorithm :

(1) initially make trav = root, top = –1 & flag = 0

(2) while trav! = NULL

      put every node on stack top

      move trav to left hand side

      make visited_right [top] = 0;

    when trav becomes NULL goto (3)

(3) if (trav == NULL)

      pop the content from the stack top and assign it to trav i.e. trav=stack [top];

      pop the contents from visited_right [top] and assign it to flag.

      i.e. flag = visited_right [top];

      goto (4) if flag == 0; else goto (3)

(4) if (flag == 0)

    move trav to its right and make the visited_right [top] = 1;

if trav is NULL goto (5) else goto (7)

(5) if (trav == NULL)

say trav = stack [top],

pop flag from the top of visited_right i.e. flag = visited_right [top];

if flag == 1 then goto (6)

(6) if (flag == 1)

pop the content from both the stack & visited_right and print the content i.e.

top − −;

cout << trav → data

trav = stack [top];   Assign stack [top] to trav & visited_right

flag = visited_right [top];   [top] to flag

go to (9)

(7) if (trav!=NULL)

break;

go to (2)

(8) if (flag !=0)

pop the content from the stack i.e. top − −;

cout << trav → data; // print data of trav

trav = stack [top];

flag = visited_right [top];

(9) if (top ==−1)

break;

go to (11) else go to (4) if (flag==0) OR go to (8) if (flag!=0)

(10) Repeat step (2) until top!=−1

i.e. while (top!=−1);

(11) if top == −1

come out from the program

else

go to step (2)

Postorder Traversal (Recursive)   **[May 10]**

Algorithm :

```
void postorder (node *root)
{
    if(root!=NULL)
    {
        postorder (root→left);
        postorder(root→right);
        cout<<root→data
    }
}
```

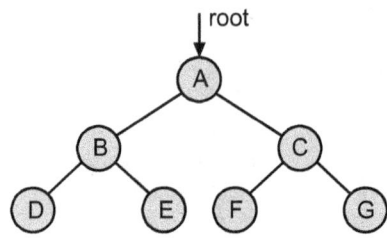

Fig. 1.31 : Binary tree

Working of Recursive Postorder Traversal :

Line No.	Code	Root	Compiler stack	Output
1	void postorder (node *root)	A	A	
3	if(root!=NULL) ------- True	A	A	
5	postorder(root→left)	A	A	
1	void postorder (node *root)	B	BA	
3	if(root!=NULL) ------- True	B	BA	
5	postorder(root→left)	B	BA	
1	void postorder (node *root)	D	DBA	
3	if(root!=NULL) ------- True	D	DBA	
5	postorder(root→left)	D	DBA	
1	void postorder (node *root)	NULL	NULL DBA	
3	if(root!=NULL) ------- False	NULL	NULL DBA	
9	}	D	DBA	
6	postorder(root→left)	D	DBA	D
1	void postorder (node *root)	NULL	NULL DBA	D
3	if(root!=NULL) ------- False	NULL	NULL DBA	D
9	}	D	DBA	D

7	cout<<root→data	D	DBA	D
9	}	B	BA	D
6	postorder(root→right)	B	BA	D
1	void postorder (node *root)	E	EBA	D
3	if(root!=NULL) ------- True	E	EBA	D
5	postorder(root→left)	E	EBA	D
1	void postorder (node *root)	NULL	NULL EBA	D
3	if(root!=NULL) ------- False	NULL	NULL EBA	D
9	}	E	EBA	D
6	postorder(root→right)	E	EBA	D
1	void postorder (node *root)	NULL	NULL EBA	D
3	if(root!=NULL) ------- False	NULL	NULL EBA	D
9	}	E	EBA	D
7	cout<<root→data	E	EBA	DE
9	}	B	BA	DE
7	cout<<root→data	B	BA	DEB
9	}	A	A	DEB
6	postorder(root→left)	A	A	DEB
1	void postorder (node *root)	C	CA	DEB
3	if(root!=NULL) ------- True	C	CA	DEB
5	postorder(root→left)	C	CA	DEB
1	void postorder (node *root)	F	FCA	DEB
3	if(root!=NULL) ------- True	F	FCA	DEB
5	postorder(root→left)	F	FCA	DEB
1	void postorder (node *root)	NULL	NULL FCA	DEB
3	if(root!=NULL) ------- False	NULL	NULL FCA	DEB
9	}	F	FCA	DEB
6	postorder(root→right)	F	FCA	DEB
1	void postorder (node *root)	NULL	NULL FCA	DEB

3	if(root!=NULL) ------- False	NULL	NULL FCA	DEB
9	}	F	FCA	DEB
7	cout<<root→data	F	FCA	DEBF
9	}	C	CA	DEBF
6	postorder(root→right)	C	CA	DEBF
1	void postorder (node *root)	G	GCA	DEBF
3	if(root!=NULL) ------- True	G	GCA	DEBF
5	postorder(root→left)	G	GCA	DEBF
1	void postorder (node *root)	NULL	NULL GCA	DEBF
3	if(root!=NULL) ------- False	NULL	NULL GCA	DEBF
9	}	G	GCA	DEBF
6	postorder(root→right)	G	GCA	DEBF
1	void postorder (node *root)	NULL	NULL GCA	DEBF
3	if(root!=NULL) ------- False	NULL	NULL GCA	DEBF
9	}	G	GCA	DEBF
7	cout<<root→data	G	GCA	DEBFG
9	}	C	CA	DEBFG
7	cout<<root→data	C	CA	DEBFGC
9	}	A	A	DEBFGC
7	cout<<root→data	A	A	DEBFGCA
9	}	-	empty	DEBFGCA

1.5.4 Creation of Binary Tree from Traversal Sequence

1.5.4.1 Creation of Binary Tree from Preorder and Inroder Traversals

Inorder	G	C	E	M	H	J	F	D	I
Preorder	H	C	G	M	E	F	J	I	D

Step 1 : Root is the first node in preorder traversal. Hence H is the root of the binary tree.

root

Step 2 : From inorder traversal mechanism we can find the left and right side childs of root.

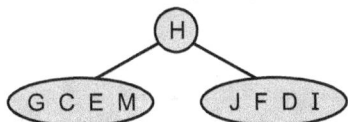

Step 3 : Now consider the left side of root node. Among GCEM, according to preorder C comes first. So 'C' is a root of the subtree having left child G and right child EM.

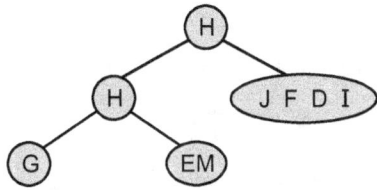

Step 4 : Among nodes EM, M comes first in preorder traversal so M will become a root of the subtree with E as a left child.

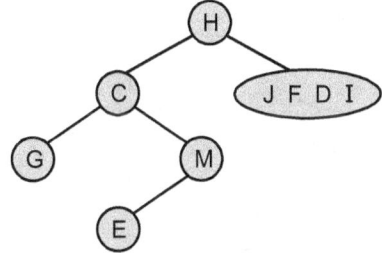

Step 5 : Among nodes J F D I (at right side of H), F comes first in preorder traversal, with J as left child and D I as its right child.

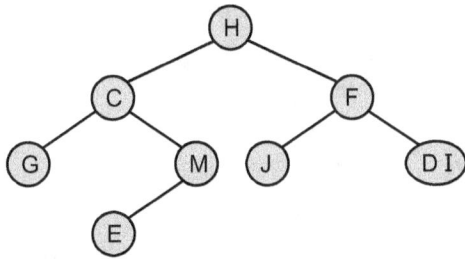

Step 6 : Among nodes D I, I comes first. So I is a root of the subtree having D as a left child.

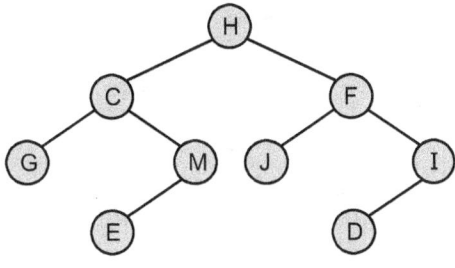

1.5.4.2 Creation of Tree from Postorder and Inorder Traversal

Inorder	B	K	D	L	C	G	E	H	F
Preorder	K	D	B	G	C	H	F	E	L

Step 1 : Using postorder traversal we can say that root is the last node. Hence L is the root of the binary tree.

root

Step 2 : From inorder traversal we can find left and right descendants of the given root L.

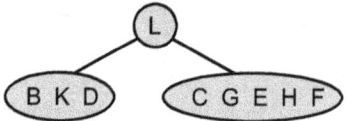

Step 3 : Among nodes B k D, B comes last in postorder traversal so B is the root of subtee with KD as its right side's descendants.

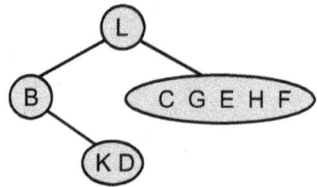

Step 4 : Among nodes KD, D comes last in postorder traversal. So D is the root of the subtree with K as its left child.

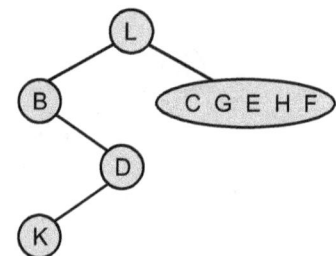

Step 5 : Among nodes C G E H F, E comes last in postorder traversal. So E is a root with C G as left side's descendants and H F as its right side's descendants.

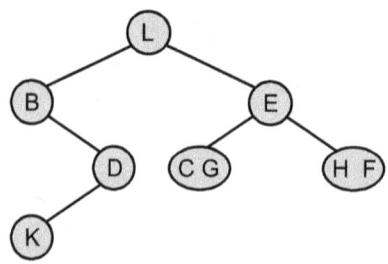

Step 6 : Among nodes C G, C comes last in postorder travers, so C will be the root of the subtree with G as its right child.

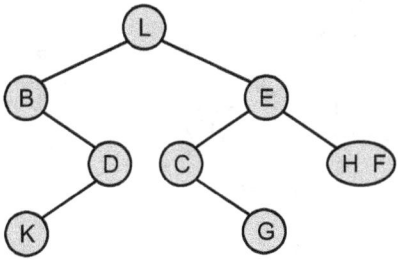

Step 7 : Among nodes H F, F comes last in the postorder traversal. So F will be the root of the subtree having H as its left child.

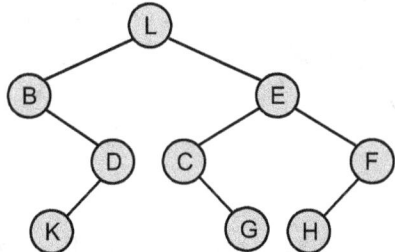

1.6 BFS TRAVERSAL   [Dec. 10]

Breadth First Search Traversal on Binary Tree :

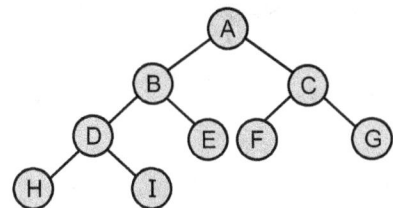

Fig. 1.32

(1) Initially trav = root;

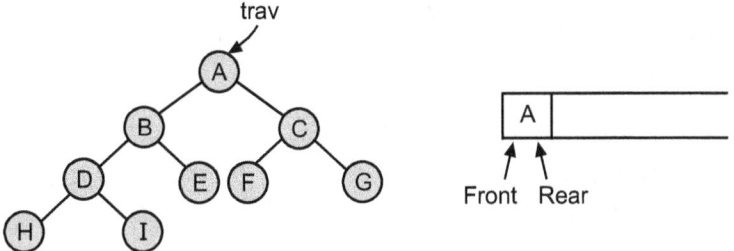

(2) Pop content from queue and print it. Push its left and right children on the queue. i.e.

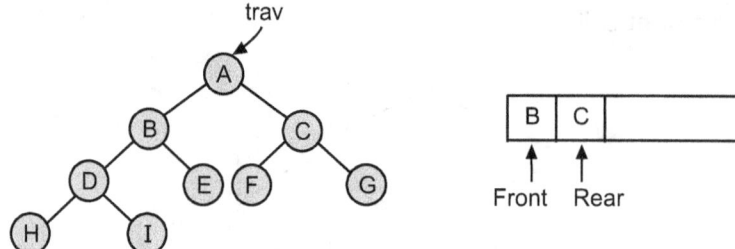

Output : A

(3) Pop the content from the stack and assign it to trav. Print trav → data. Push left and right children of trav on the queue.

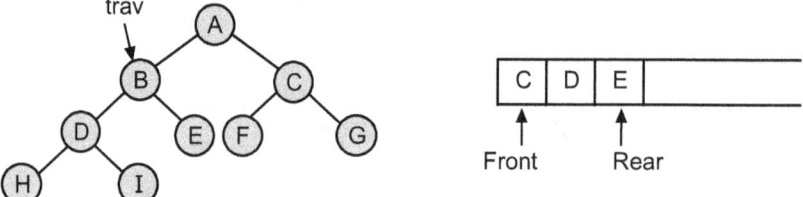

Output : A B

(4) Pop the element from queue and assign it to trav. Print trav → data. Push it's left and right children on the queue.

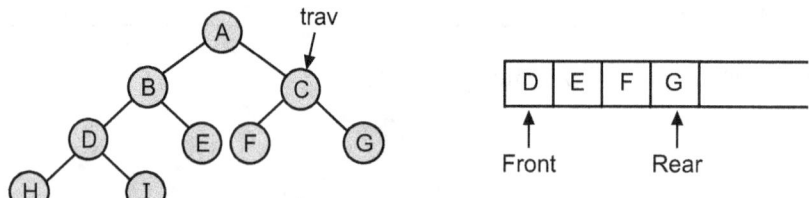

Output : A B C

(5) Pop the element from queue and assign it to trav. Print trav → data. Push it's left and right children on the queue.

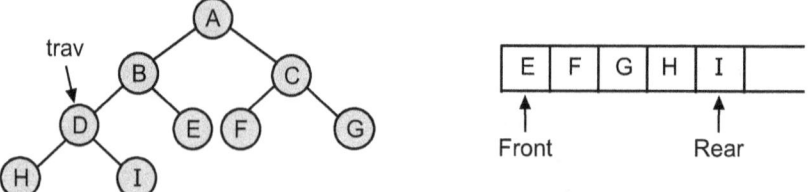

Output : A B C D

(6) Pop the element from queue and assign it to trav. Print trav → data. Push it's left and right children on the queue.

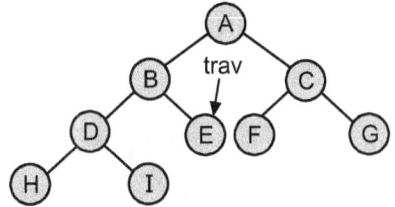 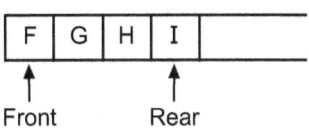

Output : A B C D E

(7) Pop the element from queue and assign it to trav. Print trav → data. Push its left a right children on the queue.

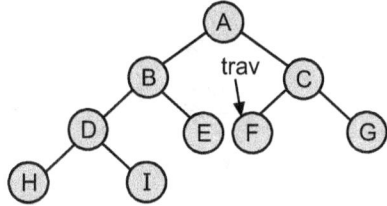 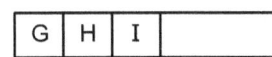

Output : A B C D E F

(8) Repeat the process, till queue becomes empty.

Final output will be : A B C D E F G H I

Algorithm :

- Push the root node in the queue

- Pop a node from queue and examine it. After poping the node, print its value and push it's left and right children (if any) in the queue.

- Repeat step (2) till queue is not empty.

Source Code :

```
void tree : :levelwise_display(tree*root)
{
    tree*queue[20],*trav;
    int choice, front=-1, rear=-1;
    clrscr();
    trav=root;

    if(front==-1)
    {
        queue[++rear]=trav;
        front++;
```

```
    }
    do
    {
        trav=queue[front];
        cout<<" "<<trav->data;
        for(int i=0;i<=rear;i++)
        {
            queue[i]=queue[i+1];
        {
        rear - -;
        if(trav->left!=NULL)
        {
        if(trav->right!=NULL)
        {
            queue[++rear]=trav->right;
        }
    }while(rear!=-1);
    getch( );
    }
    }
    }
}
```

1.7 BINARY SEARCH TREE (BST)

Binary search tree as the name suggests, is used for storing the data mainly for searching applications. We have seen that nonlinear data structures are used for speeding up the process of searching. If we store the data in binary tree in a particular way, we will be able to improve the efficiency of searching to the order of $\log_2 n$ similar to binary search. In fact, **BST** implements the same principle as that of binary search,

Definition 1 :

A binary search tree is a binary tree that is either empty or has each node that can satisfy following conditions.

- All the elements in left sub-tree of the root precede the element in the root.
- All the elements in the right sub-tree of the root succeed the element in the root.
- Left and right sub-trees are again binary search tree.

Definition 2 :

A binary search tree is a binary tree in which for each node the left sub-tree elements are less than the node element and right sub-tree elements are greater than the node element or vice versa.

The example of BST is shown in Fig. 1.33.

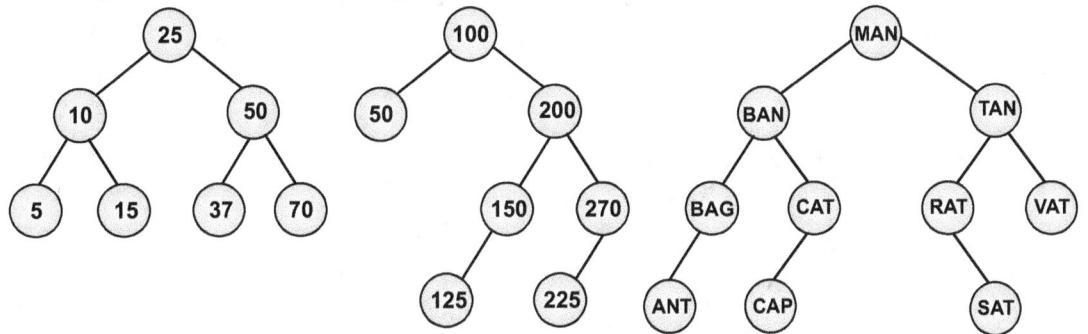

Fig. 1.33 : Binary search tree

1.8 OPERATIONS ON BINARY SEARCH TREE

We can use the traversals discussed earlier for the binary search trees. For example for first tree the traversals will be as :

Inorder	:	5 10 15 25 37 50 75
Preorder	:	25 10 5 15 50 37 75
Postorder	:	5 15 10 37 75 50 25

Note that inorder traversal of BST will result into ascending order.

We can store the elements in BST in reverse order also. i.e., smaller element on right side and larger element on left side of root. In that case, the inorder traversal will result into descending order of the elements in the tree.

The main operation that we need to do on binary search tree is searching an element. Consider tree as shown in Fig. 1.34.

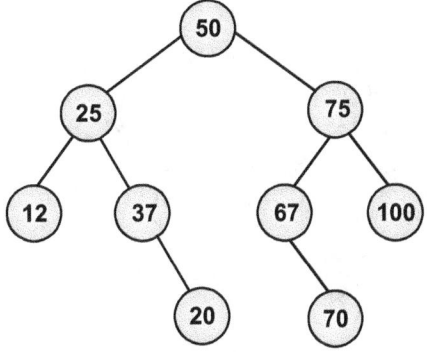

Fig. 1.34 : Binary search tree

Suppose we want to search 37 in the tree. We start from the root node and move to left or right side depending on whether the number is smaller or greater.

Step 1 : Compare whether element at current node is 37. The answer is no. Now since 37 < 50 we move to the left side.

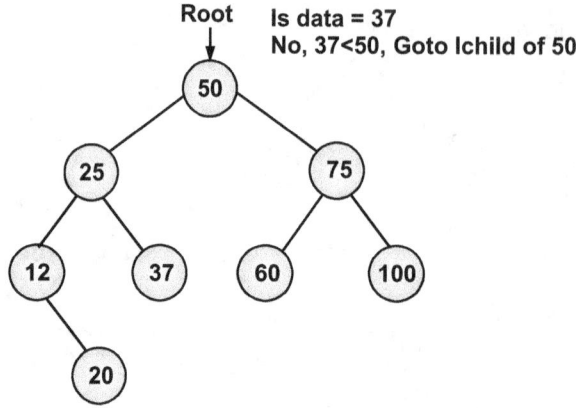

Fig. 1.35 (a) : Search operation

Step 2 :

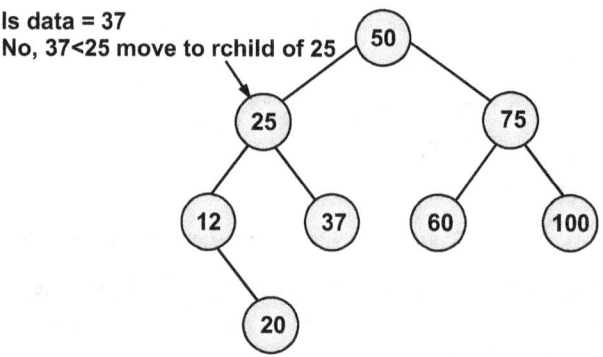

Fig. 1.35 (b) : Search operation

Step 3 :

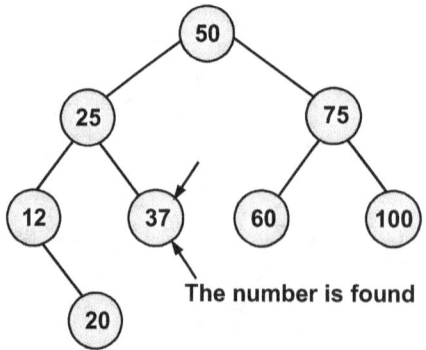

Fig. 1.35 (c) : Search operation

If the number to be searched is not there in the BST, we will reach the end of BST (i.e. Leaf node).

There are various operations that can be performed on BST viz., create, search and traverse.

Let us write the algorithms for various operations on BST.

1.8.1 Creating BST

```
Read n {Number of elements}
root=Null
Repeat Steps 4 to 2 n times.
Read x
Create a node ptr
ptr->data=x
ptr->lchild=ptr->rchild=Null
temp = root
if (temp==NULL) root=ptr
while (temp!=NULL)
    {
        prev=temp;
        if (temp->data>x)
            temp=temp->lchild; flag=1;
        else
            temp= temp->rchild; flag=0;
    }
    if (flag==1)
        prev->lchild = ptr;
    else
        prev->rchild=ptr;
```

Explanation :

1. n is number of elements to be stored in BST.

2. The root pointer points to root node which is initially null.

3. Every time we accept the data, we create a new node ptr, store the data in it and this node is to be placed in the BST.

4. When first node is created it will be pointed by root.

5. Whenever a new node is created we start from root node and find a position for this node in BST. For this we compare the element in the tree with current element and move to right or left side. Before we move, pointer prev is kept behind so that we can connect new node to the current node, in case its lchild or rchild becomes null.

6. The movement of pointer temp before it becomes null gives location where new node is to be inserted. It is tracked with the help of flag.

1.8.2 Searching in BST

```
Read s
temp=root
while (temp!=NULL)
{
    if (temp->data ==s)
    {
        printf("Found");
        break;
    }
    if (temp->data>s)
        temp=temp->lchild
    if (temp->data <s)
        temp=temp->rchild
}
if (temp==NULL)
    printf("Not found");
```

Explanation :

1. The element to be searched is s.

2. We start from the root and move into the tree either on left or right side depending on data at current node,

3. If we find the data at a particular node, we exit.

4. If we don't find the data, temp will finally become null.

1.8.3 Tree Traversal Operations

We can use recursive functions as :

Inorder (temp)

1. {

    if(temp!=NULL)

    {

        inorder (temp- >lchild)

        print temp->data

        inorder (temp->rchild).

    }

}

Explanation :

Let us take a BST as shown in Fig. 1.36 for this.

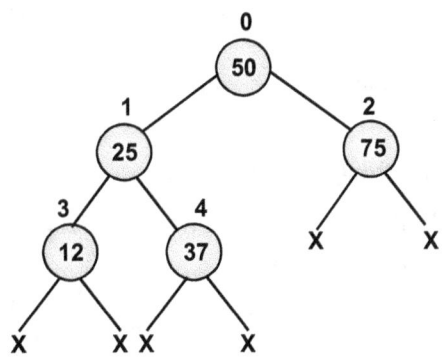

Fig. 1.36 : Binary search tree

Let 0, 1, 2, 3, 4 be the addresses of there nodes.

The function will be called as

   inorder (root) ;

The function gets address of root which is assumed to be 0. Temp is assigned this address. The following table shows how the function gets called recursively. Follow the numbered lines in that sequence.

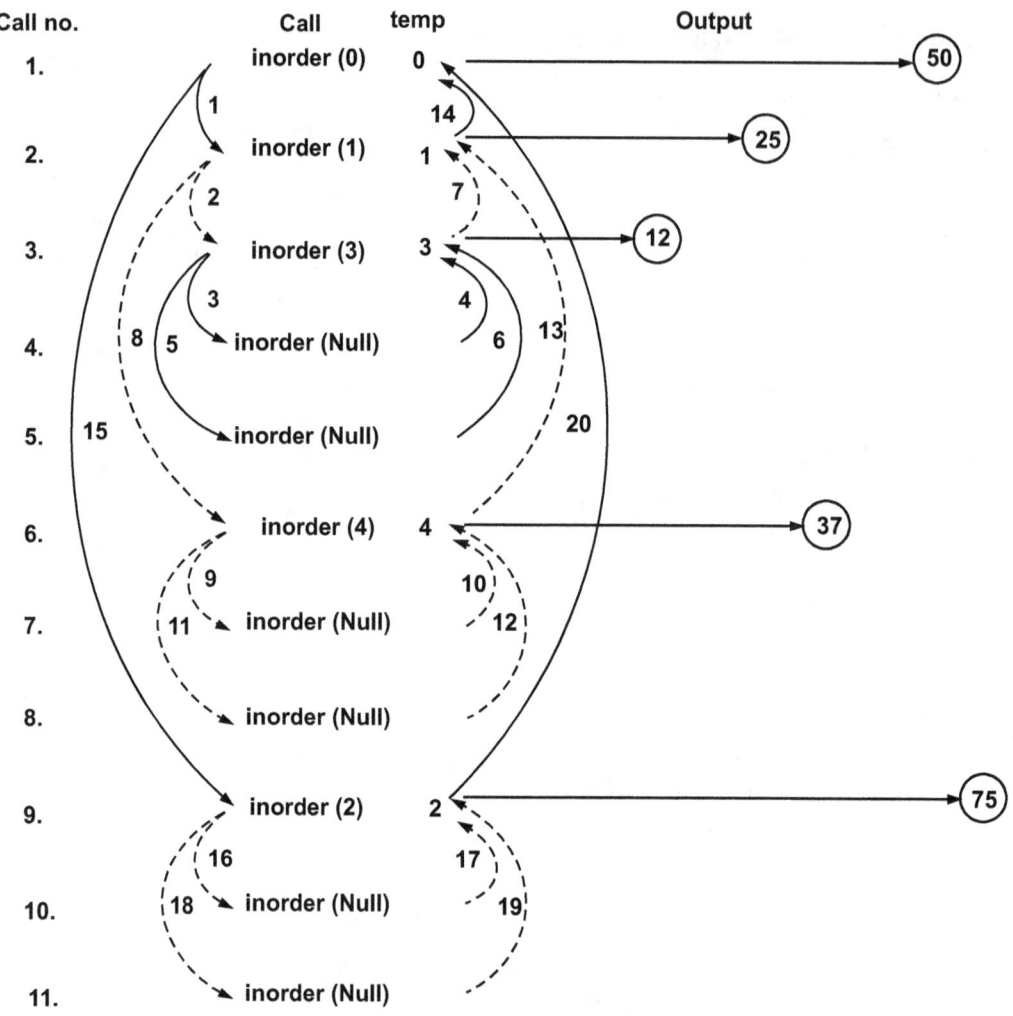

Fig. 1.37 : Recursive inorder traversal function trace

The other two traversal functions are as follows :

```
preorder (temp)
{
    if (temp!=Null)
    {
        print temp->data;
        preorder(temp->lchild);
        preorder(temp->rchild);
    }
```

```
        }
    postorder (temp)
    {
        if(temp!=Null)
        {
            postorder(temp->lchild)
            postorder(temp->rchild)
            print temp->data
```

1.8.4 Delete Operation

Deleting a node in BST is a complex operation because we need to readjust the nodes in the tree. There are four different situations in the BST for deleting a node. They are,

- The node to be deleted is leaf node.
- The node has right child only.
- The node has left child only.
- The node has both children.

Let us find out how to deal with these four cases with example

Case 1 :

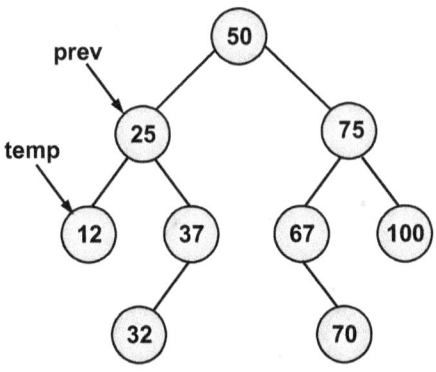

Fig. 1.38 (a) : Delete operation leaf node

Suppose, the node to be deleted is 12, we need two pointers one at 12 (temp) other at its parent node i.e. 25 (prev). We need to check whether the node to be deleted (temp) is connected to lchild or rchild of prev.

    if prev->lchild=temp make prev-lchild=Null

    if prev->rchild=temp make prev->rchild=Null

    and then free (temp)

Case 2 :

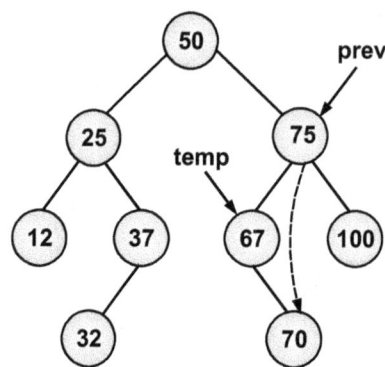

Fig. 1.38 (b) : Delete operation node with rchild

Suppose, the node to be deleted has right child as shown in Fig. 1.38 (b). In this case, since 67 is to be deleted, its successor 70 is to be made *l*child of its parent i.e. 75. The node to be deleted might be right child of its parent or left child. Hence, we have to determine this first. The code will be :

```
if (temp->rchild != NULL &&temp->lchild == NULL)
{
    if(prev-lchild==temp)
        prev-lchild=temp->rchild ;
    else
        prev->rchild=temp->rchild;
}
```

Case 3 :

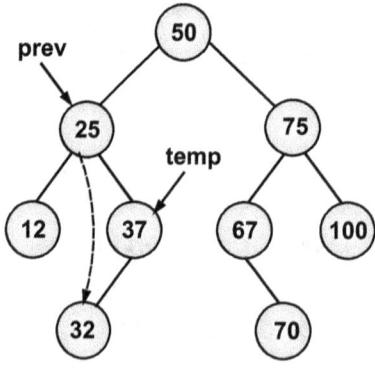

Fig. 1.38 (c) : Delete operation node with lchild

If the node to be deleted has left child as shown in Fig. 1.38 (c). If 37 is deleted, its successor should be made right child of 25. We can have the node to be deleted as right or left child of its parent node. Hence, we will have two options.'

```
if (temp->rchild==NULL &&temp->lchild!=NULL)
{
    if (prev->lchild==temp)
        prev->lchild=temp->lchild;
    else
        prev->rchild=temp->lchild;
}
```

Case 4 : The node to be deleted has both children as shown in Fig. 1.38 (d).

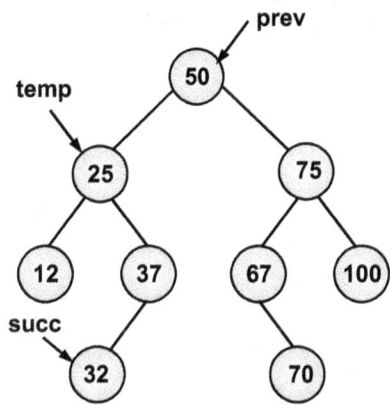

Fig. 1.38 (d) : Delete operation node with lchild and rchild

Let us say we want to delete 25. The inorder successor of 25 is 32. We can copy 32 in place of 25 and delete 32. Hence, the process is to find inorder successor of the node. Copy the successor in its place and delete the inorder successor node.

```
if (temp->lchild!=NULL, &&temp->rchild!=NULL)
{
    succ= temp;
    x=temp->rchild;
    while(x!=NULL)
    {
        prev=succ;
        succ=x;
        x=x->lchild;
    }
    temp->data=succ->data;
    temp=succ;
}
```

This will copy the value of inorder, successor into the node to be deleted. Now, that we have a pointer temp to the inorder successor node and prev to its parent node, this node will fall into one of the 3 cases considered earlier. If we write the cases after this case, automatically one of them will get executed and the-node will be deleted.

1.8.5 Insert Operation

If new data is to be inserted in already existing BST, the position for this new data has to be located. It will be inserted as a leaf node in the BST. The algorithm will be as follows :

```
Read x (Data to be added)
Create a new node ptr and store the data in it
temp=root
while(temp!=NULL)
{   prev=temp;
    if(temp->data>x)
        temp=temp->lchild; flag=1;
    else
        temp=temp->rchild; flag=0;
}
if (flag==1)
    prev->lchild=ptr;
else
    prev->rchild=ptr;
```

Explanation :

1. The new data to be inserted is accepted and stored into a new node ptr.

2. Start from root node till you go bottom of tree. Compare at each node and move to left or right. Before we move to left or right keep a pointer prev to previous node so that if you fall into null, we have a pointer to the node on whose left or right side new node is to be attached. The decision of whether the new node will be attached to right or left will be made from the value of flag.

    Now let us write a menu driven program to implement all these operations.

    The functions that we are going to write are

    (i) Create   :   Creates a binary search tree and returns address of root node,

    (ii) Search   :   Searches an element in BST.

(iii) Inorder   :   Display inorder traversal.

(iv) Preorder   :   Display preorder traversal.

(v) Postorder :   Display postorder traversal.

(vi) Delete   :   Deletes a node.

(vii) insert   :   Inserts a new node.

Program 1.1 : To create and implement binary search tree

```c
#include <stdio.h>
#include <conio.h>
typedef struct node
{
    int data;
    struct node *lchild,*rchild;
}NODE;
NODE*create( );
int search (NODE*, int);
void inorder (NODE*);
void preorder (NODE*)
void postorder (NODE*);
NODE*del(NODE*);
NODE* insert (NODE*);
void main( )
{
    int ch, s;
    NODE*root=NULL;
    do
    {
        clrscr( );
        printf("1.Create \n 2.Search \n 3.Inorder \n 4.Preorder \n 5.Postorder \n
        6.Delete \n 7.Insert \n8.Exit \n");
        printf("Enter your choice \n");
        scanf("%d", &ch);
```

```
        switch(ch)
        {
            case 1  :   root=create( );
                    break;
            case 2  :   printf("Enter number to be searched \n");
                    scanf("%d", &s);
                    search(root, s)
                    break;
            case 3  :   inorder(root);
                    break;
            case 4  :   preorder(root);
                    break;
            case 5  :   postorder(root);
                    break;
            case 6  :   root=del(root)
                    break;
            case 7  :   root=insert(root);
                    break;
        }
        getch();
    }while(ch!=8);
}
NODE *create( )
{
    int x, i, n, flag;
    NODE *root, *ptr, *temp, *prev;
    root=NULL;
    printf("How many elements? \n");
    scanf("%d", &n);
    for(i=1;i<=n;i++)
```

```
{
    printf("Enter the number");
    scanf("%d", &x);
    ptr=(NODE*)malloc(sizeof(NODE));
    ptr->data=x;
    ptr->rchild=ptr->lchild=NULL;
    if (root==NULL)
        root=ptr;
    else
    {
        temp=root;
        while (temp!=NULL)
        {
            prev=temp;
            if (temp->data>x)
            {
                temp=temp->lchild;
                flag=1;
            }
            else
            {
                temp=temp->rchild;
                flag=0;
            }
        }
        if (flag==1)
            prev->lchild=ptr;
        else
            prev->rchild=ptr;
    }
```

```c
        }
    return (root);
    }
    int search (NODE *root, int x)
    {
        NODE *temp;
        temp=root;
        while (temp!=NULL && temp->data!=x)
        {
            if(temp->data>x)
                temp=temp->lchild;
            else
                temp=temp->rchild;
        }
        if (temp!= NULL)
            return (1);
        else
            return (0);
    }
    void inorder (NODE *temp)
    {
        if (temp!= NULL)
        {
            inorder (temp->lchild);
            printf("%d \n", temp->data);
            inorder(temp->rchild);
        }
    }
    void preorder (NODE *temp)
    {
```

```c
        if (temp!=NULL)
        {
            printf("%d \n", temp->data);
            preorder(temp->lchild);
            preorder(temp->rchild);
        }
}
void postorder (NODE *temp)
{
    if (temp!=NULL)
    {
        postorder(temp->lchild);
        postorder(temp->rchild);
        printf("%d \n", temp->data);
    }
}
NODE *del(NODE*root)
{
    NODE *temp, *prev, *x, *succ;
    int s;
    printf("Enter data to be deleted \n");
    scanf("%d", &s);
    temp=root;
    prev=temp;
    while(temp!=NULL)
    {
        if (temp->data==s)
            break;
        prev=temp;
        if(temp->data>s)
```

```
            temp=temp->lchild;
        else
            temp=temp->rchild;
    }
    if(temp==NULL)
    {
        printf("Not in the BST \n");
        exit(0);
    }
    if(temp->lchild!=NULL &&temp->rchild!=NULL)
    {
        succ=temp;
        x=temp->rchild;
        while(x!=NULL)
        {
            prev=succ;
            succ=x;
            x=x-Achild;
        }
        temp->data=succ->data;
        temp=succ;
    }
    if(temp->rchild== NULL & temp->lchild!=NULL)
    {
        if(prev->lchild == temp)
            prev->rchild=temp->lchild;
        else
            prev->rchild=temp->lchild;
    }
    if(temp->rchild!=NULL &&temp->lchild==NULL)
```

```
        {
            if(prev->lchild==temp)
                prev->lchild=temp->rchild;
            else
                prev->rchild=temp->rchild;
        }
        if(temp->lchild == NULL &&temp->rchild == NULL)
        {
            if(prev->lchild==temp)
                prev->lchild=NULL;
            else
                prev->rchild=NULL;
        }
        free(temp);
        return(root);
    }
    NODE *insert(NODE *root)
    {
        NODE *temp, *prev, *ptr;
        int x, flag;
        printf("Enter data to be inserted \n");
        scanf("%d", &x);
        ptr =(NODE*)malloc(sizeof(NODE));
        ptr->data=x;
        ptr->lchild=ptr->rchild=NULL;
        temp=root;
        while (temp!=NULL)
        {
```

```
                    prev=temp;
                    if(temp->data>x)
                    {
                        temp=temp->lchild;
                        flag=1;
                    }
                    else
                    {
                        temp=temp->rchild;
                        flag=0;
                    }
                }
                if(root==NULL)
                    root=ptr;
                else
                {
                if(flag==1)
                    prev->lchild=ptr;
                else
                    prev->rchild=ptr;
                }
                return (root);
        }
```

1.9 OPERATIONS ON BINARY TREE

We have seen Binary search tree and operations on it. The BST was relatively easy to implement along with the operations such as create, insert, delete traversals, etc. It was because of the relation that exists among the elements in BST. Now, if you are given a binary tree and asked to create it as it is, we will have to ask the user to manually enter the data and their positions in the tree. The operators that we can have on this tree are insert, traversals (all three). The algorithms of these operations are as follows.

1.9.1 Creating a Binary Tree

```
Read n
root=Null
for (i=1;i<=n;i++)
{
    Read x
    Create a new node ptr
    store x in ptr->data
    if(root==NULL)
        root=ptr
    else
    {
        temp=root;
        while(temp!=NULL)
        {
            prev=temp;
            read side
            if(side=='l')
                temp=temp->lchild
            else
                temp=temp->rchild;
        }
        if(side=='l')
            prev->lchild=ptr
        else
        prev->rchild=ptr
    }
}
Stop
```

Explanation :

1. Read number of nodes (n) in the tree.

2 root=NULL.

3. Repeat for each element the following process

4. Read data and store it in a node ptr.

5. If it is first node let it be pointed by root.

6,7. If it is not first node, start from root node and traverse in the tree every time asking the user about which side of current node the new node is to be added.

8. When temp becomes NULL, prev will be at a node in the tree on whose left or right side new node is to be inserted. Insert the node accordingly.

1.9.2 Traversal Operation

The inorder, preorder and postorder traversals can be implemented in the same way as discussed in BST.

1.9.3 Insert Operation

It will be similar to create operation except that the process is to be carried out only once.

Program 1.2 : To implement a binary tree

```
typedef struct node
{
    int data;
    struct node *lchild, *rchild;
} NODE;
NODE *create( );
void       inorder(NODE*);
void       preorder (NODE*);
void    postorder(NODE*);
NODE *insert(NODE*);
void main( )
{
    int ch;
    NODE *root;
    root=NULL;
```

```
do
{
    printf("1.Create \n2. Inorder W. preorder \n4. Postorder \n5. Insert \n6.
     Exit \n");
    printf("Enter your choice \n");
    scanf("%d", &ch);
    switch(ch)
    {
        case 1  :  root=create( );
                   break;
        case 2  :  inorder(root);
                   break
        case 3  :  preorder(root);
                   break;
        case 4  :  postorder(root);
                   break;
        case 5  :  root=insert(root);
    }
    getch( );
} while(ch!=6);
}
NODE *create( )
{
    NODE *ptr, *temp, *prev;
    int x; n, i;
    char ch;
    printf("Enter number of nodes \n");
    scanf("%d",&n);
    root=NULL;
    for(i=1;i<=n;i++)
    {
```

```
            printf("Enter data \n");
            scanf("%d", &x);
            ptr=(NODE*) malloc(sizeof (NODE));
            ptr->lchild=ptr->rchild=NULL;
            if(root == NULL)
                root=ptr;
            else
            {
                temp=root;
                while(temp!=NULL)
                {   prev=temp;
                    printf("which side of %d? (l/r) \n", temp->data);
                    ch=getch( );
                    if(ch=='l' || ch=='L')
                        temp=temp->lchild;
                    else
                        temp=temp->rchild;
                }
                if(ch=='l' || ch=='L')
                    prev->lchild=ptr;
                else
                    prev->rchild=ptr;
            }
        }
        return (root);
    }
    void inorder(NODE*root)
    {   NODE *temp;
        temp=root;
        if (temp!=NULL)
```

```
        {
            inorder(temp->lchild);
            printf("%d \n", temp->data);
            inorder(temp->rchild);
        }
    }
    void preorder(NODE*root)
    {   NODE *temp;
        temp=root;
        if (temp!=NULL)
        {
            printf("%d \n", temp->data);
            preorder(temp->lchild);
            preorder(temp->rchild);
        }
    }
    void postorder(NODE*root)
    {
        NODE*temp;
        temp=root;
            if(temp!=NULL)
            {
                postorder(temp->lchild);
                postorder(temp->rchild);
                printf("%d \n", temp->data);
            }
    }
    NODE *insert(NODE*root)
    {
        NODE *temp,*ptr, *prev;
```

```
int x;
char ch;
printf("Enter data \n");
scanf("%d", &x);
ptr=(NODE*)malloc(sizeof(NODE));
ptr->data=x;
ptr->child=ptr->rchild=NULL;
if (root==NULL)
    root=ptr;
else
{
    temp=root;
    while(temp!=NULL)
    {
        printf("which side of %d (l/r) \n", temp->data);
        ch=getch( );
        if(ch=='l' || ch=='L')
            temp=temp->lchild;
        else
            temp=temp->rchild;
    }
    if(ch=='l' || ch=='L')
        prev->lchild=ptr;
    else
        prev->rchild=ptr;
}
return(root);
}
```

1.9.4 Non-Recursive Traversal

The recursive inorder, preorder and postorder traversals use the program's recursion stack. The recursion can be removed by implementing user defined stack. Let us see, how we can write inorder and preorder traversals using stack.

1. Inorder Traversal

Algorithm : Inorder traversal

```
1.  temp=root
2.  do
    {
        while(temp!=NULL)
        {
            push(temp);
            temp=temp->lchild;
        }
            temp=pop( );
            print temp->data
            temp=temp->rchild;
    }while(stack is not empty OR temp!=NULL);
3.  Stop.
```

Explanation :
1. Start with root node.
2. Traverse on left side while storing the address of each node on stack.
3. Pop the address of a node from stack (it will be left most node). Display the data.
4. Move to right side.
5. Repeat above till all nodes are traversed.
6. The stack will be stack of pointers as it has to store addresses of nodes.

Consider a binary tree as :

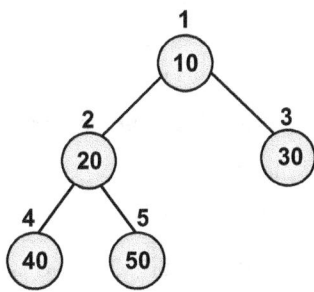

Fig. 1.39 (a) : Binary tree

Let 1, 2, 3, 4, 5, be the addresses of the nodes.

1. We start with root node and move to left pushing every time address of node on the stack. At the end of inner while, the stack will be

```
┌───┐
│ 4 │
├───┤
│ 2 │
├───┤
│ 1 │
└───┘
```

Fig. 1.39 (b) : Stack contents for non-recursive inorder traversal

2.   temp=pop( ) will pop node 4.

   data at node 4 i.e. 40 will be displayed.

3.   temp will be Null as rchild of 4 is Null.

   Since temp is NULL, 2 is poped.

   Data at 2 i.e. 20 is displayed.

   temp will move to rchild of 2.

   Hence, 5 will be pushed and stack will be

```
┌───┐
│   │
├───┤
│   │
├───┤
│ 5 │
├───┤
│ 1 │
└───┘
```

Fig. 1.39 (c) : Stack contents for non-recursive inorder traversal

4.   5 is popped and data at 5 is displayed i.e. 50.

   Since temp is NULL

   1 is popped and data 1 is displayed i.e. 2.

   temp will move to rchild 3.

   3 is pushed and stock will be

```
┌───┐
│   │
├───┤
│   │
├───┤
│ 3 │
└───┘
```

Fig. 1.39 (d) : Stack contents for non-recursive inorder traversal

3 is popped data at 3. i.e. 30 displayed.

stack becomes empty and temp is null hence the function gets over.

2.   **Preorder Traversal :** For preorder traversal (VLR) we used to make only one change the print statement will be written before left move as follows :

```
temp=root;
do
```

```
{    while(temp!=NULL)
    {
        print temp->data;
        push(temp);
        temp=temp->lchild;
    }
    temp=pop( );
    temp=temp->rchild;
}    while (stack is not empty OR temp!=NULL)
Stop
```

1.10 THREADED BINARY TREE

"A binary tree is *threaded* by making all right child pointers that would normally be null point to the inorder successor of the node, and all left child pointers that would normally be null point to the inorder predecessor of the node."

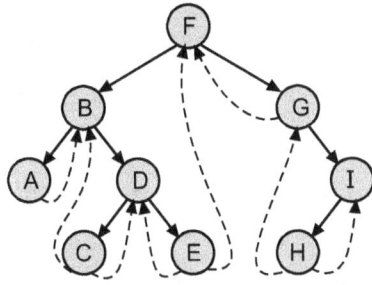

Fig. 1.40

Advantages :   **[May 11]**

• The traversal operation is faster than that of its unthreaded version, because with threaded binary tree non-recursive implementation is possible which can run faster and does not require the help of stack.

• The second advantage is more subtle with a threaded binary tree; we can efficiently determine the predecessor and successor nodes starting from any node. A stack is required to provide upward pointing information in the tree whereas in a threaded binary tree, without having to incur the overload of using a stack mechanism the same can be carried out with the threads.

• Any node can be accessible from any other node. Threads are usually more to upward whereas links are downward. Thus in a threaded tree, one can move in either direction and nodes are in fact circularly linked. This is not possible in unthreaded counter part because there we can move only in downward direction starting form root.

- Insertion into and deletions from a threaded tree are all although time consuming operations (since we have to manipulate both links and threads).

Disadvantages :   **[May 11]**

- Insertion and deletion operation becomes more difficult.

- Tree traversal becomes difficult.

- Memory required to store a node increases. Each node has to store the information whether the links are normal or they are threads.

1.10.1 Memory Representation of Threaded Binary Tree

Basically in normal binary tree representation there are two links i.e. left and right link. Right link of node is points to address of right sub-tree and left link of node is points to address of left sub-tree. But when there is no sub-tree on its right or left then that link is replaced by NULL i.e. if left sub-tree is absent then left link of node is replaced by NULL, if right sub-tree is absent then right link of node is replaced by NULL.

In threaded binary tree the NULL links are replaced by threads, where the right (NULL) link of the node will point to its inorder successor and left (NULL) link points to inorder predecessor.

So, in the class of TBT along with the left and right pointers of the node we will require left and right flags, which will differentiate between the regular link and thread.

The class declaration of threaded binary tree will be

```
Class TBT
{
    int data;
    TBT*l_link,*r_link;
    int l_flag,r_flag;
};
```

Whenever the values of l_flag and r_flag will be 0, it means that there is a normal link (not a thread), otherwise there is a thread.
In the diagram the threads are always shown by dotted lines.

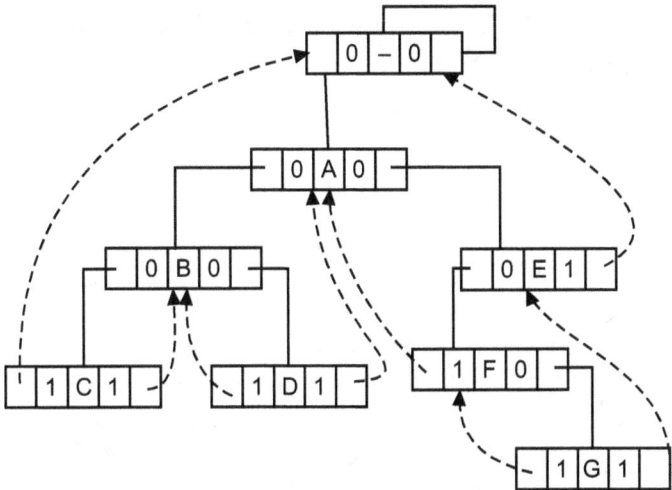

Fig. 1.41 : Threaded binary tree

1.10.2 Creation of TBT

The class required for the creation of TBT is shown below. Nodes of TBT majorly contains (1) data (2) left flag (3) right flag (4) left link and (5) right link along with the functions for tree creation and tree traversal.

```
class TBT
{
    private :
        int data;
        int l_flag,r_flag;
        TBT*l_link,*r_link;
    public :
        TBT*create_TBT(TBT*,TBT*);
        void inorder_TBT(TBT*,TBT*);
        void preorder_TBT(TBT*,TBT*);
        void postorder_TBT(TBT*,TBT*);
};
```

Create_TBT function accepts two parameters

1. Root node
2. Header node

1. If root==NULL, then create root, set its left and right flag and also make its left and right links to point to header node.

```
if(root==NULL)
{
    temp=new TBT();
    cout<<"\nEnter the data ";
    cin>>temp->data;
    temp->l_flag=1;
    temp->r_flag=1;
    temp->l_link=header;
    temp->r_link=header;
    root=temp;
}
```

header

l_link	l_flag	data	r_flag	r_link
~	1	15	1	~

2. If root!=NULL, create a temporary node and assign 0 to attached_flag, make attached_flag=1 when the node gets successfully attached to the TBT.

```
temp=new TBT();
cout<<"\nEnter the data ";
cin>>temp->data;
temp->l_flag=1;
temp->r_flag=1;
attached_flag=0;
```

3. Make trav=root so that trav will point to very first node of the tree.

If trav->data < temp->data && trav->r_flag==0 move trav to its right side. i.e. trav=trav->r_link.

4. If trav->data < temp->data && trav->r_flag==1, attach the temp node to the right side of the trav, as soon as the node is attached, set the value of attached_flag.

```
if(trav->data<temp->data&&trav->r_flag==0)
{
    trav=trav->r_link;
}
else
```

```
    if(trav->data<temp->data&&trav->r_flag==1)

    {

        trav->r_flag=0;

        p=trav->r_link;

        trav->r_link=temp;

        temp->r_link=p;

        temp->l_link=trav;

        attached_flag=1;

    }
```

5. If trav->data > temp->data && trav->l_flag==0 move trav to its left side. i.e. trav=trav->l_link.

    If trav->data > temp->data && trav->l_flag==1, attach the temp node to the left side of the trav, as soon as the node is attached, set the value of attached_flag.

```
        if(trav->data>temp->data&&trav->l_flag==0)

        {

            trav=trav->l_link;

        }

        else

        if(trav->data>temp->data&&trav->l_flag==1)

        {

            trav->l_flag=0;

            p=trav->l_link;

            trav->l_link=temp;

            temp->l_link=p;

            temp->r_link=trav;

            attached_flag=1;

        }
```

Function for TBT Creation :

```
TBT*TBT : :create_TBT(TBT*root,TBT*header)

{

    TBT*trav,*temp,*p;
```

```
int attached_flag=0;
char ans;
while(1)
{
trav=root;
if(root==NULL)
{
    temp=new TBT();
    cout<<"\nEnter the data ";
    cin>>temp->data;
    temp->l_flag=1;
    temp->r_flag=1;
    temp->l_link=header;
    temp->r_link=header;
    root=temp;
}
else
{
        temp=new TBT();
        cout<<"\nEnter the data ";
        cin>>temp->data;
        temp->l_flag=1;
        temp->r_flag=1;
        attached_flag=0;

        trav=root;
        while(attached_flag==0)
        {
            if(trav->data<temp->data&&trav->r_flag==0)
            {
                trav=trav->r_link;
            }
```

```
        else
        if(trav->data<temp->data&&trav->r_flag==1)
        {
            trav->r_flag=0;
            p=trav->r_link;
            trav->r_link=temp;
            temp->r_link=p;
            temp->l_link=trav;
            attached_flag=1;
        }

        if(trav->data>temp->data&&trav->l_flag==0)
        {
            trav=trav->l_link;
        }
        else
        if(trav->data>temp->data&&trav->l_flag==1)
        {
            trav->l_flag=0;
            p=trav->l_link;
            trav->l_link=temp;
            temp->l_link=p;
            temp->r_link=trav;
            attached_flag=1;
        }
    }
    attached_flag=0;
}
cout<<"\nDo you want to attach more nodes [y/n] ";
cin>>ans;
```

```
    if(ans=='n'||ans=='N')
    break;
    }
    return root;
}
```

1.10.2.1 Algorithm for Preorder Traversal of TBT

Initialize flag = 0 and trav = root.

- While trav !=header goto step 2 else go to step 8
- While flag==0&&trav->l_flag==0, move trav to its left side and **print** its data. Repeat step 2. (this loop will be terminated when trav will reach at leftmost node, where ( ) trav->l_flag will be 1)
- If flag==0 print trav->data
- If flag==0, move trav to its right side if there exists a right child and go to step 1. Else go to step 5.
- If flag==1 and there exists a right child to trav, move trav to its right side and make flag=0 and go to step 1. Else goto step 6.
- If flag==0 and trav is not having right child, move trav to its right side (using thread) and make flag=1 and go to step1. Else goto step 7.
- If flag==1 and trav is not having right child, move trav to its right side (using thread) and go to step1.
- Stop

Working :

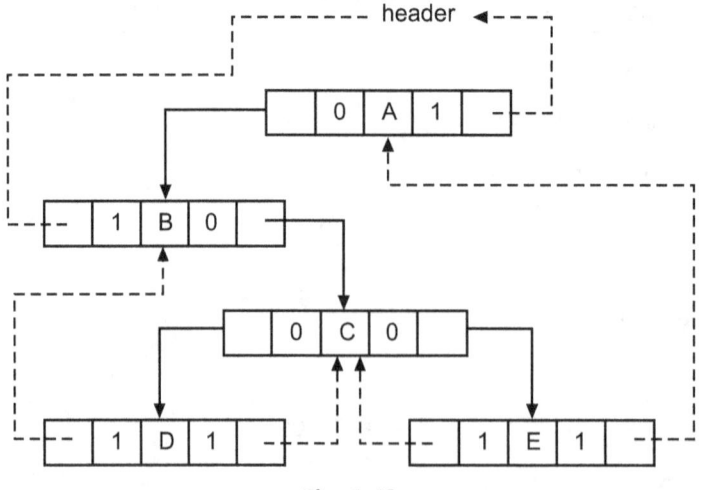

Fig. 1.42

- Initially, flag = 0, trav will point to A.
- As (flag==0 && trav → l_flag ==0)

  print trav → data.

  current output will be : A

  move trav to its left side. Now trav will point to B.
- As trav → l_flag !=0, we will come out of while loop, but here if (flag==0) condition is true, so print trav → data.

  Therefore, current output will be : A   B
- Now, as trav → r_flag==0 && flag==0, we will move trav to it's right side, [Now trav is pointing to c]
- Here trav → l_flag==0 && flag==0 print trav → data & move trav to its left side.

  therefore current output will be : A   B   C

  [trav is pointing to D]
- As flag==0

  print trav → data

  therefore current output will be : A   B   C   D

  [trav is pointing to D]
- Here (trav → r_flag==1 && flag==0)

  move trav to its right side & make flag = 1

  [trav is pointing to c & flag = 1]
- Now (trav → r_flag==0 && flag==1)

  move trav to its right side & make flag = 0

  [trav is pointing to E & flag = 0]
- Here flag==0

  print trav → data

  therefore current output will be : A B C D E
- Here (trav → r_flag==1 && flag==0)

  move trav to its right side & make flag=1

  [trav will point to A]
- Now (trav → r_flag==1 && flag==1)

  move trav to right side

  [trav will point to header]

- As (trav==header) exit from the code so after successful execution of the algorithm, the output for the preorder traversal of above tree is : A B C D E

Function for Preorder Traversal of TBT :

```
void TBT : :preorder_TBT(TBT*root,TBT*header)
{
    TBT*trav;
    int flag=0;
    trav=root;
    while(trav!=header)
    {
        while(trav->l_flag==0&&flag==0)
        {
            cout<<" "<<trav->data;
            trav=trav->l_link;
        }
        if(flag==0)
        cout<<" "<<trav->data;
        if(trav->r_flag==0&&flag==0)
        {
            trav=trav->r_link;
        }
        else
        {
            if(trav->r_flag==0&&flag==1)
            {
                trav=trav->r_link;
                flag=0;
            }
            else
            {
                if(trav->r_flag==1&&flag==0)
                {
                    trav=trav->r_link;
                    flag=1;
```

```
        }
        else
        {
            if(trav->r_flag==1&&flag==1)
            {
            trav=trav->r_link;
            }
        }
    }
   }
  }
}
```

1.10.2.2 Algorithm for Inorder Traversal of TBT

- If trav!=header go to step 2 else go to step 6

- Move to the leftmost element of the tree when flag==0;

- Print trav->data

- If trav is having right child then move trav to its right side.   i.e. trav=trav->right. Make flag=1

- Move to step 1.

- Stop.

Refer the following TBT :

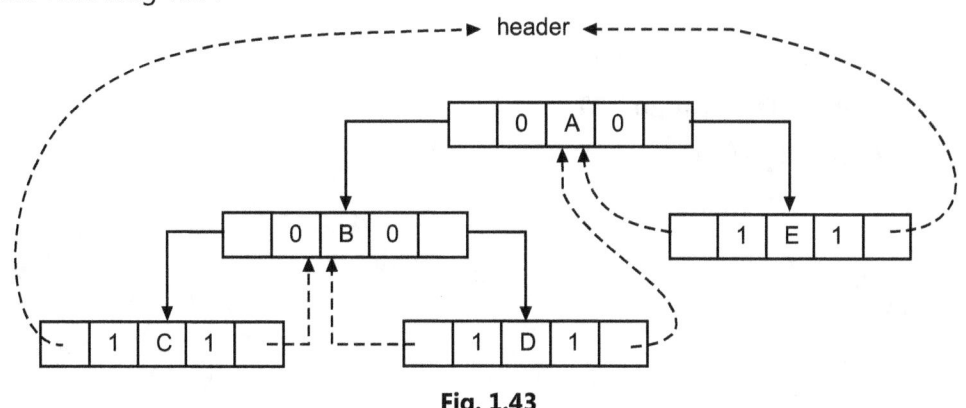

Fig. 1.43

Working of Algorithm :

- Initially flag = 0 & trav will point to (A)

- As trav!=header goto (3)
- As trav → l_flag!=1 && flag==0, move trav to trav → l_link i.e. trav will point to (B) repeat step (3) till trav points to (c). At (c) trav → l_flag is 1, so we will come out of while loop.
- Print trav → data.

  i.e. current output will be : C
- As trav → r_flag !=0 move trav to right side, so trav will point to B, & make flag = 1.
- Print trav → data

  current o/p will be : C   B
- Now trav → r_flag==0, so move to its right side. Now trav will point to (D), make flag=0 [previously it was 1].
- Print trav → data

  current o/p will be : C   B   D
- At (D) trav → r_flag !=0, so move trav to its right, as well as make flag = 1, [Now trav will point to (A)].
- Print trav → data

  current output will be : C   B   D   A
- Trav is pointing to (A) & trav → r_flag is 0, so move trav to it's right side & make flag = 0. [Now trav will point to E]
- Print trav → data

  current output will be : C   B   D   A   E
- Now trav → r_flag !=0, move trav to right side & make flag=1. [Now trav will point to header]
- As trav==header, exit from the function.

Function for Inorder Traversal of TBT :

```
void TBT : :inorder_TBT(TBT*root,TBT*header)
{
    int flag=0;
    TBT*trav;
    trav=root;


    while(trav!=header)
    {
```

```
        while(trav->l_flag!=1&&flag==0)
        {
            trav=trav->l_link;
        }

        cout<<" "<<trav->data;

        if(trav->r_flag==0)
        {
            trav=trav->r_link;
            flag=0;
        }
        else
        {
            trav=trav->r_link;
            flag=1;
        }
    }
}
```

Program : Threaded Binary Tree :

```
#include<iostream.h>
#include<conio.h>
#include<process.h>

class TBT
{
    private :
        int data;
        int l_flag,r_flag;
        TBT*l_link,*r_link;
```

```cpp
    public :
        TBT*create_TBT(TBT*,TBT*);
        void inorder_TBT(TBT*,TBT*);
        void preorder_TBT(TBT*,TBT*);
};

void TBT : :preorder_TBT(TBT*root,TBT*header)
{
    TBT*trav;
    int flag=0;
    trav=root;
    while(trav!=header)
    {
        while(trav->l_flag==0&&flag==0)
        {
            cout<<" "<<trav->data;
            trav=trav->l_link;
        }
        if(flag==0)
        cout<<" "<<trav->data;

        if(trav->r_flag==0&&flag==0)
        {
            trav=trav->r_link;
        }
        else
        {
            if(trav->r_flag==0&&flag==1)
            {
                trav=trav->r_link;
```

```
                flag=0;
            }
        else
        {
            if(trav->r_flag==1&&flag==0)
            {
                trav=trav->r_link;
                flag=1;
            }
            else
            {
                if(trav->r_flag==1&&flag==1)
                {
                trav=trav->r_link;

                }
            }
        }
    }
}

}

void TBT : :inorder_TBT(TBT*root,TBT*header)
{
    int flag=0;
    TBT*trav;
    trav=root;

    while(trav!=header)
```

```
    {
        while(trav->l_flag!=1&&flag==0)
        {
            trav=trav->l_link;
        }

        cout<<" "<<trav->data;

        if(trav->r_flag==0)
        {
            trav=trav->r_link;
            flag=0;
        }
        else
        {
            trav=trav->r_link;
            flag=1;
        }
    }
}

TBT*TBT : :create_TBT(TBT*root,TBT*header)
{
    TBT*trav,*temp,*p;
    int attached_flag=0;
    char ans;

    while(1)
    {
    trav=root;
```

```cpp
if(root==NULL)
{
    temp=new TBT();
    cout<<"\nEnter the data ";
    cin>>temp->data;
    temp->l_flag=1;
    temp->r_flag=1;
    temp->l_link=header;
    temp->r_link=header;
    root=temp;
}
else
{
        temp=new TBT();
        cout<<"\nEnter the data ";
        cin>>temp->data;
        temp->l_flag=1;
        temp->r_flag=1;
        attached_flag=0;

        trav=root;
        while(attached_flag==0)
        {
            if(trav->data<temp->data&&trav->r_flag==0)
            {
                trav=trav->r_link;
            }
            else
            if(trav->data<temp->data&&trav->r_flag==1)
```

```
                {
                    trav->r_flag=0;
                    p=trav->r_link;
                    trav->r_link=temp;
                    temp->r_link=p;
                    temp->l_link=trav;
                    attached_flag=1;
                }

                if(trav->data>temp->data&&trav->l_flag==0)
                {
                    trav=trav->l_link;
                }
                else
                if(trav->data>temp->data&&trav->l_flag==1)
                {
                    trav->l_flag=0;
                    p=trav->l_link;
                    trav->l_link=temp;
                    temp->l_link=p;
                    temp->r_link=trav;
                    attached_flag=1;
                }
            }

        attached_flag=0;
}
cout<<"\nDo you want to attach more nodes [y/n] ";
cin>>ans;
if(ans=='n'||ans=='N')
```

```
        break;
    }
    return root;
}


void main()
{
    int choice;
    TBT*root=NULL,obj,*header=NULL;

    while(1)
    {
        cout<<"\n1.Create TBT";
        cout<<"\n2.Inorder TBT";
        cout<<"\n3.Preorder TBT";
        cout<<"\n4.Exit";
        cout<<"\nEnter your choice :";
        cin>>choice;
        switch(choice)
        {
            case 1 : root=obj.create_TBT(root,header);
                break;
            case 2 : obj.inorder_TBT(root,header);
                break;
            case 3 : obj.preorder_TBT(root,header);
                break;
            case 4 :
                exit(0);
        }
    }
}
```

Postorder Traversal TBT :

Note : Postorder traversal of TBT is implemented using different method than that of inorder and preorder.

- Accept head as a function parameter.

- t = head → l_link.

  so t will point to the root node of the tree.

- Move t to its left or right depending on if it is having left or right child associated with it. i.e.

```
while (t → l_flag ==0 || t → r_flag == 0)
{
     if (t → l_flag == 0)
          t = t → l_link;
     else
          t = t → r_link;
}
while(t! = head)
{
     print data of t
     Then find out it's postorder successor. i.e.
     t = postorder_successor (t);
}
```

Function for Postorder Traversal of TBT :

```
void TBT : :postorder(tbtnode *head)
{
   tbtnode *t;
   t=head->l_link;
while(t->l_flag==0||t->r_flag==0)
{
  if(t->l_flag==0)
   t=t->l_link;
  else
```

```
 t=t->r_link;
}
while(t!=head)
{
cout<<" "<<t->data;
t=postorder_successor(t);
}
}
```

Find Post-Order Successor for the Given Node :

1. If t is a right child of its parent then do the following else goto (2).

    move to the left most child of t. i.e.

    ```
    while (t → l_flag ==0)
    t = t → l_link;
    return (t → l_link);
    ```

2.

    ```
    while (t → r_flag ==0)
    t = t → r_link;
    t = t → r_link;
    if (t → r_flag ==1)
    {
        return (t)
    }
    else
    {
        t = t → r_link;
        while (t → l_flag ==0 || t → r_flag == 0)
        {
            if (t → l_flag ==0)
                t = t → l_link;
            else
    ```

```
        t = t → r_link;
    }
    return (t);
}
```

Code for Postorder_Successor Function :

```
tbtnode *TBT : :postorder_successor(tbtnode *t)
{
if(t->child==1)
 {
while(t->l_flag==0)
 t=t->l_link;
 return(t->l_link);
 }
 else
 {
 while(t->r_flag==0)
 t=t->r_link;
 t=t->r_link;
   if(t->r_flag==1)
     return(t);
   else
   {
    t=t->r_link;
    while(t->l_flag==0||t->r_flag==0)
    {
    if(t->l_flag==0)
    t=t->l_link;
    else
     t=t->r_link;
    }
```

```
    return(t);
}
}
}
```

Consider the following example to understand the working of postorder.

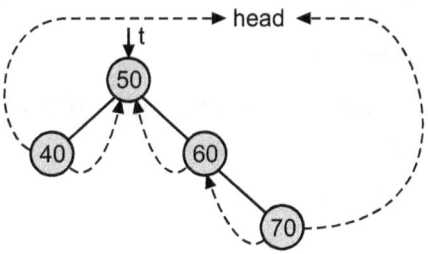

Fig. 1.44

- Initially t will point to root.
- t → l_flag == 0, move t to its left side.

  Now t will point to 40.

  t → r_flag && t → l_flag will now become1, so we will come out of while loop.
- As, t! = head

  print t → data i.e. 40.

  Output : 40

  Pass t to postorder_successor function.
- In postorder successor function, as t is not a right child of its parent node so if (t → child ==1) condition will be false and we will goto else part.

  t → r_flag is not a

  move t to its right side. Now t will point to 50.

  As r_flag of 50 is not 1 so goto the else part move t to its right side. So t will point to 60.

  Now as r_flag of 60 is 0 go in to the while loop. here, t → l_flag is not equal to 0 so goto else part and move t to its right. t will now point to 70. As left and right flag of 70 is not 0 so we will be out of while loop.

  After coming out of while loop return t (currently t is pointing to 70).
- Collect value of t into postorder function as :

  t = postorder_successor (t);

  and print t → data.

Output : 40, 70.

pass 70 to postorder_successor function.

- In postorder_successor function, as t i.e. 70 is right child of its parent return (t → l_link) so it will return 60 to the postorder function.

- In the postorder function collect 60 and print it.

Output : 40, 70, 60.

pass 60 to postorder_successor function.

- In postorder_successor function, as t i.e. 60 is right child of its parent return (t → l_link) so it will return 50 to the postorder function.

- In the postorder function collect 50 and print it.

Output : 40, 70, 60, 50

Pass 50 to postorder_successor function.

- In postorder_successor function as t i.e. 50 is not right child of its parent node, then move to the rightmost child by

while (t → r_flag ==0)

      t = t → r_link;

after this while loop t will point to 70. Now move t to it's right side once again. So t will point to head node.

Now t → r_flag == 1 when t points to head node.

As t → r_flag ==1, return head node to the postorder function.

- as t ==head, come out of the while loop of the postorder function.

Final output will be : 40, 70, 60, 50.

Source Code of TBT

```
#include<stdio.h>
#include<iostream.h>
#include<conio.h>
#include<stdlib.h>
#include<process.h>
class tbtnode
  {
  public :
    int data;
```

```
        tbtnode *l_link,*r_link;
        int l_flag,r_flag,flag;
        int child;
    };
class TBT
 {
  tbtnode *root;
  tbtnode *preorder_successor(tbtnode *t);
  tbtnode *inorder_successor(tbtnode *t);
  tbtnode *postorder_successor(tbtnode *t);
  public :
    TBT()
     {
     root=NULL;
     }
  void preorder(tbtnode *);
  void inorder(tbtnode *);
  void postorder(tbtnode *);
  void create(tbtnode *);
 };
void main()
 {
   TBT tbt;
   int op,x,n;
   char ch;
   clrscr();
   tbtnode *head,*root;      //here head indicates dummy variable
   head= new tbtnode();
   head->l_link=head;
   head->r_link=head;
```

```cpp
head->l_flag=1;
head->r_flag=1;
clrscr();
 do
 {
 cout<<"\n****Threaded binary tree operations****";
 cout<<"\n1)create\n2)preorder\n3)inorder\n4)postorder\n5)exit";
 cout<<"\nEnter ur choice";
 cin>>op;
switch(op)
{
 case 1 :
  cout<<"nEnter Number Of Nodes";
  cin>>n;
  cout<<"\nEnter root data :";
   cin>>x;
   root=new tbtnode();
   root->data=x;
   root->l_flag=root->r_flag=1;
   root->child=0;
   root->l_link=head->l_link;
   head->l_link=root;
   head->l_flag=0;
   root->r_link=head->r_link;
   for(int i=0;i<n-1;i++)
   tbt.create(root);
   break;
  case 2 :
   cout<<"\nPreorder Traversal Is :\n";
   tbt.preorder(head);
```

```
            break;
    case 3 :
    cout<<"\nInorder Traversal Is :\n";
        tbt.inorder(head);
        break;
    case 4 :
        cout<<"\nPostorder Traversal Is :\n";
        tbt.postorder(head);
        break;
    case 5 :
        exit(0);
        break;
    }
}while(op<=5);
}
void TBT : :create(tbtnode *root)
{
    int x,op,flag,y;
    flag=0;
    char ch;
    tbtnode *curr=root;
    tbtnode *q,*p;
    do
    {
        cout<<"\nCurrent   node   :\t"<<curr->data<<"\n\n1.l_link   direction"<<"\n\n2.r_link
direction";
        cout<<"\nEnter ur choice";
        cin>>op;
switch(op)
{
case 1 :
```

```
if(curr->l_flag==1)
{
cout<<"enter l_link child of "<<curr->data<<" :-";
 cin>>x;
 q=new tbtnode();
 q->data=x;
 q->l_flag=q->r_flag=1;
 q->l_link=curr->l_link;
 q->r_link=curr;
 curr->l_link=q;
 curr->l_flag=0;
 q->child=0;
  flag=1;
 }
 else
 curr=curr->l_link;
 break;
case 2 :
 if(curr->r_flag==1)
 {
   cout<<"enter r_link child of "<<curr->data<<" :-";
   cin>>x;
   q=new tbtnode();
   q->data=x;
   q->l_flag=q->r_flag=1;
   q->l_link=curr;
   q->r_link=curr->r_link;
   curr->r_link=q;
   curr->r_flag=0;
   q->child=1;
```

```
       flag=1;
  }
    else
    curr=curr->r_link;
    break;
    }
 }while(flag==0);
}
void TBT : :preorder(tbtnode *head)
{
  tbtnode *t;
  t=head->l_link;
    cout<<"\n";
  while(t!=head)
   {
   cout<<" "<<t->data;
    t=preorder_successor(t);
   }
}
tbtnode* TBT : :preorder_successor(tbtnode *t)
{
if(t->l_flag==0)
  return(t->l_link);
if(t->r_flag==0)
  return(t->r_link);
do
{
t=t->r_link;
}while(t->r_flag==1);
  return(t->r_link);
```

```
}
void TBT : :postorder(tbtnode *head)
{
   tbtnode *t;
   t=head->l_link;
while(t->l_flag==0||t->r_flag==0)
 {
  if(t->l_flag==0)
   t=t->l_link;
  else
   t=t->r_link;
 }
  while(t!=head)
 {
 cout<<" "<<t->data;
 t=postorder_successor(t);
 }
}
tbtnode *TBT : :postorder_successor(tbtnode *t)
{
if(t->child==1)
 {
while(t->l_flag==0)
 t=t->l_link;
 return(t->l_link);
 }
  else
  {
  while(t->r_flag==0)
  t=t->r_link;
```

```
 t=t->r_link;
   if(t->r_flag==1)
      return(t);
    else
    {
     t=t->r_link;
    while(t->l_flag==0||t->r_flag==0)
    {
    if(t->l_flag==0)
    t=t->l_link;
    else
      t=t->r_link;
     }
     return(t);
   }
   }
 }
void TBT : :inorder(tbtnode *head)
  {
   tbtnode *t;
   t=head->l_link;
   cout<<"\n";
   while(t->l_flag==0)
   t=t->l_link;
    while(t!=head)
    {
    cout<<" "<<t->data;
    t=inorder_successor(t);
    }
  }
```

```
tbtnode *TBT : :inorder_successor(tbtnode *t)
  {
   if(t->r_flag==0)
    {
     t=t->r_link;
    while(t->l_flag==0)
     t=t->l_link;
     return(t);
    }
   else
     return(t->r_link);
  }
```

/*==================== Threaded binary tree operations ==========================

1) create

2) preorder

3) inorder

4) postorder

5) exit

Enter ur choice1

nEnter Number Of Nodes8

Enter root data : 50

Current node :   50

1.l_link direction

2.r_link direction

Enter ur choice1

enter l_link child of 50 :-25

Current node :   50

1.l_link direction

2.r_link direction

Enter ur choice1

Current node :   25

1.l_link direction

2.r_link direction

Enter ur choice2

enter r_link child of 25 :-30

Current node :   50

1.l_link direction

2.r_link direction

Enter ur choice 2

enter r_link child of 50 :-75

Current node :   50

1.l_link direction

2.r_link direction

Enter ur choice 2

Current node :   75

1.l_link direction

2.r_link direction

Enter ur choice1

enter l_link child of 75 :-60

Current node :   50

1.l_link direction

2.r_link direction

Enter ur choice 2

Current node :   75

1.l_link direction

2.r_link direction

Enter ur choice1

Current node :   60

1.l_link direction

2.r_link direction

Enter ur choice2

enter r_link child of 60 :-63

Current node :   50

1.l_link direction

2.r_link direction

Enter ur choice 2

Current node :　75

1.l_link direction

2.r_link direction

Enter ur choice1

Current node :　60

1.l_link direction

2.r_link direction

Enter ur choice2

Current node :　63

1.l_link direction

2.r_link direction

Enter ur choice 1

enter l_link child of 63 :-61

Current node :　50

1.l_link direction

2.r_link direction

Enter ur choice 2

Enter ur choice2

Current node :　75

1.l_link direction

2.r_link direction

Enter ur choice2

enter r_link child of 75 :-85

****Threaded binary tree operations****

1) create

2) preorder

3) inorder

4) postorder

5) exit

Enter ur choice 2

Preorder Traversal Is :

 50 25 30 75 60 63 61 85

****Threaded binary tree operations****

1) create

2) preorder

3) inorder

4) postorder

5) exit

Enter ur choice3

Inorder Traversal Is :

 25 30 50 60 61 63 75 85

****Threaded binary tree operations****

1) create

2) preorder

3) inorder

4) postorder

5) exit

Enter ur choice4

Postorder Traversal Is :

 30 25 61 63 60 85 75 50

****Threaded binary tree operations****

1) create

2) preorder

3) inorder

4) postorder

5) exit

Enter ur choice 5*/

Questions :

It is worthwhile to use threaded trees to avoid recursive postorder or preorder traversals?

Justify your answer.

Answer :

1. TBT mainly uses threads to replace the NULL links.

2. Left "NULL" link is replaced by the address of its inorder predecessor and that of the right "NULL" link is replaced by the address of its inorder successor.

3. We can implement all the traversals on TBT without using stack, but the memory requirement for storing the node increase.

4. Also timing complexity of preorder and postorder traversal on TBT is worse than that of the recursive traversal on binary trees without threads.

5. Also insertion and deletion operations becomes complex in TBT.

1.11 CASE STUDY

In computer science, trees have number of applications because they are most efficient for searching the data. Hence, they are used to store large databases. Some of the applications are as below.

1. Expression Tree :

The compilers and interpreters evaluate the expression based on the precedence of operators. Any arithmetic expression can be represented using binary tree. The evaluation of the expression becomes convenient with such representation. For example, the expression a + b * c/d can be represented as below :

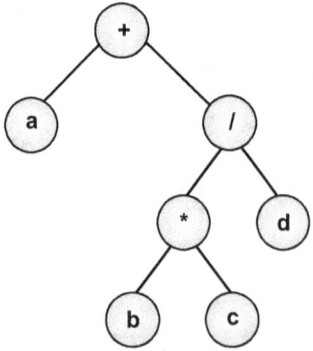

Fig. 1.45 : Expression tree for a + b * c/d

The expression 3 * 4 + (8 + 7) can be represented as

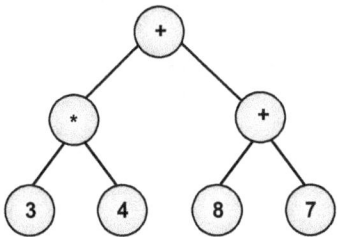

Fig. 1.46 : Expression for tree 3 * 4 + (8 + 7)

Inorder traversal of tree will result into evaluation of the expression. Some more examples are as below.

d=a * b/d − 4.

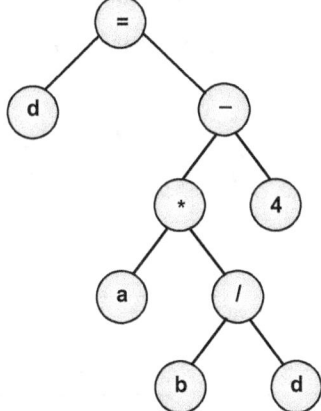

Fig. 1.47 : Expression tree for d = a * b/d − 4

x=4 * 5 + 6 * 7 − 3/2

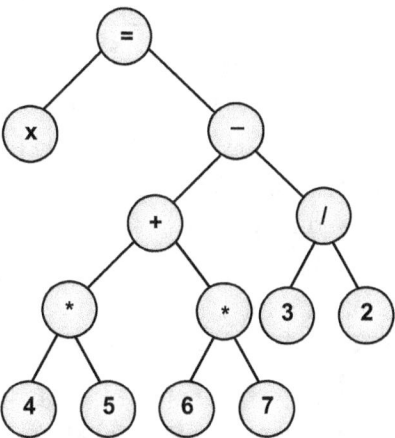

Fig. 1.48 : Expression tree for x = 4 * 5 + 6 * 7 − 3/2

2. Huffman's Coding :

Why Huffman Coding??

- Huffman coding is a technique used to compress files before transmission
- Uses statistical coding
  - ➤ More frequently used symbols have shorter code words by making the use of prefix codes.
- Works well for text and fax transmissions.

One of the most important applications of binary tree is in communication (sending and receiving data).

Consider an example of transmitting an English text made up from a, b, c, d, e, f, g, h.

We are going to represent these characters in binary numbers.

As there are 8 characters, we can use three bits for generating unique codes for them, which are shown in the following table.

Table 1.1

Character	Code/Seq.
a	000
b	001
c	010
d	011
e	100
f	101
g	110
h	111

Let us consider that sequence of 1000 character is to be send. Hence total bits transmitted will be 1000*3=3000 (as every character in the sequence will be represented by 3 bits).

It may happen that, among these 1000 characters, the letters b, d and f are appeared maximum number of times in the sequence.

So in such transmissions, we represent the letters having more frequent occurrence with shorter sequences (using less no. of bits) and less frequently used letters with longer sequences (using more no. of bits). So that the overall length of the string will be reduced.

In the above example, if b, d and f are represented by sequence of 2 bits and each of them appeared in the sequence 150 times then, 3*150*2=900 bits will be formed for transmission. But before shortening them, each letter we were representing by 3 bits that time we would have required 3*150*3= 1350 bits.

It means that after shortening the sequence of letters b, d and f, we are transmitting 1350-900=450 less bits. This means we have done data compression compared to the first regular technique.

Such a coding is called as 'variable length coding', even though variable length coding reduces the overall length of the sequence to be transmitted, the interesting problem arises :

Problem Due to Variable Length Coding :

Lets us the following sequences :

Table 1.2

Character	Sequence/code
a	00
n	01
t	0001

- We will transmit 'an' letters by sending the sequence 0001
- At receiving end it is difficult to determine whether the transmitted sequence is 'an' or 't'.
- This is because 00 is a prefix of code 0001.
- For that while assigning the variable sequence to letters, we must take care that no code should be prefix of the other.

Prefix Code :

A set of sequence is said to be a prefix code, if no sequence in the set is a prefix of another sequence in the set. E.g. see the following table,

Table 1.3

Character	Sequence/code
a	000
b	001
c	01
d	10

The sequence codes in the above table are called as prefix codes.

Now see the following table

Table 1.4

Character	Sequence/code
a	1
b	00
c	000
d	0001

The sequence codes in the above table are not prefix codes. Huffman had given a very elegant procedure to construct optimal binary tree for generating the prefix codes of variable lengths for the letters from the point of unambiguous data transmission.

1.12 HUFFMAN'S ALGORITHM

- Organize the data into a row as ascending order of their frequency of occurrence in the given sequence of letters.

- Find two nodes with smaller weights, join them to form the third node. This will form a new two level tree. The weight of new third node is addition of weights of two nodes.

- Repeat step 2 till all nodes on every level are combined to form a single tree.

Huffman's Coding :

Example 1.9 : For the given data, build the Huffman's tree and find out prefix code for each letter.   [IT 08]

Table 1.5

Data	Weight
A	22
B	5
C	11
D	19
E	2
F	11
G	25
H	5

Solution :

Step 1 :

E	B	H	C	F	D	A	G
2	5	5	11	11	19	22	25

Step 2 :

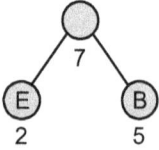

		H	C	F	D	A	G
E	B	5	11	11	19	22	25
2	5						

Step 3 :

Sort the list in ascending order.

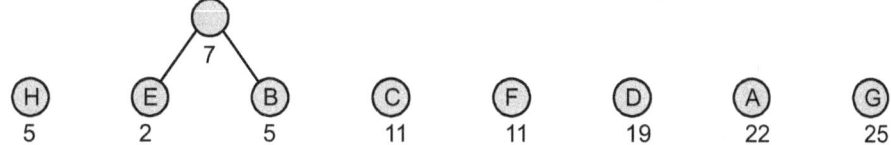

Step 4 :

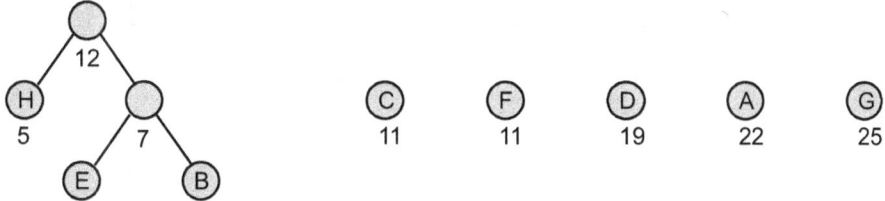

Step 5 : Arrange the list in ascending order

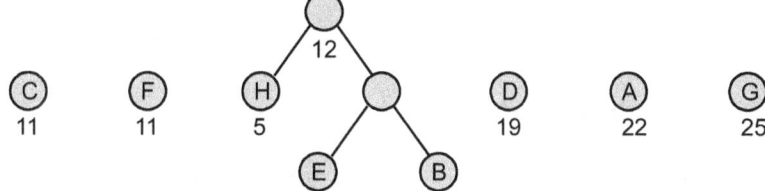

Step 6 :

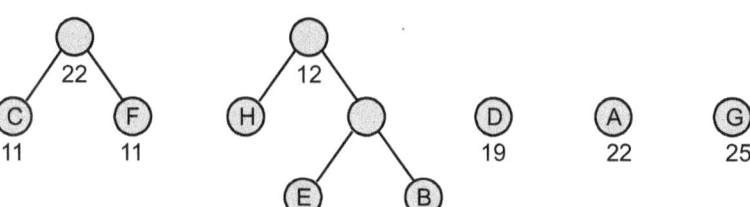

Step 7 :

Sort the list in ascending order.

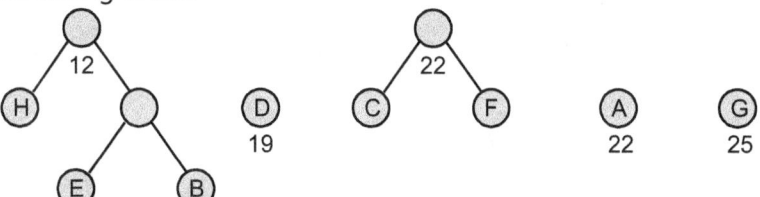

Step 8 :

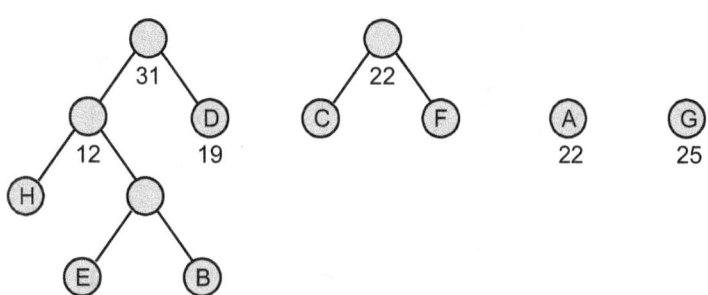

Step 9 :

Sort the list in ascending order.

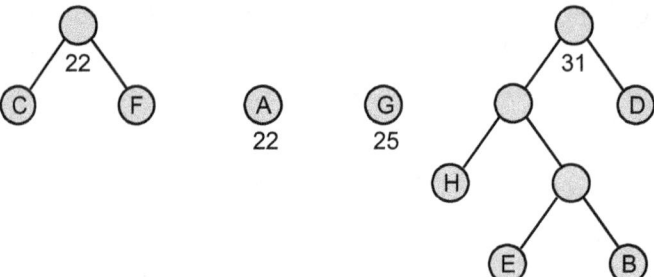

Step 10 :

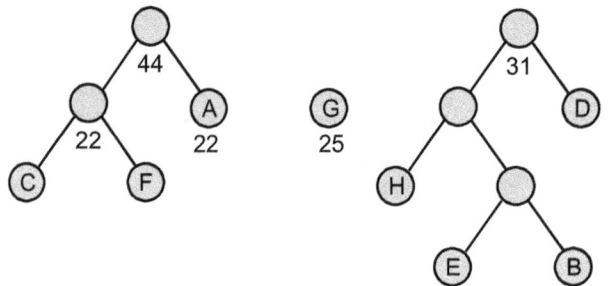

Step 11 :

Sort the list in ascending order

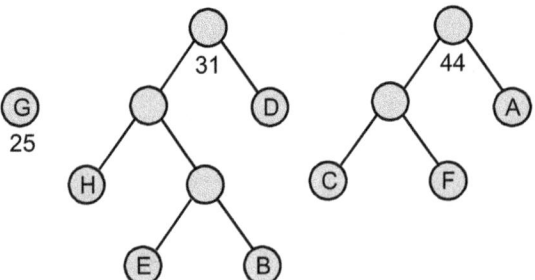

Step 12 :

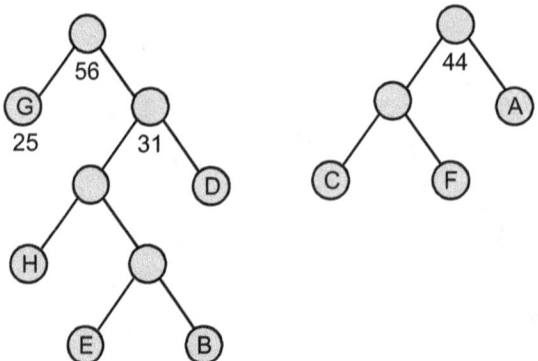

Step 13 :

Sort the list according to its ascending order.

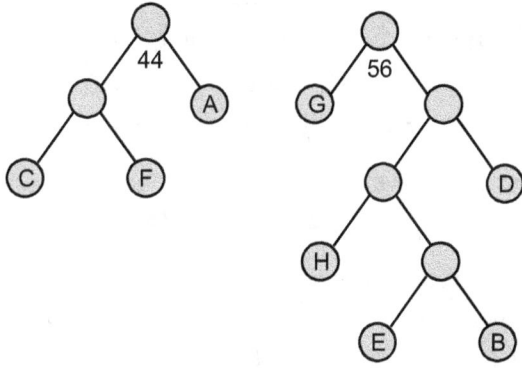

Step 14 :

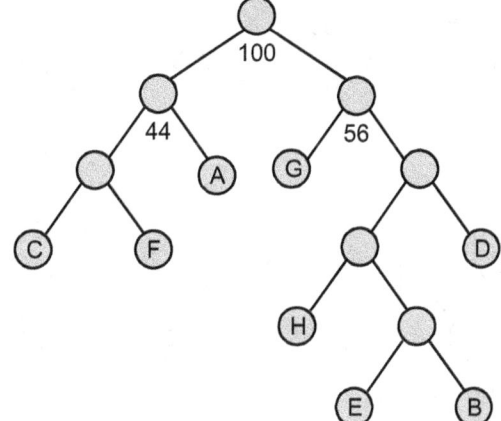

Huffman's codes will be as follows :

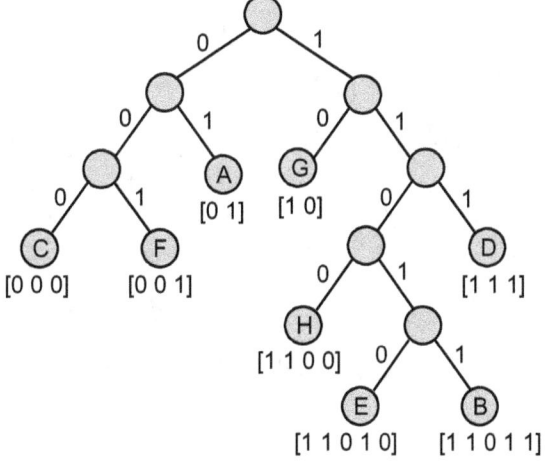

Note : See the Huffman codes carefully, the number of bits required to represent A and G (having weights 22 and 25 respectively) are only 2, while that of E and B (having weights 2 and 5) are 5.

Example 1.10 : Construct Huffman tree based on the following character weights :**[Dec. 11]**

E = 15	T = 12	A = 10	O = 08	R = 07	N = 06	S = 05
U = 05	I = 04	D = 04	M = 03	C = 03	G = 02	K = 02

Also give Huffman code assignment at each node.

Solution :

Step 1 : Each node is represented as tree

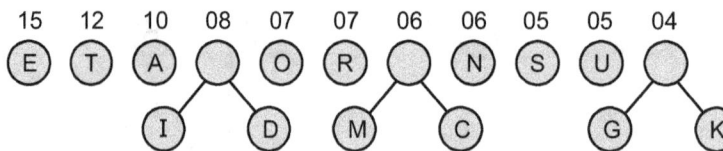

Step 2 : Merge G.K. (Trees of minimum weights)

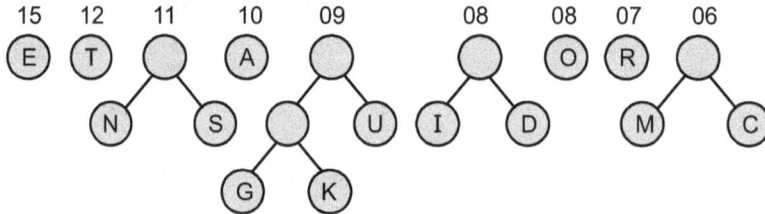

Step 3 : Merge M, C and I, D

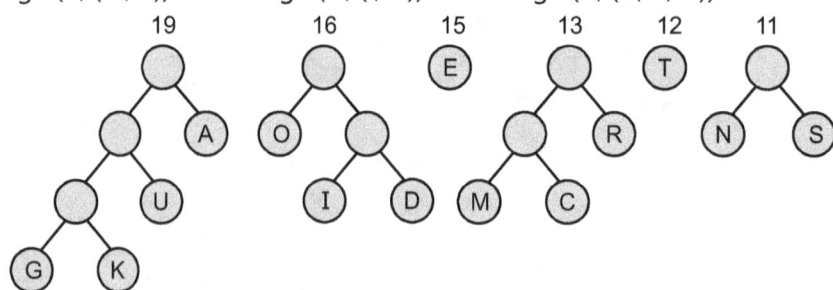

Step 4 : Merge (U, (G, K)) and Merge (N, S)

Step 5 : Merge (R, (M, C)) and Merge (O, (I, D)) and merge (A, (G, K, U))

Step 6 : Merge (T, (N, S)) and Merge (E, (M, C, R)) and Merge ((G, K, U, A), (O, I, D))

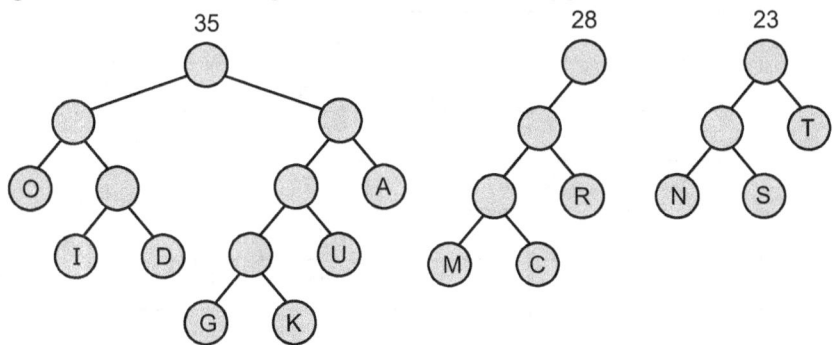

Step 7 : Merge ((M, C, R, E), (N, S, T))

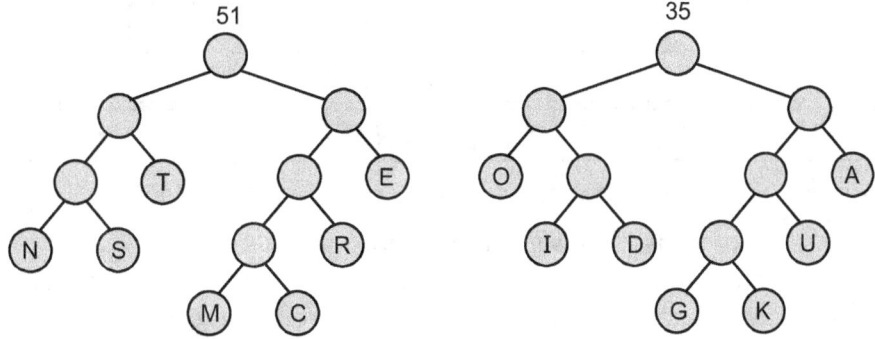

Step 8 : Merge ((N, S, T, M, C, R, E), (O, I, D, G, K, U, A))

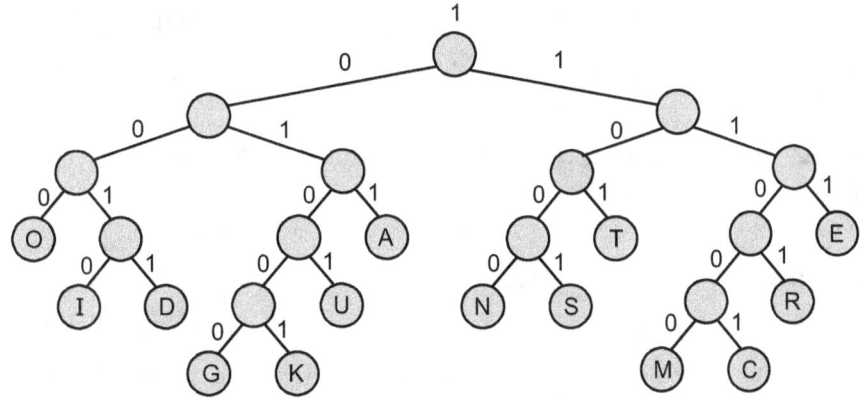

Table 1.6

Symbol	Huffman Code
E	111
T	101
A	011

O	000
R	1101
N	1000
S	1001
U	0101
I	0010
D	0011
M	11000
C	11001
G	01000
K	01001

SUMMARY

- Tree is a nonlinear data structure used for efficient access or retrieval of elements.

- A tree (T) is a set of nodes. The set can be empty. If it is non-empty set, it consists of a specially designated node called root node and zero or more sub-trees (T_1, T_2, ..., T_n) each whose roots are connected by a directed edge from the root of T.

- Binary tree is a tree in which no node has more than two sub-trees.

- A binary tree can be represented using array or linked representation.

- A binary tree can be traversed in three different ways inorder (LVR), preorder (VLR) and postorder (LRV).

- A Binary Search Tree (BST) is used to store data for searching applications. A binary search tree is a binary tree in which for each node, the left sub-tree elements are less than the node elements and right sub-tree elements are greater than the node element.

- If binary search tree is height balanced, the time complexity of search is $0(\log_2 n)$.

- The traversals of binary tree can be implemented using recursive or non-recursive ways.

- A threaded binary tree makes use of NULL fields in the nodes of binary tree for spreading up the operations on binary tree.

- A height balanced or AVL tree is a binary tree with T_l and T_r as left and right sub-trees having heights h_l and h_r such that $|h_l - h_r| \leq 1$.

- In order to make a binary tree height balanced, we can use one of the four rotations LL, RR, LR or RL.

- Trees can be used for expression storage and evaluation and gaming applications.

SOLVED PROBLEMS

1. Write a recursive function to print leaf nodes of binary tree.

Solution :

```
void leaf node_check(NODE *temp)

{

    printf("The leaf nodes are \n");

    if (temp!=NULL)

    {

        leaf-node-check (temp->lchild);

        if(temp->lchild==NULL && temp->rchild=NULL)

        {

            printf("%d \n", temp->data);

        }

        leaf_node_check(temp->rchild);

    }

}
```

2. Write Inorder, Preoder and Postorder traversals for following tree.

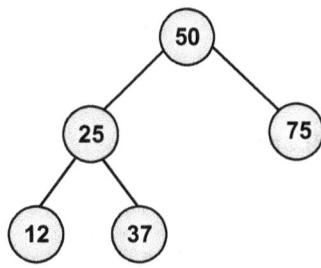

Fig. 1.49 : Binary tree

Solution :

Inorder   12 25 37 50 75

Preoder   50 25 12 37 75

Postorder 12 37 25 75 50

3. For the following data draw a binary search tree. Show all steps.

50 80 30 20 100 75 25 15 68

Solution : A binary search tree is shown in Fig. 1.49.

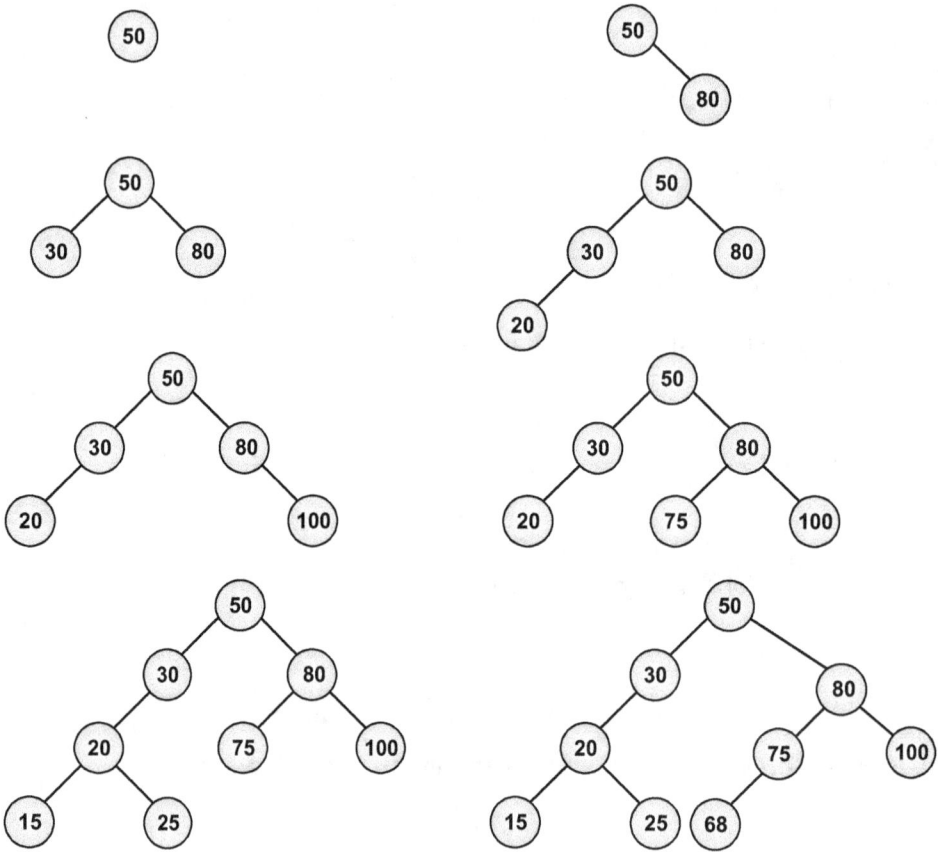

Fig. 1.50

4. Write Inorder, Preoder and Postorder traversals for the following. [May 10]

Solution :

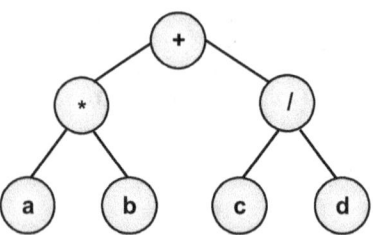

Fig. 1.51

Solution :

     Inorder   :   + *ab/cd

     Preoder   :   a * b + c/d

     Postorder   :   ab * cd \+

5. **From gives traversal, construct the binary tree.**   **(May 05, May 08, May 09)**

     Inorder   :   DBFEAGCLJHK

     Preorder   :   DFEBGLJKHCA

Solution :

Step I : From postorder we can see last element is root.

       Hence, the left sub-tree and right sub-tree from inorder traversal is

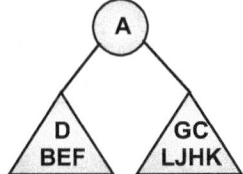

Step II :

    D   (B)   F   E   (A)   G   (C)   L   J   H   K

    D   F   E   (B)   G   L   J   K   H   (C)   (A)

Step III :

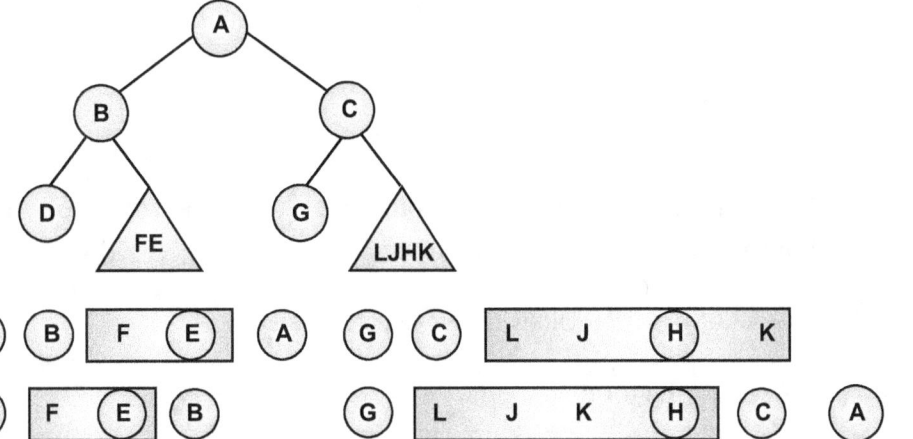

Step IV :

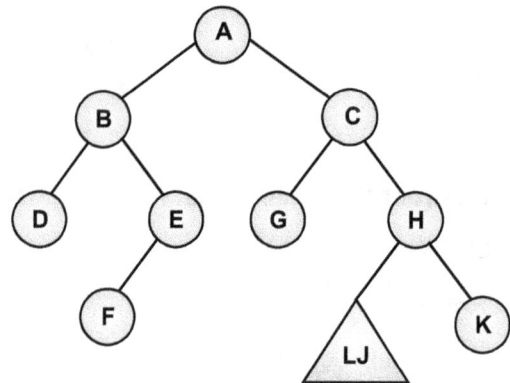

Step V :

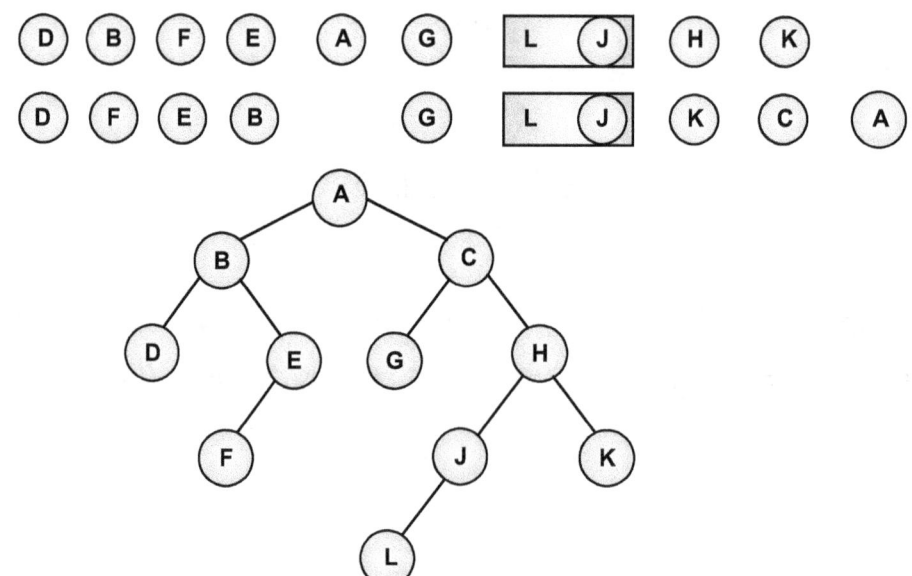

Fig. 1.52

6. **Define binary search tree. Construct binary search tree from following set of strings. Show all steps. Also write height of final tree.** **[May 05, 06, 08, 09]**

JAN FEB MAR APR MAY JUN JUL AUG SEP OCT NOV DEC

Solution : (Refer section 1.4 for definition)

Steps for creation of BST.

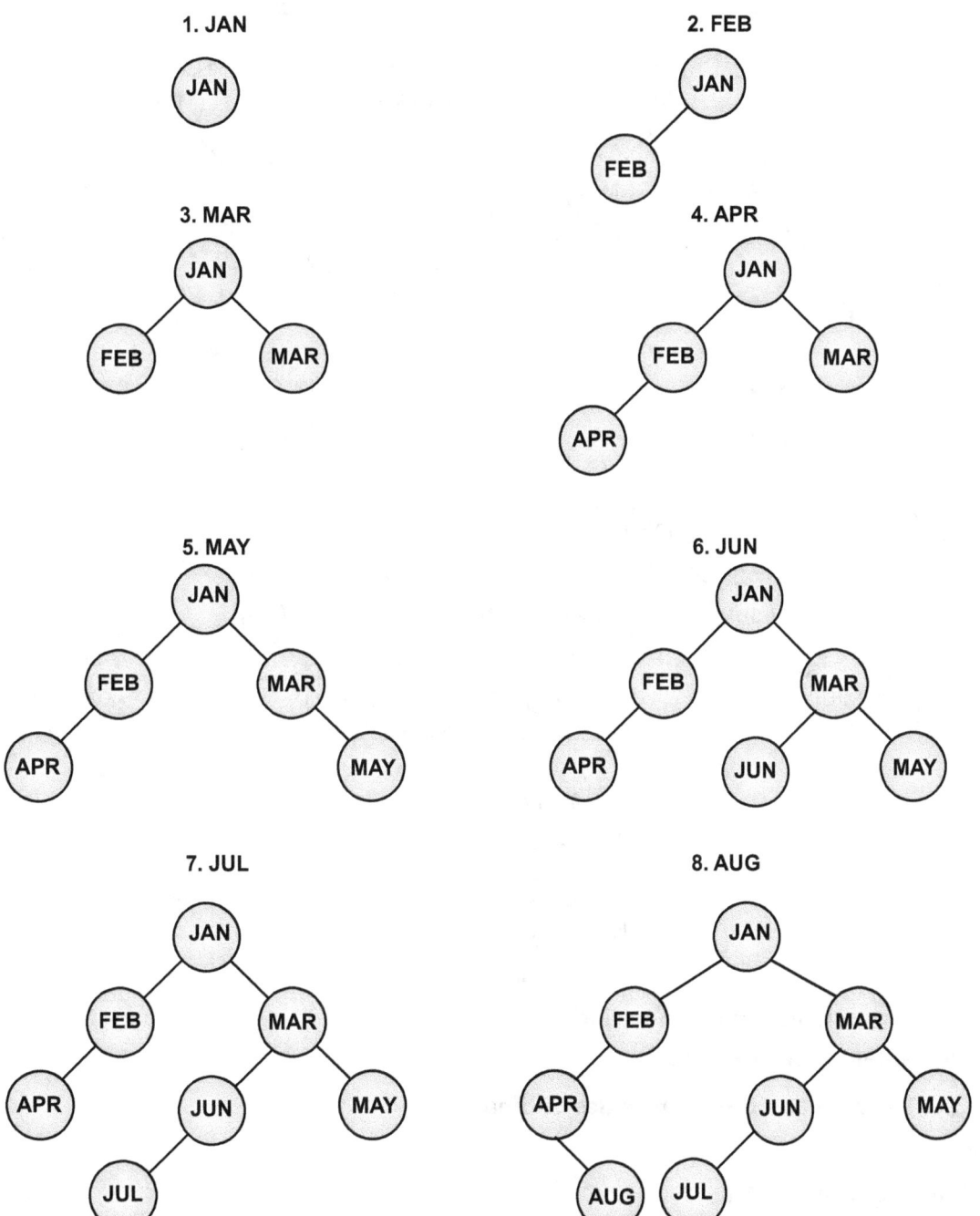

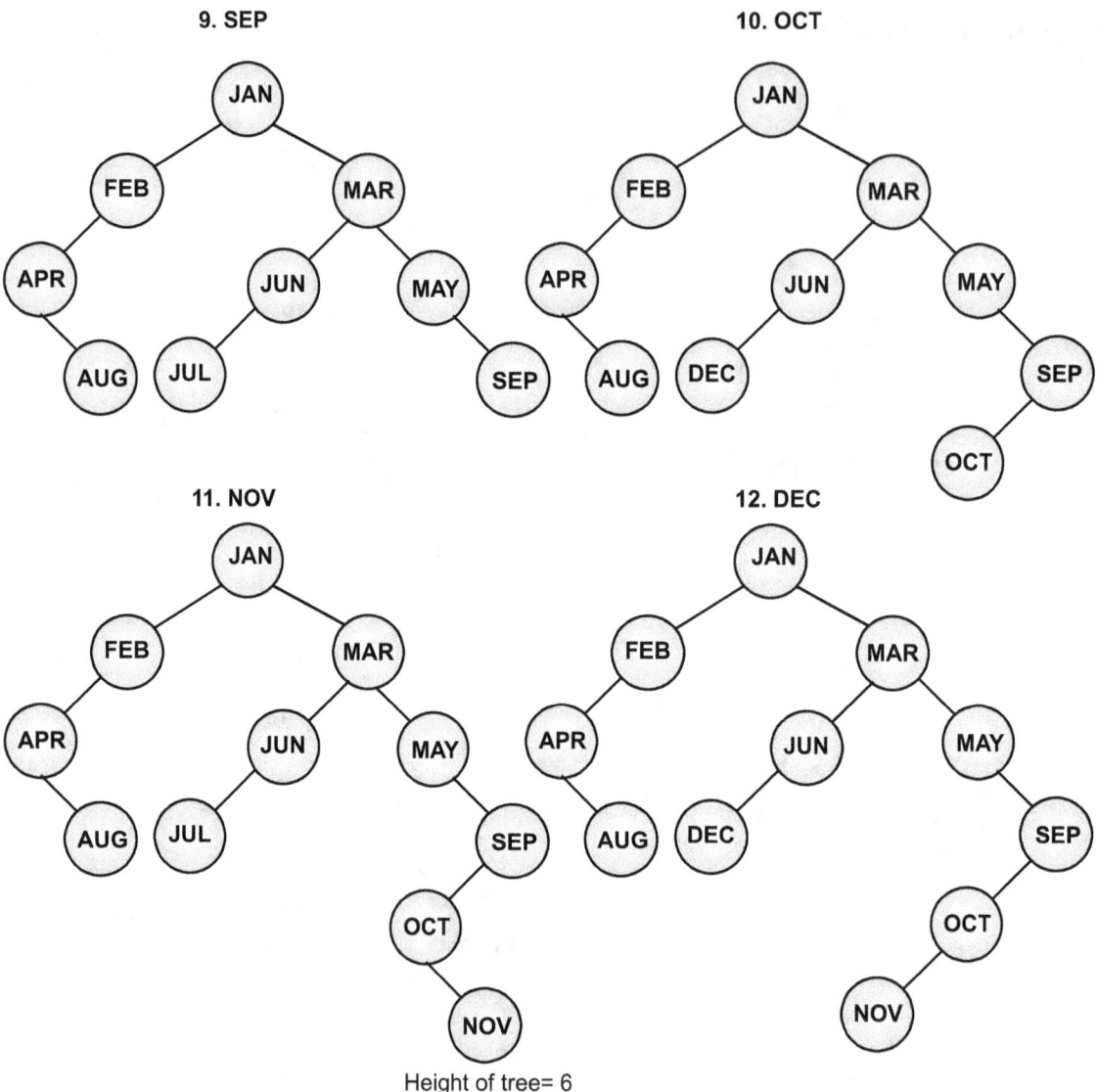

9. SEP

10. OCT

11. NOV

12. DEC

Height of tree= 6

Fig. 1.53

7. **Write a recursive function to find.**

   (i) Height of a binary tree.

   (ii) To count and print leaf nodes of binary tree.

Solution :

(i) int height(NODE *root)

     {

          int c;

```
    if (root== NULL)
        return(0);
    if (root->lchild==NULL & root->rchild==NULL)
        return(0);
    hl=height(root->lchild);
    hr=height(root->rchild);
    if(hl>hr)
        return(1 + hl)
    else
        return(1 + hr);
}
```

(ii) Refer solved problem 3.

8. Give pseudo code to print the leaves of tree using any traversal.

Solution :

```
void print_leaves(NODE *root)
{

    if (root!=NULL)
        print_leaves(root->lchild);
    if (root->lchild == NULL & root->rchild == NULL)
    printf("%d \n", root->data);
    print_leaves(root->rchild);

}
```

9. Explain any one application of binary tree with suitable example.

Solution : There are two applications of binary tree that we can list out.

  (i) Binary search tree.

  (ii) Expression tree.

(i) **Binary Search Tree :** We can use binary tree to store data in such a way that it will be easier to search required data. We can store the binary search tree such that at each node on the left side we will have smaller numbers and on right side we will have larger numbers than the data at node.

(ii) **Expression Tree :** Another application can be expression tree. We can store an infix expression into the binary tree so that we can have its prefix or postfix conversion using preorder or postorder traversal.

10. Write a non-recursive function to count number of leaf nodes in a binary tree.

Solution :

We can use non-recursive inorder traversal function. In place of print statement, we can use following statement.

```
if (temp->lchild==NULL&&temp->rchild==NULL)
    count=count + 1;
int count_leaves(NODE *root)
{   NODE *temp;  int count;
    temp=root;
    do
    {
        while(temp!=NULL)
        {
            push(temp);
            temp temp->lchild;
        }
        temp=pop( );
        if(temp-lchild==NULL && temp->rchild==NULL)
            count=count + 1;
        temp=temp->rchild;
    } while(!stack empty( ) || temp!=NULL);
    return(count);
}
```

EXERCISE

1. Define the following related to tree:

   1. Complete binary tree,

   2. Siblings,

   3. Non-terminals, (All non-leaf nodes are known as non-terminals)

   4. Forest,

   5. Height or Depth,

   6. Ancestors. (All nodes on the path joining the current node and the root node are ancestors of the current node.)

2. Define following terms with example.

   (i) Complete binary tree.

   (ii) Siblings.

   (iii) Height.

   (iv) Binary search tree.

   (v) Forest.

3. Define the following terms.

   1. Binary tree,

   2. Complete Binary tree,

   3. Threaded Binary Tree.

   4. What is binary tree?

5. Define the following:

   (a) Binary tree,

   (b) Complete binary tree,

   (c) Full binary, tree,

   (d) Sibling.

6. Define the following terms with respect to tree.

   (i) Complete binary tree.

   (ii) Forest.

   (iii) Height of binary tree.

(iv) Skewed binary tree.

(v) Full binary tree.

7. Explain the sequential representation of binary tree with example.

8. Define the term binary search tree. Give a 'C' declaration to define a node structure for the same. Write a function in 'C' to insert a node in a binary search tree.

9. What do you mean by binary search tree? Write a C function to search an element from a given binary search tree.

10. What is binary search tree? Explain its application.

11. What is binary search tree? Explain its application.

12. What is Binary search tree? Explain the application of BST.

13. Define binary search tree. Write a function to delete a node from a BST. Consider all possible cases.

14. Write necessary 'C' functions to search given data in BST.

15. Write a function to search an element in BST.

16. Traverse the tree built in Q. 47 in inorder, postorder and preorder and display the sequence of numbers.

17. Write a 'C' function (non-recursive) for deleting a node from binary search tree.

18. Write a C function to delete a node from binary search tree. Consider all cases.

19. Write necessary 'C' functions to delete a node in BST.

20. Write a non-recursive function to delete a node from BST. Explain all cases with suitable example.

21. Define binary search tree. Write a function to delete a node from BST.

22. Write a C function to insert a node in binary search tree.

23. Write a function to insert an element in BST.

24. Write necessary 'C' functions to implement inorder traversal in a binary tree non-recursively.

25. Write a non-recursive C function to traverse a binary tree in in-order traversal.

26. Write a non-recursive function in 'C' to perform a pre-order traversal on a binary tree.

27. Write necessary 'C' functions to implement preorder traversal in a binary tree non-recursively.

28. Write a pseudo code to traverse a given binary tree in preorder without recursion.

29. Write a non-recursive 'C' function to traverse binary tree in preorder. Explain with suitable example.

30. Explain non-recursive inorder traversal of binary tree.

31. Write an algorithm to implement non-recursive inorder traversal of binary tree.

32. Comment on "Threaded binary tree can be traversed without using stack".

33. What is threaded binary tree? State its advantage and disadvantages.

34. What is threaded binary tree? State its advantages and disadvantages.

35. State and explain the advantages of threaded binary tree.

36. Explain the term threaded binary tree. Give a 'C declaration to define the node structure of a threaded binary tree. What are the advantages of threaded binary trees over normal binary trees?

37. What do you mean by threaded binary tree? Also write pseudo code to perform non-recursive preorder traversal of TBT without using stack.

38. What is threaded binary tree? Explain its application.

39. What is threaded binary tree? Explain the application of threaded binary tree.

40. (i)   Give declaration in 'C' for TBT.

    (ii) Write a function in 'C' to perform traversal of threaded binary tree.

    (iii) Compare traversal of TBT with binary tree.

41. List the advantages of using a threaded binary tree. Give node structure for defining a threaded binary tree. Write a function in 'C' to find the pre-order successor of any node pointed by P in a threaded binary tree.

42. List advantages of threaded binary tree. Give its node structure. Write a function in 'C' to find preorder successor of any node pointed by 7 in TBT.

43. What is threaded binary tree? Explain its advantages/applications.

44. Comment on "Threaded binary tree can be traversed without stack".

45. Write a non-recursive algorithm for pre-order traversal of a binary tree.

46. What is AVL tree? Explain RR and LL rotations with example.

47. Build a binary search tree from the following set of elements: -

    100, 50, 200, 300, 20, 150, 70, 180, 120, 30

48. Construct binary search tree from the following set of strings:

    JAN, FEB, MAR, APR, MAY, JUN, JUL, AUG, SEP, OCT, NOV and DEC.

49. Construct Binary tree if following traversals are give.

    Inorder   : D, F, E, G, A, H, I, C

    Postorder   : D, F, G, E, B, I, H, C, A

50. Construct BST from following elements:

    (i)   MAT, TAN, BAN, BAT, SUN, CAT, RAT Show all steps.

    (ii) 100, 50, 200, 300, 20, 150, 70, 180, 120, 30

51. Construct binary search tree from the following set of strings:

    MAR, MAY, NOV, AUG, APR, JAN, DEC, JUL, FEB, JUN, OCT and SEP. Show all steps.

52. Create Binary Search Tree for the following data and print the tree using all tree traversals.

    MAR, OCT, JAN, APR, NOV, FEB, MAY, DEC, JUN, AUG, JUL, SEP.

53. Write a recursive function to count and print leaf nodes of binary tree.

54. Write a recursive function to find height of binary tree.

55. Write recursive functions to obtain:

    (i)   Height of a binary tree,

    (ii) To count and print the leaf nodes of a binary tree.

56. Explain any one application of binary tree with suitable example.

57. Construct a threaded binary search tree for the following set of elements:

    100, 50, 200, 300, 20, 150, 150, 70, 180, 120, 30 show all steps

GRAPHS

2.1 INTRODUCTION

Graph is a nonlinear data structure used in many applications. These applications include finding shortest path in a network analysis of electrical circuits, project planning, genetics, identification of chemical compounds etc. Many problems can be modeled as graph and solved.

2.2 BASIC CONCEPTS

Definition : A graph can be defined as set of nodes or vertices or points (V) and set of arcs or edges (E), such that each edge e is identified with unique ordered pair [u, v] of nodes in V.

A graph is denoted as G (V, E) where V is set of vertices and E is set of edges.

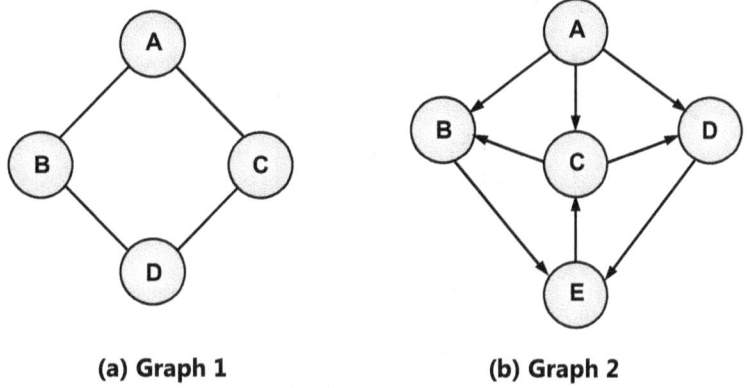

(a) Graph 1   (b) Graph 2

Fig. 2.1 : Example of graph

Graph 1 consists of vertices {A, B, C, D} and edges {(A, B) (A, C), (B, D), (C, D) }

Graph 2 consists of set of vertices {A, B, C, D, E} and set of edges {<A, B>, <A, D>, <A, C>, <C, D>, <C, B>, <B, E>, <E, C>, <D, E>}

If e = [u, v] is an edge, then the nodes u and v are called end points of e. Also u and v are said to be adjacent nodes or neighbours.

A Graph can be of Two Types :

1. Directed graph or digraph

2. Undirected graph.

Directed graph is a graph in which each edge has direction or we say that the pair of vertices in the graph is ordered Fig. 2.1 (b) is a directed graph.

The set of edges in such graph are written in <> sign.

Suppose G is directed graph with edge e = <v, u>, then e is also called an arc.

Following terminology is used.

•   e begins at u and ends at v.

•   u is origin and v is destination of e.

•   u is predecessor and v is successor or neighbour of e.

•   u is adjacent to v and v is adjacent to u.

Undirected graph is a graph in which the edges do not have direction. The flow between two edges can be in both directions. In undirected graph, the set of edges are written in ( ) sign. Fig. 2.1 (a) is an undirected graph.

The vertices in undirected graph are said to be unordered. If (v, u) is an edge and (u, v) represents same edge.

A graph sometimes has weight or cost specified for each edge as shown in Fig. 2.2. Such graph is said to be labelled or weighted graph.

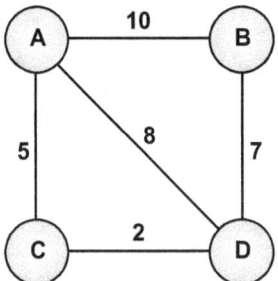

Fig. 2.2 : Weighted graph

Tree also can be termed as graph as it has set of edges and vertices.

There are some terms used with graph. Let us understand them.

•   A graph is said to be complete if it has n(n – 1)/2 number of district unordered pairs, where n is number of vertices. For a directed graph maximum number of edges will be n(n – 1).

•   If (u) is an edge of graph, we say that u and v are adjacent (vertices) and we say that edge (u) is incident on vertices u and .

•   A graph G1 is a subgraph of Graph G, in which all vertices of G1 belong to G and all edges of G1 belong to G.

Following Fig. 2.3 show graph G and its sub-graph.

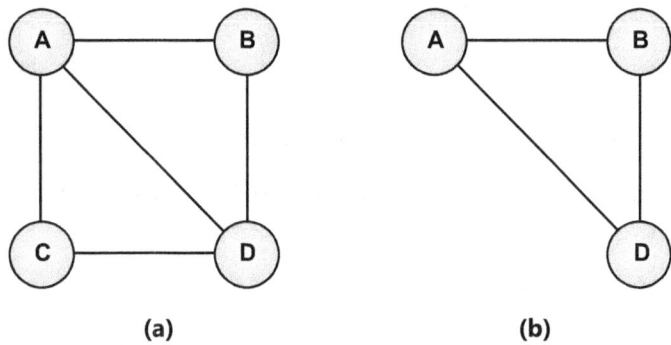

(a)   (b)

Fig. 2.3 : Graph and its sub-graph

- A path in a graph (G) is a sequence of vertices $v_1, v_2, v_3, \ldots v_m, v_n$ where (v_1, v_2) (v_2, v_3) (v_m, v_n) are edges in the graph.

- A simple path is a path such that all vertices are distinct except first and last which could be same.

- A graph can have an edge from a vertex to same vertex called self edge as shown in Fig. 2.4. The path from A to A is called loop.

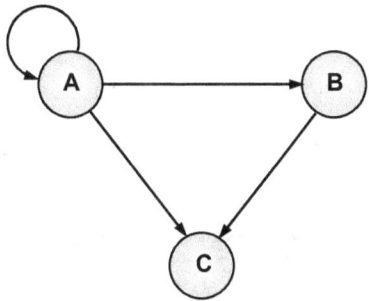

Fig. 2.4 : Graph with self edge node

- A cycle in a directed graph is a path of length at least 1 such that $v_1 = v_n$ i.e. the first and last vertex is same.

- In undirected graph for a cycle, the edges are to be distinct. Otherwise edge (u) will also be cycle.

- A directed graph is called acyclic if it has no cycles. It is denoted as DAG.

- An undirected graph is said to be connected if there is path from every vertex to all other vertices.

- A directed graph is said to be connected or strongly connected if for every pair of distinct vertices in graph G there is directed path in both direction i.e. v_i to v_j and v_j to v_i.

- Strongly connected component of undirected graph (G) is maximal connected sub-graph of G.

- Indegree of vertex in a graph is number of incoming edges at that vertex.

- Out-degree of vertex is the number of outgoing edges from that vertex.

- Total degree of vertex is sum of indegree and outdegree.

- A graph is said to be complete if every node in G is adjacent to every other node. A complete graph with n nodes will have n (n − 1)/2 edges.

- A graph without any cycle is called tree graph or free tree or simply tree.

- Distinct edges e and e' are called multiple edges if they connect same end points, that is, if e = [u, v] and e' = [u, v].

- An edge e is called a loop if it has identical endpoints, that is, if e = [u, u].

- A graph having multiple edges and loops is called multigraph.

- A multigraph with finite number of edges is called finite multigraph.

- A directed graph is said to be simple if G has no parallel edges. It means a simple graph can have loops but it cannot have more than one loop at a given node.

- A directed Acyclic Graph (DAG) can be used to solve problems like critical path analysis, expression free evaluation etc. A sink vertex is a vertex with only single edge ending on it. A source vertex is a vertex having edges starting from it.

- A Biconnected graph is a connected graph which cannot be broken down further by deletion of any single vertex (and incident edges).

2.3 GRAPH STORAGE REPRESENTATION

A graph can be represented using two different ways :

1. Adjacency matrix

2. Adjacency list.

The choice of particular representation depends on application or function to be performed.

2.3.1 Representation of Graph using Adjacency Matrix

The adjacency matrix representation is the simplest representation in which we use a two dimensional array of integers. The elements in the two dimensional array represent the information about edges and vertices in the graph. Suppose, a graph has an edge (v_1, v_2) then the element in the matrix in row no. v_1 and column No. v_2 will be 1. If there is no edge between v_1 and v_2 the element will be 0.

Let us consider two graphs as shown in Fig. 2.5.

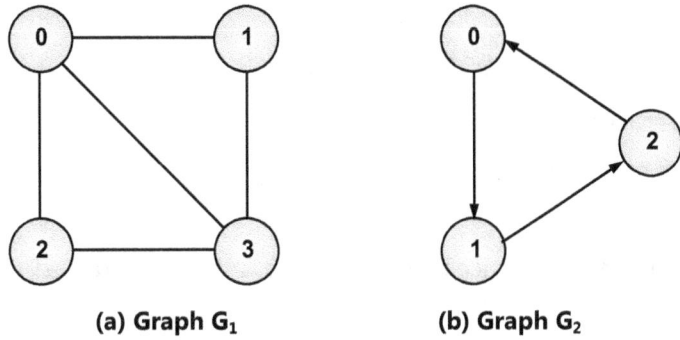

(a) Graph G_1 (b) Graph G_2

Fig. 2.5

The adjacency matrix for graph G_1 will have 4 rows and 4 columns as there are 4 vertices. The elements in the matrix will be as shown in Fig. 2.6.

$$
\begin{array}{c}
\begin{array}{cccc} 0 & 1 & 2 & 3 \end{array} \\
\begin{array}{c} 0 \\ 1 \\ 2 \\ 3 \end{array}
\left[\begin{array}{cccc}
0 & 1 & 1 & 1 \\
1 & 0 & 0 & 1 \\
1 & 0 & 0 & 1 \\
1 & 1 & 1 & 0
\end{array} \right]
\end{array}
$$

Fig. 2.6 : Adjacency matrix for G_1

Note that the graph G_1 is undirected graph. Hence, the matrix is symmetric. We can store only upper or lower triangular matrix to reduce the space requirements. The adjacency matrix for graph G_2 is shown in Fig. 2.7.

$$
\begin{array}{c}
\begin{array}{ccc} 0 & 1 & 2 \end{array} \\
\begin{array}{c} 0 \\ 1 \\ 2 \end{array}
\left[\begin{array}{ccc}
0 & 1 & 0 \\
0 & 0 & 1 \\
1 & 0 & 0
\end{array} \right]
\end{array}
$$

Fig. 2.7 : Adjacency matrix for graph G_2

From adjacency matrix we can find whether there is an edge between given two vertices or not.

We can find indegree of vertices by counting number of 1's in corresponding column and out-degree by counting number of 1's in corresponding row.

For example, Indegree of vertex 1 in G_1 = 2

Outdegree of vertex 1 in G_1 = 2

If the cost or weight is specified on the edges of graph, we can put the cost or weight in place of 1.

The advantage of adjacency matrix representation is its simplicity but requires more space of the order of n^2.

Let us write a program to represent a graph in adjacency matrix format. The program accepts from user number of vertices and edges in the graph and prints the matrix. It also calculates indegree, outdegree and total degree of a given vertex.

Explanation :

int g[MAX][MAX] is the 2-D array for storing matrix.

n is number of vertices.

There are three functions used

(i)   create_graph ( )

It accepts the number of vertices of n. If the graph is undirected, their reverse edge corresponding to two vertices is also stored.

(ii) disp ( )

This function displays the matrix.

(iii) calc( )

This function calculates indegree, outdegree and total degree of a given vertex.

Program 2.1 : To represent graph using adjacency matrix, display it and calculate indegree - outdegree of nodes.

```
#define MAX 10,

int g[MAX] [MAX];

int n;

void create_graph ( );

void disp( );

void calc( );

void main
{
    create_graph( );
    disp( );
    calc( );
}
void create_graph( )
{
    char ch, type;
    printf("How many vertices\n");
    scanf("%d", &n);
```

```
        printf("Enter type of graph directed or undirected \n");
        type = getch( );
        do
        {
            printf("Enter edge");
            scanf("%d %d", &v1, &v2);
                g[v1] [v2] = 1;
            if(type=='u'||type=='U')
            g[v2] [v1] = 1;
            printf("Do you want to continue? \n");
            ch = getch( );
        }   while (ch=='y'||ch=='y');
}
void disp( );
{
    int i, j;
    for(i=0; i<n; i++)
    {
        for(j=0; j<n; j++)
        {
            printf(%d", g[i][j]);
        }
        printf("\n");
    }
}
void calc( );
{
    int c1 = 0, c2 = 0, c3 = 0, v;
```

```
    printf("Enter vertex \n");
    scanf("%d", &v);
    for (i=0; i<n; i++)
    {
        if (g[i][v]==1)
        c1++;
    }
    for(i=0, i<n; i++)
    {
        if(g[v] [i] ==1)
        c2++;
    }
    c3 = c1 + c2;
    printf("Indegree =%d\n", c1);
    printf("outdegree=%d\n", c2);
    printf("Total degree = %\n", c3);
}
```

2.3.2 Representation of Graph Using Adjacency List

This is linked list representation of graph. The n rows of adjacency matrix are represented as n linked lists. For each vertex there will be one list. The list contains adjacent vertices of that vertex. Let us consider two graphs and their adjacency list representations.

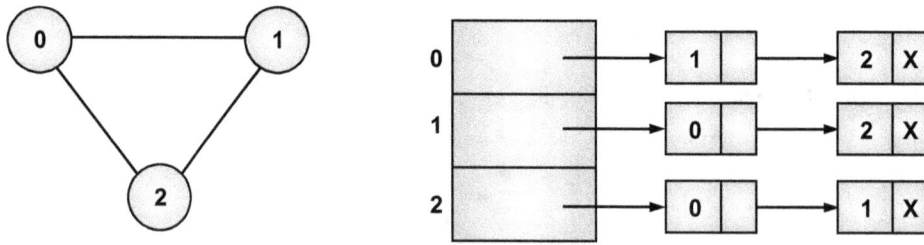

Fig. 2.8 : Graph and its adjacency list

As seen in the graph, vertex 0 has adjacent vertices 1 and 2. Hence, the list corresponding to vertex 0 has two nodes with 1 and 2 in its list and list 2 has vertices 0 and 1.

Another example is directed graph.

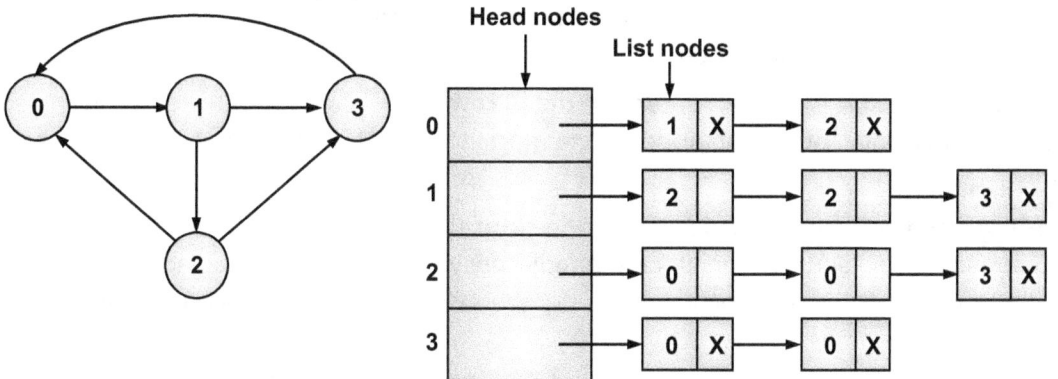

Fig. 2.9 : Graph and its adjacency list

Each list has head node which stores the address of the list. For directed graph if there are n vertices and e edges, the adjacency list will have n head nodes and e list nodes.

For undirected graph if there are n vertices and e edges the list will have n head nodes and 2e list nodes.

The indegree of a vertex in undirected graph is number of nodes in the corresponding list.

The outdegree of a vertex in undirected graph is number of nodes in list.

The outdegree of a vertex in directed graph is number of nodes in the corresponding list.

The indegree of a vertex is calculated by examining the entire adjacency list. The number of nodes of that vertex in adjacency list is the indegree of that vertex.

The comparison of adjacency list with adjacency matrix is

- The adjacency list consists of dynamic allocation hence, space requirement for adjacency list will be less compared to matrix representation.

- The adjacency list is complex structure and difficult to implement whereas adjacency matrix is simple and easy to implement.

Operations on Graph : There are various operations such as searching, inserting and deleting nodes and edges in the graph.

Searching in a Graph : We can find the location, loc of a node N in a graph G. This can be accomplished easily with both representations that is adjacency matrix or adjacency list.

In adjacency matrix, the row number or column number responds to node. In adjacency list, the list address corresponds to node.

We can also find the location, loc of a edge (v_i, v_j) in the graph. In adjacency matrix if the ij^{th} entry in the matrix is 1 the edge is present otherwise absent.

In adjacency list representation, we can search the edge, (v_i, v_j) in the ith row of the list.

Inserting a Graph : To insert a node N in the graph, in adjacency matrix, we can increase row number and column number in the matrix. In the adjacency list, we can increase one more element in the list of pointers.

To insert an edge (v_i, v_j) we can enter 1 in the ith row and j^{th} column of the adjacency matrix. In case of adjacency list we can append one more node at the end (append) in the ith row of the list.

Deleting from a Graph : To delete a node from the graph, we can insert all zeros in the corresponding row and column, in case of adjacency matrix. In case of adjacency list, we can delete entire list corresponding to the node. We also have to delete all nodes in the other lists corresponding this vertex.

2.3.3 Adjacency Multi list

In the adjacency-list representation of an undirected graph each edge (u, v) is represented by two entries one on the list for u and the other on that list for v.

As we shall see in some situations it is necessary to be able to determine entry for a particular edge and mark that edge as having been examined. This can be accomplished easily if the adjacency lists are actually maintained as multi lists (i.e., lists in which nodes may be shared among several lists). For each edge there will be exactly one node but this node will be in two lists (i.e. the adjacency lists for each of the two nodes to which it is incident).

The new node structure is

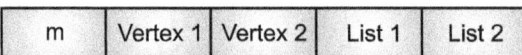

Where m is a Boolean mark field that may be used to indicate whether or not the edge has been examined. The storage requirements are the same as for normal adjacency lists, except for the addition of the mark bit m.

2.3.4 Inverse adjacency list

Determining the in-degree of a vertex is a little more complex. In case there is a need to repeatedly access all vertices adjacent to another vertex then it may be worth the effort to keep another set of lists in addition to the adjacency lists. This set of lists, called inverse adjacency lists, will contain one list for each vertex.

Fig. 2.10 : Graph G

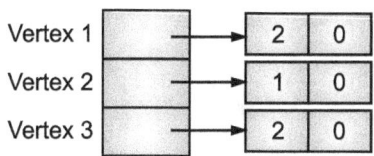

Vertex 1
Vertex 2
Vertex 3

Fig. 2.11 : Inverse adjacency list for Graph G

2.4 TRAVERSALS OF GRAPH (DFS AND BFS)

The graph can be traversed in two different ways :

- Depth first search,

- Breadth first search.

Traversal means visiting each vertex in the graph once. The tree traversals were studied in Unit 1. In the starting point of the traversals, there was root node. In case of graph, starting point may be any vertex. Now traversing in case of graph means, visiting all vertices that are reachable from the starting vertex because every vertex may not be reachable from a given vertex.

2.4.1 Depth First Search (DFS) Traversal

As the name suggests, starting from a given vertex we go till the depth of the vertex and then go back to traverse another path till its depth.

Suppose we start at a vertex v1, process it, we go to its adjacent vertex say v2, process it, then we move to adjacent vertex of v2 say v3. Like this, we continue till there is no vertex left with adjacent vertex. After this we come back to the previous vertex (last but one processed). If there is any other adjacent vertex, we move to that vertex, process and keep on going forward. When we have reached a vertex with no adjacent vertices, we keep coming back. Thus, when we start with a vertex we keep on going forward to its descendants. While doing this, every vertex should be processed only once in the entire traversal.

Let us take a graph and see the DFS traversal of it.

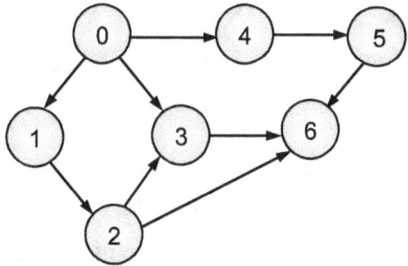

Fig. 2.12 : Graph

Suppose our starting vertex is 0 (process it)

From 0 we can go to 1 or 3 or 4 (Adjacent vertex).

Let us select 1 (process it)

From 1 we can to 2 (process it)

From 2 we can go to 3 or 6.

Let us select 3 (process it).

From 3 we can go to 6 (process it)

From 6 you cannot reach any node, which is not processed or visited.

Hence, go back to 3 (previous vertex)

There is no other vertex connected to 3.

Go back to 2.

From 2 we can go to 6 but it is already processed.

Go back to 0.

From 0 we can go to 3 but it is already processed.

From 0 we can go to 4. (Process it)

From 4 we can go to 5. (Process it).

From 5 we can go to 6 but it is already processed.

Go back to 0.

There is no other vertex left out

Hence the Traversal is 0, 1, 2, 3, 6, 4, 5.

The traversal is shown in Fig. 2.13.

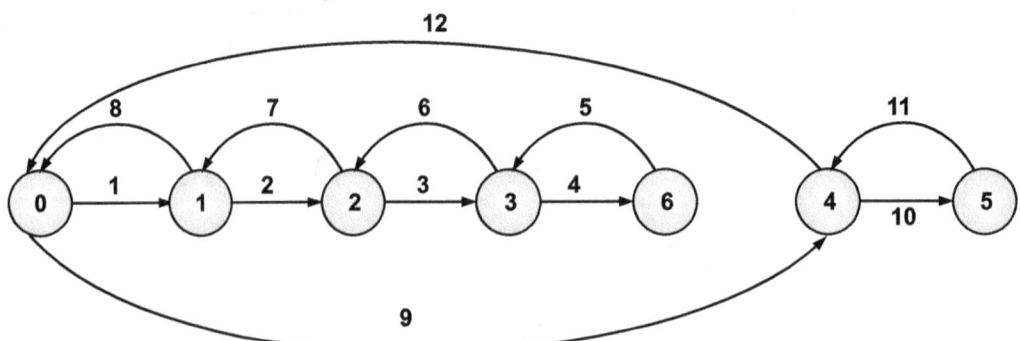

Fig. 2.13 : DFS traversal of graph in Fig. 2.10

Let us take one more graph and see its DFS Traversal.

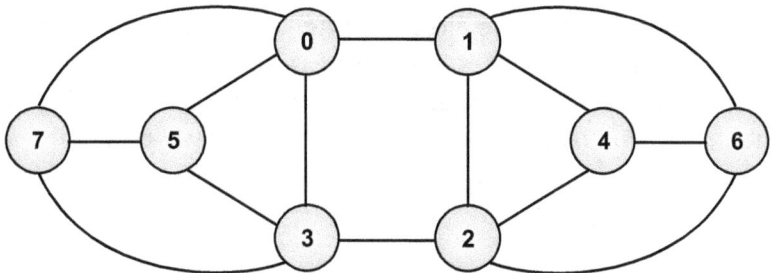

Fig. 2.14 : Graph

The traversal path is shown in Fig. 2.15.

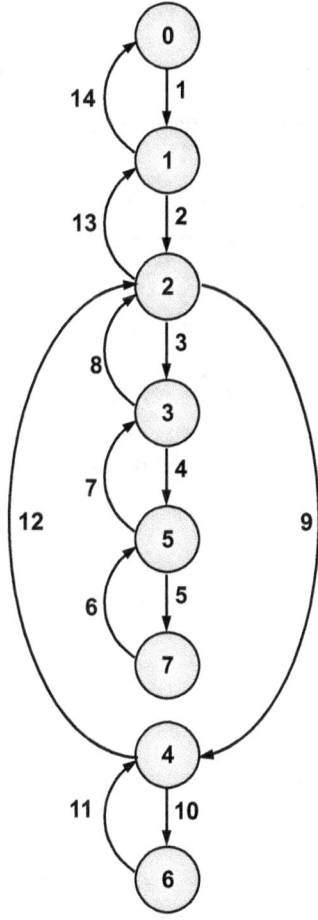

Fig. 2.15 : DFS traversal of graph in Fig. 2.14

The DFS traversal is 0 1 2 3 5 7 4 6.

Algorithm for DFS Traversal :

DFS is a recursive process. We can either use recursive function or stack to implement DFS. The algorithm we are going to write is for adjacency matrix representation. The create_graph( ) function which we have already written will be used here for storing graph in the 2-D array int g[MAX] [MAX] and n is number of vertices. We require an additional array to store the information about status of each vertex whether it is visited or not. Let us have the array int visited[MAX]. Initially, the elements of this array will be 0. Whenever a vertex is visited the corresponding element will be made 1. The algorithm is as follows :

```
void dfs(int v1)

{

    print v1;        // visit or process

    visited [v1] = 1; // mark as visited

    for(v2=0; v2<n; v2++)// check all adjacent vertices edge for a (v1, v2)

    {

        if (g[v1] [v2]==1)

        {

            if(visited [v2]==0)   // if not visited

                dfs (v2);// Repeat dfs again

        }

    }

}
```

Explanation :

1. We start with source vertex v1 in the graph. It is processed (display) and marked as visited.

2. In the loop we are finding an adjacent vertex of v1 (verifying g[v1] [v2] ==) say v2 and if it is not visited yet, the function DFS will be called to process visit that node. This process continues recursively as explained in example.

Analysis :

The total time to determine adjacent vertices of a vertex is n and for each vertex we have to do this. Hence time complexity of this algorithm is $O(n^2)$. The space required for this algorithm is the array visited and stack (of program) a part from the array.

Let us consider DFS traversal of the following graph.

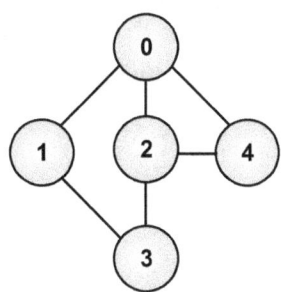

Fig. 2.16

Table 2.1 DFS Traversal of Fig. 2.16

Call No.	V₁	Output	Visited array					V₂
1	0	0	0	1	2	3	4	
			1	0	0	0	0	0
								1
2	1	1	0	1	2	3	4	
			1	1	0	0	0	0
								1
								2
			0	1	2	3	4	3
3	3	3	1	1	0	1	0	0
								1
			0	1	2	3	4	2
4	2	2	1	1	1	1	0	0
								1
								2
								3
			0	1	2	3	4	4
5	4	4	1	1	1	1	1	0
								1
								2
								3
								4
								5 →

After call number 5, control goes back to 4 $V_2 = 5$

Control goes back to call 3 $V_2 = 3, 4, 5$

Control goes back to call 2 $V_2 = 4, 5$

Control goes back to call 1 $V_2 = 2, 3, 4, 5$

Following is the algorithm for non-recursive traversal of DFS.

```
void dfs(int v1)

{

    push v1;              // Store v1 in stack

    visited [v1] = 1;     // Mark it as visited

    while(stack not empty)

    {


        v1 =pop( );       // Remove the vertex in stack

        print v1;         // Process or visit

        for(v2=0;v2<n;v2++)// Check all adjacent vertices

        {

            if (g[v1][v2]==1 && visited [v2]==0)// If there is edge v1 – v2 and V2 is not
visited

            {

                visited [v2] == 1;        // Mark it as visited

                push (v2);// Store the vertex on stack

            }

        }

    }

}
```

2.4.2 Breadth First Search (BFS) Traversal

In BFS, we go to the breadth of the current vertex every time we come to a new vertex and then take up the next vertex.

Suppose we start with vertex v_1, process it, then we visit all the adjacent vertices of v_1 say v_{11}, v_{12}, v_{13}, v_{1n}. Then we visit all the adjacent vertices of v_{11}, then of v_{12} so on upto v_{1n}. This is continued till there is not vertex left out to be visited. Let us consider a graph given in Fig. 2.17.

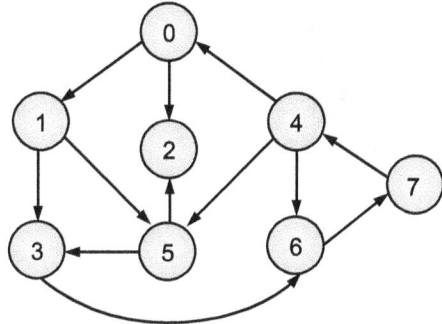

Fig. 2.17 : Graph

For the graph, we start with say vertex 0.

Mark it as visited.

The adjacent vertices are 1 and 2.

Mark them as visited

The adjacent vertices of 1 are 3, 5

Mark them as visited

The adjacent vertices of 2 is 5 (already visited)

The adjacent vertices of 3 is 6

Mark it as visited.

The adjacent vertices of 5 is 2 and 3 already visited

The adjacent vertices of 6 is 7

Mark it as visited.

The adjacent vertices 7 is 4

Mark it as visited

The adjacent vertices of 4 are 0, 5 (already visited)

Hence, the BFS traversal is 0, 1, 2, 3, 5, 6, 7, 4.

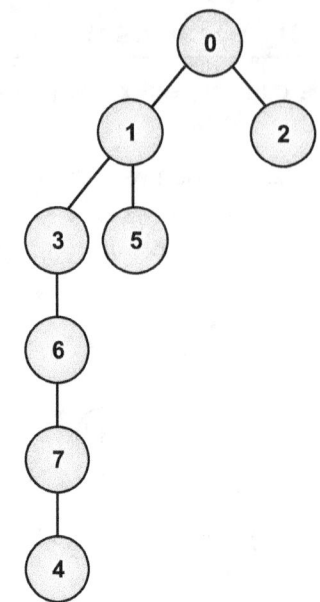

Fig. 2.18 : BFS traversal of graph in Fig. 2.17

Now consider an undirected graph shown in Fig. 2.19.

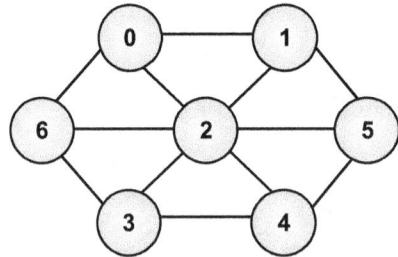

Fig. 2.19 : Graph

If starting vertex is 0.

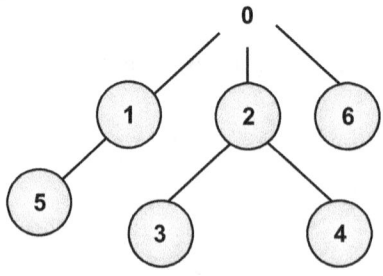

Fig. 2.20 : BFS traversal of graph in Fig. 2.19

Hence, the BFS Traversal is 0, 1, 2, 6, 5, 3, 4.

Algorithm for BFS Traversal :

For implementing BFS traversal, we have to use queue for storing the adjacent vertices of current vertex being visited.

The create_graph ( ) function which was written earlier will be used here for storing graph in 2-D array int g[MAX] [MAX] and n is number of vertices. An additional array int visited [MAX] is used to store the information about status of each vertex whether it is visited or not. Initially, the elements of this array will be 0. Whenever a vertex is visited corresponding element will be made 1.

The algorithm is as below.

```
void bfs(int v1)
{
    insertq(v1);
    visited[v1] = 1;
    while (Queue is not empty)
    {
        v1=delq( );
        print v1
        for(v2=0;v2<n;v2++)
        {
            if(g[v1] [v2]==1)                // If there is edge v1 – v2
            {
                if(visited [v2]==0)          // If there is not yet visited
                {
                    insertq (v2)
                    visited[v2] = 1;
                }
            }
        }
    }
}
```

Explanation :

1. In above function, it is assumed that the queue is defined with an array of int, along with two functions insertq and delq. The detailed program is given at the end of this section.

2. We start with source vertex v1 in the graph. It is inserted in the queue and marked as visited.

3. A vertex in the queue is removed and it is processed i.e. displayed.

All adjacent vertices of this current vertex are inserted in the queue and marked them as visited.

This process is repeated until the queue becomes empty.

Let us consider a graph given in Fig. 2.21.

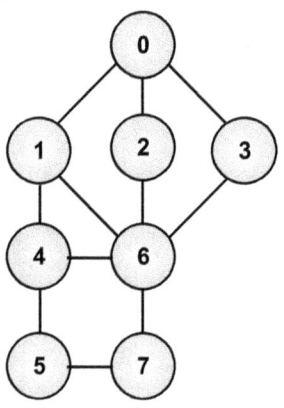

Fig. 2.21 : Graph

Table 2.2 BFS Traversal of Fig. 2.21

0	Suppose our starting vertex is 0, it is inserted in queue and marked as visited.	q	0							
		visited	1	0	0	0	0	0	0	0
			0	1	2	3	4	5	6	7
1	Remove 0 from queue and display. Output is 0. Insert adjacent vertices of 0 i.e. 1, 2, 3 on queue and mark them as visited.	q	X	1	2	3				
		visited	1	1	1	1	0	0	0	0
			0	1	2	3	4	5	6	7
2	Remove 1 from queue and display. Output is 1. Insert adjacent vertices of 1 i.e. 4 and 6 on queue and mark them as visited.	q	X	X	2	3	4	6		
		visited	1	1	1	1	1	0	1	0
			0	1	2	3	4	5	6	7
3	Remove 2 from queue and display Output is 2. There is no adjacent vertex of 2 not yet visited.	q	X	X	X	3	4	6		
		visited	1	1	1	1	1	0	1	0
			0	1	2	3	4	5	6	7

4	Remove 3 from queue and display. Output is 3. There is no adjacent vertex of 3 not yet visited.	q: X X X X 4 6 _ _ visited: 1(0) 1(1) 1(2) 1(3) 1(4) 0(5) 1(6) 0(7)
5	Remove 4 from queue and display. Output is 4. Insert 5 on queue. Mark it as visited.	q: X X X X X 6 5 _ visited: 1(0) 1(1) 1(2) 1(3) 1(4) 1(5) 1(6) 0(7)
6	Remove 6 from queue and display. Output is 6. Insert adjacent vertex of 6 i.e. 7 on queue and mark it as visited.	q: X X X X X X 5 7 visited: 1(0) 1(1) 1(2) 1(3) 1(4) 1(5) 1(6) 1(7)
7	Remove 5 from queue and display. Output is 5. There is no adjacent vertex of 3 not yet visited.	q: X X X X X X X 7 0 1 2 3 4 5 6 7
8	Remove 7 from queue and display. Output is 7. There is no adjacent vertex of 3 not yet visited and queue is empty. The BFS traversal is 1, 2, 3, 4, 6, 5, 7	q: X X X X X X X X 0 1 2 3 4 5 6 7

Program 2.2 : To create a given graph using adjacency matrix and display BFS and DFS traversals.

```
# define MAX 10

int g[MAX] [MAX]

int n;

void create_graph( );

void disp( );

void bfs (int);

void dfs (int);

int q[MAX];
```

```
int rear = -1, front = -1;
void insertq (int);
int delq (int);
int visited [MAX];
void main( )
    {
        int ch, v1;
        do
        {
            for(i=0,i<n;i++)
                visited [v1] = 0;
                clrscr();
                printf("1. create\n 2. Disp\n3. DFS\n4. BFS\n5. Exit\n")
                printf("Enter your choice\n");
                scanf("%d", &ch);
                switch(ch)
                {
                    case1 :  creat_graph();
                        break;
                    case2 :  disp( );
                        break;
                    case3 :  printf("Enter starting vertex\n");
                    scanf("%d, &v1);
                        dfs(v1);
                        break;
                    case4 :  printf("Enter starting vertex");
```

```
                    scan("%d", &v2);
                        bfs(v2);
                }
            getch( );
        } while (ch!=5);
}
void create_graph ()
{
    int v1, v2, i;
    char type, ch;
    printf("Enter type of graph\n");
    type = getch( );
    printf("Enter number of vertices\n");
    scanf("%d", &n);
    do
    {
        printf("Enter edge\n");
        scanf("%d%d", &v1, &v2);
        g [v1] [v2] = 1;
        if(type=='u'||type=='u')
            g[v2] [v1] = 1;
        printf("Do you want to continue ?\n");
        ch = getch( );
    }   while(ch=='y'||ch=='Y')
}
void disp( )
```

```c
{
    int i;
    printf("Adjacency matrix is\n");
    for(i=0;i<n;i++)
    {
        for(j=0;j<n;j++)
        {
            printf("%d",g[i][j]);
        }
        printf("\n");
    }
}
void dfs (int v1)
{
    int i, v2;
    printf("%d\n", v1)
    visited [v1] = 1;
    for (v2=0; v2<n; v2++)
    {
        if (g[v1] [v2]==1)
        {
            if (visited [v2]==0)
            dfs (v2);
        }
    }
}
```

```
void bfs (int v1)
{
    int v2;
    insertq (v1)
    visited[v1] = 1;
    while (front ! = rear)
    {
        v1 = delq ();
        printf("%d\n", v1);
        for(v2=0; v2<n; v2++)
        {
            if (g[v1] [v2]==1)
            {
                if(visited [v2]==0)
                {
                insertq(v2);
                visited [v2] = 1;
                }
            }
        }
    }
}
void insertq(int v1)
{
    if (rear==MAX - 1)
        printf("Q full\n");
    else
    {
```

```
                     rear++;
                     q[rear] = v1;
               }
        }
        int delq( )
        {
               int v1;
               if (front==rear)
                     printf("Q empty");
               else
               {
                     front ++;
                     v1 = q[front];
                     return(v1);
               }
        }
```

Explanation :

1. Most of the variables in the program are declared as global because they are required in at least one of function.

2. The initialization of array visited[ ] is required because it is going to be modified in BFS and DFS functions.

3. The variables front and rear of the queue are global and can be used directly in BFS to check whether q is empty or full.

4. We can write separate functions for insertq, delq etc.

2.5 INTRODUCTION TO GREEDY STRATEGY

Greedy algorithm is designed to achieve optimum solution for a given problem. In greedy algorithm approach, decisions are made from the given solution domain. As being greedy, the closest solution that seems to provide an optimum solution is chosen.

Greedy algorithms suggests that one can devise an algorithm which works in stages, considering one input at a time.

Examples

Most networking algorithms use the greedy approach. Here is a list of few of them −

*   Travelling Salesman Problem
*   Prim's Minimal Spanning Tree Algorithm
*   Kruskal's Minimal Spanning Tree Algorithm

- Dijkstra's Minimal Spanning Tree Algorithm
- Graph - Map Coloring
- Graph - Vertex Cover
- Knapsack Problem
- Job Scheduling Problem

2.5.1 Minimum Spanning Tree

An undirected graph is said to be connected if for every pair of distinct vertices there is a path.

For a connected undirected graph if we carry out DFS traversal from any vertex as source, all the vertices in the graph can be traversed.

Hence, for a connected undirected graph we can form set of edges which will include all the vertices. Moreover it is possible for trees with the edges that include all the vertices. A tree is a graph in which there is no cycle (closed path).

Any tree that has set of edges in the graph and includes all the vertices is called spanning Tree.

Consider a graph given in Fig. 2.22 with cost/weights.

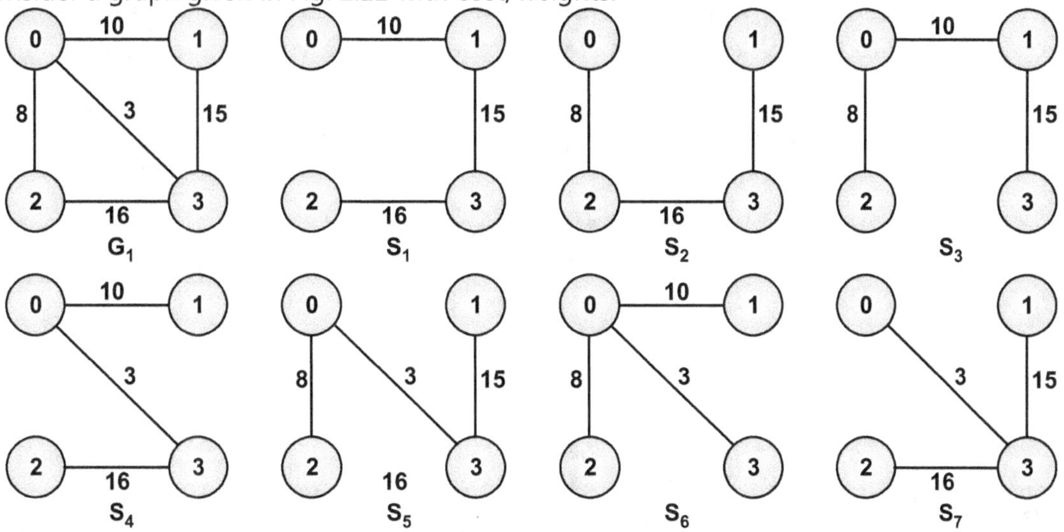

Fig. 2.22 : Graph G_1 and its spanning trees

The cost of spanning tree is total weights of all the edges in the spanning tree.

The cost of spanning trees shown in the graph of Fig. 2.19 are

$$
\begin{array}{ll}
S_1 & 41 \\
S_2 & 39 \\
S_3 & 33 \\
S_4 & 29 \\
S_5 & 26 \\
S_6 & 21 \\
S_7 & 34
\end{array}
$$

The minimum cost is 21 for spanning tree S_6. It is called as minimal cost spanning tree or minimal spanning tree.

Definition :

The spanning tree of a graph whose sum of the costs or weights is minimum is called minimum spanning tree.

There are two algorithms which are used to find minimum spanning tree.

1.   Prim's algorithm

2.   Kruskal's algorithm

1. Prim's Algorithm

In this algorithm, we start with any arbitrary vertex in the graph as the root of the tree. Then we find the vertex adjacent to this root vertex which has an edge with minimum cost or weight. Now we have two vertices in the tree. Find all the out-going edges from these two vertices and select an edge with minimum cost among these such that the addition of this edge should not form a cycle. Like this we continue till all the vertices are included in the tree.

Let us consider an example i.e. the same graph we had in Fig. 2.3 (a).

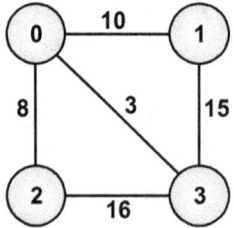

Fig. 2.23 (a) : Graph

Let us start with vertex 0.

The outgoing edges from this vertex and selected vertex is shown in Fig. 2.23 (b).

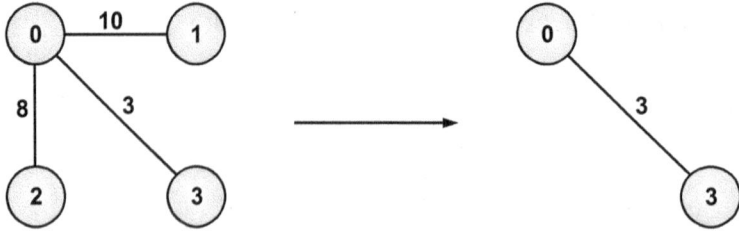

Fig. 2.23 (b) : Step 1 for MST

Now find the outgoing edges of 0 and 3 and select minimum of the edges.

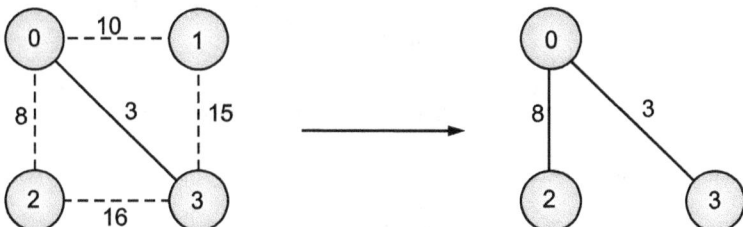

Fig. 2.23 (c) : Step 2 for MST

Now find the outgoing edges of 0, 2, and 3.

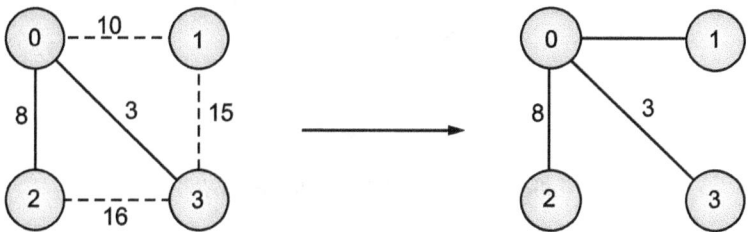

Fig. 2.23 (d) : Step 3 for MST

Since above graph includes all vertices it is the MST.

SOLVED EXAMPLES

Example 2.1 : Show the stepwise construction of minimum spanning tree for the given graph using Prim's algorithm. [Fig. 2.24 (a)]

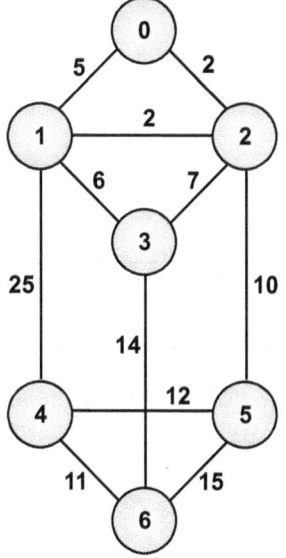

Fig. 2.24 (a) : Graph

Step 1 : Let us start from vertex 0

Fig. 2.24 (b) : Prim's algorithm

Step 2 : The adjacent vertices with cost are

$$0 - 1 \rightarrow 5$$

$$0 - 2 \rightarrow 2 \text{ (minimum)}$$

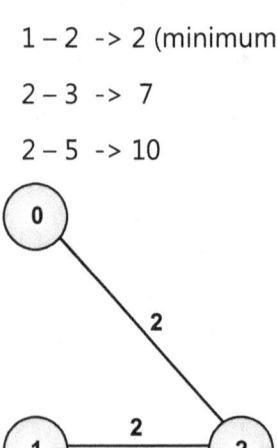

Fig. 2.24 (c) : Prim's algorithm

Step 3 : The adjacent vertex of 0 and 2 not forming cycle are

$$0 - 1 \rightarrow 5$$

$$1 - 2 \rightarrow 2 \text{ (minimum)}$$

$$2 - 3 \rightarrow 7$$

$$2 - 5 \rightarrow 10$$

Fig. 2.24 (d) : Prim's algorithm

Step 4 : The adjacent vertex of 0, 1, 2 not forming cycle are

$$2 - 5 \rightarrow 10$$

$$2 - 3 \rightarrow 7$$

$$1 - 3 \rightarrow 6 \text{ (minimum)}$$

$$1 - 4 \rightarrow 25$$

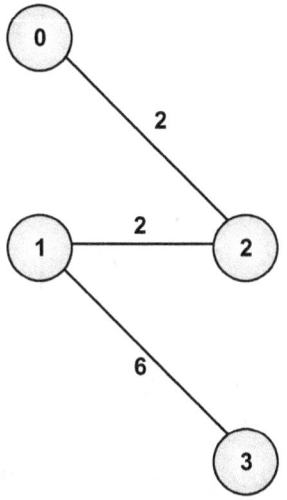

Fig. 2.24 (e) : Prim's algorithm

Step 5 : The adjacent vertex of 0, 1, 2, 3 are

$$2 - 5 \ \text{->} \ 10 \ (\text{minimum})$$
$$1 - 4 \ \text{->} \ 25$$
$$3 - 6 \ \text{->} \ 14$$

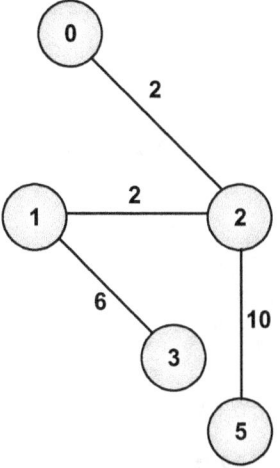

Fig. 2.24 (f) : Prim's algorithm

Step 6 : The adjacent vertex of 0, 1, 2, 3, 5 are

$$1 - 4 \ \text{->} \ 25$$
$$5 - 4 \ \text{->} \ 12 \ \ (\text{minimum})$$
$$3 - 6 \ \text{->} \ 14$$
$$5 - 6 \ \text{->} \ 15$$

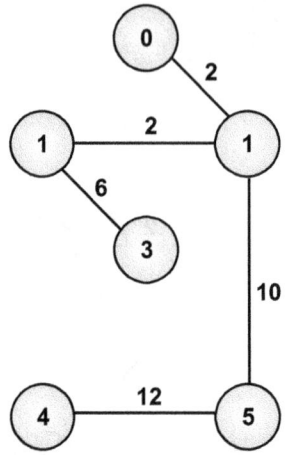

Fig. 2.24 (g) : Prim's algorithm

Step 7 : The adjacent vertex of 0, 1, 2, 3, 4, are

$$5 - 6 \rightarrow 15$$
$$4 - 6 \rightarrow 11 \ (minimum)$$

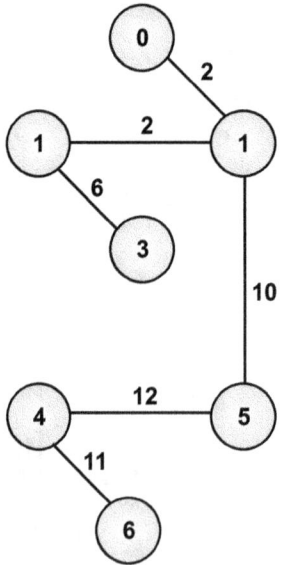

Fig. 2.24 (h) : Prim's algorithm

This is spanning tree of given graph the total cost is 2 + 2 + 6 + 10 + 12 + 11 = 43.

The algorithm can be written as below.

Prim's algorithm :

```
1.  T = { }
2.  S = {0}
3.  While(uv)
```

```
        {
                Let (u, ) be lowest cost edge such that u is in S and is in V - S
                T = T { (c, )}
                S = S {}
        }
    4.  Stop
```

Explanation :

1. T is the set of edges of the minimum spanning tree to be constructed. Initially, it will be empty set.

2. S is the set of vertices of the minimum spanning tree. Initially, it will be having starting vertex say 0.

3. At each step we find shortest edge (u) that connects S and remaining vertices of the graph G i.e. V – S. The edge is added to T and vertex to S.

This process is continued until S becomes V (i.e. all vertices of graph are included in the tree).

Analysis :

When we start with particular vertex, we examine the edges connected to it. For this we have to check connectivity to all vertices and then select minimum cost edge. This process is repeated for all vertices. Hence, it is nested loop where outer, and inner loop will run for n times; where n is number of vertices. Hence, time complexity of algorithm will be $O(n^2)$.

2. Kruskal's Algorithm

This algorithm also finds minimum spanning tree. If we are given a graph G (V, E), we start taking all vertices of the graph initially and no edges. We keep on adding the edges to the spanning tree in order of increasing cost in the MST, till all vertices are in one component.

Algorithm :

1. G (V, E).

2. We start with a graph T (V,) consisting of n vertices of G and no edges.

3. Examine edges from E. Repeat 4 and 5 in increasing order of cost of edges.

4. Add edge e_i to T if it connects two vertices in two different connected components of T. Otherwise discard e_i.

5. Take next edge and go to 3, if the vertices are not in one connected component.

Analysis :

A priority queue can be used to store the edges and taking them in increasing cost order. The formation of priority queue of e edges will require $O(e\log_2 e)$. Hence, there are n vertices and e edges assuming n < e. This algorithm will have time complexity $O(e\log_2 e)$.

Consider following example :

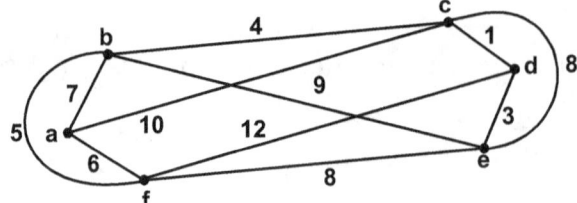

Fig. 2.25 (a) : Graph

We start with all vertices in the graph a, b, c, d, e, f as follows :

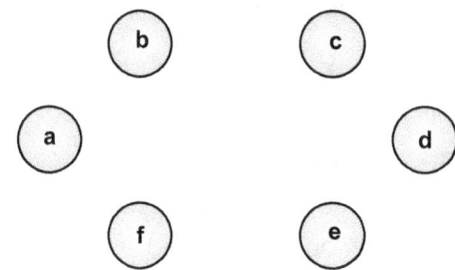

Fig. 2.25 (b) : Kruskal's algorithm

Step 1 : The edges with cost 1 are c – d include it in MST.

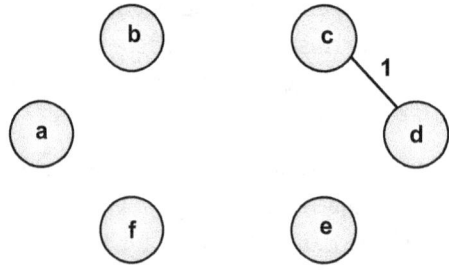

Fig. 2.25 (c) : Kruskal's algorithm

Step 2 : Edges with cost 2 Nil

Edges with cost 3 d – e

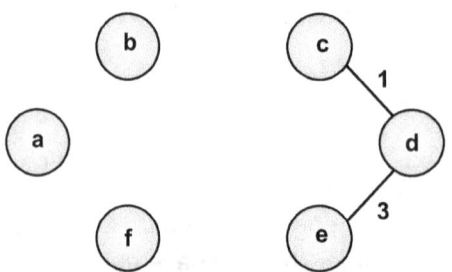

Fig. 2.25 (d) : Kruskal's algorithm

Step 3 : Edges with cost 4 : b – c

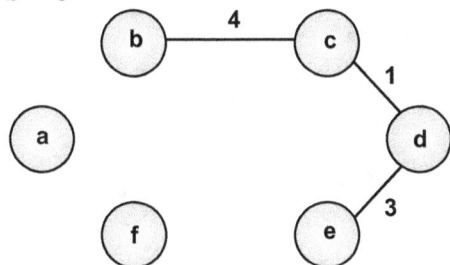

Fig. 2.25 (e) : Kruskal's algorithm

Step 4 : Edges with cost 5 : b – f

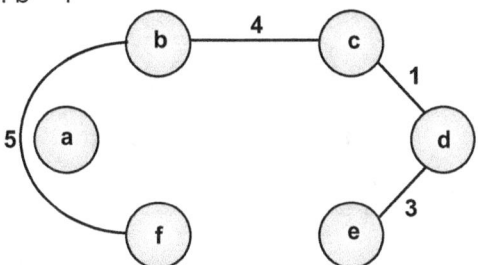

Fig. 2.25 (f) : Kruskal's algorithm

Step 5 : Edges with cost 6 : f – a

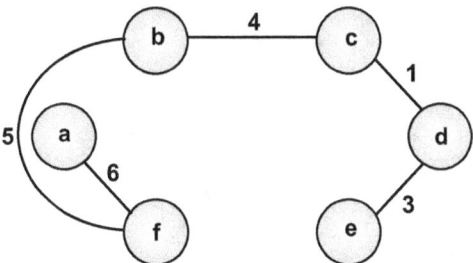

Fig. 2.25 (g) : Kruskal's algorithm

This is minimum spanning tree. Total cost is 19.

Example 2.2 : Find minimum spanning tree for following graph using *Kruskal's* algorithm

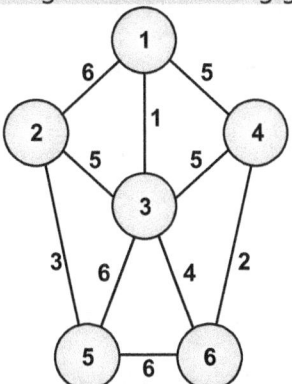

Fig. 2.26 (a) : Graph

Solution :

We start with all vertices in the graph.

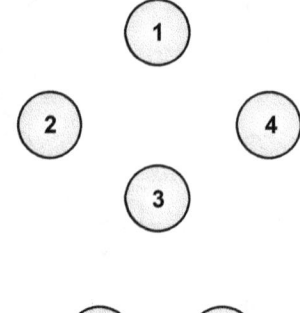

Fig. 2.26 (b) : Kruskal's algorithm

Step 1 : Edges with cost = 1 are 1 – 3

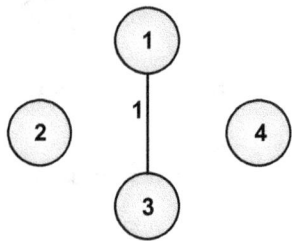

Fig. 2.26 (c) : Kruskal's algorithm

Step 2 : Edges with cost = 2 are 4 – 6

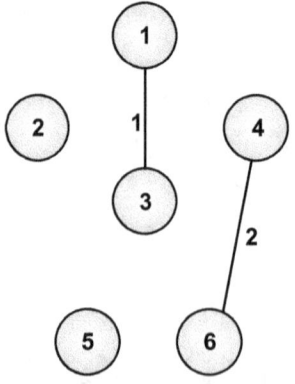

Fig. 2.26 (d) : Kruskal's algorithm

Step 3 : Edges with cost = 3 are 2 – 5

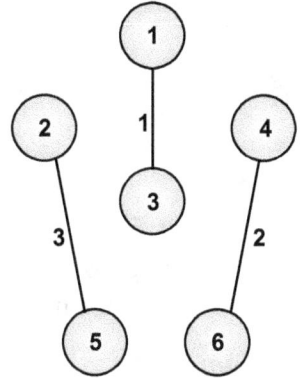

Fig. 2.26 (e) : Kruskal's algorithm

Step 4 : Edges with cost = 4 are 3 – 6

    Vertices are not in one component.

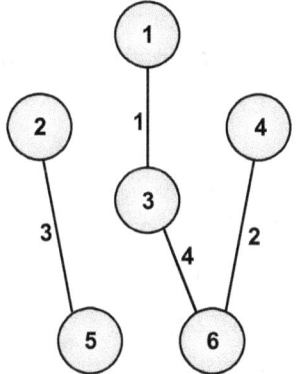

Fig. 2.26 (f) : Kruskal's algorithm

Step 5 : Edges with cost = 5 are 2 – 3 and 3 – 4

    3, 4 are in same connected component hence include.

    2, 3 are in different connected component hence include.

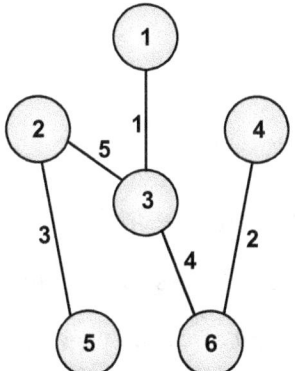

Fig. 2.26 (g) : Kruskal's algorithm

All vertices are in are connected component.

Hence this is minimum spanning tree.

The cost of MST is 15.

2.5.2 Shortest Paths

The **shortest path** between two nodes of a graph is a sequence of connected nodes so that the sum of the edges that inter-connect them is minimal.

Shortest Path using Dijkstra's Algorithm

Dijkstra's algorithm solves the single-source shortest-path problem when all edges have non-negative weights. It is a greedy algorithm and similar to Prim's algorithm. Algorithm starts at the source vertex, s, it grows a tree, T, that ultimately spans all vertices reachable from S. Vertices are added to T in order of distance i.e., first S, then the vertex closest to S, then the next closest, and so on. Following implementation assumes that graph G is represented by adjacency lists.

DIJKSTRA (G, w, s)

- INITIALIZE SINGLE-SOURCE (G, s)

- S ← { }   // S will ultimately contains vertices of final shortest-path weights from s

- Initialize priority queue Q i.e., Q ← V[G]

- while priority queue Q is not empty do

- u ← EXTRACT_MIN(Q)   // Pull out new vertex

- S ← S È {u}
  // Perform relaxation for each vertex v adjacent to u

- for each vertex v in Adj[u] do

- Relax (u, v, w)

Analysis

Like Prim's algorithm, Dijkstra's algorithm runs in O(|E|lg|V|) time.

Example 2.3 : Step by Step operation of Dijkstra algorithm.

Note: Bold arrow are green arrow, light arrow are red arrows.

Step 1 : Given initial graph G=(V, E). All nodes have infinite cost except the source node, s, which has 0 cost.

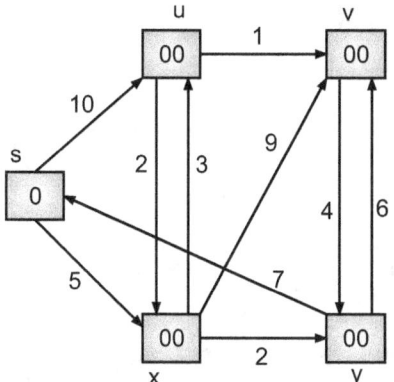

Fig. 2.27 : Graph

Step 2 : First we choose the node, which is closest to the source node, s. We initialize d[s] to 0. Add it to S. Relax all nodes adjacent to source, s. Update predecessor (see red arrow in diagram below) for all nodes updated.

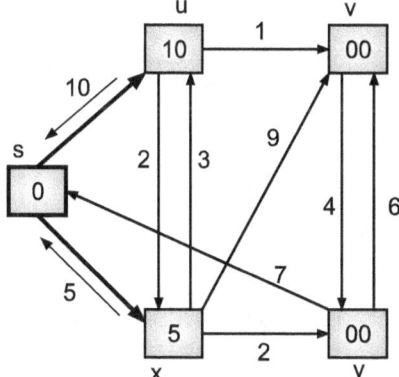

Fig. 2.28 : Dijkstra's algorithm

Step 3 : Choose the closest node, x. Relax all nodes adjacent to node x. Update predecessors for nodes u, v and y (again notice red arrows in diagram below).

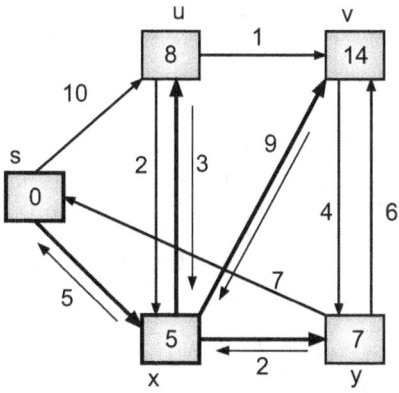

Fig. 2.29 : Dijkstra's algorithm

Step 4 : Now, node y is the closest node, so add it to S. Relax node v and adjust its predecessor (red arrows remember!).

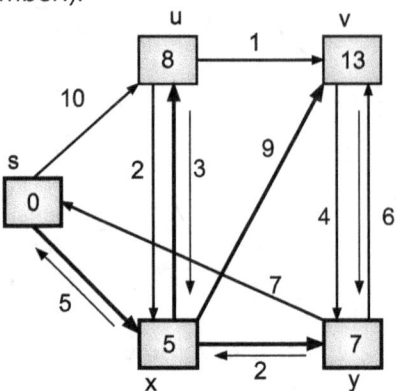

Fig. 2.30 : Dijkstra's algorithm

Step 5 : Now we have node u that is closest. Choose this node and adjust its neighbor node v.

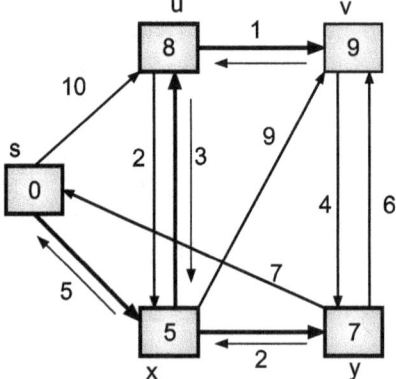

Fig. 2.31 : Dijkstra's algorithm

Step 6 : Finally, add node v. The predecessor list now defines the shortest path from each node to the source node, s.

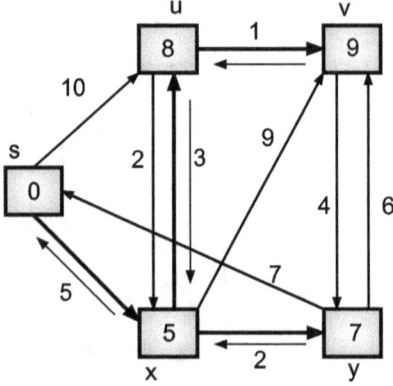

Fig. 2.33 : Dijkstra's algorithm

2.6 TOPOLOGICAL SORTING

We can represent the activities related to a task or project in the form of a graph. The activities in the task are interrelated. Suppose certain project has 5 activities to be completed in order to complete the project. They are represented by graph. The order of completion of the activities is also important, for example, unless we complete activities A and D we cannot start activity C.

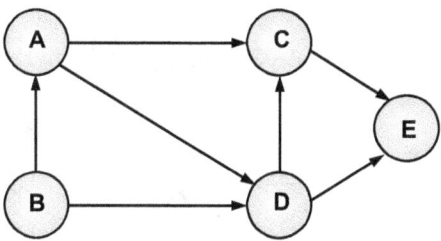

Fig. 2.33 : Activity graph

The topological sort is a process of assigning a linear ordering to the vertices of DAG so that if there is an arc from vertex i to vertex j, than i appears before j in the linear ordering.

The topological sort for graph in Fig. 2.31 will be B, A D, C, E.

Note that the graph has to be directed acyclic graph.

The directed graph has vertices representing activities and the edges represent precedence relationship between the activities is called Activity On Vertex Network (AOV).

The algorithm for topological sort is as below.

1.   Input AOV network.

2.   Let n be number of vertices.

3.   For i = 1 to n do

     If every vertex has predecessor stop (exit)

4.   Pick a vertex v which has no predecessor.

5.   Print v.

6.   Delete all edges starting from v.

7.   End (of for)

8.   Stop.

The topological sort for graph in Fig. 2.33 will be as below.

1.   We start with vertex B which has no predecessor.

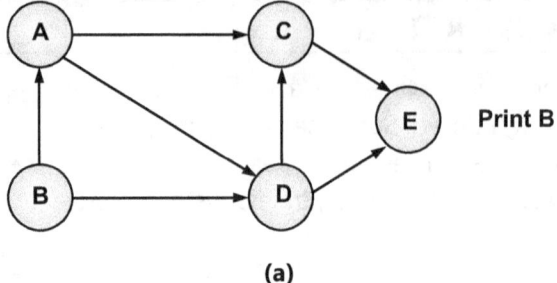

Print B

(a)

Output B-and delete the two outgoing edges from B.

2.

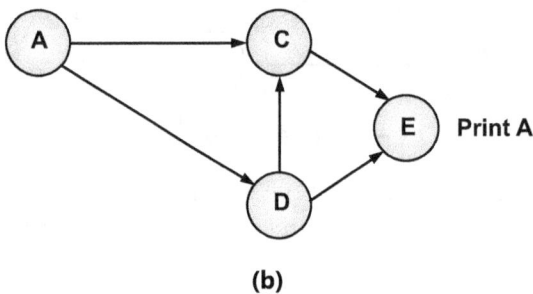

Print A

(b)

We select vertex A which has no predecessor and delete outgoing edges from A.

3.

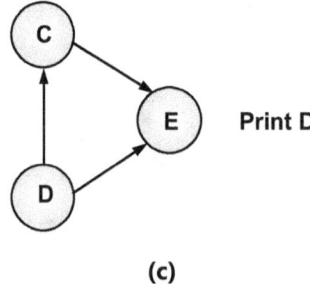

Print D

(c)

We select vertex D and delete the outgoing edges.

4.

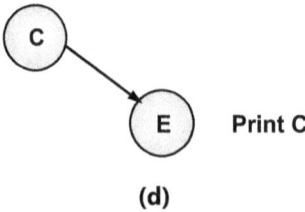

Print C

(d)

We select vertex C and delete outgoing edges.

5.

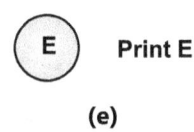

(e)

Thus the topological sort can be represented as

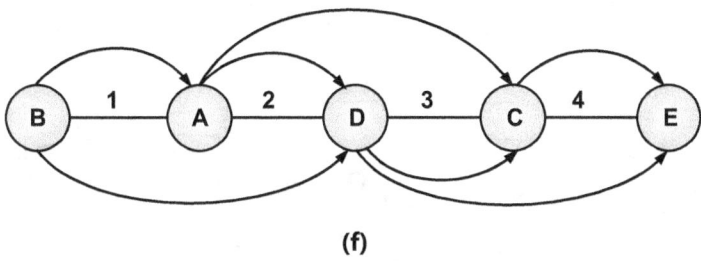

(f)

Fig. 3.34 : Topological sorts

Note : For a graph there can be multiple topological sort order.

Example 2.4 : Find topological sort for the graph given in Fig. 2.35

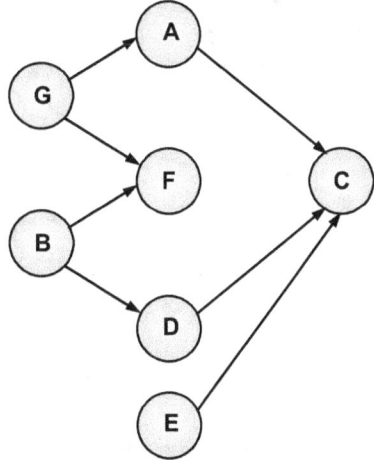

Fig. 2.35

Solution : We can start with either B, E or G. Hence there can be 3 different topological sorts.

If we start with B. It will be

B, D, G, A, F, E, and C. It is shown in Fig. 2.36 (a)

If we start with E it will be

E, G, B, A, D, F and C. It is shown in Fig 2.36 (b)

If we start with G it can be

G, B, A, F, D, E and C

It is shown in Fig. 2.36 (c)

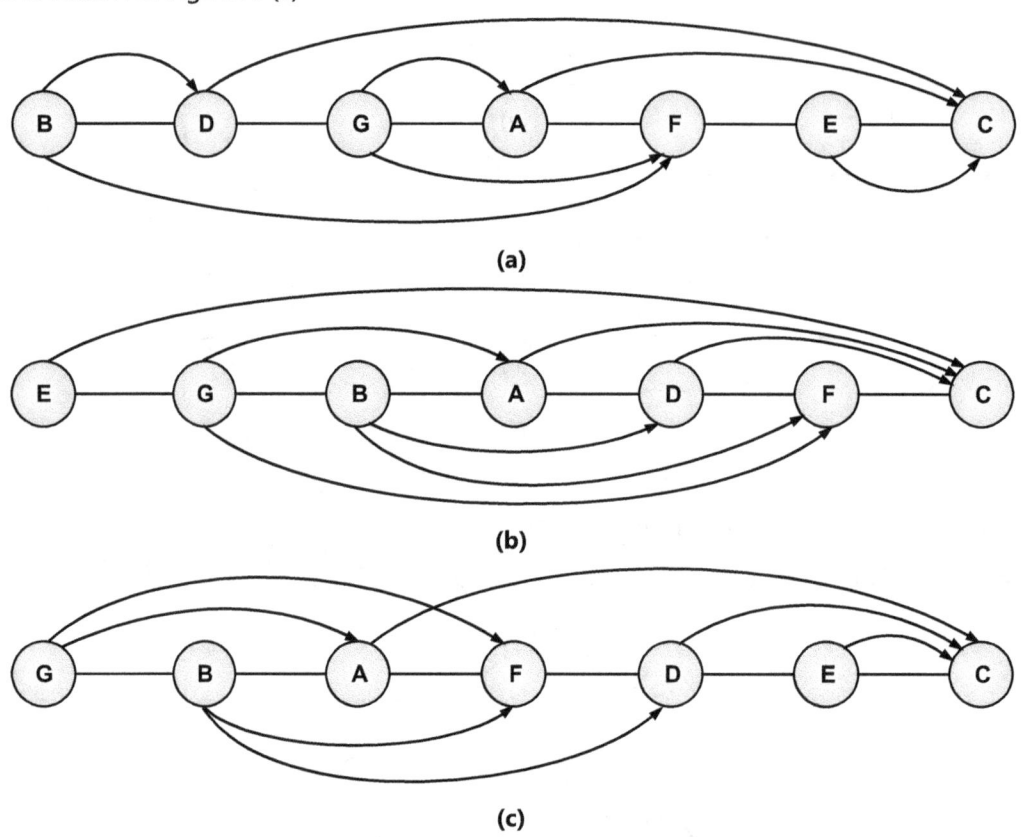

(a)

(b)

(c)

Fig. 2.36 : Topological sorts

2.7 CASE STUDY-DATA STRUCTURES USED IN WEBGRAPH AND GOOGLE MAP

Google Map:

- Google Maps is a web mapping service developed by Google.
- It offers satellite imagery, street maps, 360° panoramic views of streets (Street View), real-time traffic conditions (Google Traffic), and route planning for traveling by foot, car, bicycle (in beta), or public transportation.
- Google Maps' satellite view is a "top-down" or "birds eye" view; most of the high-resolution imagery of cities is aerial photography taken from aircraft flying at 800 to 1,500 feet (240 to 460 m), while most other imagery is from satellites.
- Google Map uses Polyline Algorithm with varied structures as per needs.
- For Geographical mapping google map uses R-tree, R* tree data structures.
- Technologies Used by Google Map is JavaScript's,
- Google Indoor Maps uses JPG, .PNG, .PDF, .BMP, or .GIF, for floor plan.

Web Graph:

WebGraph is a framework for graph compression aimed at studying web graphs. It provides simple ways to manage very large graphs, exploiting modern compression techniques. More precisely, it is currently made of:

- A set of flat codes, called ζ codes, which are particularly suitable for storing web graphs (or, in general, integers with power-law distribution in a certain exponent range). The fact that these codes work well can be easily tested empirically, but we also try to provide a detailed mathematical analysis.

- Algorithms for accessing a compressed graph without actually decompressing it, using lazy techniques that delay the decompression until it is actually necessary.

- Datasets for very large graph (e.g., a billion of links). These are either gathered from public sources (such as WebBase), or produced by UbiCrawler.

With Web Graph you can access and analyze very large web graphs. Using Web Graph is as easy as installing a few jar files and downloading a dataset. This makes studying phenomena such as Page Rank, distribution of graph properties of the web graph, etc. very easy.

Applications of Web Graph:

- The web graph is used for computing the Page Rank of the WWW pages.

- The web graph is used for computing the personalized Page Rank.

- The web graph can be used for detecting web pages of similar topics, through graph-theoretical properties only, like co-citation.

SUMMARY

- Graph is a non linear data structure which may be used in project planning, genetics, network analysis etc.

- A graph can be directed (digraph) or undirected graph.

- Operations on graph can be searching, inserting and deleting nodes and edges in the graph.

- In DFS, from the given vertex we go till the depth of the vertex and then go back to traverse another path till its depth.

- In BFS, we go to the breadth of the current vertex every time we come to a new vertex and then take up the next vertex.

- An undirected graph is said to be connected if for every pair of distinct vertices there is a path.

- Prim's algorithm is a greedy algorithm that finds a minimum spanning tree for a weighted undirected graph.

- Kruskal's algorithm is a minimum-spanning-tree algorithm which finds an edge of the least possible weight that connects any two trees in the forest

- Dijkstra's algorithm is an algorithm for finding the shortest paths between nodes in a graph, which may represent, for example, road networks.

EXERCISE

1. Define the term graph. With the help of suitable example give adjacency matrix representation and adjacency list representation for the same.

2. Explain how graph is represented using suitable example.

3. Take your own example of graph and represent it using matrix and adjacency linked list. Give 'C' declaration for the above mentioned representation.

4. Write non-recursive pseudo-c algorithm for depth first search of a graph.

5. Write non-recursive pseudo-c algorithm for BFS of a graph.

6. Describe the following with suitable examples.

    Depth first search

7. Write an algorithm for Depth First Search for a graph.

8. What is Depth First Search? What are the advantages and disadvantages of DFS? Give pseudo-code to implement DFS on any graph.

9. Explain what are BFS and DFS. Write a pseudo-c to traverse a graph using BFS.

10. Write necessary C functions to implement BFS of graph.

11. Define DFS and BFS for graph.

12. What do you mean by spanning tree? Explain Kruskal's algorithm to find minimum spanning tree with the help of suitable example.

13. What is spanning tree? What is minimum spanning tree?

14. What is minimum spanning tree? Explain Prim's algorithm.

15. Explain Prim's algorithm.

16. Explain Kruskal's algorithm.

17. Write pseudo-c code to find minimum spanning tree using Kruskal's algorithm. Explain all steps with suitable example. What is time complexity of algorithm?

18. Construct minimum spanning tree (step-by-step) from the following graph using Kruskal's algorithm.

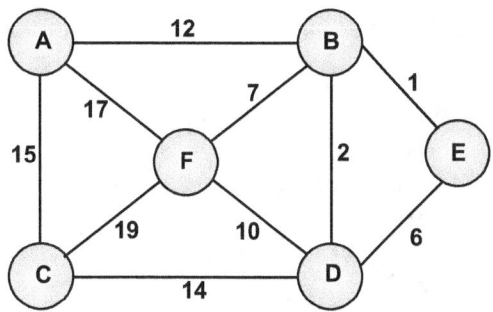

Fig. 2.37 : Graph

19. Determine minimum spanning tree for the following graph using Kruskal's algorithm. Show all the steps.

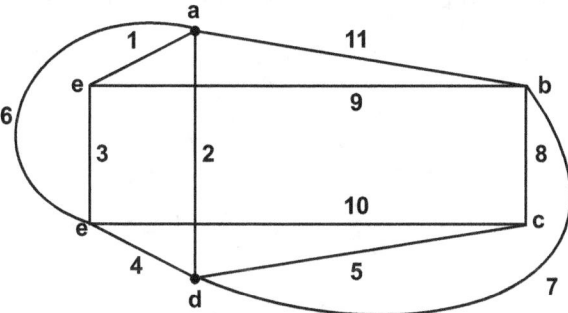

Fig. 2.38 : Graph

20. Construct minimum spanning tree using Kruskal's algorithm for the following graph :

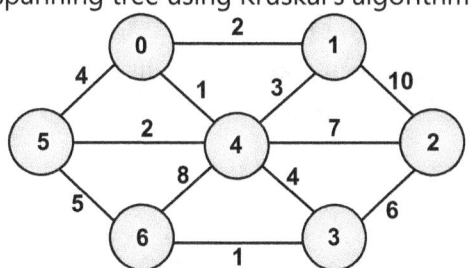

Fig. 2.39 : Graph

21. What is minimum spanning tree? Find minimum spanning tree of the following graph using Kruskal's algorithm.

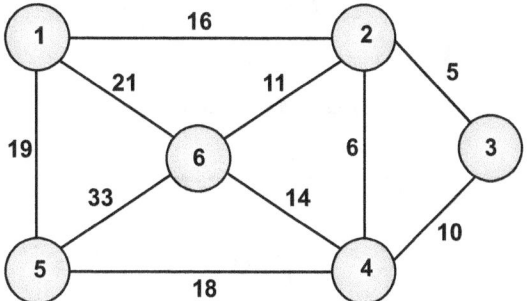

Fig. 2.40 : Graph

22. What is minimum spanning tree? Find minimum spanning tree of the following graph using Kruskal's algorithm.

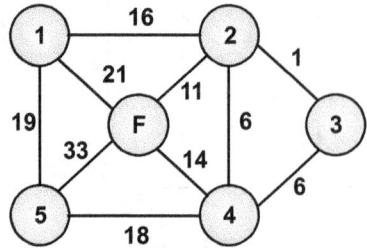

Fig. 2.41 : Graph

23. Define DFS and BFS for graph. Show DFS and BFS for the graph given below :

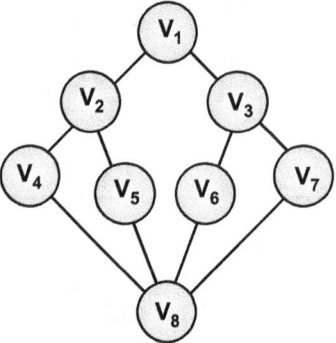

Fig. 2.42 : Graph

24. What do you mean by adjacency matrix and adjacency list? Give the adjacency matrix and adjacency list of the following graph :

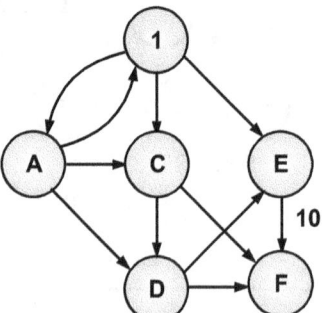

Fig. 2.43 : Graph

◈ ◈ ◈

HASHING

3.1 INTRODUCTION

Hashing is the transformation of a string of characters into a usually shorter fixed-length value or key that represents the original string. Hashing is a effective way to reduce the storage space requirements and to reduce number of comparisons for searching.

3.2 HASH TABLE

Hash tables are the data structures which favor efficient storage and retrieval of data elements which are **linear** in nature.

Dictionaries :

Dictionaries is a collection of data elements uniquely identified by a field called **key**. A dictionary supports operations of search, insert and delete.

A dictionary supports both **sequential and random access**. A sequential access is the process in which the data elements of the dictionary are **ordered** and accessed according to the order of the keys (ascending/descending). A random access is the process in which the data elements of the dictionary are not accessed according to a particular order.

Hash tables are ideal data structures for dictionaries.

Hash Search :

Hash search is a search in which the key, through an algorithmic function, determines the location of the data.

Hashing it is a key to address transformation in which the keys map to addresses in a list.

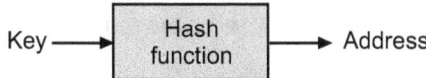

Fig. 3.1 (a) : Hash search

Hash Functions :

A hash function is a mathematical function which maps a given key of the dictionary to its corresponding location in the storage table (known as hash table).

The process of mapping the keys to their respective position in the hash table is called as **hashing**.

The choice of the hash function plays a significant role in the performance of the hash table. It is therefore essential that a hash function satisfies following characteristics :

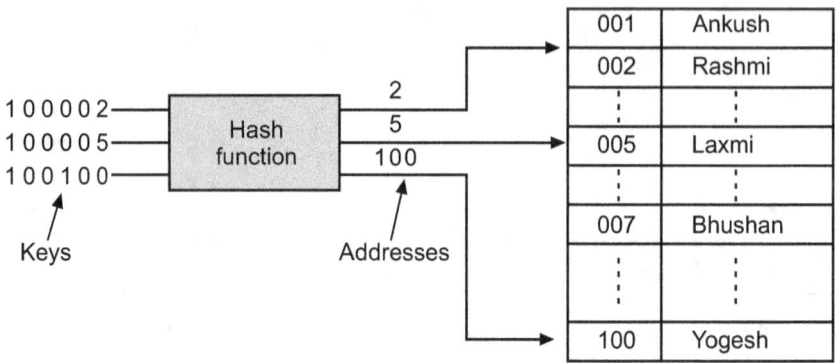

Fig. 3.2 : Hash search

Characteristics of Hash Functions :

- Easy and quick to compute.
- Even distribution of keys across the hash table.
- A hash function must minimize collisions.

Basic Definitions of Hashing :

- **Synonyms :** The set of **keys** that hash to the **same location** in our list is called as synonyms.
- **Collision :** Collision is the event that occurs when a hashing algorithm produces an address for an insertion key and that address is already occupied.
- **Home Address :** The address produced by the hashing algorithm is known as home address.
- **Prime Area :** The memory that contains all of the home addresses is known as the prime area.
- **Probe :** Each calculation of an address and test for success is known as a probe.
- **Bucket :** A hash table uses a hash function to compute an index into an array of buckets or slots, from which the desired value can be found.
- **Overflow :** An overflow occurs when the home bucket for a new pair (key, element) is full.
- **Open hashing:** In open hashing, keys are stored in linked lists attached to cells of a hash table.
- **Closed Hashing :** In closed hashing, all keys are stored in the hash table itself without the use of linked lists.
- **Load Density /Load Factor :** The loading density or loading factor of a hash table is a = n/(sb)
  - s is the number of slots
  - b is the number of buckets

3.2.1 Issues in Hashing

Following are the some basic issues which are consider while hashing.

1. Computing the hash function

2. Collision resolution: Algorithm and data structure to handle two keys that hash to the same index.

3. Equality test: Method for checking whether two keys are equal.

3.2.2 Properties of Good Hashing Function

Hash fuctions should have the following properties:

1.   Fast computation of the hash value (O(1)).

2.   Hash values should be distributed (nearly) uniformly:

   -   Every hash value (cell in the hash table) has equal probabilty.

   -   This should hold even if keys are non-uniformly distributed.

3.   The goal of a hash function is: 'disperse' the keys in an apparently random way

4.   A hash function must minimize collisions.

3.2.3 Basic Hashing Techniques

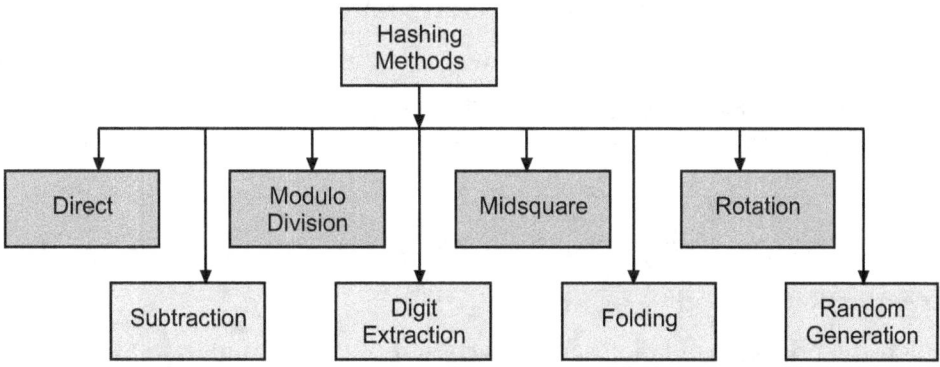

(1) Direct Hashing :

In direct hashing, address for a key is generated without any algorithmic manipulation. Therefore the data structure must contain an address for every possible key.

Example : A small organization has 100 employees. Each employee is assigned an employee number between 1 to 100. Hence we create an array of 100 employee records; the employee number can be directly used as the address of any individual record.

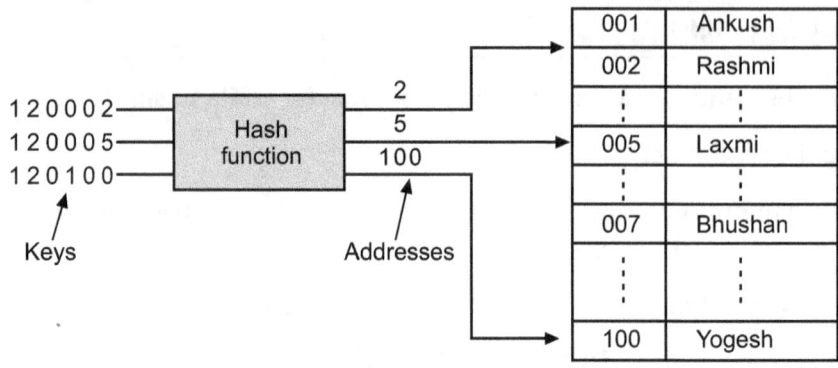

Fig. 3.3

(2) Subtraction Method :

Sometimes we have keys that are consecutive but do not start from one. This method is simple and it guarantees no collisions. Limitation is this method can be used for small lists in which the keys map to a densely filled list.

Example : Consider a company has 100 employees, but their employee number starts from 1000 up to 1100 consecutively. Then we use a very simple hashing function that subtracts 1000 from the key to determine the address.

(3) Modulo-Division Method/Division Remainder :

This method divides the key by an array or bucket size and uses the remainder plus one for the address.

$$\therefore \quad\quad\quad \text{Address} = (\text{key} \% \text{ list size}) + 1$$

A list size that is a prime number produces fewer collisions than other list sizes.

Example : Suppose we have 300 employees. The first prime number greater than 300 is 307. We therefore choose 307 as our list size.

$$\therefore \quad\quad\quad \text{Employee number} - 121267$$

$$\therefore \quad\quad\quad (121267 \% 307) + 1 = 2 + 1 = 3$$

(4) Digit Extraction Method :

Using digit extraction, selected digits are extracted from the key and used as the address.

Example :
$$3\underline{79}4\underline{52} \rightarrow 394$$
$$\underline{12}1\underline{2}67 \rightarrow 112$$
$$3\underline{78}8\underline{45} \rightarrow 388$$
$$1\underline{60}2\underline{52} \rightarrow 102$$
$$\underline{0}4\underline{51}28 \rightarrow 051$$

(5) Midsquare Method :

Key is squared and the address is selected from the middle of the squared number.

Example : 9452 * 9452 = 89**3403**04

Address is 3403

(6) Folding Method :

There are 2 folding methods :

(a) Fold Shift : The key value is divided into parts whose size matches the size of the required address. Then the left and right parts are shifted and added with middle part.

Example : Suppose we have 3-digit addresses and key is 123456789

$$
\begin{array}{r}
1\ 2\ 3 \\
+\ 4\ 5\ 6 \\
+\ 7\ 8\ 9 \\
\hline
(1)\ 3\ 6\ 8
\end{array}
$$

Discard (1) so address is 368.

(b) Fold Boundary : Left and right numbers are folded on a fixed boundary between them and the center number. This results in the two outside values being reversed.

Example : Suppose we have 3 digit addresses and key is 123456789.

$$
\begin{array}{r}
3\ 2\ 1 \\
+\ 4\ 5\ 6 \\
+\ 9\ 8\ 7 \\
\hline
(1)\ 7\ 6\ 4
\end{array}
$$
→ Reversed digits of 123

→ Reversed digits of 789

Discard (1). So address is 764.

(7) Rotation Method :

Rotation method is incorporated in combination with other hashing methods. it is most useful when keys are assigned serially, such as we often see in employee numbers and part numbers.

Example :

Original Key	Rotation	Rotated Key
6 0 0 1 0 1	6 0 0 1 0 [1]	[1] 6 0 0 1 0
6 0 0 1 0 2	6 0 0 1 0 [2]	[2] 6 0 0 1 0
6 0 0 1 0 3	6 0 0 1 0 [3]	[3] 6 0 0 1 0
6 0 0 1 0 4	6 0 0 1 0 [4]	[4] 6 0 0 1 0

(8) Pseudorandom Method :

The key is used as the seed in pseudorandom number generator and the resulting random number then scaled into the possible address range using modulo division. Common random generator is Y = ax + c.

Example : Consider a = 17 and c = 7. Also consider list size is 307. Key is 121267.

$$\therefore \qquad y = ((17 * 121267) + 7)\ \%\ 307 + 1$$
$$y = (2061539 + 7)\ \%\ 307 + 1$$
$$y = (2061546\ \%\ 307) + 1$$
$$y = 41 + 1$$
$$y = 42$$

∴   Address is 42.

(9) Multiplicative Hash Function

e.g. H(k)= floor(p * fractionalpart of key * A)

Where,

P = constant integer

A = constant real number

e.g.

k = 107, p = 50,

A = 0.61803398987

∴   H(k) = floor (50 * (107 * 0.61803398987))

= floor (3306.4818458045)

∴ H(k) = 3306

3.2.4 Forms of Hashing Data Structure

(1) Linear Open Addressing : It allows any number of records to be stored, because the space is dynamic.

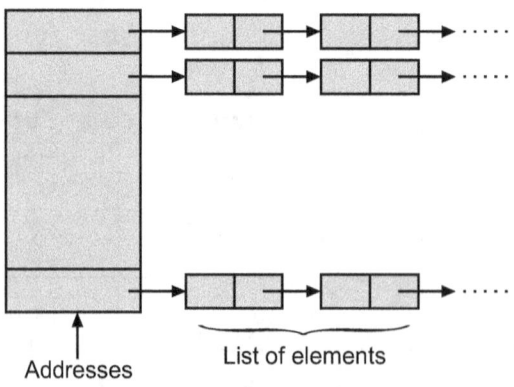

Fig. 3.4 : Linear open addressing

(2) Linear Closed Addressing : It uses a fixed space for storage and hence this limits the size of hash table.

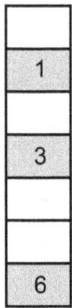

Fig. 3.5 : Linear closed Addressing

In this case maximum 7 elements can be stored as array size is only 7 and that is fixed.

3.3 COLLISION RESOLUTION METHODS

To avoid the collision we can use different collision resolution methods which are

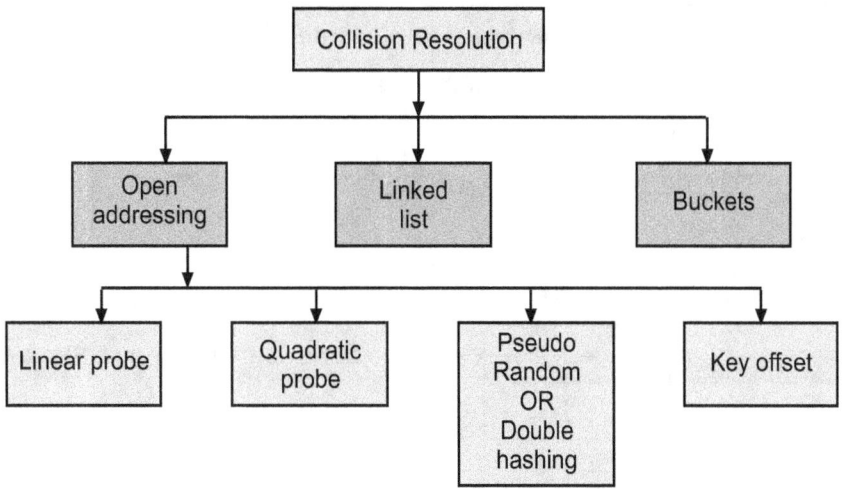

Open Addressing :

In open addressing when a collision occurs, the home area addresses are searched for an unoccupied element where the new data can be placed.

(1) Linear Probe :

(a) Linear Probing without Chaining :

When collision occurs, we resolve the collision by finding the next empty cell.

Example : Keys 3, 33, 42, 63, 89, 45, 93

Hash function = Key % 10

	Empty	After 3	After 33	After 42	After 63	After 89	After 45	After 93
0	-	-	-	-	-	-	-	-
1	-	-	-	-	-	-	-	-
2	-	-	-	**42**	42	42	42	42
3	-	**3**	3	3	3	3	3	3
4	-	-	**33**	33	33	33	33	33
5	-	-	-	-	**63**	63	63	63
6	-	-	-	-	-	-	**45**	45
7	-	-	-	-	-	-	-	**93**
8	-	-	-	-	-	-	-	-
9	-	-	-	-	-	**89**	89	89

(b) Linear Probing with Chaining (without Replacement) :

Excessive collisions can be dealt by means of chaining. All the records mapped to same location are stored in a chain.

Example : Keys – 3, 33, 42, 63, 89, 45, 93

Hash function $\Rightarrow$ key % 10.

Index	Key	Chain	
0	-	− 1	⟶ −1 shows there is no chaining yet.
1	-	− 1	
2	-	− 1	
3	-	− 1	
4	-	− 1	
5	-	− 1	
6	-	− 1	
7	-	− 1	
8	-	− 1	
9	-	− 1	

Index	Key	Chain
0	-	− 1
1	-	− 1
2	42	− 1
3	3	4 ──→ index of 33
4	33	5 ──→ index of 63
5	63	7 ──→ index of 93
6	45	− 1
7	93	− 1
8	-	− 1
9	**89**	− 1

Here 3, 33, 63 and 93 are supposed to be mapped at location 3. Hence all these are chained by index number at chain column.

(c) Linear Probing with Chaining (with Replacement) :

In above example, key 45 has misplaced its starting location is at index 5. So to overcome this issue we replace key at index 5 by 45 and shift 63 to another subsequent empty location.

Example : Keys – 3, 33, 42, 63, 89, 45, 93.

Hash function = key % 10.

Index	Key	Chain
0	-	− 1
1	-	− 1
2	**42**	− 1
3	**3**	4 ──→ index of 33
4	**33**	5 ──→ index of 63
5	**63**	− 1
6	-	− 1
7	-	− 1
8	-	− 1
9	**89**	− 1

Now to insert 45, we have shift 63 to next index 6 and place 45 at index 5.

After arrival of 45 and 93 :

Index	Key	Chain
0	-	− 1
1	-	− 1
2	42	− 1
3	3	4 ⟶ index of 33
4	33	**6** ⟶ new index of 63
5	**45**	− 1
6	63	7 ⟶ index of 93
7	**93**	− 1
8	-	− 1
9	89	− 1

Program to implement Direct Access File, collision handling through linear probing with chaining and without replacement.

Program 3.1 : Hash Table-Linear Probing without Chaining :

```
/*   To implement Direct Access File ,Collision handling through linear probing with
chaining and without replacement.  */

#include <iomanip.h>
#include <iostream.h>
#include <fstream.h>
#include <conio.h>
#include <string.h>
#define SIZE 10
#define h(x) x%SIZE
struct student
{
        int rollno;
        char name[20];
        float marks;
        int status;
        int link;
};

class lin_probe
```

```
{
  char table[30];
  fstream tab;
  student rec;
  public :
          lin_probe(char *a);

          void displayall();
          void insert(student rec1);
          void  Delete(int rollno);
          int  search(int rollno);
          void display(int recno)
            {
                int i=recno;
                tab.open(table,ios : :binary | ios : :in | ios : :nocreate);
                tab.seekg(recno*sizeof(student),ios : :beg);
                tab.read((char*)&rec,sizeof(student));
                if(rec.status==0)
                    {
                        cout<<"\n"<<i<<")        "<<rec.rollno<<"                "<<rec.name<<"
"<<setprecision(2)<<rec.marks;
                        cout<<" "<<rec.link;
                    }
                else
                        cout<<"\n"<<i<<") ***** Empty ********";
                tab.close();
            }
          void read(int recno)
            {
                tab.open(table,ios : :binary | ios : :in  );
                tab.seekg(recno*sizeof(student),ios : :beg);
                tab.read((char*) &rec,sizeof(student));
                tab.close();
            }
           void write(int recno)
            {
                tab.open(table,ios : :binary | ios : :nocreate | ios : :out | ios : :in);
                tab.seekp(recno*sizeof(student),ios : :beg);
                tab.write((char*)&rec,sizeof(student));
```

```
                    tab.close();
                }


};
void lin_probe : :lin_probe(char *a)
{
        int i;
        strcpy(table,a);
        rec.status=1;rec.link=-1;
        tab.open(table,ios : :binary | ios : :out);
        tab.close();
        for(i=0;i<SIZE;i++)
                    write(i);


}
void lin_probe : :displayall()
{
        int i=1,n;
        cout<<"\n*********Data File*********\n";
        for(i=0;i<SIZE;i++)
                    display(i);
}

void lin_probe : :insert(student rec1)
{
        int n,i,j,start,k;
        rec1.status=0;
        rec1.link=-1;
        start=h(rec1.rollno);
        for(i=0;i<SIZE;i++)
          {
                    j=(start+i)%SIZE;
                    read(j);
                    if(rec.status==0 && h(rec.rollno)==start)
                       break;
          }
        if(i<10)
          {
                while(rec.link!=-1)
```

```
            {
                    j=rec.link;
                    read(j);
            }
            for(i=0;i<SIZE;i++)
            {
                    k=(start+i)%SIZE;
                    read(k);
                    if(rec.status==1)
                      {
                                rec=rec1;
                                write(k);
                                read(j);
                                rec.link=k;
                                write(j);
                                return;

                      }
            }
          cout<<"\nTable is full ";
        }
    else
      {
          for(i=0;i<SIZE;i++)
            {
                    k=(start+i)%SIZE;
                    read(k);
                    if(rec.status==1)
                      {
                                rec=rec1;
                                write(k);
                                return;

                      }
            }
          cout<<"\nTable is full ";
      }

}

void lin_probe : :Delete(int rollno)
```

```
{
        student rec1;
        int recno;
        int i,j,start,k;
        start=h(rollno);
        for(i=0;i<SIZE;i++)
         {
                j=(start+i)%SIZE;
                read(j);
                if(rec.status==0 && h(rec.rollno)==start)//synonim found
                  break;
         }
        if(i<10)
        {
            if(rec.rollno==rollno )
                {
                        rec.status=1;
                        write(j);
                }
            else
                {
                        while(rec.rollno !=rollno && rec.link!=-1)
                          {
                            k=j;
                        j=rec.link;
                          read(j);
                          }

                        if(rec.rollno==rollno)
                          {   rec.status=1;
                              write(j);
                              int nextlink=rec.link;
                              read(k);
                              rec.link=nextlink;
                              write(k);
                          }
                        else
                        cout<<"\nElement not found";
                }
```

```
                }
        else
                        cout<<"\nRecord Not Found ";
}
int lin_probe : :search(int rollno)
{
        int start,i,j;
        start=h(rollno);
        for(i=0;i<SIZE;i++)
          {
                j=(start+i)%SIZE;
                read(j);
                if(rec.status==0 && h(rec.rollno)==start)//synonim found
                  break;
          }
        if(i<10)
          {
                        while(rec.rollno !=rollno && rec.link!=-1)
                          {
                        j=rec.link;
                          read(j);
                          }

                        if(rec.rollno==rollno)
                        return(j);

                        else
                        return -1;
          }
        else
                        return -1;
}


void main()
 {
   lin_probe object("table.txt");
   int rollno,op,recno;
   student rec1;
```

```
clrscr();
do
 {
   cout<<"\n\n1)Print\n2)Insert\n3)Delete";
   cout<<"\n4)Search\n5)Quit";
   cout<<"\nEnter Your Choice :";
   cin>>op;
   switch(op)
       {
         case 1 : object.displayall();
                 break;
         case 2 :
         cout<<"\nEnter a record to be inserted(roll no,name,marks) : ";
                 cin>>rec1.rollno>>rec1.name>>rec1.marks;
                 object.insert(rec1);
                  break;
         case 3 :
                 cout<<"\nEnter the roll no. :";
                 cin>>rollno;
                 object.Delete(rollno);
                  break;
          case 4 :
                 cout<<"\nEnter a roll no. : ";
                 cin>>rollno;
                 recno=object.search(rollno);
                 if(recno>=0)
                  {
                         cout<<"\n Record No. :  "<<recno;
                         object.display(recno);
                  }
                 else
                         cout<<"\nRecord Not Found ";
                 break;
       }
   }while(op!=5);
}

/**************OUTPUT***************/
1)  Print
```

2) Insert
3) Delete
4) Search
5) Quit
Enter Your Choice :2

Enter a record to be inserted(roll no,name,marks) : 155 ABC 76

1) Print
2) Insert
3) Delete
4) Search
5) Quit

Enter Your Choice :2

Enter a record to be inserted(roll no,name,marks) : 45 LMN 88

1) Print
2) Insert
3) Delete
4) Search
5) Quit

Enter Your Choice :2

Enter a record to be inserted(roll no,name,marks) : 90 XYZ 70

1) Print
2) Insert
3) Delete
4) Search
5) Quit

Enter Your Choice :4

Enter a roll no. : 45

Record No. : 6

6) 45 Komal 88 -1

1) Print
2) Insert
3) Delete
4) Search
5) Quit
Enter Your Choice :1

*********Data File*********

0) 90 XYZ 70 -1
1) ***** Empty ********
2) ***** Empty ********
3) ***** Empty ********
4) ***** Empty ********
5) 155 ABC 76 6
6) 45 LMN 88 -1
7) ***** Empty ********
8) ***** Empty ********
9) ***** Empty ********

1) Print
2) Insert
3) Delete
4) Search
5) Quit

Enter Your Choice :3

Enter the roll no. :45

1) Print
2) Insert
3) Delete
4) Search
5) Quit
Enter Your Choice :1

```
*********Data File*********

0)  90  XYZ  70 -1
1)  ***** Empty ********
2)  ***** Empty ********
3)  ***** Empty ********
4)  ***** Empty ********
5)  155  ABC  76 -1
6)  ***** Empty ********
7)  ***** Empty ********
8)  ***** Empty ********
9)  ***** Empty ********


1)  Print
2)  Insert
3)  Delete
4)  Search
5)  Quit

Enter Your Choice :5
```

(2) Quadratic Probe :

In quadratic probe, the increment is the collision probe number squared. Thus for 1st probe we add 1^2; for 2nd probe we add 2^2; for 3rd probe we add 3^2; and so forth until we find an empty element or we exhaust the possible elements.

This probe does not ensure that all cells will be examined to find empty cell. Thus it may be possible that key wont be inserted even if there is an empty cell in the table.

Probe Number	Collision Location	(Probe)^2 and Increment	New Address
1	1	$(1)^2 = 1$	1 + 1 = 2
2	2	$(2)^2 = 4$	2 + 4 = 6
3	6	$(3)^2 = 9$	6 + 9 = 15
4	15	$(4)^2 = 16$	15 + 16 = 31
5	31	$(5)^2 = 25$	31 + 25 = 56

Quadratic collision resolution increments.

Example : Keys – 4371, 1323, 6173, 4199, 4344, 9679, 1989.

Hash function = Key % 10.

Index	Key
0	9679
1	4371
2	-
3	1323
4	6173
5	4344
6	-
7	-
8	1989
9	4199

i)   4371 % 10 = 1   (1st location is empty, put the element directly)

ii) 1323 % 10 = 3   (3rd location is empty, put the element directly)

iii) 6173 % 10 = 3   (3rd location is not empty)

$\therefore$ 6173 % 10 = 3 + (1)^2 = 4   (4th location is empty, put the element directly)

iv) 4199 % 10 = 9   (9th location is empty, put the element directly)

v)   4344 % 10 = 4   (4th location is not empty)

$\therefore$ 4344 % 10 = 4 + (1)^2 = 5   (5th location is empty, put the element directly)

vi) 9679 % 10 = 9   (9th location is not empty)

$\therefore$ 9679 % 10 = 9 + (1)^2 = 10 % 10 = 0   (0th location is empty, So put the element directly)

vii) 1989 % 10 = 9   (9th location is not empty)

$\therefore$ 1989 % 10 = 9 + (1)^2 = 10% 10 = 0 (0th location is not empty)

$\therefore$ 1989 % 10 = 9 + (2)^2 = 9 + 4 = 13 % 10 = 3   (3rd location is not empty)

$\therefore$ 1989 % 10 = 9 + (3)^2 = 9 + 9 = 18 % 10 = 8   (8th location is empty. So put the element there)

(3) Pseudorandom / Double Hashing :

Rather than using an arithmetic probe function, the address is rehashed. This means if first hash function yields an address which is already occupied then apply second hash function to get the different address for a key.

Example : keys – 4371, 1323, 6173, 4199, 4344, 9679

First hash function = key % 10

Second hash function = 7 – (key % 7)

Index	Key	To insert
0		(a) 6173 $\rightarrow$
1	4371	$7 - (6173 \% 7) = 7 - 6 = 1$
2		$\therefore 6173 \% 10 = 3 + (1)^{\times 1} = 4$
3	1323	(b) 4344 $\rightarrow$
4	6173	$7 - (4344 \% 7) = 7 - 4 = 3$
5	9679	$\therefore 4344 \% 10 = 4 + (3)^{\times 1} = 7$
6		(c) 9679 $\rightarrow$
7	4344	$7 - (9679 \% 7) = 7 - 5 = 2$
8		$\therefore 9679 \% 10 = 9 + (2)^{1} = 11 \% 10 = 1$
9	4199	Again $9679 \% 10 = 9 + (2)^{2} = 13 \% 10 = 3$
		Again $9679 \% 10 = 9 + (2)^{3} = 15 \% 10 = 5$

(4) Key Offset :

Key offset is a double hashing method that produces different collision paths for different keys. Key offset calculates the new address as a function of the old address and the key.

Offset = [Key / Listsize]

Address = [(Offset + Old address) % List size] + 1

Example :   key $\rightarrow$ 166702

$$\text{size} \rightarrow 307$$

$$1^{\text{st}} \text{ hash function } = \text{ key } \% \text{ 10}$$

$$\therefore \qquad 166702 \% 10 = 2$$

$$\therefore \qquad \text{Offset } = (166702/307) = 543$$

$$\text{Address } = [(543 + 002) \% 307] + 1 = 239$$

If at 239 there is also a collision then repeat the process to locate next address.

$$\therefore \qquad \text{Offset } = (166702/307) = 543$$

$$\text{Address } = [(543 + 239) \% 307] + 1 = 169$$

(5) Linked List Resolution/Dynamic Hashing :

Linked list is an ordered collection of data in which each element contains the location of the next element.

Linked list resolution uses a separate area to store collisions and chairs all synonyms together in a linked list. It uses two storage areas, prime area and overflow area.

When a collision occurs one element is stored in prime area and chained to its corresponding linked list in overflow area.

Example : Keys – 3, 33, 42, 63, 89, 45, 93.

Hash Function = key % 10.

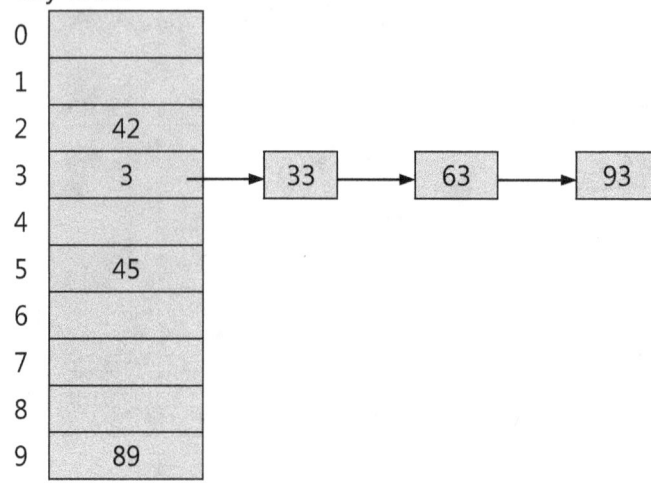

(6) Bucket Hashing :

Bucket nodes that accommodate **multiple data occurrences**. Because a bucket can hold multiple pieces of data, collision are postponed until the bucket is full.

Example : Keys – 3, 33, 42, 63, 89, 45

Hash Function = key % 10.

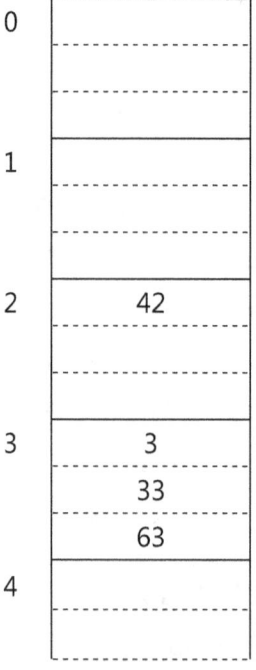

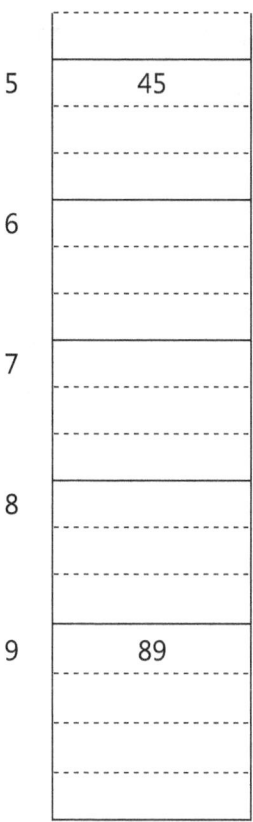

(7) Rehashing

Rehashing tells us what to do when the hash table gets full instead of waiting for the hash table to get completely full, it is more efficient to rehash when the table is about 70% or 80% full.

The most common rehashing technique is to construct a new table of approximately double size of the original hash table.

e.g. Insert 13 15 6 24 23 into an initially empty hash table. Assume table size= 7 & use linear probing for collision resolution.

Since table size=7

Hash(x)= x mod 7

After 23 is inserted table is 70% full.

Rehash: New table size =7 * 2=14

14 is not a prime number.

So, we select the prime number closest to & greater than 14 i.e.17 as the new table size. New hash function is : hash(x)= x mod 17.

When to Rehash:

1) Rehash when table is half full
2) Rehash as soon as insertion fails
3) Rehash beyond a certain load factor.

SOLVED EXAMPLES

Example 3.1 : Explain linear probing with and without replacement using the following data : 12, 01, 04, 03, 07, 08, 10, 02, 05, 14, 06, 28. Assume buckets from 0 to 9 and each bucket has one slot. Calculate average cost or number of comparison for both.

Solution : (a) Linear probing without replacement.

Index	Key	Chain
0	**10**	- 1
1	**01**	- 1
2	**12**	- 1
3	**03**	- 1
4	**04**	- 1
5	-	- 1
6	-	- 1
7	07	- 1
8	08	- 1
9	-	- 1

After insertion of 1st 7 keys.

Total comparisons = 7 × 1 = 7

Index	Key	Chain
0	10	- 1
1	01	- 1
2	12	5
3	03	- 1
4	04	- 1
5	02	- 1
6	05	- 1
7	07	- 1
8	08	- 1
9	-	- 1

After insertion of 02 and 05

For 2 Total comparisons are = 4

For 5 Total comparisons are = 2

Index	Key	Chain
0	10	- 1
1	01	- 1
2	12	5
3	03	- 1
4	04	_9_
5	02	- 1
6	05	- 1
7	07	- 1
8	08	- 1
9	_14_	- 1

After insertion of 14

(6 comparisons - 1st at 4, 2nd at 5, 3rd at 6 and 4th at 7, 5th at 8 and 6th at 9th position)

Keys 06 and 28 cannot be inserted as the bucket size of hash table is full.

So, therefore total number of comparisons.

$$= (7 \times 1) + 4 + 2 + 6$$
$$= 19$$

(b) Linear Probing with Replacement :

Index	Key	Chain
0	_10_	- 1
1	_01_	- 1
2	_12_	- 1
3	_03_	- 1
4	_04_	- 1
5	-	- 1
6	-	- 1
7	_07_	- 1
8	_08_	- 1
9	-	- 1

After insertion of 1st 7 keys which are 12, 01, 04, 03, 07, 08, 10.

(Each with 1 comparison only at 2, 1, 4, 3, 7, 8, and 0 respectively)

Index	Key	Chain
0	10	- 1
1	01	- 1
2	12	_5_

After insertion of 02

(4 comparisons – 1st at 2, 2nd at 3, 3rd at 4 and 4th at 5th position)

3	03	- 1
4	04	- 1
5	02	- 1
6	-	- 1
7	07	- 1
8	08	- 1
9	-	- 1

Index	Key	Chain
0	10	- 1
1	01	- 1
2	12	6
3	03	- 1
4	04	9
5	05	- 1
6	02	- 1
7	07	- 1
8	08	- 1
9	14	- 1

After insertion of 5

(3 comparisons – 1st at 5, 2nd at 6 to

remove 2 at 6th position

3rd at 2nd to change chain number)

and After insertion of 14

(6 comparisons – 1st at 4, 2nd at 5,

3rd at 6, 4th at 7, 5th at 8, and 6th at 9th

position)

Keys 06 and 28 cannot be inserted as the bucket size 9 of hash table is full.

So, therefore total number of comparisons.

$$= 7 \times 1 + 4 + 3 + 6$$

$$= 20$$

Example 3.2 : Given the input {4371, 1323, 6173, 4199, 4344, 9679, 1989} and hash function $h(x) = (x \bmod 10)$, show the results for the following :

(a) Open addressing hash table using linear probing.

(b) Open addressing hash table with quadratic probing.

(c) Open addressing hash table with second hash function.

which is $h2(x) = 7 - (x \bmod 7)$.

Solution :

(a) Open Addressing has Table with Linear Probing :

Index	4371	1323	6173	4199	4344	9679	1989
0	-	-	-	-	-	9679	9679
1	**4371**	4371	4371	4371	4371	4371	4371
2	-	-	-	-	-	-	**1989**
3	-	**1323**	1323	1323	1323	1323	1323
4	-	-	**6173**	6173	6173	6173	6173
5	-	-	-	-	**4344**	4344	4344
6	-	-	-	-	-	-	-
7	-	-	-	-	-	-	-
8	-	-	-	-	-	-	-
9	-	-	-	**4199**	4199	4199	4199

(b) Open Addressing Hash Table with Quadratic Probing :

Index	4371	1323	6173	4199	4344	9679	1989
0	-	-	-	-	-	**9679**	9679
1	**4371**	4371	4371	4371	4371	4371	4371
2	-	-	-	-	-	-	-
3	-	**1323**	1323	1323	1323	1323	1323
4	-	-	**6173**	6173	6173	6173	6173
5	-	-	-	-	**4344**	4344	4344
6	-	-	-	-	-	-	-
7	-	-	-	-	-	-	-
8	-	-	-	-	-	-	**1989**
9	-	-	-	**4199**	4199	4199	4199

- Key 6173 to be mapped to
  $$(6173 \% 10 + (1)^2) = 3 + 1 = 4$$
- Key 4344 to be mapped to
  $$(4344 \% 10 + (1)^2) = 4 + 1 = 5$$
- Key 9679 to be mapped to
  $$(9679 \% 10 + (1)^2) = 9 + 1 = 10 \% 10 = 0$$
- Key 1989 to be mapped to
  $$(1989 \% 10 + (1)^2) = 9 + 1 = 10 \% 10 = 0$$

0th position not available

So $(1989 \% 10 + (2)^2) = 9 + 4 = 13 \% 10 = 3$

3rd position not available

So $(1989 \% 10 + (3)^2) = 9 + 9 = 18 \% 10 = 8.$

8th position is empty. So insert 1989 at 8th position

(c) Open Addressing Hash Table with 2nd Hash Function

$$h2(x) = 7 - (x \bmod 7)$$

Index	4371	1323	6173	4199	4344	9679	1989
0	-	-	-	-	-	-	-
1	**4371**	4371	4371	4371	4371	4371	4371
2	-	-	-	-	-	-	**1989**
3	-	**1323**	1323	1323	1323	1323	1323
4	-	-	**6173**	6173	6173	6173	6173
5	-	-	-	-	-	**9679**	9679
6	-	-	-	-	-	-	-
7	-	-	-	-	**4344**	4344	4344
8	-	-	-	-	-	-	-
9	-	-	-	**4199**	4199	4199	4199

Here 1989 is not mapped.

- h2 (6173) = 7 – 6173 % 7 = 7 – 6 = 1

  So 6173 to be mapped to 6173%10 + (1 × h2(6173) = 3 + 1 = 4

- h2 (4344) = 7 – 4344 % 7 = 7 – 4 = 3

  So 4344 to be mapped to 4344 % 10 + (1 × h2 (4344) = 4 + 3 = 7

- h2 (9679) = 7 – 9679 % 7 = 7 – 5 = 2

  So 9679 to be mapped to 9679 % 10 + (1 × h2 (9679)) = 9 + 2 = 11% 10 = 1

  9679 % 10 + (2 × h2 (9679)) = 9 + 4 = 13% 10 = 3

  9679 % 10 + (3 × h2 (9679)) = 9 + 6 = 15% 10 = 5

- h2 (1989) = 7 – 1989 % 7 = 7 – 1 = 6

  This key cannot be inserted as any location of (9 + 6 × i) % 10 is not empty.

Example 3.3 : Assume (a) hash table of size 9 and hash function H(x) = x mod 10 performs linear probing with and without replacement for the given set of values.

0, 1, 4, 72, 65, 85, 87, 90, 58

Solution :

(a) Linear Probing without Replacement :

Index	Key	Chain
0	**0**	- 1
1	**1**	- 1
2	**72**	- 1
3	-	- 1
4	**4**	- 1
5	**65**	- 1
6	-	- 1
7	-	- 1
8	-	- 1
9	-	- 1

After insertion of 1st 5 keys,

Index	Key	Chain
0	0	- 1
1	1	- 1
2	72	- 1
3	-	- 1
4	4	- 1
5	65	- 1
6	**85**	6
7	**87**	- 1
8	-	- 1
9	-	- 1

After insertion of 85 and 87

Index	Key	Chain
0	0	3
1	1	- 1
2	72	- 1
3	**90**	- 1
4	4	- 1
5	65	6

After insertion of 90 and 58

6	85	- 1
7	87	- 1
8	**58**	- 1
9	-	- 1

(b) Linear Probing with Replacement :

Index	Key	Chain	
0	**0**	- 1	After insertion of 1st 5 keys.
1	**1**	- 1	
2	**72**	- 1	
3	-	- 1	
4	**4**	- 1	
5	**65**	- 1	
6	-	- 1	
7	-	- 1	
8	-	- 1	
9	-	- 1	
Index	**Key**	**Chain**	
0	0	- 1	After insertion of 85 and 87
1	1	- 1	
2	72	- 1	
3	-	- 1	
4	4	- 1	
5	65	6	
6	**85**	- 1	
7	**87**	- 1	
8	-	- 1	
9	-	- 1	
Index	**Key**	**Chain**	
0	0	- 1	After insertion of 90 and 58
1	1	- 1	
2	72	- 1	

3	**90**	- 1
4	4	- 1
5	65	6
6	85	- 1
7	87	- 1
8	**58**	- 1
9	-	- 1

Example 3.4 : Explain linear probing, chaining with replacement and chaining without replacement using the following data -

   10, 12, 22, 23, 14, 6, 5, 3, 9, 11

Assume buckets from 0 to 9 and each bucket has one slot. Hash function is key % 10. Calculate average number of comparisons for all.

Solution :

(a) Linear Probing, Chaining without Replacement :

Index	Key	Chain
0	**10**	- 1
1	-	- 1
2	**12**	- 1
3	-	- 1
4	-	- 1
5	-	- 1
6	-	- 1
7	-	- 1
8	-	- 1
9	-	- 1

After insertion of 1st 2 keys which are 10 and 12. (Each with 1 comparison only at 0th and 2nd index position)

Index	Key	Chain
0	10	- 1
1	-	- 1
2	12	3
3	**22**	- 1
4	**23**	- 1
5	**14**	- 1
6	**6**	- 1

After insertion of 22, 23, 14 and 6. (2 comparisons for 22 at 2nd and 3rd position, for 23 at 3rd and 4th position, for 14 at 4th and 5th position and 1 comparison for 6 at 6th position only)

Index	Key	Chain
7	-	- 1
8	-	- 1
9	-	- 1
Index	**Key**	**Chain**
0	10	- 1
1	**11**	- 1
2	12	3
3	22	- 1
4	23	8
5	14	- 1
6	6	- 1
7	**5**	- 1
8	**3**	- 1
9	**9**	- 1

After insertion of 5, 3, 9, and 11.
(3 comparisons for 5 at 5th, 6th and 7th position, 6 comparisons for 3 at 3, 4, 5, 6, 7 and 8th position, 1 comparison each for 9 and 11)

So therefore total number of comparisons :

$$= 2 + 6 + 1 + 3 + 6 + 2$$

$$= 20$$

(b) Linear Probing Chaining with Replacement :

Index	Key	Chain
0	**10**	- 1
1	-	- 1
2	**12**	3
3	**22**	- 1
4	-	- 1
5	-	- 1
6	-	- 1
7	-	- 1
8	-	- 1
9	-	- 1

After insertion of 10, 12 and 22.
(1 comparison for 10 and 12 at 0 and 2nd position respectively. 2 comparisons for 22 at 2nd and 3rd position)

Index	Key	Chain
0	10	- 1
1	-	- 1
2	**12**	**4**
3	**23**	- 1
4	22	- 1
5	-	- 1
6	-	- 1
7	-	- 1
8	-	- 1
9	-	- 1

After insertion of 23 (3 comparisons at 3rd, at 4th to shift 22 and at 2nd to change chain number)

Index	Key	Chain
0	10	- 1
1	-	- 1
2	12	**5**
3	23	- 1
4	**14**	- 1
5	22	- 1
6	**6**	- 1
7	-	- 1
8	-	- 1
9	-	- 1

After insertion of 14 and 6.
(3 comparisons for inserting 14 and one comparison for inserting 6)

Index	Key	Chain
0	10	- 1
1	**11**	- 1
2	12	**7**
3	23	**8**
4	14	- 1
5	**5**	- 1

After insertion of 5, 3, 9 and 11
(4 comparisons for inserting 5
6 comparisons for inserting 3
1 comparison each for inserting 9 and 11)

6	6	- 1
7	22	- 1
8	3	- 1
9	9	- 1

So, therefore total number of comparisons

$$= 2 + 2 + 3 + 3 + 1 + 4 + 6 + 2$$
$$= 23.$$

O(1) access to files means that no matter how big the file grows, access to a record always takes the same, small number of seeks. By contrast, sequential searching gives us O(N) access, where in the number of seeks grow in proportion to the size of the files. As we shall study in preceding chapters, B trees improve on this greatly, providing $O(\log_k N)$ access, the number of seeks increases as the logarithm to the base k of the number of records, where k is a measure of the leaf size. $O(\log_k N)$ access provide very good retrieval performance, even for very large files, but it is still not O(1) access.

3.4 EXTENDIBLE HASHING

Extendible hashing is a type of **hash** system which treats a hash as a bit string, and uses a **trie** for bucket lookup. Because of the hierarchical nature of the system, re-hashing is an incremental operation (done one bucket at a time, as needed). This means that time-sensitive applications are less affected by table growth than by standard full-table rehashes.

e.g.

Assume that the hash function h(k) returns a string of bits. The first i bits of each string will be used as indices to figure out where they will go in the "directory" (hash table). Additionally, i is the smallest number such that the index of every item in the table is unique.

Keys to be used:

$$h(k1) = 100100$$

$$h(k2) = 010110$$

$$h(k3) = 110110$$

Let's assume that for this particular example, the bucket size is 1. The first two keys to be inserted, k_1 and k_2, can be distinguished by the most significant bit, and would be inserted into the table as follows:

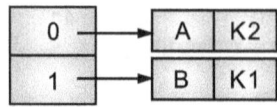

Now, if k_3 were to be hashed to the table, it wouldn't be enough to distinguish all three keys by one bit (because both k_3 and k_1 have 1 as their leftmost bit). Also, because the bucket size is one, the table would overflow. Because comparing the first two most significant bits would give each key a unique location, the directory size is doubled as follows:

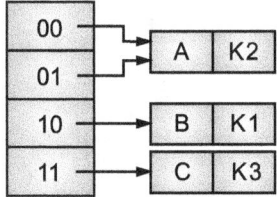

And so now k_1 and k_3 have a unique location, being distinguished by the first two leftmost bits. Because k_2 is in the top half of the table, both 00 and 01 point to it because there is no other key to compare to that begins with a 0.

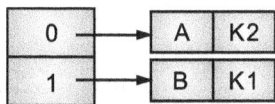

3.5 DICTIONARY

Dictionaries is a collection of data elements uniquely identified by a field called **key**. A dictionary supports operations of search, insert and delete.

A dictionary supports both **sequential** and **random access**. A sequential access is the process in which the data elements of the dictionary are **ordered** and accessed according to the order of the keys (ascending/descending). A random access is the process in which the data elements of the dictionary are not accessed according to a particular order.

Hash tables are ideal data structures for dictionaries.

3.5.1 Dictionary as ADT

Operations

- **Dictionary create()**

    creates empty dictionary

- **Boolean is Empty(Dictionary d)**

    tells whether the dictionary **d** is empty

- **put(Dictionary d, Key k, Value v)**

    associates key **k** with a value **v;**

    if key **k** already presents in the dictionary

    old value is replaced by **v**

- **Value get(Dictionary d, Key k)**

  returns a value, associated with key **k**

  or null, if dictionary contains no such key

- **remove(Dictionary d, Key k)**

  removes key **k** and associated value

- **destroy(Dictionary d)**

  destroys dictionary **d**

3.6 SKIP LIST

An interesting data structure for efficiently realizing the ordered map ADT is the **skip list.** This data structure makes random choices in arranging the entries in such a way that search and update times are O(logn) on **average,** where **n** is the number of entries in the dictionary.

A **skip list** S for a map M consists of a series of lists $\{S_0, S_1,.. ., S_h\}$. Each list Si stores a subset of the entries of M sorted by increasing keys plus entries with two special keys, denoted $-\infty$ and $+\infty$, where $-\infty$ is smaller than every possible key that can be inserted in M and $+\infty$ is larger than every possible key that can be inserted in M. In addition, the lists in S satisfy the following :

- List So contains every entry of the map M (plus the special entries with keys $-\infty$ and $+\infty$).
- For i = 1,. . . , h - 1, list Si contains (in addition to $-\infty$ and $+\infty$) a randomly generated subset of the entries in list S_{i-1}.
- List S_h, contains only $-\infty$ and $+\infty$.
- An example of a skip list is shown in Fig. 3.5. It is customary to visualize a skip list **S** with list So at the bottom and lists S_1,. . . S_h, above it. Also, we refer to h as the **height** of skip list S.

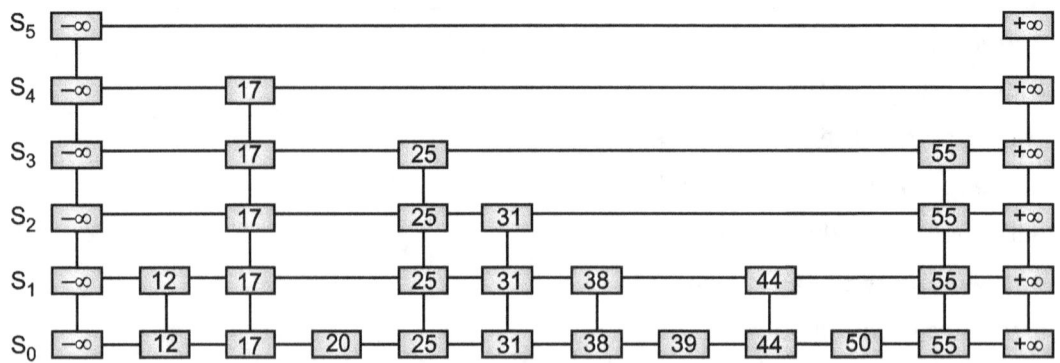

Fig. 3.6 : Example of a skip list storing 10 entries

3.6.1 Search and Update Operations in a Skip List

The skip list structure allows for simple map search and update algorithms. In fact, all of the skip list search and update algorithms are based on an elegant **SkipSearch** method that takes a key **k** and finds the position **p** of the entry **e** in list **So** such that **e** has the largest key (which is possibly -∞) less than or equal to k .

Searching in a Skip List

Suppose we are given a search key **k.** We begin the **SkipSearch** method by setting a position variable **p** to the top-most, left position in the skip list **S,** called the **start position** of **S.** That is, the start position is the position of S_h storing the special entry with key -∞. We then perform the following steps (see Fig. 3.6), where *key(p)* denotes the key of the entry at position *p* :

- If S.below(p) is null, then the search terminates-we are at the bottom and have located the largest entry in S with key less than or equal to the search key k. Otherwise, we drop down to the next lower level in the present tower by setting p <- S. below(p) .

- Starting at position p, we move p forward until it is at the right-most position on the present level such that key(p) <= k. We call this the scan forward step.

Note that such a position always exists, since each level contains the keys -∞ and +∞. In fact, after we perform the scan forward for this level, p may remain where it started. In any case, we then repeat the previous step.

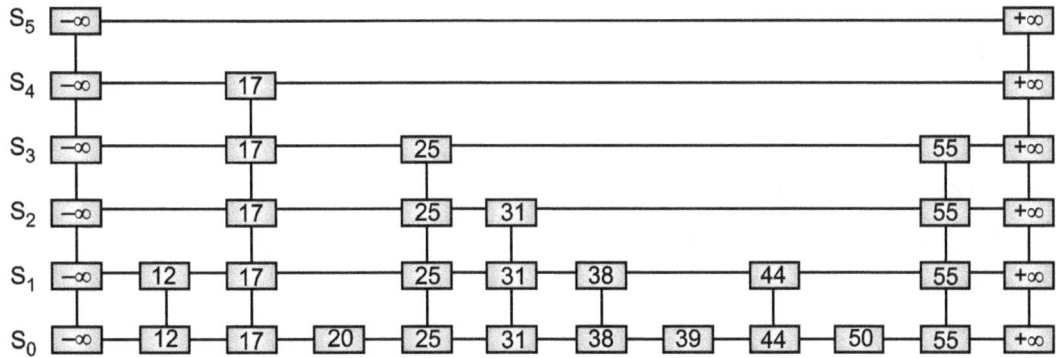

Fig. 3.7 : Example of a search in a skip list

Insertion in a Skip List

The insertion algorithm for skip lists uses randomization to decide the height of the tower for the new entry. We begin the insertion of a new entry (k, v) by performing a SkipSearch(k) operation. This gives us the position p of the bottom-level entry with the largest key less than or equal to k (note that p may hold the special entry with key -∞). We then insert (k, v) immediately after position p. After inserting the new entry at the bottom level, we "flip" a coin. If the flip comes up tails, then we stop here. Else (the flip comes up heads), we backtrack to the previous (next higher) level and insert (k,v) in this level at the appropriate position. We again flip a coin; if it comes up heads, we go to the next higher level and repeat. Thus, we continue to insert the new entry (k,v) in lists until we finally get a flip that comes up tails. We link together all the references to the new entry (k,v) created in this process to create the tower for the new entry. A coin flip can be simulated with Java's built-in pseudo-random number generator java.util.Random by calling nextInt(2), which returns 0 of 1, each with probability 1/2. We give the insertion algorithm for a skip list S in Code Fragment and we illustrate it in Fig. 3.7. The algorithm uses method insertAfterAbove(p, q, (k, v)) that inserts a position storing the entry (k, v) after position p (on the same level as p) and above position q, returning the position r of the new entry (and setting internal references so that next, prev, above, and below methods will work correctly for p, q, and r). The expected running time of the insertion algorithm on a skip list with n entries is O(logn),

Algorithm SkipInsert(k, v) :

Input : Key **k** and value **v**

Output : Topmost position of the entry inserted in the skip list

p <- SkipSearch(k)

q <- null

e <- **(k, v)**

i <- - 1

repeat

i<- i+l

if i > h **then**

h<-h+1 {add a new level to the skip list)

t <- **next(s)**

s <- insertAfterAbove(null,s, (-∞, null))

insertAfterAbove(s, t ,(+∞, null))

while above(p) = null do

P<- prev(P)   {scan backward)

p <- **above(p)**   {jump up to higher level)

q<- insertAfterAbove(p,q, e) {add a position to the tower of the new entry}

until coin Flip() = tails

n<- n+l

return q

Insertion in a skip list. Method **coinflip()** returns "heads" or "tails", each with probability **112.** Variables **n, h,** and **s** hold the number of entries, the height, and the start node of the skip list.

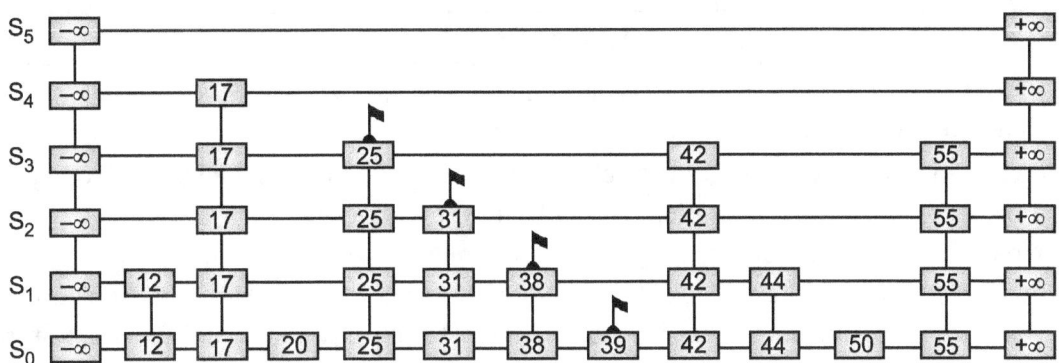

Fig. 3.8 : Insertion of an entry with key 42 into the skip list of Fig. 3.6

We assume that the random "coin flips" for the new entry came up heads three times in a row, followed by tails. The positions visited are highlighted in blue. The positions inserted to hold the new entry are drawn with thick lines, and the positions preceding them are flagged.

Removal in a Skip List

Like the search and insertion algorithms, the removal algorithm for a skip list is quite simple. In fact, it is even easier than the insertion algorithm. That is, to perform a remove(k) operation, we begin by executing method SkipSearch(k). If the position p stores an entry with key different from k, we return **null.** Otherwise, we remove p and all the positions above p, which are easily accessed by using above operations to climb up the tower of this entry in S starting at position p. The removal algorithm is illustrated in Fig. 3.8.

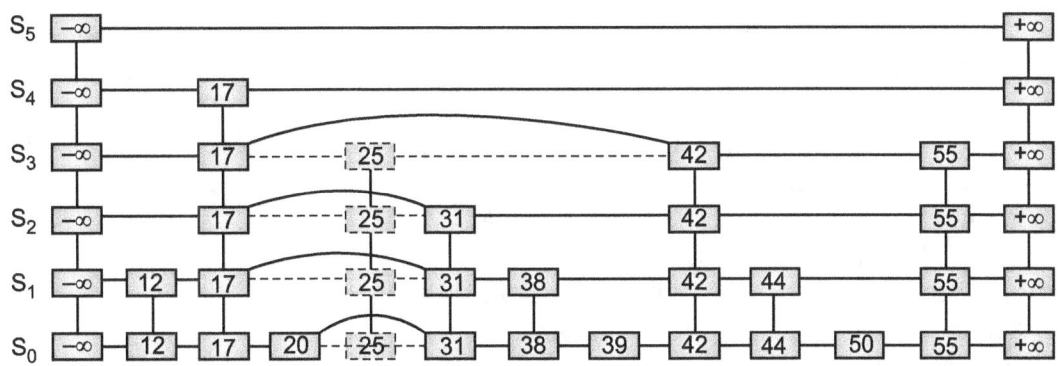

Fig. 3.9 : Removal of the entry with key 25 from the skip list of Fig. 3.8

The positions visited after the search for the position of So holding the entry are highlighted in blue. The positions removed are drawn with dashed lines.

SUMMARY

- Hash tables are data structures which favor efficient storage and retrieval of data elements which are linear in nature.
- Dictionaries are a collection of data elements uniquely identified by a field called key.
- A dictionaries supports operations of search, insert and delete.
- A hash function distributes the keys evenly and must have minimum collisions.
- In direct hashing, address of a key is generated without any algorithmic manipulation.
- The linear probing hash table is a fairly simple structure where data items are stored directly inside the hash element array.
- Linked list resolution or dynamic hashing uses a separate area to store collisions and chairs all synonyms together in linked list.
- Extendible hashing is a type of hash system which treats a hash as a bit string, and uses a trie for bucket lookup..
- Re-hashing is done when hash table is filled beyond certain number-Load Factor.
- A closed hash table keeps the members of the set in the bucket table rather than using that table to store list headers.

EXERCISE

1. What is a Hashing function ? Explain any 4 types of Hashing functions.   **(6 M)**
2. What is collision? What are different collision resolution techniques? Explain any two methods in detail.   **(8 M)**
3. What is hashing ? What are the characteristics of good hash function ? Explain any two types of hash functions.   **(6 M)**
4. Explain linear probing, chaining with replacement and chaining without replacement using the following data 10, 12, 22, 23, 14, 6, 5, 3, 9, 11. Assume buckets from 0 to 9 and each bucket has one slot. Hash function is key % 10. Calculate average number of comparisons for all.   **(10 M)**
5. What is hash function ? What are issues in hashing ? What are rules for designing hash function? Give types of uninform hash functions.   **(8 M)**
6. What is bucket hashing? Explain with example.   **(8 M)**
7. What is hash function? Explain the following hash function :   **(8 M)**
    (i) Mid-square   (ii) Modulo Division
    (iii) Folding Method   (iv) Digit Analysis.
8. What is the use of hash tables? Explain the characteristics of a good hash function.
9. Assume a hash table of size 10 and hash function H(X)=X mod 10 performs linear probing with and without replacement for the given set of values. 0, 1, 2, 4, 72, 65, 85, 87, 90, 58.
10. What is skip list? Explain different operations of skip list with example.   **(8 M)**

SEARCH TREES

4.1 SYMBOL TABLE

While compilers and assemblers scan a program, each identifier must be examined to determine if it is a keyword. This information concerning the keywords in a programming language is stored in a **symbol table.**

Keyed tables are very useful structures of the same. The keyed table stores **<key, information>** pairs with no additional logical structure.

The operations on symbol tables are :

- The pairs <key, information> are inserted into the collection.
- The pair <key, information> removed by specifying the key.
- Search for particular key.
- Retrieve the information associated with a key.

For Example :

Symbol	Information
A	------
B	------
Sum	------

Any time compiler wants to store information that can be retrieved by some unique key value, it means we are using a keyed table. The field that contains the value by which we want to retrieve the information is the key field.

Keyed tables are used in assemblers, where the key (the symbol) is the programmer's identifier and the information is the location assigned by the assembler to that identifier. The keyed tables are also called as symbol tables.

4.1.1 Representation of Symbol Table

There are two different techniques for implementing the keyed tables; symbol table and tree tables.

Static Tree Tables : Static tree tables are used when symbols are known in advance and no insertion and deletion is allowed. An example of this type of table is reserved word table in a compiler. This table is searched once for every occurrence of an identifier in a program. If an identifier is not in the reserved word table, then it is looked for in another table. To optimize a table knowing what keys are in the table and what the probable distribution is of those that are not in the table, we build an Optimal Binary Search Tree (OBST).

- Stored as sorted sequential list and binary search ($O(\log_2 n)$)can be used to search a symbol.
- Balanced BST can be used to find symbols having equal probabilities.
- OBST (Optimal Binary Search Tree) is to be used when different symbols are searched with different probabilities.
- Hash tables can be used to store symbol table having search time O(1).

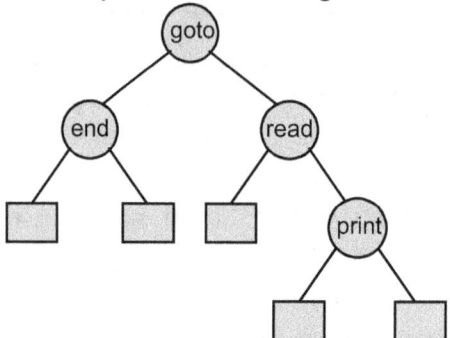

Fig. 4.1 : Optimal binary search tree

Dynamic Tree Table : Dynamic tree tables are used when symbols are not known in advance and inserted as they come and deleted if not required. Dynamic keyed tables are those that are built on the fly. The keys have no history associated with their use. As we know nothing about them, not even how many symbols are there, so balanced binary search tree is a good choice for Dynamic tree tables.

AVL tree is an example of dynamic tree table.

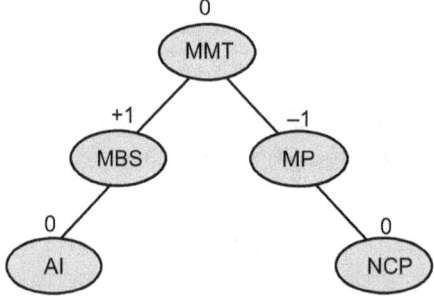

Fig. 4.2 : AVL tree (Balance factor (0 or -1 or 1))

4.2 INTRODUCTION TO DYNAMIC PROGRAMMING

Dynamic programming (DP) is a technique to solve a particular class of problems. The idea is very simple, if you have solved a problem with the given input, then save the result for future reference, so as to avoid solving the same problem again. If the given problem can be broken up in to smaller sub-problems and these smaller sub problems are in turn divided into still-smaller ones, and in this process, if you observe some over-lapping sub problems, then it's a big hint for Dynamic Programming.

Example :

Fibonacci Series.

4.2.1 Dynamic Programming Approaches

- Top-Down
- Bottom-Up

- **Top-Down :** Start solving the given problem by breaking it down into sub problems. If you see that the problem has been solved already, then just return the saved answer. If it has not been solved, solve it and save the answer. This is called as Memoization.

```
Public int fibTD(int m) {
        if (m==0) return 1;
        if(m==1) return 1;
        if(fib[m]!=0){
            return fib[m];
        }else{
            fib[m] = fibTD(m-1) + fibTD(m-2);
            return fib[n];
        }
}
```

- **Bottom-Up** : Identify the problem and check the order in which the sub-problems are solved and start solving from the minor sub-problem, up towards the given problem. In this process, it is guaranteed that the sub-problems are solved before solving the problem. This is referred to as **Dynamic Programming**.

```
Public int fiboBU(int y) {
        int fibo[] = new int[y + 1];
        fibo [0] = 0;
        fibo [1] = 1;
        for (int i = 2; i < y + 1; i++) {
        fibo[i] = fibo[i - 1] + fibo[i - 2];
        }
        return fibo[y];
}
```

4.3 WEIGHT BALANCED TREE (WBT)

Weight Balanced Tree is designed by Nievergelt and Reingold in 1972. Weight Balanced Tree (WBT) is a Binary Search Tree (BST) which is majorly used to implement finite maps and sets. Other BST's like AVL or Red Black tree used height of a sub tree for balancing while WBT considers the sizes (no. of elements) of the sub trees below each node. In order to ensure performance, the algorithm keeps the height of a tree logarithmic to its size by balancing the sizes of the sub trees in each node.

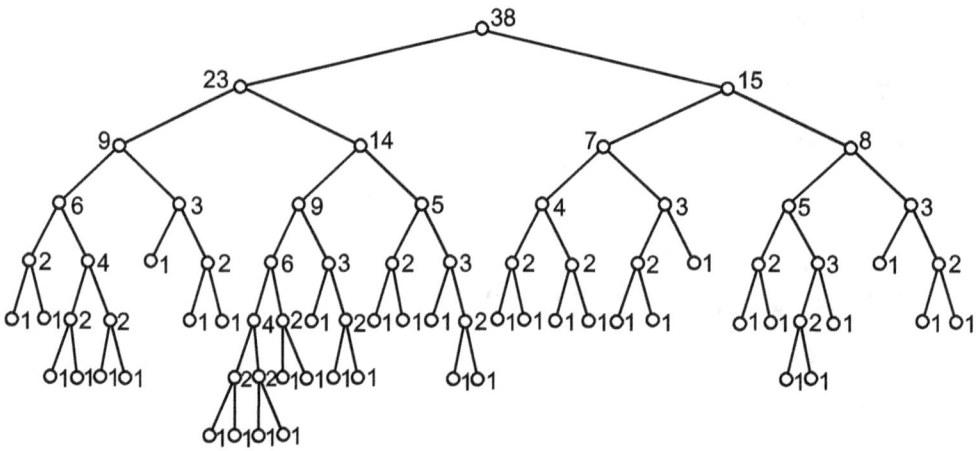

Fig. 4.3 : WBT with node heights

WBT is a binary search tree satisfying an extra condition.

- The size of a sub tree is the number of keys in the sub tree.

- The size at a node is the size of the sub tree rooted at that node.

- Size (null) = 0 for the empty tree, is a null node.

The extra condition :

For every node v, "v is balanced", means

$$\frac{1}{3} \leq \frac{\text{size (v. left)} + 1}{\text{size (v.right)} + 1} \leq 3$$

Similarly the inequalities can be

$$\text{size (v.left)} + 1 \leq (\text{size (v.right)} + 1) \times 3$$

$$(\text{size (v.left)} + 1) \times 3 \geq \text{size (v.right)} + 1$$

4.4 OPTIMAL BINARY SEARCH TREES

A binary search tree is one of the most important data structures in computer science. When array is used to store ordered data, we can use very efficient searching technique binary search, but insertion and deletion algorithms are inefficient. They require shifting of data in the array. The alternative is use of linked list to store ordered data, which provide efficient insertion and deletion algorithms, but now searching algorithm used should be sequential search which is inefficient. The binary search tree is a data structure that has an efficient searching algorithm and also efficient insertion and deletion algorithms.

BST Definition : A binary search tree is a binary tree. It may be empty. If not, then it satisfies the following properties :

* Every element has a key and no two elements have the same key (i.e. the keys are distinct).

* The keys (if any) in the left subtree are smaller than the key in the root.

* The keys (if any) in the right subtree are greater than or equal to the key in the root.

* Each subtree is itself a binary search tree.

For example, consider the following binary search tree.

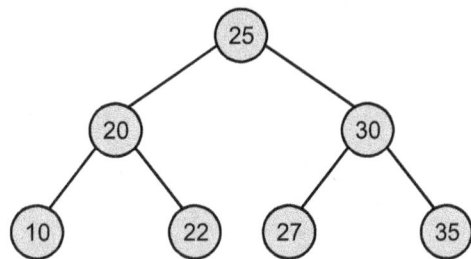

Fig. 4.4 : Binary Search Tree

The inorder traversal of the above binary search tree produces an ordered list – 10, 20, 22, 25, 27, 30, 35.

One of the important application of binary search tree is to arrange a set of keys from some linear ordered set to minimize the average search time. If probabilities of searching for elements of a set are known from some previous searches, then an optimal binary search tree can be obtained for which the average number of comparisons in a search is the smallest possible.

For Example : If four keys P, Q, R, S are to be searched with probabilities 0.1, 0.2, 0.4, and 0.3 respectively, then there are 14 possible binary search trees. Few of them are shown in the figure 4.5. Out of these 14 we have to find out which is optimal. One way is to construct all possible binary search trees and find the optimal one. But as the number of keys n increases, the total number of search trees also increases. So this approach is unrealistic for large n. Therefore the alternative is to use a general algorithm.

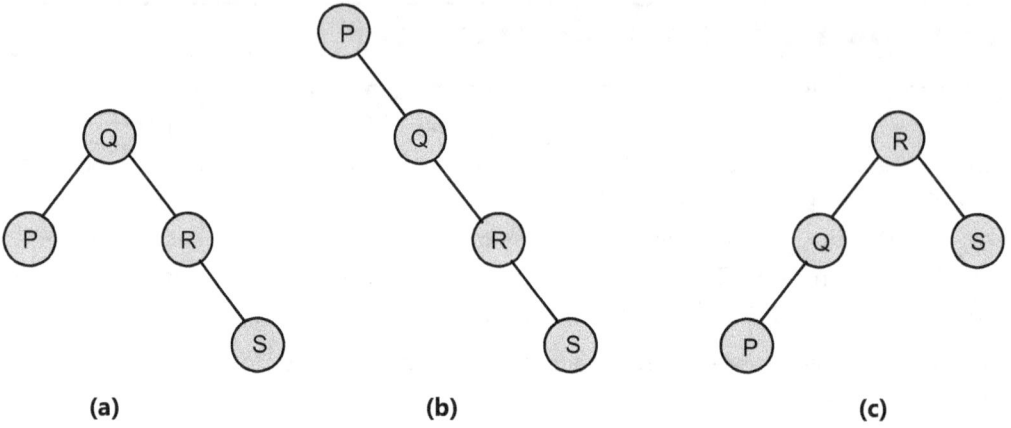

Fig. 4.5 : Possible Binary Search Tree

Let a_1, a_2, ..., a_n be distinct keys ordered with a_1 being smallest and a_n being largest. Let p_1, p_2, ..., p_n be the probabilities for searching them. Let C[i,j] be the smallest average number of comparisons made in a successful search in a binary tree T_i^j having keys a_i, ..., a_j, where i, j are integer indices, $1 \leq i \leq j \leq n$.

First using the dynamic programming algorithm, we shall find values of C[i,j] for all smaller instances of the problem. Consider all possible ways to choose a_k as the root among the keys a_i, ..., a_j. See the following figure.

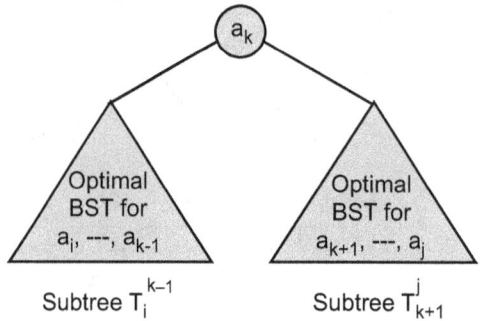

Fig. 4.6 : Possible Ways of choosing a_k

In such a binary search tree, a_k is the root, T_i^{k-1} is the left subtree which contains a_i, ..., a_{k-1} keys optimally arranged and T_{k+1}^j is the right subtree which contains a_{k+1}, ..., a_j keys optimally arranged. Let tree levels are counted from 1. Assume that C[i, i − 1] = 0 for $1 \leq i \leq n + 1$, which means that number of comparisons is 0 in the empty tree. The *recurrence relation* is,

$$C[i,j] = \min_{i \leq k \leq j} \{C[i,k-1]+C[k+1,j]\} + \sum_{s=i}^{j} P_s \text{ for } 1 \leq i \leq j \leq n$$

From this formula, we can obtain formula for a one-mode binary tree containing key a_i, as given below :

$$C[i,i] = P_i \text{ for } 1 \le i \le n.$$

The initial cost table of the dynamic programming algorithm for constructing optimal binary search tree is shown below :

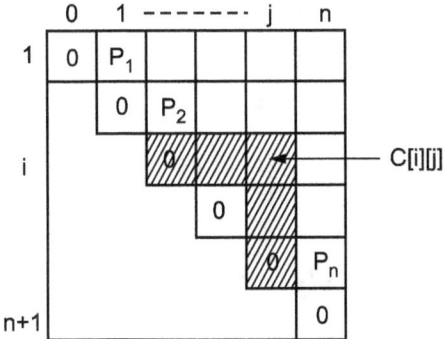

Fig. 4.7 : Initial cost Table

The values needed for computing C[i][j] are shaded in the above table. They are in row i and the columns to the left of column j, and the values in column j and the rows below row i.

The pseudocode of the dynamic programming algorithm to find an optimal binary search tree is given below :

Algorithm OptBST(P[1...n])

Input : An array P[1...n] of search probabilities for a sorted list of n keys.

Output : Two dimensional arrays C and R of size (n + 2) ∞ (n + 1), 0 based. For the subrange of key a_i, ..., a_j C[i,j] gives the minimum weighted search cost and R[i,j] gives the best choice of the root for the binary search tree on this subrange of keys. The optimal cost for whole tree is C[1,n]

Algorithm for OBST :

```
    for i=1 to n do
    begin
        C[i,i–1]=0
        C[i,i]=P[i]
        R[i,i]=i
    end
    C[n+1,n]=0
    for d=1 to n–1 do          // diagonal count
```

```
    begin
        for i=1 to n-d do
        begin
            j=i+d
            minval=oo
            for k=i to j do
            begin
                if C[i,k-1]+C[k+1,j]<minval
                begin
                    minval=C[i,k-1]+C[k+1,j]
                    kmin=k
                end
            end
        R[i,j]=k
        sum=P[i]
        for s=i+1 to j do
        begin
            sum=sum+P[s]
        end
        C[i,j]=minval+sum
        end
    end
    return C[1,n],R
```

Let us see one example to illustrate the above algorithm.

For the 4 keys

Keys	P	Q	R	S
Probabilities	0.1	0.2	0.4	0.3

	0	1	2	3	4
1	0	0.1			
2		0	0.2		
3			0	0.4	
4				0	0.3
5					0

Initial Cost Table C

	0	1	2	3	4
1		1			
2			2		
3				3	
4					4
5					

Initial Root Table R

Diagonal count 'd' will vary from 1 to 3. i will vary from 1 to n–d.

Initially d=1, i will vary from 1 to 3.

[A] For i = 1, j = i + d = 1 + 1 = 2

Let us find C[1,2] for k=1 and k=2.

For k = 1,

$$C[i,j]=C[i,k-1]+C[k+1,j]+ \sum_{s = i}^{j} Ps$$

$$C[1,2] = C[1,0]+C[2,2]+ \sum_{s = 1}^{2} Ps$$

$$= 0+0.2+(P_1 + P_2)$$

$$= 0+0.2+(0.1+0.2)$$

$$= 0+0.2+0.3$$

$$= 0.5$$

Similarly for k=2

$$C[1,2] = C[1,1]+C[3,2]+ \sum_{s = 1}^{2} Ps$$

$$= 0.1+0+(0.1+0.2)$$

$$= 0.4$$

Select minimum value.

$$\therefore \qquad C[1,2] = 0.4 \text{ for } k=2$$

$$\therefore \qquad \text{Put } R[1,2] = k=2$$

[B] For i=2, j=i+d=2+1=3

Let us find C[2,3] for k=2,3.

For k=2,

$$C[2,3] = C[2,1]+C[3,3]+ \sum_{s=2}^{3} Ps$$

$$= 0+0.4+(P2+P3)$$

$$= 0+0.4+(0.2+0.4)$$

$$= 1.0$$

For k=3,

$$C[2,3] = C[2,2]+C[4,3]+ \sum_{s=2}^{3} Ps$$

$$= 0.2+0+(0.2+0.4)$$

$$= 0.8$$

∴ Select minimum value.

$$C[2,3] = 0.8 \text{ for k=3}$$

∴ $$R[2,3] = 3$$

[C] For i=3,j=i+d=3+1=4

Let us find C[3,4] for k=3,4.

For k=3,

$$C[3,4] = C[3,2]+C[4,4]+ \sum_{s=3}^{4} Ps$$

$$= 0+0.3+(P3+P4)$$

$$= 0+0.3+(0.4+0.3)$$

$$= 1.0$$

$$C[3,4] = C[3,3]+C[5,4]+ \sum_{s=3}^{4} Ps$$

$$= 0.4+0+(0.4+0.3)$$

$$= 1.1$$

Select minimum value.

∴ $$C[3,4] = 1.0 \text{ for k=3}$$

∴ $$R[3,4] = 3$$

	0	1	2	3	4
1	0	0.1	0.4		
2		0	0.2	0.8	
3			0	0.4	1.0
4				0	0.3
5					0

Cost Table C

	0	1	2	3	4
1		1	2		
2			2	3	
3				3	3
4					4
5					

Root Table R

[D] Now d=2 and i will vary from 1 to 2.

For i=1, j=i+d=1+2=3.

Let us find C[1,3] for k=1,2,3.

For k=1,

$$C[1,3] = C[1,0]+C[2,3]+ \sum_{s=1}^{3} Ps$$

$$= 0+0.8+(P1+P2+P3)$$

$$= 0+0.8+(0.1+0.2+0.4)$$

$$= 1.5$$

For k=2,

$$C[1,3] = C[1,1]+C[3,1]+C[3,3]+ \sum_{s=1}^{3} Ps$$

$$= 0.1+0.4+(0.1+0.2+0.4)$$

$$= 1.2$$

For k=3,

$$C[1,3] = C[1,2]+C[4,3]+ \sum_{s=1}^{3} Ps$$

$$= 0.4+0+(0.1+0.2+0.4)$$

$$= 1.1$$

Select minimum value

$\therefore$ C[1,3] = 1.1 for k=3

$\therefore$ Set R[1,3] = 3

[E] Now i=2, j=i+d=2+2=4.

Let us find C[2,4] for k=2,3,4

For k=2,

$$C[2,4] \; = \; C[2,1]+C[3,4] + \sum_{s=2}^{4} Ps$$

$$= \; 0+1.0+(P2+P3+P4)$$

$$= \; 0+1.0+(0.2+0.4+0.3)$$

$$= \; 1.9$$

For k=3,

$$C[2,4] \; = \; C[2,2]+C[4,4] + \sum_{s=2}^{4} Ps$$

$$= \; 0.2+0.3+(0.2+0.4+0.3)$$

$$= \; 1.4$$

For k=4,

$$C[2,4] \; = \; C[2,3]+C[5,4] + \sum_{s=2}^{4} Ps$$

$$= \; 0.8+0+(0.2+0.4+0.3)$$

$$= \; 1.7$$

Select minimum value.

∴   C[2,4] = 1.4 for k=3

∴   Set R[2,4] = 3

	0	1	2	3	4
1	0	0.1	0.4	1.1	
2		0	0.2	0.8	1.4
3			0	0.4	1.0
4				0	0.3
5					0

Cost Table C

	0	1	2	3	4
1		1	2	3	
2			2	3	3
3				3	3
4					4
5					

Root Table R

[F] Now d=3, i=1, j=i+d=1+3=4.

Let us find C[1,4] for k=1 to 4.

For k=1,

$$C[1,4] = C[1,0]+C[2,4] + \sum_{s=1}^{4} Ps$$

$$= 0+1.4+(P1+P2+P3+P4)$$

$$= 0+1.4+(0.1+0.2+0.4+0.3)$$

$$= 2.4$$

For k=2,

$$C[1,4] = C[1,1]+C[3,4]+ \sum_{s=1}^{4} Ps$$

$$= 0.1+1.0+(0.1+0.2+0.4+0.3)$$

$$= 2.1$$

For k=3,

$$C[1,4] = C[1,2]+C[4,4]+ \sum_{s=1}^{4} Ps$$

$$= 0.4+0.3+(0.1+0.2+0.4+0.3)$$

$$= 1.7$$

For k=4,

$$C[1,4] = C[1,3]+C[5,4]+ \sum_{s=1}^{4} Ps$$

$$= 1.1+0+(0.1+0.2+0.4+0.3)$$

$$= 2.1$$

Select minimum value.

$\therefore$ $\qquad$ C[1,4] = 1.7 for k=3

$\therefore$ $\qquad$ Set R[1,4] = 3

	0	1	2	3	4
1	0	0.1	0.4	1.1	1.7
2		0	0.2	0.8	1.4
3			0	0.4	1.0
4				0	0.3
5					0

Final Cost Table C

	0	1	2	3	4
1			1	2	3	3
2				2	3	3
3					3	3
4						4
5						

Final Root Table R

Finally, C[1,4]=1.7 & R[1,4]=3

So for the four keys P, Q, R, S, the optimal BST has root at index 3 (i.e. key R) and the average number of comparisons in a successful search in this tree is 1.7. The following figure shows the optimal BST for the above example.

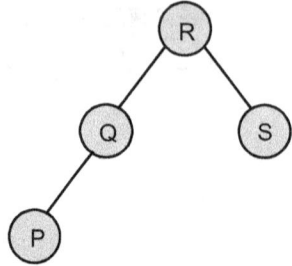

Fig. 4.8 : Optimal BST

The algorithm given above has quadratic space efficiency and cubic time efficiency.

4.5 HEIGHT BALANCED TREE (AVL TREE)

A binary search tree (BST) is used to store and retrieve data. The maximum number of comparisons required for searching in a binary search tree depends on how data is stored in a tree. If tree is well balanced as shown figure 4.9 the number of comparisons will be minimum.

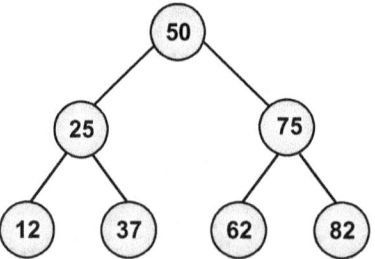

Fig. 4.9 : Balanced binary tree

If the tree is right or left skewed it will require same number of comparison as that of sequential search.

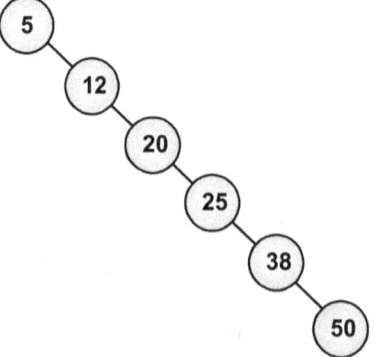

Fig. 4.10 : Unbalanced binary tree

Imagine a situation where the BST is dynamic means the elements of the tree are getting deleted or new elements getting added to it. Average and maximum search time will be minimized, if tree is maintained as complete binary tree at all times. It will require restructuring of tree to accumulate new entry, so that both average and worst case search time will be $O(\log_2 n)$ for the tree of n nodes.

Adelson-Velskii and *Landis* (AVL) in 1962 introduced a Binary Tree that is balanced with respect to height of sub-trees.

Definition : An empty tree is height balanced. If T is non-empty binary tree with T_l and T_r as left and right sub-tree, then T is said to be height balanced if.

1. T_l and T_r is height balanced.

2. $|h_l - h_r| \leq 1$.

    Where, h_f and h_r are heights of T_l and T_r.

The tree in Fig. 4.9 is height balanced.

Restructuring of BST is done so that tree becomes height balanced. When we add a node to a particular tree its height may change. This change can disturb the balancing also. In order to verify whether a tree is height balanced or not, we need to find out balance factor of every node.

Balanced Factor :

Balance factor of a node is defined as $h_l - h_r$ where h_l and h_r are heights of T_l and T_r.

When a new node is added in BST one of the four types of situations can arise in the tree. In other words, there are 4 ways in which rebalancing can be done. These are called Rotations. They are RR, LL, RL, LR rotations.

(1) RR Rotation : If the newly inserted node (say Y) is in right sub-tree of right sub-tree of the nearest ancestor (say A) whose | balance factor | >= 2.

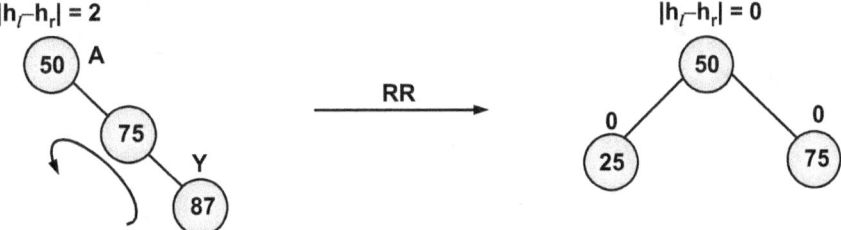

Fig. 4.11 : RR rotation

(2) LL Rotation : The newly inserted node Y is the left sub-tree of left sub-tree of A.

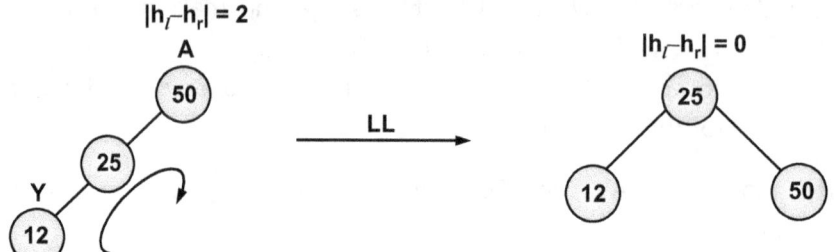

Fig. 4.12 : LL rotation

(3) LR Rotation : Y is inserted in right sub-tree of left sub-tree of A.

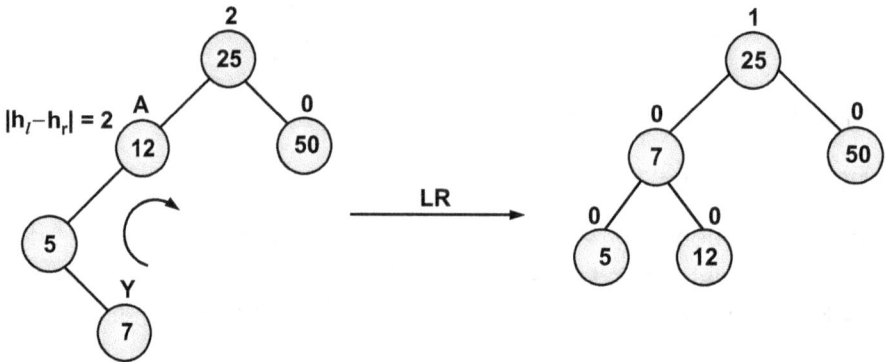

Fig. 4.13 : LR rotation

(4) RL Rotation : Y is inserted in left sub-tree of right sub-tree of A.

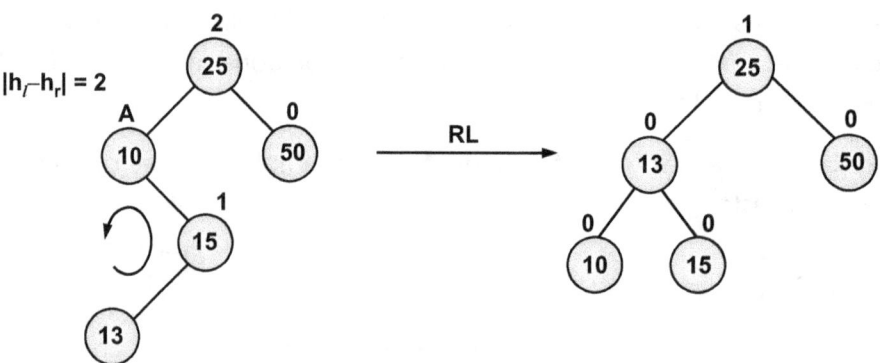

Fig. 4.14 : RL rotation

Let us look into some more examples. Each rotation type has two different situations. First is the simple and the other is complex.

- **Case I : LL Rotation**

Situation 1

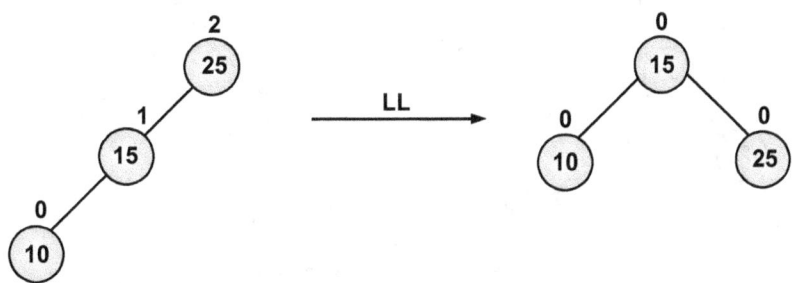

Fig. 4.15 (a) : LL rotation

Situation 2

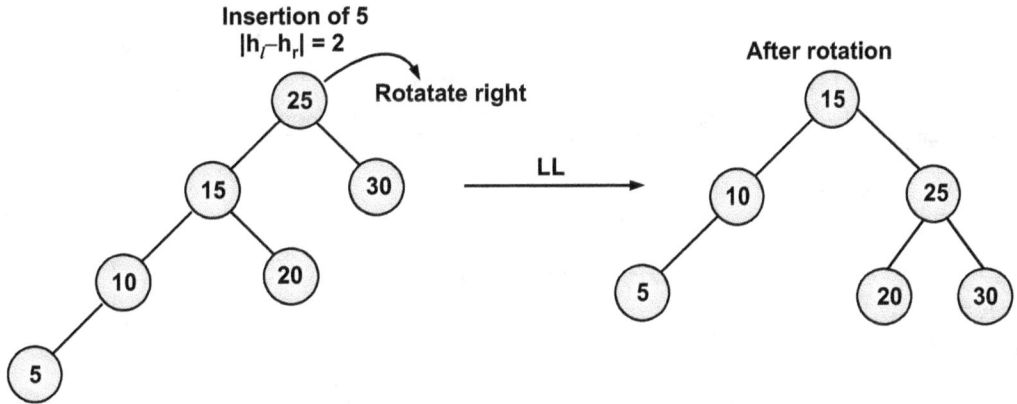

Fig. 4.15 (b) : LL rotation

- **Case II : RR Rotation**

Situation 1

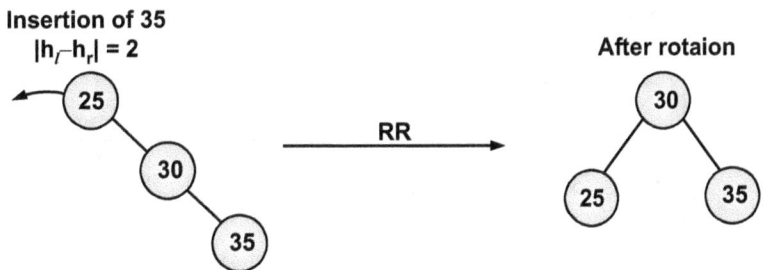

Fig. 4.15 (c) : RR rotation

Situation 2

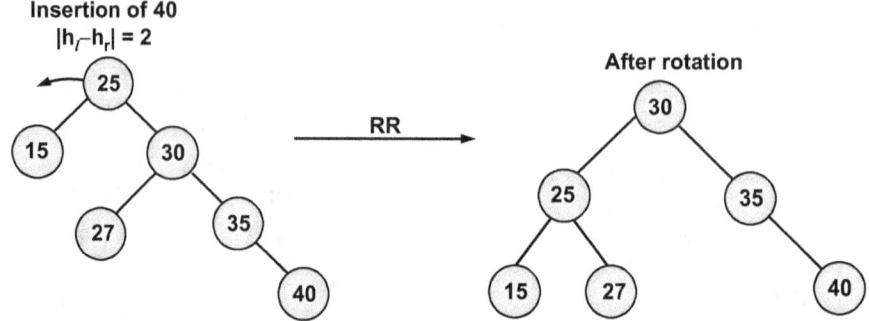

Fig. 4.15 (d) : RR rotation

Actually, the RL and LR rotations are carried out in two steps. Following examples illustrate how exactly these rotations are done.

- **Case III : LR Rotation**

Situation 1

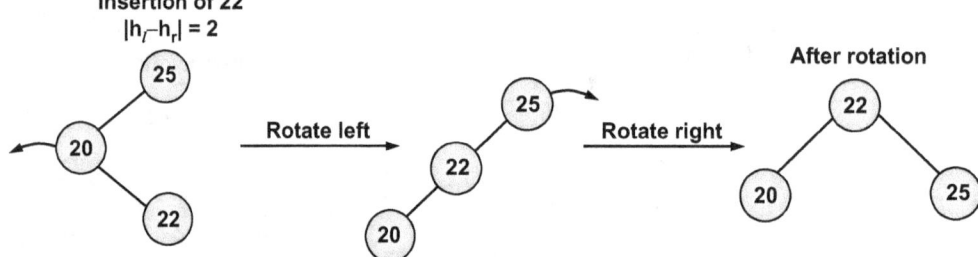

Fig. 4.15 (e) : LR rotation

Situation 2

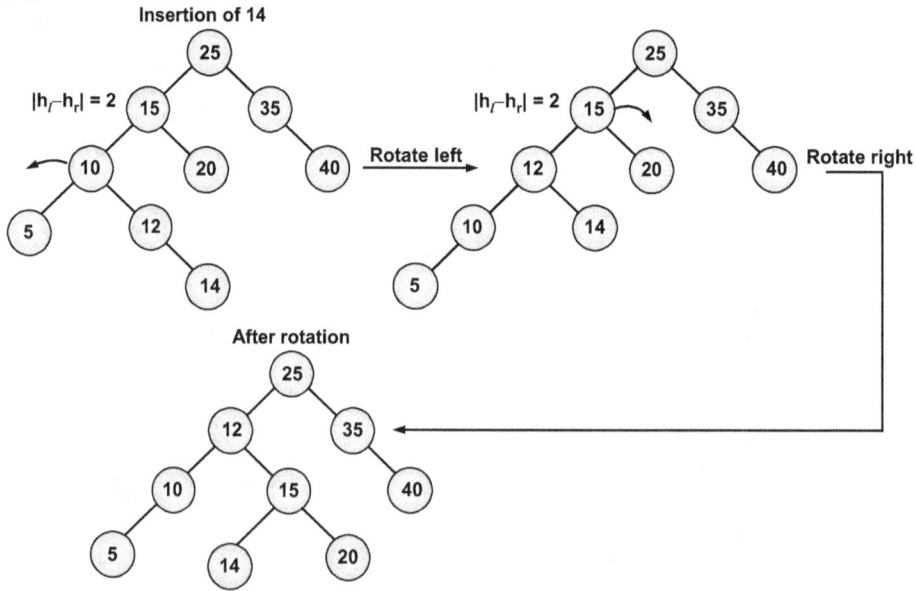

Fig. 4.15 (f) : LR rotation

Case IV : RL Rotation
Situation 1

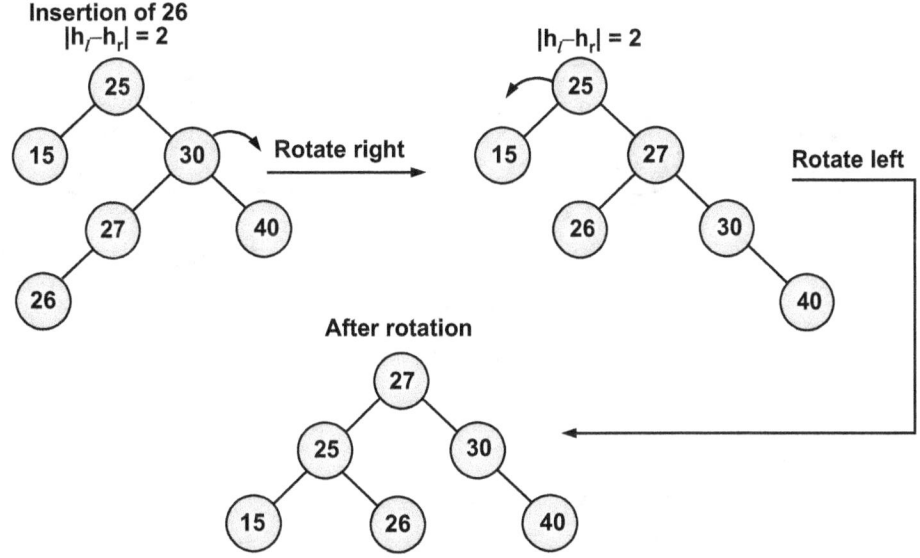

Fig. 4.15 (g) : RL rotation

Situation 2

Fig. 4.15 (h) : RL rotation

SOLVED EXAMPLES

Example 4.1 : Create AVL tree for the following elements :

Solution :

Note : The figures shown in nodes are balance factors

1.

2.

...Conti.

3.

4.

5.

6.

7.

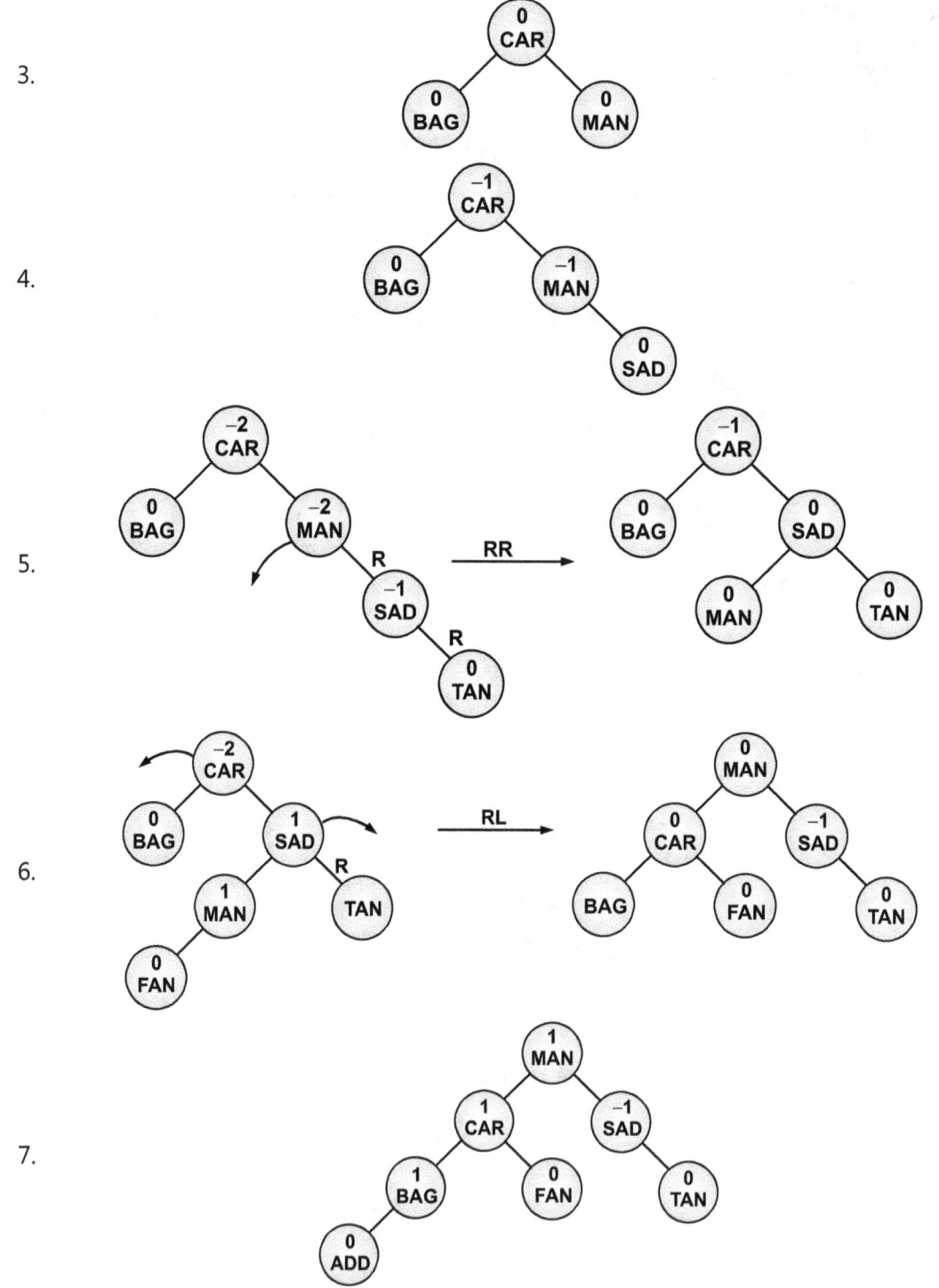

Fig. 4.16 : Creating height balance (AVL) binary tree

Example 4.2 : Create AVL tree for the following elements :

MAR MAY NOV AUG APR JAN DEC JUL FEB

Solution :

Note : The figures shown in nodes are balance factors.

1.

2.

3.

RR

4.

5.

LL

...Conti.

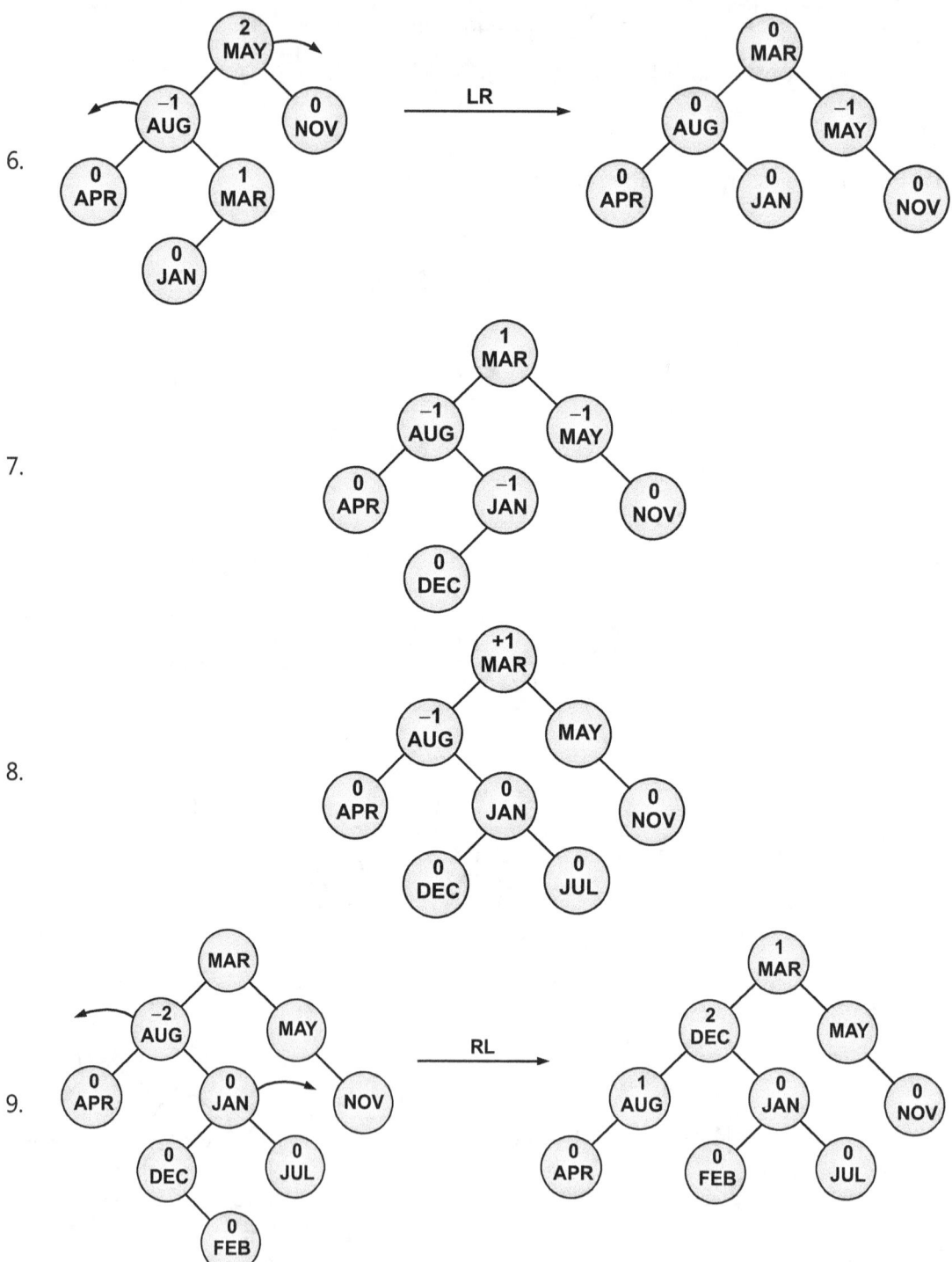

Fig. 4.17 : Creating height balance (AVL) binary tree

SUMMARY

- Keyed tables are implemented using symbol table and tree tables.

- Top down and Bottom up are the two dynamic programming approaches.

- In top down approach, start solving the given problem by breaking it down. If you see that the problems has been solved already, and then just return the saved answer. If it has not been solved, solve it and save the answer.

- In bottom up approach, Analyze the problem and see the order in which the sub-problems are solved and start solving from the trivial sub problem, up towards the given problem.

- Weighted binary tree considers sizes (no. of elements) of the search tree.

- A weight-balanced tree has fields like key, value, left, right and size (integer).

- OBST is a binary search tree which provides the smallest possible search time (or expected search time) for a given sequence of accesses.

- AVL tree is a self-balancing Binary Search Tree (BST) where the difference between heights of left and right sub trees cannot be more than one for all nodes.

- AVL trees are often compared with red–black trees because both support the same set of operations and take O (log n) time for the basic operations.

EXERCISE

1. What is symbol table? What are operations on symbol table? Give complete specification of symbol table ADT.

2. Explain static and dynamic tree tables.

3. Explain dynamic programming.

4. Explain weight balanced tree using proper example.

5. What is an optimal binary search tree? What is its use?

6. Give any 3 points of comparison between Binary search tree, OBST.

7. Obtain the height balance tree for the following sequence of data December, January, April, March, July, August, October, November, May, June. Show all steps.

8. Write a Pseudo 'C' algorithm for LL, RR, LR and RL rotations for AVL tree.

9. Explain different types of rotation for AVL tree with suitable example.

INDEXING AND MULTIWAY TREES

5.1 INDEXING AND INDEXING TECHNIQUES

An index is an arrangement of entries designed to enable end users to locate information in a document. The process of creating an index is called indexing, and a person who does it is called an indexer.

A last few pages of many books contains an index which contains list of topics and number of pages where the topic is available.

- An index is a table containing a list of keys associated with a reference field pointing to the record where the information referenced by the key can be found.

- An index lets you impose order on a file without rearranging the file.

- A simple index is simply an array of (key, reference) pairs.

- You can have different indexes for the same data : multiple access paths.

- Indexing give us keyed access to variable-length record files.

Fig. 5.1 (a) shows index containing key and reference field and Fig. 5.1 (b) contains actual data records. Reference field is treated as addresses for record to access records.

Example : Key= Abhi, Reference field for Abhi=10. Now 10 will be considered as an address where the actual data is stored.

INDEX	
Key	Reference Field
Abhi	10
Poonam	11
Bhagwat	12
Pratik	13
Tejas	14
Panchu	15
Raju	16

Fig. 5.1 (a) : Index

Address of Records	Actual Data Record
10	Abhi | 25 |Pune |India
11	Poonam| 20 |Mumbai |India
12	Bhagwat| 21 |Kolkata |India
13	Pratik| 20 |Pune |India
14	Tejas| 20 |Chennai |India
15	Panchu| 22|Pune |India
16	Raju| 24 |Delhi |India

Fig. 5.1 (b) : Actual data record

Choosing Indexing Techniques :

Following factors must be considered while choosing indexing technique

- access type
- overhead
- access time
- insertion time
- deletion time

Indexing Techniques :

- B tree
- B+ tree
- Hashing

Note : For hashing refer unit no. 3 and for B & B+ tree refer 5.2.2 and 5.27.

5.2 TYPE OF SEARCH TREE

5.2.1 Multiway Search Tree

A multiway tree is a generalized binary tree that can have more than two children's. If a multiway tree having m children's then it is called as m-way tree. The keys in a node are maintained in order.

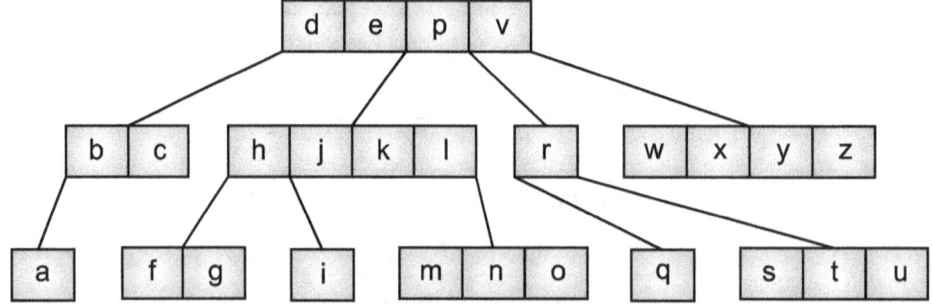

Fig. 5.2 : Multiway search tree

For the processing of m-way trees particular order will be imposed on the keys within each node that results in a multi way search tree of order m.

Definition of M-Way Search Tree :

- It is m-way tree.

- The keys in each node are in ascending order.

- Each node has m-1 key fields.

- Each node has m children's.

- The keys in the first i children are smaller than the ith key.

- The keys in the last m-i children are larger than the ith key.

4-way Search Tree :

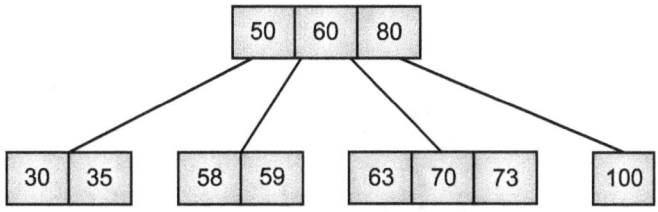

Fig. 5.3 : 4-way search tree

M-way search trees provides fast information retrieval and modification. But, the disadvantage of m-way search trees is that they can be unbalanced.

Searching an M-Way Search Tree :

```
Mway *search (Mway *tree, int n, keytype key, int *pos)

{

Mway *p = tree;

While (p! = null) {          // search a node

i = searchfornode (p, key);

if (i<numtrees(p) –1 && key == key(p, i))

{

*pos = i; return p;

}

p = son (p, i);

}
```

pos = -1;

return (-1);

}

5.2.2 B Trees

For a B-tree of order m :

It is an m way search tree that can be either empty or satisfies the following properties.

• The root node has at least two children's.

• All external nodes are at same level.

• All nodes other than the root node and external nodes have at least [m/2] children.

Example :

The following is an example of a B-tree of order 4. Hence, 3 is the maximum number of keys.

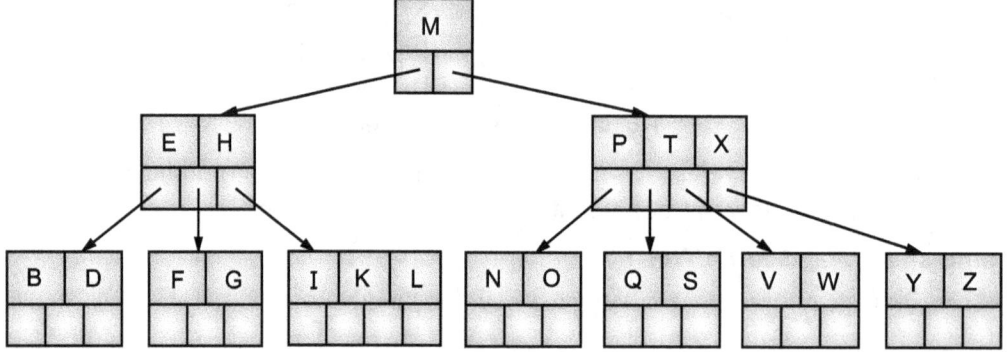

*Note that all the leaves are at the same level

Fig. 5.4 : B tree of order 5

5.2.2.1 Constructing a B Tree :

• We want to construct a B-tree of order 5

• Start with an empty B-tree and keys arrive in the following order :1 12 8 2 25 5 14 28 17 7 52 16 48 68 3 26 29 53 55 45

• B tree of order 5 means maximum number of keys are 4. Hence all the internal nodes should have at least 3 childrens (5/2=2.5 means 3) and hence at least 2 keys.

• So, the first four items go into the root :

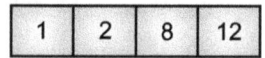

Fig. 5.5

• To put the fifth item in the root would violate condition 5

- Therefore, when 25 arrives, pick the middle key to make a new root

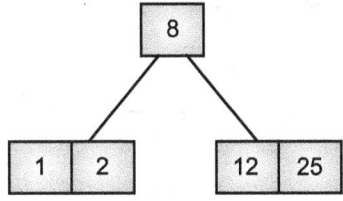

Fig. 5.6

- 6, 14, 28 get added to the leaf nodes :

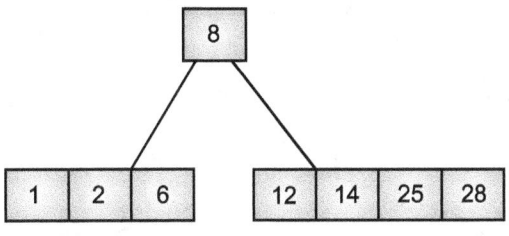

Fig. 5.7

Adding 17 to the right leaf node would over-fill it, so we take the middle key, promote it (to the root) and split the leaf.

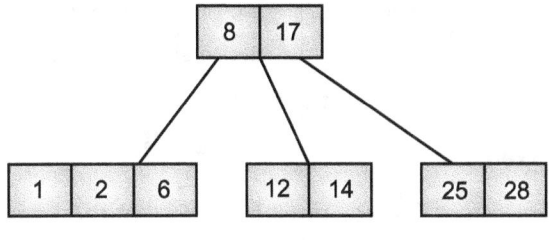

Fig. 5.8

7, 52, 16, 48 get added to the leaf nodes.

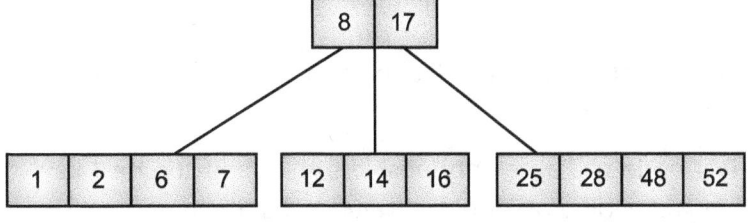

Fig. 5.9

Adding 68 causes us to split the right most leaf, promoting 48 to the root, and adding 3 causes us to split the left most leaf, promoting 3 to the root; 26, 29, 53, 55 then go into the leaves.

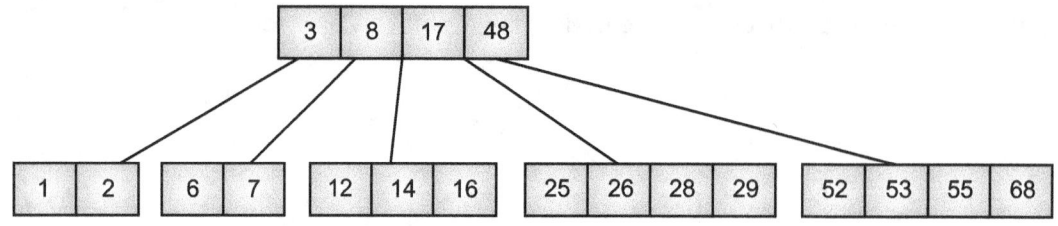

Fig. 5.10

Adding 45 causes a split of

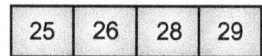

Fig. 5.11

and promoting 28 to the root then causes the root to split

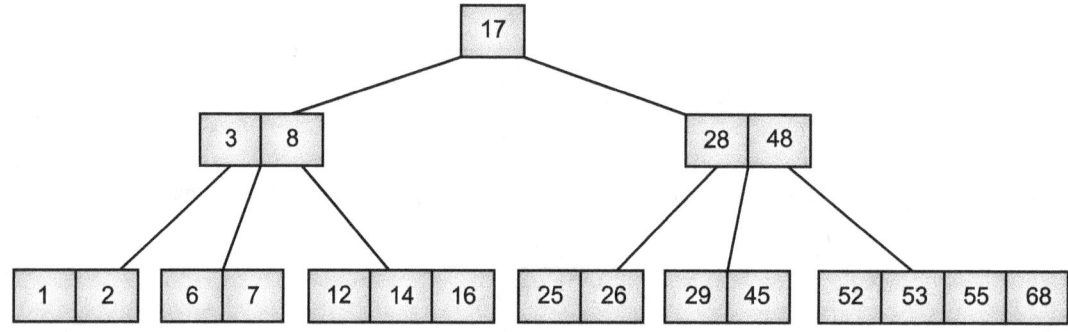

Fig. 5.12

5.2.2.2 Insertion into B Tree :

Steps for inserting a key in B tree. The key must be added at the leaf nodes.

Step 1 : Check whether tree is Empty.

Step 2 : If tree is Empty, then create a new node with new key value and insert into the tree as a root node.

Step 3 : If tree is Not Empty, then find a leaf node to which the new key value can be added using Binary Search Tree logic.

Step 4 : If that leaf node has an empty position, then add the new key value to that leaf node by maintaining ascending order of key value within the node.

Step 5 : If that leaf node is already full, then split that leaf node by sending middle value to its parent node. Repeat the same until sending value is fixed into a node.

Step 6 : If the silting is occurring to the root node, then the middle value becomes new root node for the tree and the height of the tree is increased by one.

5.2.2.3 Deletion from B Tree :

During insertion, the key always goes into a leaf. For deletion we wish to remove from a leaf. There are three possible ways we can do this :

(1) If the key is already in a leaf node, and removing it doesn't cause that leaf node to have too few keys, then simply remove the key to be deleted.

(2) If the key is not in a leaf then it is guaranteed (by the nature of a B-tree) that its predecessor or successor will be in a leaf -- in this case we can delete the key and promote the predecessor or successor key to the non-leaf deleted key's position.

• If (1) or (2) lead to a leaf node containing less than the minimum number of keys then we have to look at the siblings immediately adjacent to the leaf in question :

(3) If one of them has more than the min. number of keys then we can promote one of its keys to the parent and take the parent key into our lacking leaf.

(4) If neither of them has more than the min. number of keys then the lacking leaf and one of its neighbours can be combined with their shared parent (the opposite of promoting a key) and the new leaf will have the correct number of keys; if this step leave the parent with too few keys then we repeat the process up to the root itself, if required.

Case 1 : Assuming a B tree of order 5. Delete 2.

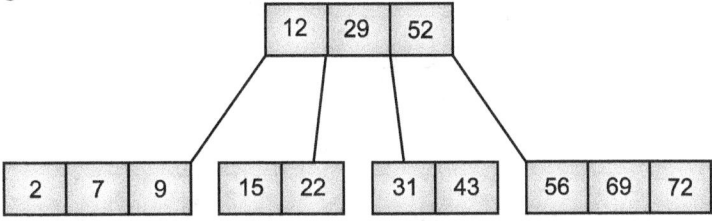

Fig. 5.13

Since there are enoughkeys in the node, just delete it

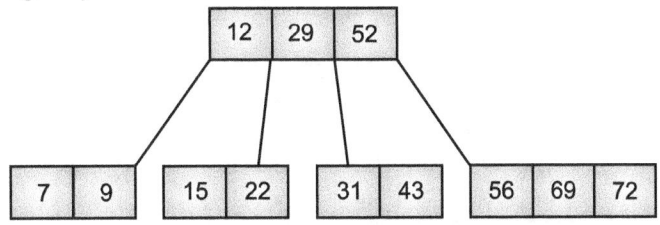

Fig. 5.14

Case 2 : Delete 52

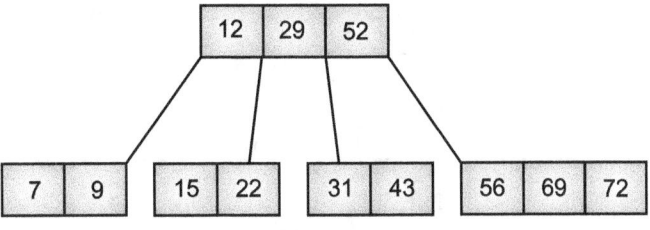

Fig. 5.15

Delete 52 and borrow the successor that is 56 into the root.

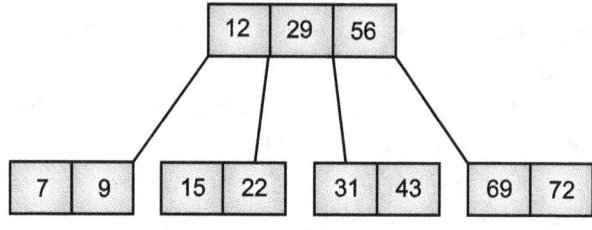

Fig. 5.16

Case 3 : Delete 72

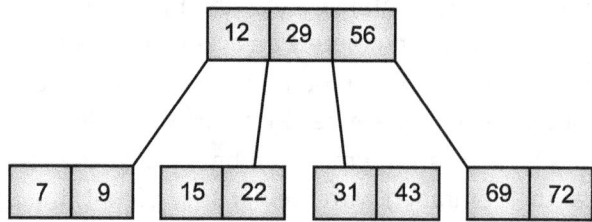

Fig. 5.17

After deletion of 72, only one key is remain that 69. But it violates B tree properties. So the solution is to join back 31, 43, 56 and 69 together.

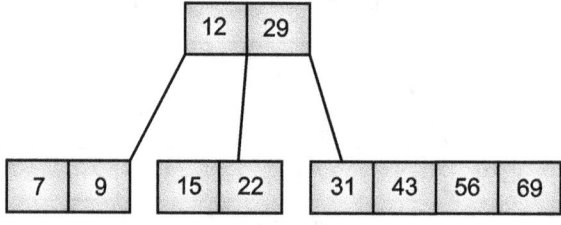

Fig. 5.18

Case 4 : Delete 22.

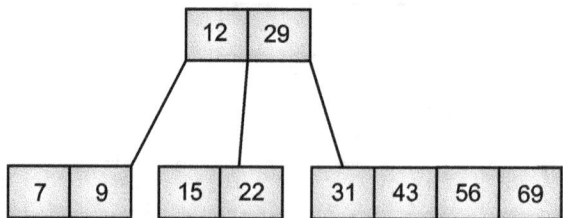

Fig. 5.19

Demote 29 and promote 31.

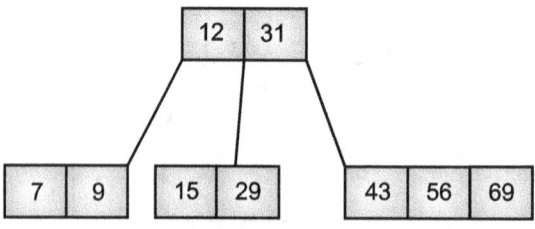

Fig. 5.20

5.2.3 Trie Trees

In computer science a trie, or strings over an alphabet. Unlike a binary search tree, no node in the tree stores the key associated with that node; instead, its position in the tree shows what key it is associated with. Pointers, one pointer for each character in the alphabet and all the descendants of a node have common prefix of the string associated with that node. The root is associated with empty string and values not associated with every node, only with leaves.

A trie is a tree data structure that allows string with similar character prefixes to use the same prefix data and store only the tails as separate data. One character of the string is stored at each level of the tree, with the first character of the string stored at the root.

Following example illustrates an example trie for alphabetical keys. The trie stores the keys Bauer, Baum, Feld, Hahn, Haus, Huhn, and Hund.

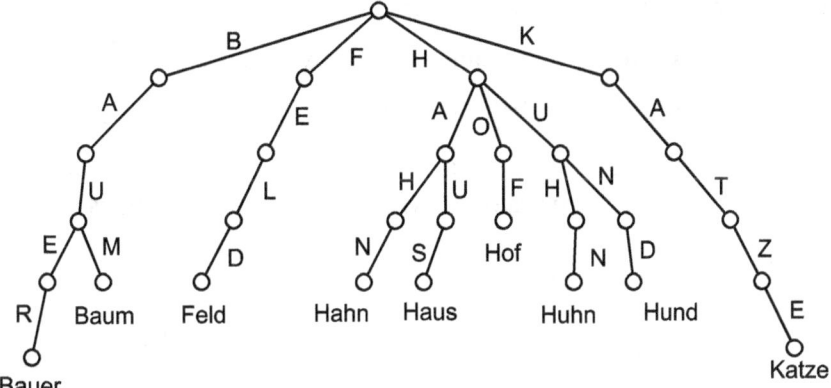

Fig. 5.21 : Trie tree

5.2.4 AA Tree

AA trees are named for their inventors Arne Andersson. An **AA tree** is a variation of red-black tree and a form of BST. AA tree are used for storing and retrieving ordered data efficiently. In AA tree, red nodes can only be added as a right sub child.

An AA tree needs to consider two shapes because right links can always be red :

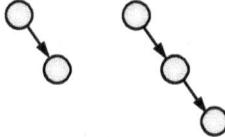

Fig. 5.22

AA Tree Properties :

An AA-Tree is a BST with the same ordering properties as a red-black tree :

• Every node is colored either red or black.

- The root is black.
- If a node is red, its children must be black.
- All simple paths from any node x to a descendent leaf must contain the same number of black nodes = black-height(x).
- Left children may not be red.

Implication of Ordering Links :

- Horizontal links are right links.
  - ➢ because only right children may be red.
- There may not be two consecutive horizontal links.
  - ➢ because there cannot be consecutive red nodes.
- Nodes at level 2 or higher must have two children.
- If a node does not have a right horizontal link, its two children are at the same level.
- Any simple path from a black node to a leaf contains one black node on each level.

To satisfy all the above properties split and skew is required. Split is a rotation done when there are two reds in a row and skew is done when too many black nodes on one path.

AA Tree Insertion :

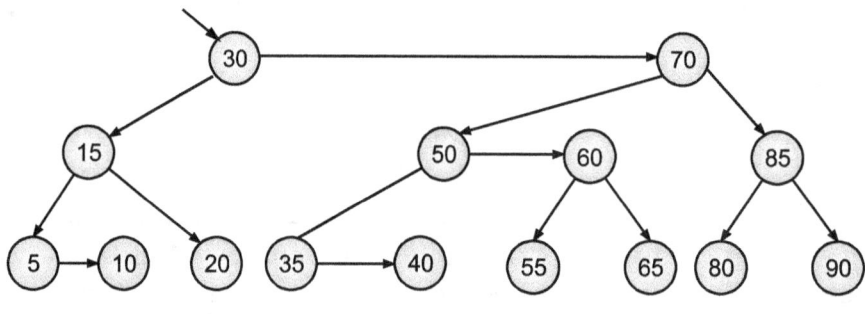

Fig. 5.23

Insert 45 : Insert same as BST

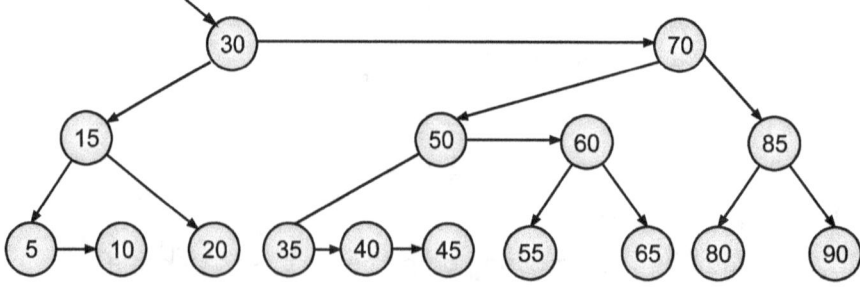

Fig. 5.24

Problem : Consecutive horizontal links starting at 35, so need split

After Split at 35

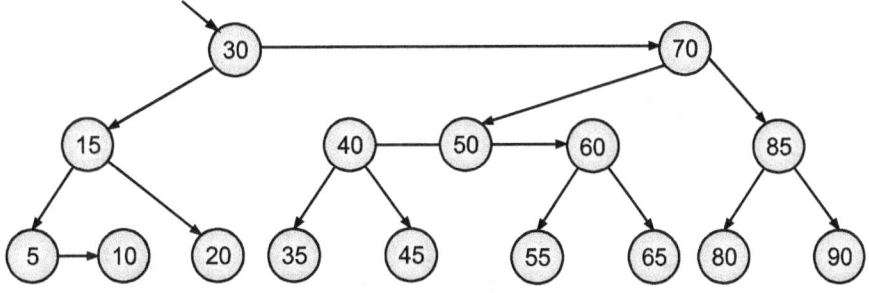

Fig. 5.25

Problem : Left horizontal link at 50 is introduced, so need skew

After Skew at 50

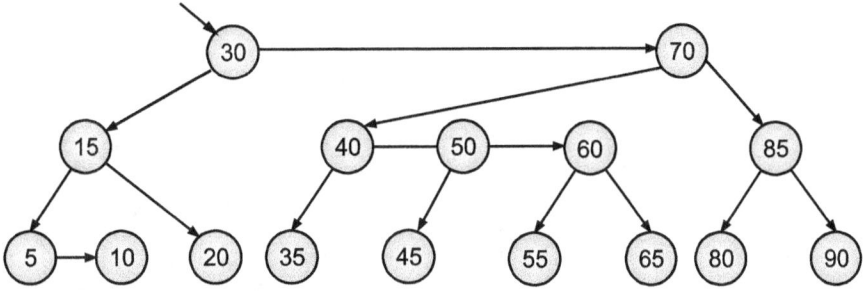

Fig. 5.26

Problem : Consecutive horizontal links starting at 40, so need split

After Split at 40

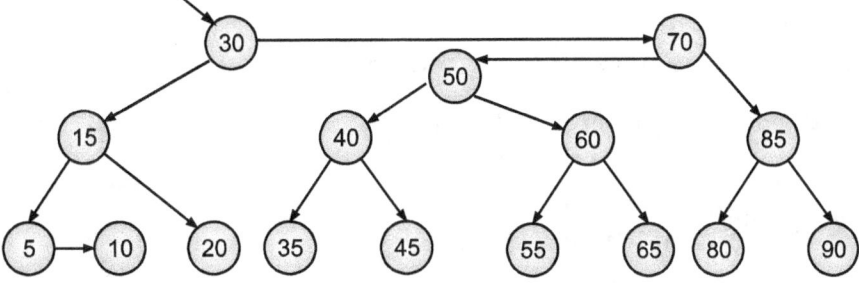

Fig. 5.27

Problem : Left horizontal link at 70 is introduced (50 is now on same level as 70), so need skew

After Skew at 70

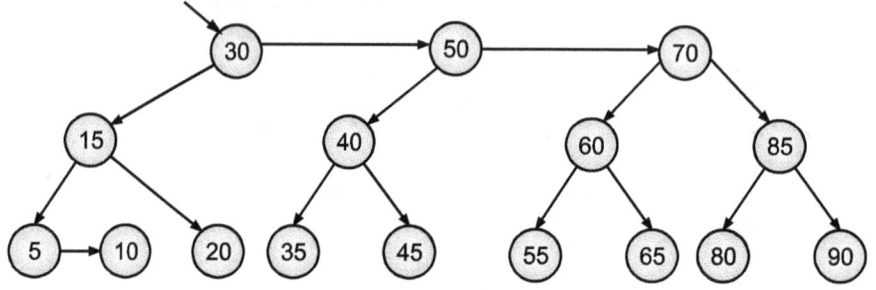

Fig. 5.28

Problem : Consecutive horizontal links starting at 30, so need split

After Split at 30

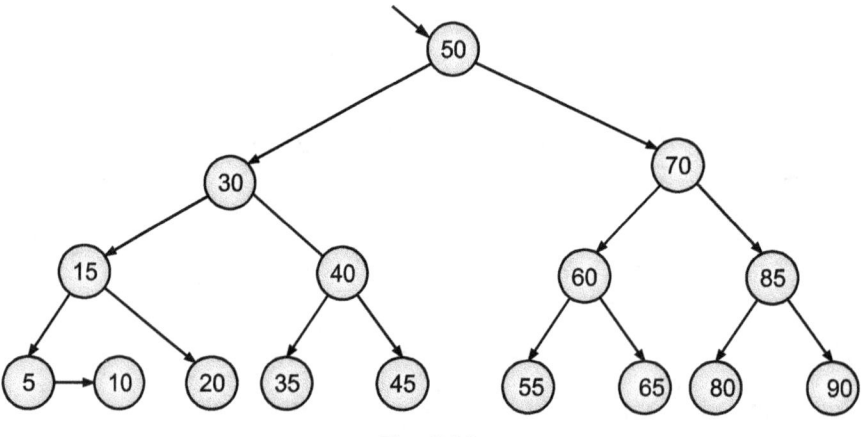

Fig. 5.29

Here, Insertion is completed.

Insertion Algorithm :

// Inserts node n into AA-Tree rooted at node m

// only for tree nodes with no pointer to parent

Insert (m, n)

        if (m = NIL) // have found where to insert y

            then m ← n

        else if key[n] < key[m]

```
        then Insert( left[ m ], n )

    else if key[ y ] > key[ m]

        then Insert( right[ m ], n )

    else

        n is a duplicate; handle duplicate case

    skew ( m )   // Do skew and split at each level

    split ( m )
```

5.2.5 K-Dimensional Tree

In k dimensional tree, k is dimension of data. For example 2d tree or 4d tree.

- Kd- trees are binary trees.
- Node consists of
  - ➢ Two child pointers,
  - ➢ Satellite information (such as name).
  - ➢ A key : Either a single float representing a coordinate value, or a pair of floats (representing a dimension of a rectangle)

Steps for Construction of K Dimensional Tree :

Construct a binary tree

- At each step, choose one of the coordinate as a basis of dividing the rest of the points.
- For example, at the root, choose x as the basis,
  - ➢ Like binary search trees, all items to the left of root will have the x-coordinate less than that of the root.
  - ➢ All items to the right of the root will have the x-coordinate greater than (or equal to) that of the root.
- Choose y as the basis for discrimination for the root's children.
- And choose x again for the root's grandchildren Note : Equality (corresponding to right child) is significant.

5.2.5.1 Construct 2D Tree for the Given Points :

- Coordinates of points are (35, 90), (70, 80), (10, 75) (80, 40), (50, 90), (70, 30), (90, 60), (50, 25), (25, 10), (20, 50), and (60, 10)

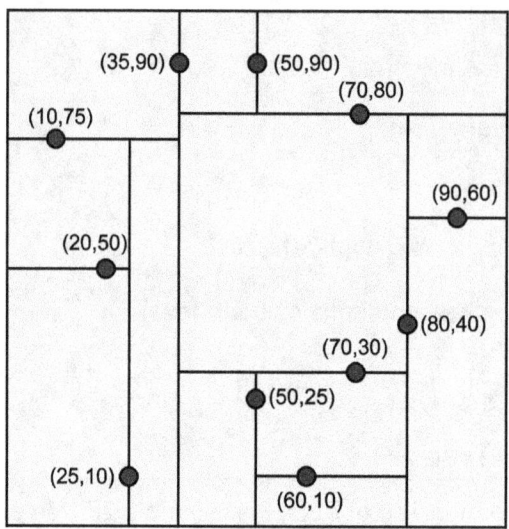

Fig. 5.30

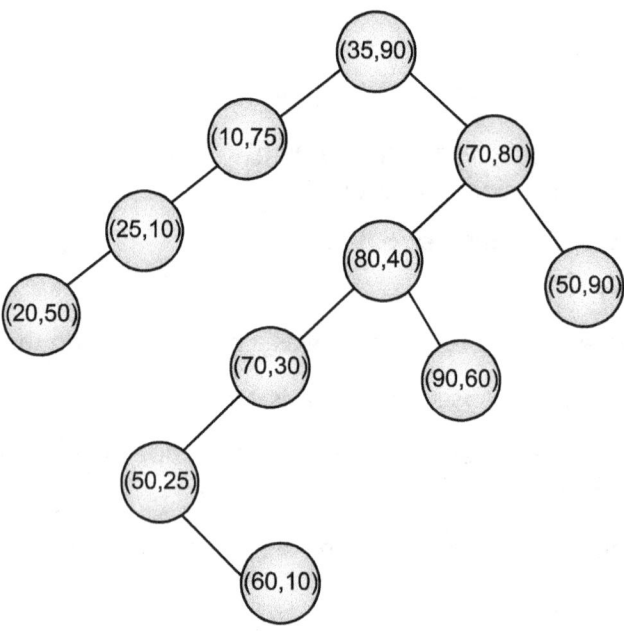

Fig. 5.31

5.2.6 Red-Black Trees

A red-black tree is a binary search tree with one extra attribute for each node : the colour, which is either red or black. We also need to keep track of the parent of each node, so that a red-black tree's node structure would be :

```
structt_red_black_node {
enum { red, black } colour;
void *item;
structt_red_black_node *left,
            *right,
            *parent;
  }
```

For the purpose of this discussion, the NULL nodes which terminate the tree are considered to be the leaves and are coloured black.

5.2.6.1 Definition of a Red-Black Tree

A red-black tree is a binary search tree which has the following red-black properties :

- Every node is either red or black.

- Every leaf (NULL) is black.

- If a node is red, then both its children are black.

- Every simple path from a node to a descendant leaf contains the same number of black nodes.

- Implies that on any path from the root to a leaf, red nodes must not be adjacent. However, any number of black nodes may appear in a sequence.

Note : Dark coloured blocks are black. Light coloured blocks are red.

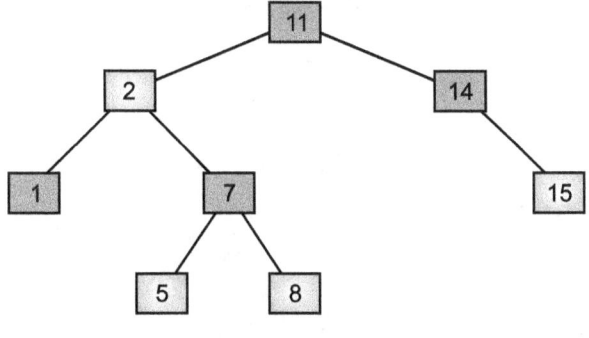

Fig. 5.32

5.2.6.2 A Basic Red-Black Tree.

Basic red-black tree with the **sentinel** nodes added. Implementations of the red-black tree algorithms will usually include the sentinel nodes as a convenient means of flagging that you have reached a leaf node.

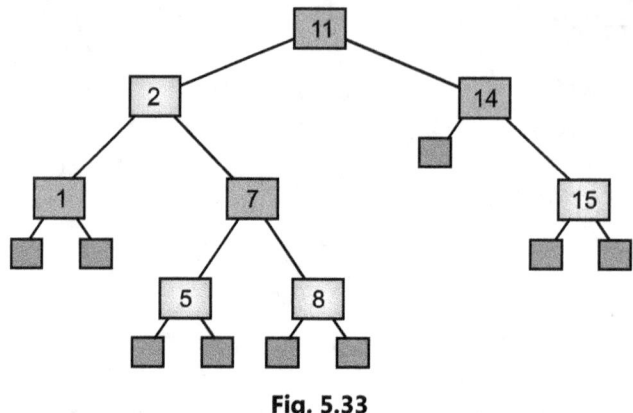

Fig. 5.33

They are the NULL Black Nodes of Property 2.

The number of black nodes on any path from, but not including, a node **x** to a leaf is called the black-height of a node, denoted **bh(x)**. We can prove the following lemma :

Lemma

A red-black tree with **n** internal nodes has height at most **2log(n+1)**. (For a proof, see Cormen, p 264)

This demonstrates why the red-black tree is a good search tree : it can always be searched in **O(log n)** time.

As with heaps, additions and deletions from red-black trees destroy the red-black property, so we need to restore it. To do this we need to look at some operations on red-black trees.

5.2.6.3 Rotations

A rotation is a local operation in a search tree that preserves in-order traversal key ordering.

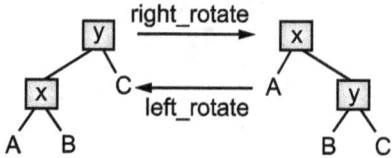

Fig. 5.34

Note that in both trees, an in-order traversal yields :

A x B y C

The left_rotate operation may be encoded :

left_rotate(Tree T, node x) {

node y;

        y = x->right;

            /* Turn y's left sub-tree into x's right sub-tree */

```
                        x->right = y->left;
                                if ( y->left != NULL )
            y->left->parent = x;
                                /* y's new parent was x's parent */
            y->parent = x->parent;
                                /* Set the parent to point to y instead of x */
                                /* First see whether we're at the root */
    if ( x->parent == NULL ) T->root = y;
else
    if ( x == (x->parent)->left )
                                /* x was on the left of its parent */
    x->parent->left = y;
else
                                /* x must have been on the right */
    x->parent->right = y;
                                /* Finally, put x on y's left */
                y->left = x;
                x->parent = y;
    }
```

5.2.6.4 Insertion

Insertion is somewhat complex and involves a number of cases. Note that we start by inserting the new node, x, in the tree just as we would for any other binary tree, using the tree_insert function. This new node is labelled red, and possibly destroys the red-black property. The main loop moves up the tree, restoring the red-black property.

```
rb_insert( Tree T, node x ) {
                            /* Insert in the tree in the usual way */
tree_insert( T, x );
                            /* Now restore the red-black property */
x->colour = red;
while ( (x != T->root) && (x->parent->colour == red) ) {
if ( x->parent == x->parent->parent->left ) {
```

```
                                    /* If x's parent is a left, y is x's right 'uncle' */
                        y = x->parent->parent->right;
if ( y->colour == red ) {
                                    /* case 1 - change the colours */
x->parent->colour = black;
y->colour = black;
x->parent->parent->colour = red;
                                    /* Move x up the tree */
                        x = x->parent->parent;
            }
else {
                                    /* y is a black node */
if ( x == x->parent->right ) {
                                    /* and x is to the right */
                                    /* case 2 - move x up and rotate */
                        x = x->parent;
left_rotate( T, x );
                }
                                    /* case 3 */
x->parent->colour = black;
x->parent->parent->colour = red;
right_rotate( T, x->parent->parent );
                }
            }

else {
                                    /* repeat the "if" part with right and left
exchanged */
            }
        }
                                    /* Colour the root black */
    T->root->colour = black;
    }
```

5.2.7 B+tree

Most queries can be executed more quickly if the values are stored in order. But it's not practical to hope to store all the rows in the table one after another, in sorted order, because this requires rewriting the entire table with each insertion or deletion of a row.

This leads us to instead imagine storing our rows in a tree structure. Our first instinct would be a balanced binary search tree like a red-black tree, but this really doesn't make much sense for a database since it is stored on disk. You see, disks work by reading and writing whole **blocks** of data at once — typically 512 bytes or four kilobytes. A node of a binary search tree uses a small fraction of that, so it makes sense to look for a structure that fits more neatly into a disk block.

Hence the B+-tree, in which each node stores up to d references to children and up to d − 1 keys. Each reference is considered "between" two of the node's keys; it references the root of a subtree for which all values are between these two keys.

Here is a fairly small tree using 4 as our value for d.

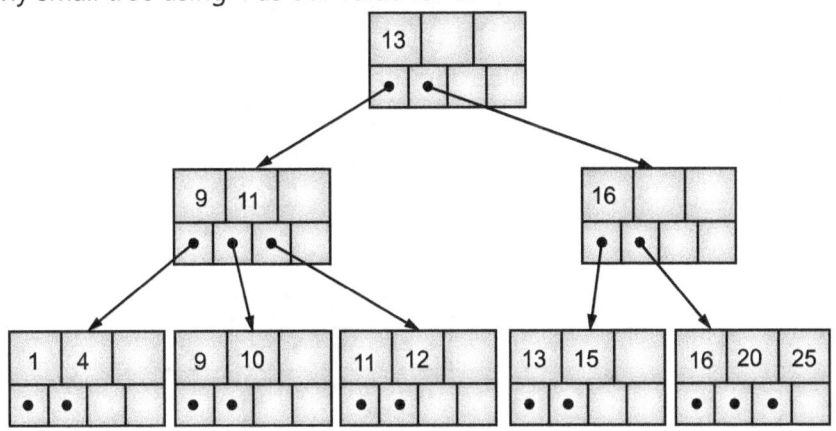

Fig. 5.35

A B+-tree requires that each leaf be at the same distance from the root, as in this picture, where searching for any of the 11 values (all listed on the bottom level) will involve loading three nodes from the disk (the root block, a second-level block, and a leaf).

In practice, d will be larger — as large, in fact, as it takes to fill a disk block. Suppose a block is 4KB, our keys are 4-byte integers, and each reference is a 6-byte file offset. Then we'd choose d to be the largest value so that $4(d − 1) + 6d \leq 4096$; solving this inequality for d, we end up with $d \leq 410$, so we'd use 410 for d. As you can see, d can be large.

A B+-tree maintains the following invariants :

- Every node has one more references than it has keys.
- All leaves are at the same distance from the root.
- For every non-leaf node N with k being the number of keys in N : all keys in the first child's subtree are less than N's first key; and all keys in the ith child's subtree $(2 \leq i \leq k)$ are between the $(i − 1)$th key of n and the ith key of n.

- The root has at least two children.
- Every non-leaf, non-root node has at least floor(d / 2) children.
- Each leaf contains at least floor(d / 2) keys.
- Every key from the table appears in a leaf, in left-to-right sorted order.

In our examples, we'll continue to use 4 for d. Looking at our invariants, this requires that each leaf have at least two keys, and each internal node to have at least two children (and thus at least one key).

1. Insertion Algorithm

Descend to the leaf where the key fits.

- If the node has an empty space, insert the key/reference pair into the node.
- If the node is already full, split it into two nodes, distributing the keys evenly between the two nodes. If the node is a leaf, take a copy of the minimum value in the second of these two nodes and repeat this insertion algorithm to insert it into the parent node. If the node is a non-leaf, exclude the middle value during the split and repeat this insertion algorithm to insert this excluded value into the parent node.

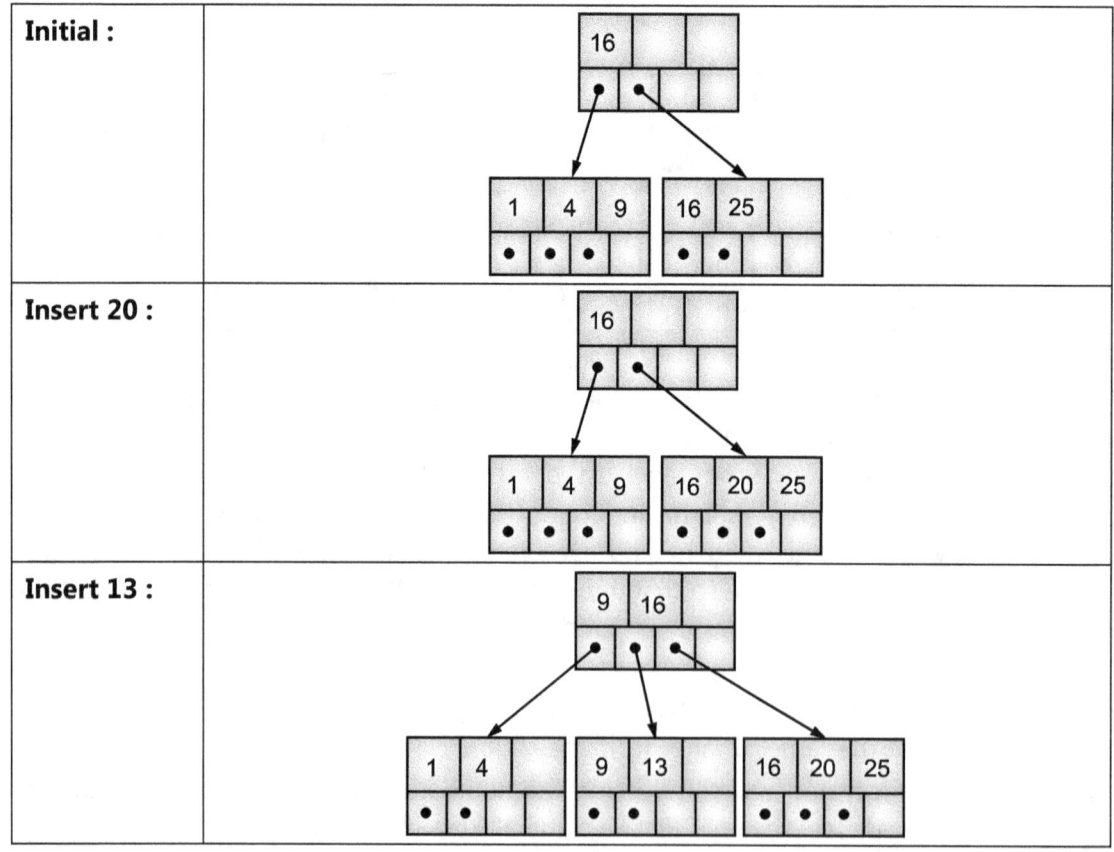

...Conti.

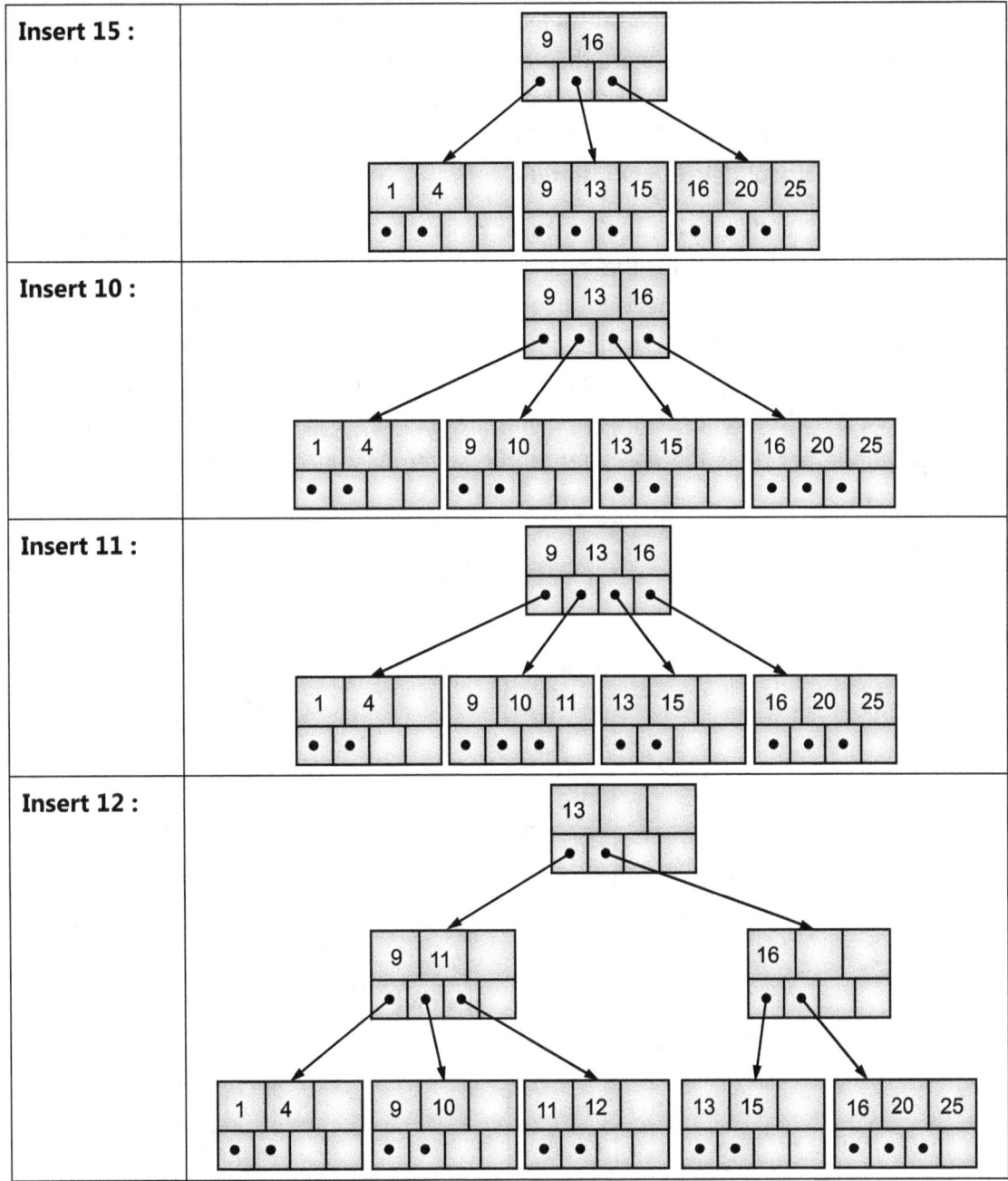

2. Deletion Algorithm

Descend to the leaf where the key exists.

- Remove the required key and associated reference from the node.
- If the node still has enough keys and references to satisfy the invariants, stop.

- If the node has too few keys to satisfy the invariants, but its next oldest or next youngest sibling at the same level has more than necessary, distribute the keys between this node and the neighbor. Repair the keys in the level above to represent that these nodes now have a different "split point" between them; this involves simply changing a key in the levels above, without deletion or insertion.

- If the node has too few keys to satisfy the invariant, and the next oldest or next youngest sibling is at the minimum for the invariant, then merge the node with its sibling; if the node is a non-leaf, we will need to incorporate the "split key" from the parent into our merging. In either case, we will need to repeat the removal algorithm on the parent node to remove the "split key" that previously separated these merged nodes — unless the parent is the root and we are removing the final key from the root, in which case the merged node becomes the new root (and the tree has become one level shorter than before).

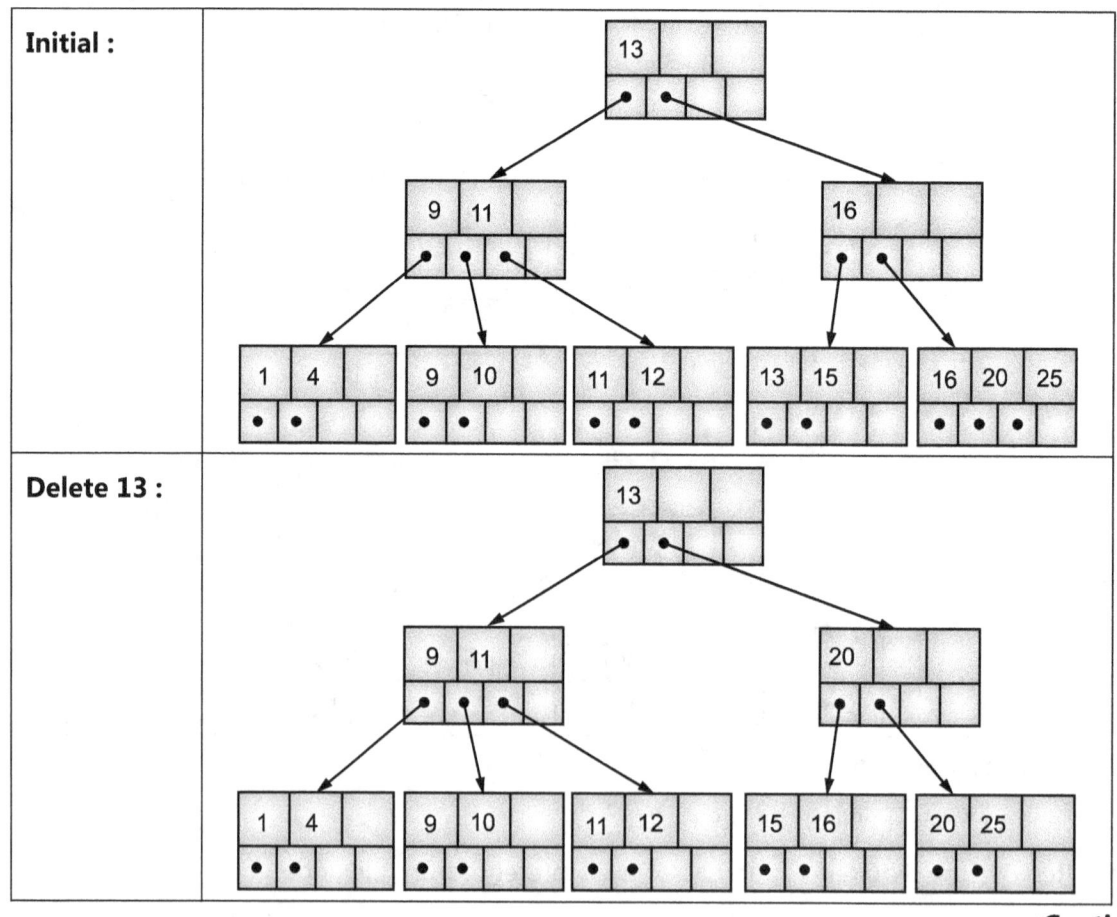

...Conti.

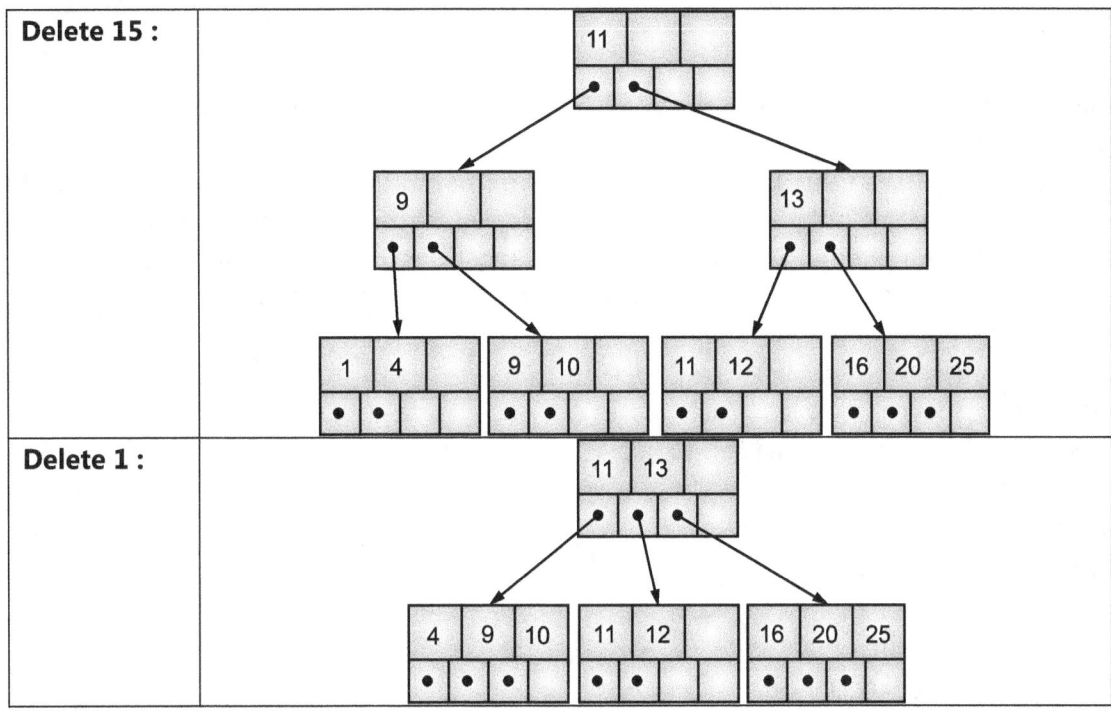

Delete 15 :

Delete 1 :

The order, or branching factor, b of a B+ tree measures the capacity of nodes (i.e., the number of children nodes) for internal nodes in the tree. The actual number of children for a node, referred to here as m, is constrained for internal nodes so that The root is an exception : it is allowed to have as few as two children. For example, if the order of a B+ tree is 7, each internal node (except for the root) may have between 4 and 7 children; the root may have between 2 and 7. Leaf nodes have no children, but are constrained so that the number of keys must be at least and at most. In the situation where a B+ tree is nearly empty, it only contains one node, which is a leaf node. (The root is also the single leaf, in this case.) This node is permitted to have as little as one key if necessary, and at most b.

Node Type	Children Type	Min Number of Children	Max Number of Children	Example b = 7	Example b = 100
Root Node (when it is the only node in the tree)	Records	1	b - 1	1 - 6	1 - 99
Root Node	Internal Nodes or Leaf Nodes	2	b	2 - 7	2 - 100
Internal Node	Internal Nodes or Leaf Nodes		b	4 - 7	50 - 100
Leaf Node	Records		b - 1	3 - 6	49 - 99

Algorithms :

Search :

The root of a B+ Tree represents the whole range of values in the tree, where every internal node is a subinterval.

We are looking for a value k in the B+ Tree. Starting from the root, we are looking for the leaf which may contain the value k. At each node, we figure out which internal pointer we should follow. An internal B+ Tree node has at most d ≤ b children, where every one of them represents a different sub-interval. We select the corresponding node by searching on the key values of the node.

Function : search (k)

returntree_search (k, root);

Function : tree_search (k, node)

if node is a leaf **then**

return node;

switch k **do**

case $k < k\_0$

returntree_search(k, p_0);

case$k\_i \le k < k\_{i+1}$

returntree_search(k, p_{i+1});

case$k\_d \le k$

returntree_search(k, p_{d+1});

5.2.8 Splay Trees

- A **splay tree** is an efficient implementation of a balanced binary search tree that takes advantage of locality in the keys used in incoming lookup requests. For many applications, there is excellent key locality. A good example is a network router. A network router receives network packets at a high rate from incoming connections and must quickly decide on which outgoing wire to send each packet, based on the IP address in the packet. The router needs a big table (a map) that can be used to look up an IP address and find out which outgoing connection to use. If an IP address has been used once, it is likely to be used again, perhaps many times. Splay trees can provide good performance in this situation.

- Importantly, splay trees offer amortized O(logn) performance; a sequence of M operations on an n-node splay tree takes O(Mlogn) time.

- Splay tree is a self-balancing data structure where the last accessed key is always at root. The insert operation is similar to Binary Search Tree insert with additional steps to make sure that the newly inserted key becomes the new root.

- A splay tree is a self-adjusting search algorithm for placing and locating files (called records or keys) in a database. The algorithm finds data by repeatedly making choices at decision points called nodes.

- In a splay tree, as in a binary tree, a node has two branches (also called children). Records are stored in locations called leaves. This name derives from the fact that records always exist at end points; there is nothing beyond them. The starting point is called the root. The number of access operations required to reach the desired record is called the depth. In a practical tree, there can be thousands, millions, or billions of nodes, children, leaves, and records. Not every leaf necessarily contains a record, but more than half do. A leaf that does not contain data is called a null.

- The splay tree scheme is unique because the tree organization varies depending on which nodes are most frequently accessed. This structural change takes place by means of so-called splaying operations, also called rotations. (In general, to splay is to spread or extend out or apart.) There are several ways in which splaying can be done. It always involves interchanging the root with the node in question. One or more other nodes might change position as well. The purpose of splaying is to minimize the number of access operations required to recover desired data records over a period of time.

- A splay tree is a binary search tree. It has one interesting difference, however : whenever an element is looked up in the tree, the splay tree reorganizes to move that element to the root of the tree, without breaking the binary search tree invariant. If the next lookup request is for the same element, it can be returned immediately. In general, if a small number of elements are being heavily used, they will tend to be found near the top of the tree and are thus found quickly.

- We have already seen a way to move an element upward in a binary search tree : tree rotation. When an element is accessed in a splay tree, tree rotations are used to move it to the top of the tree. This simple algorithm can result in extremely good performance in practice. Notice that the algorithm requires that we be able to update the tree in place, but the abstract view of the set of elements represented by the tree does not change and the rep invariant is maintained. This is an example of a benign side effect, because it does not change the value represented by the data structure.

- There are three kinds of tree rotations that are used to move elements upward in the tree. These rotations have two important effects : they move the node being splayed upward in the tree, and they also shorten the path to any nodes along the path to the splayed node. This latter effect means that splaying operations tend to make the tree more balanced.

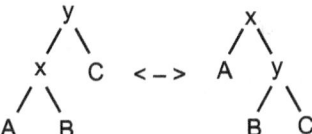

Rotation 1 : Simple Rotation

The simple tree rotation used in AVL trees and treaps is also applied at the root of the splay tree, moving the splayed node x up to become the new tree root. Here we have A < x < B < y < C, and the splayed node is either x or y depending on which direction the rotation is. It is highlighted in red.

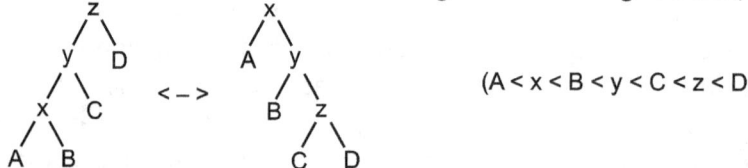

Rotation 2 : Zig-Zig and Zag-Zag

Lower down in the tree rotations are performed in pairs so that nodes on the path from the splayed node to the root move closer to the root on average. In the "zig-zig" case, the splayed node is the left child of a left child or the right child of a right child ("zag-zag").

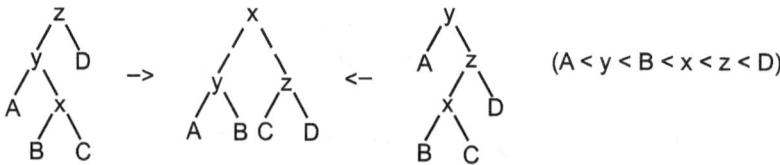

$(A < x < B < y < C < z < D)$

Rotation 3 : Zig-Zag

In the "zig-zag" case, the splayed node is the left child of a right child or vice-versa. The rotations produce a subtree whose height is less than that of the original tree. Thus, this rotation improves the balance of the tree. In each of the two cases shown, y is the splayed node :

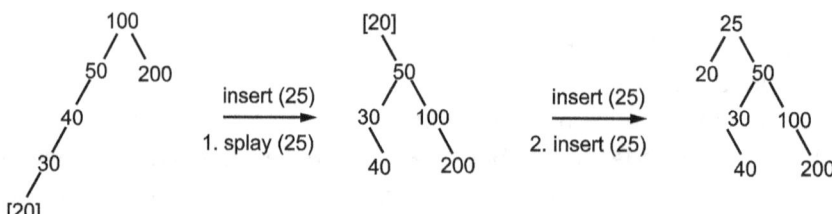

$(A < y < B < x < z < D)$

Following are different cases to insert a key k in splay tree.

- Root is NULL : We simply allocate a new node and return it as root.
- Splay the given key k. If k is already present, then it becomes the new root. If not present, then last accessed leaf node becomes the new root.
- If new root's key is same as k, don't do anything as k is already present.
- Else allocate memory for new node and compare root's key with k.
  - ➤ If k is smaller than root's key, make root as right child of new node, copy left child of root as left child of new node and make left child of root as NULL.
  - ➤ If k is greater than root's key, make root as left child of new node, copy right child of root as right child of new node and make right child of root as NULL.
- Return new node as new root of tree.

Example :

```
        100
       /   \
     50     200
      \
      40
       \
       30
        \
       [20]
```
insert (25)
───────────→
1. splay (25)

```
      [20]
         \
         50
        /   \
      30     100
        \      \
        40     200
```
insert (25)
───────────→
2. insert (25)

```
        25
       /   \
     20     50
           /   \
         30     100
           \      \
           40     200
```

```c
#include<stdio.h>
#include<stdlib.h>
// An AVL tree node
struct node
{
    int key;
    struct node *left, *right;
};
/* Helper function that allocates a new node with the given key and
   NULL left and right pointers. */
struct node* newNode(int key)
{
    struct node* node = (struct node*)malloc(sizeof(struct node));
    node->key   = key;
    node->left  = node->right  = NULL;
    return (node);
}
// A utility function to right rotate subtree rooted with y
// See the diagram given above.
struct node *rightRotate(struct node *x)
{
    struct node *y = x->left;
    x->left = y->right;
    y->right = x;
    return y;
}
// A utility function to left rotate subtree rooted with x
// See the diagram given above.
struct node *leftRotate(struct node *x)
{
    struct node *y = x->right;
    x->right = y->left;
    y->left = x;
    return y;
```

```
}
// This function brings the key at root if key is present in tree.
// If key is not present, then it brings the last accessed item at
// root.  This function modifies the tree and returns the new root
struct node *splay(struct node *root, int key)
{
    // Base cases : root is NULL or key is present at root
    if (root == NULL || root->key == key)
        return root;
    // Key lies in left subtree
    if (root->key > key)
    {
        // Key is not in tree, we are done
        if (root->left == NULL) return root;
        // Zig-Zig (Left Left)
        if (root->left->key > key)
        {
            // First recursively bring the key as root of left-left
            root->left->left = splay(root->left->left, key);
            // Do first rotation for root, second rotation is done after else
            root = rightRotate(root);
        }
        else if (root->left->key < key) // Zig-Zag (Left Right)
        {
            // First recursively bring the key as root of left-right
            root->left->right = splay(root->left->right, key);
            // Do first rotation for root->left
            if (root->left->right != NULL)
                root->left = leftRotate(root->left);
        }
        // Do second rotation for root
        return (root->left == NULL)? root : rightRotate(root);
    }
    else // Key lies in right subtree
```

```
{
    // Key is not in tree, we are done
    if (root->right == NULL) return root;

    // Zig-Zag (Right Left)
    if (root->right->key > key)
    {
        // Bring the key as root of right-left
        root->right->left = splay(root->right->left, key);
        // Do first rotation for root->right
        if (root->right->left != NULL)
            root->right = rightRotate(root->right);
    }
    else if (root->right->key < key)// Zag-Zag (Right Right)
    {
        // Bring the key as root of right-right and do first rotation
        root->right->right = splay(root->right->right, key);
        root = leftRotate(root);
    }
    // Do second rotation for root
    return (root->right == NULL)? root : leftRotate(root);
}
}
// Function to insert a new key k in splay tree with given root
struct node *insert(struct node *root, int k)
{
    // Simple Case : If tree is empty
    if (root == NULL) return newNode(k);
    // Bring the closest leaf node to root
    root = splay(root, k);
    // If key is already present, then return
    if (root->key == k) return root;
```

```
    // Otherwise allocate memory for new node
    struct node *newnode  = newNode(k);


    // If root's key is greater, make root as right child
    // of newnode and copy the left child of root to newnode
    if (root->key > k)
    {
        newnode->right = root;
        newnode->left = root->left;
        root->left = NULL;
    }
    // If root's key is smaller, make root as left child
    // of newnode and copy the right child of root to newnode
    else
    {
        newnode->left = root;
        newnode->right = root->right;
        root->right = NULL;
    }
    return newnode; // newnode becomes new root
}
// A utility function to print preorder traversal of the tree.
// The function also prints height of every node
void preOrder(struct node *root)
{
    if (root != NULL)
    {
        printf("%d ", root->key);
        preOrder(root->left);
        preOrder(root->right);
    }
}


/* Drier program to test above function*/
```

```
int main()
{
    struct node *root = newNode(100);
    root->left = newNode(50);
    root->right = newNode(200);
    root->left->left = newNode(40);
    root->left->left->left = newNode(30);
    root->left->left->left->left = newNode(20);
    root = insert(root, 25);
    printf("Preorder traversal of the modified Splay tree is \n");
    preOrder(root);
    return 0;
}
```

Output :

Preorder traversal of the modified Splay tree is

25 20 50 30 40 100 200

5.2.8.1 Search Operation

The search operation in Splay tree does the standard BST search, in addition to search, it also splays (move a node to the root). If the search is successful, then the node that is found is splayed and becomes the new root. Else the last node accessed prior to reaching the NULL is splayed and becomes the new root.

There are following cases for the node being accessed.

- **Node is root:** We simply return the root, don't do anything else as the accessed node is already root.

- **Zig : Node is child of root** (the node has no grandparent). Node is either a left child of root (we do a right rotation) or node is a right child of its parent (we do a left rotation). T1, T2 and T3 are subtrees of the tree rooted with y (on left side) or x (on right side)

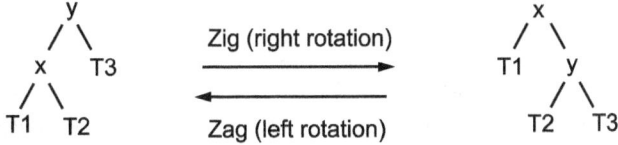

- **Node has Both Parent and Grandparent** : There can be following subcases.

  ➢ **Zig-Zig and Zag-Zag** Node is left child of parent and parent is also left child of grand parent (Two right rotations) OR node is right child of its parent and parent is also right child of grand parent (Two Left Rotations).

Zig-Zig (Left Left Case) :

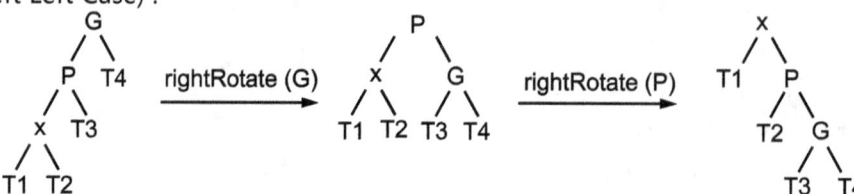

Zag-Zag (Right Right Case) :

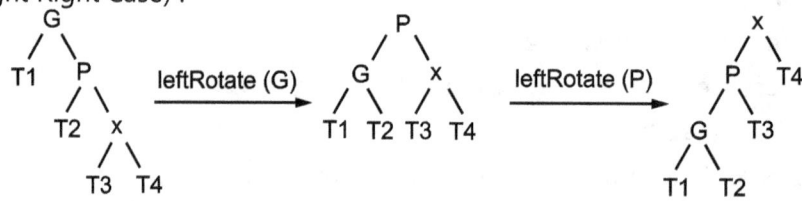

➢ **Zig-Zag and Zag-Zig** Node is left child of parent and parent is right child of grand parent (Left Rotation followed by right rotation) OR node is right child of its parent and parent is left child of grand parent (Right Rotation followed by left rotation).

Zig-Zag (Left Right Case) :

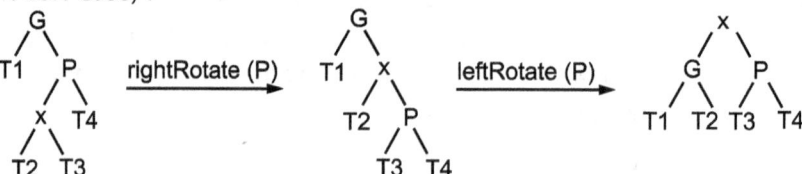

Zag-Zig (Right Left Case) :

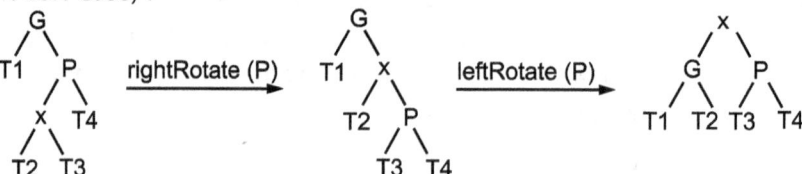

Example :

```
        100                              100                          [20]
       /  \          search (20)        /  \        search (20)          \
     50    200      ─────────────>    50    200     ─────────────>        50
     /              1. Zig-Zig          \           1. Zig-Zig           /  \
    40                at 40            [20]            at 100           30    100
   /                                     \                               \      \
  30                                      30                             40      200
 /                                         \
[20]                                        40
```

The important thing to note is, the search or splay operation not only brings the searched key to root, but also balances the BST. For example in above case, height of BST is reduced by 1.

Implementation :

```
// The code is adopted from
#include<stdio.h>
#include<stdlib.h>
```

```c
// An AVL tree node
struct node
{
   int key;
   struct node *left, *right;
};
/* Helper function that allocates a new node with the given key and
   NULL left and right pointers. */
struct node* newNode(int key)
{
   struct node* node = (struct node*)malloc(sizeof(struct node));
   node->key   = key;
   node->left  = node->right  = NULL;
   return (node);
}
// A utility function to right rotate subtree rooted with y
// See the diagram given above.
struct node *rightRotate(struct node *x)
{
   struct node *y = x->left;
   x->left = y->right;
   y->right = x;
   return y;
}
// A utility function to left rotate subtree rooted with x
// See the diagram given above.
struct node *leftRotate(struct node *x)
{
   struct node *y = x->right;
   x->right = y->left;
   y->left = x;
   return y;
}
```

```c
// This function brings the key at root if key is present in tree.
// If key is not present, then it brings the last accessed item at
// root.  This function modifies the tree and returns the new root
struct node *splay(struct node *root, int key)
{
    // Base cases : root is NULL or key is present at root
    if (root == NULL || root->key == key)
        return root;
    // Key lies in left subtree
    if (root->key > key)
    {
        // Key is not in tree, we are done
        if (root->left == NULL) return root;
        // Zig-Zig (Left Left)
        if (root->left->key > key)
        {
            // First recursively bring the key as root of left-left
            root->left->left = splay(root->left->left, key);
            // Do first rotation for root, second rotation is done after else
            root = rightRotate(root);
        }
        else if (root->left->key < key) // Zig-Zag (Left Right)
        {
            // First recursively bring the key as root of left-right
            root->left->right = splay(root->left->right, key);3
            // Do first rotation for root->left
            if (root->left->right != NULL)
                root->left = leftRotate(root->left);
        }
        // Do second rotation for root
```

```
        return (root->left == NULL)? root : rightRotate(root);
    }
    else // Key lies in right subtree
    {
        // Key is not in tree, we are done
        if (root->right == NULL) return root;
        // Zag-Zig (Right Left)
        if (root->right->key > key)
        {
            // Bring the key as root of right-left
            root->right->left = splay(root->right->left, key);
            // Do first rotation for root->right
            if (root->right->left != NULL)
                root->right = rightRotate(root->right);
        }
        else if (root->right->key < key)// Zag-Zag (Right Right)
        {
            // Bring the key as root of right-right and do first rotation
            root->right->right = splay(root->right->right, key);
            root = leftRotate(root);
        }
        // Do second rotation for root
        return (root->right == NULL)? root : leftRotate(root);
    }
}
// The search function for Splay tree.  Note that this function
// returns the new root of Splay Tree.  If key is present in tree
// then, it is moved to root.
struct node *search(struct node *root, int key)
{
```

```
    return splay(root, key);
}
// A utility function to print preorder traversal of the tree.
// The function also prints height of every node
void preOrder(struct node *root)
{
  if (root != NULL)
  {
    printf("%d ", root->key);
    preOrder(root->left);
    preOrder(root->right);
  }
}
/* Drier program to test above function*/
int main()
{
  struct node *root = newNode(100);
  root->left = newNode(50);
  root->right = newNode(200);
  root->left->left = newNode(40);
  root->left->left->left = newNode(30);
  root->left->left->left->left = newNode(20);
  root = search(root, 20);
  printf("Preorder traversal of the modified Splay tree is \n");
  preOrder(root);
  return 0;
}
```

Output :

Preorder traversal of the modified Splay tree is

20 50 30 40 100 200

Summary :

- Splay trees have excellent locality properties. Frequently accessed items are easy to find. Infrequent items are out of way.

- All splay tree operations take O(Logn) time on average. Splay trees can be rigorously shown to run in O(log n) average time per operation, over any sequence of operations (assuming we start from an empty tree)

- Splay trees are simpler compared to AVL and Red-Black Trees as no extra field is required in every tree node.

- Unlike AVL tree, a splay tree can change even with read-only operations like search.

5.3 SET ABSTRACT DATA TYPE (ADT)

A set is an Abstract Data Type (ADT) that can store some values which are not repeated, without any particular order. The mathematical concept of a finite set are computer implemented in set ADT.

An abstract data structure is a collection, or aggregate, of data. The data may be booleans, numbers, characters, or other data structures. If one considers the structure yielded by packaging or indexing, there are four basic data structures :

- unpackaged, unindexed : bunch

- packaged, unindexed : set

- unpackaged, indexed : string (sequence)

- packaged, indexed : list (array)

In this view, the contents of a set are a bunch, and isolated data items are elementary bunches (elements). Whereas sets contain elements, bunches consist of elements.

Further structuring may be achieved by considering the multiplicity of elements (sets become multisets, bunches become hyper bunches)˙ or their homogeneity (a record is a set of fields, not necessarily all of the same type).

Operations

Core Set Theoretical Operations

One may define the operations of the algebra of sets :

- Union(S, T) returns the union of sets S and T.

- Intersection (S, T) : returns the intersection of sets S and T.

- Difference(S, T) : returns the difference of sets S and T.

- Subset (S, T) : a predicate that tests whether the set S is a subset of set T.

Static Sets :

Typical operations that may be provided by a static set structure S are :

- is-element_of(x , S) : checks whether the value x is in the set S.
- is-empty(S) : checks whether the set S is empty.
- Size(S) : returns the number of elements in S.
- iterate(S) : returns a function that returns one more value of S at each call, in some arbitrary order.
- enumerate(S) :returns a list containing the elements of S in some arbitrary order.

Dynamic Sets :

Dynamic set structures typically add :

- create( ) : creates a new, initially empty set structure.
- add(S,x) adds the element x to S, if it is not present already.
- remove(S, x) removes the element x from S, if it is present.
- capacity(S) : returns the maximum number of values that S can hold.

Some set structures may allow only some of these operations. The cost of each operation will depend on the implementation, and possibly also on the particular values stored in the set, and the order in which they are inserted.

Additional Operations :

There are many other operations that can (in principle) be defined in terms of the above, such as :

- **pop(S):** returns an arbitrary element of S, deleting it from S.
- map(F,S) : returns the set of distinct values resulting from applying function F to each element of S.
- filter(P, S) : returns the subset containing all elements of S that satisfy a given predicate P.
- clear(S) :delete all elements of S.
- equal(S1, S2) : checks whether the two given sets are equal (i.e. contain all and only the same elements).

5.4 HEAP

Heap is a special tree-based data structure, that satisfies the following special heap properties :

- **Shape Property :** Heap data structure is always a Complete Binary Tree, which means all levels of the tree are fully filled.

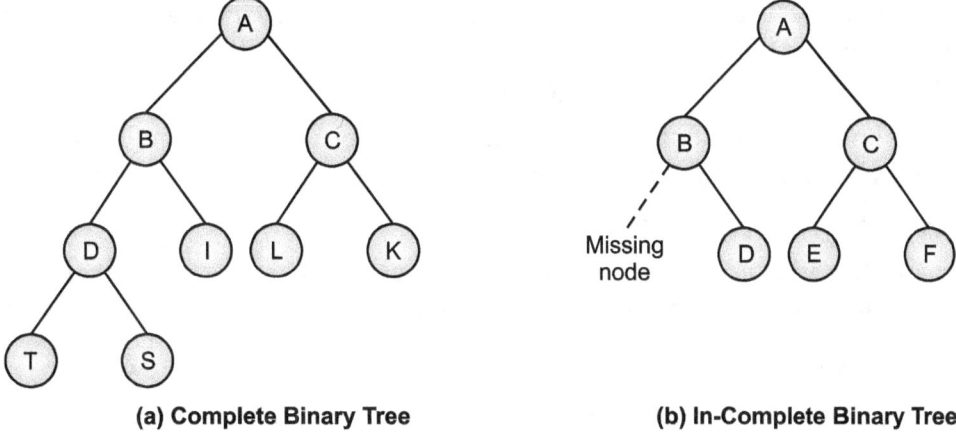

(a) Complete Binary Tree   **(b) In-Complete Binary Tree**

Fig. 5.36

- **Heap Property :** All nodes are either [greater than or equal to] or [less than or equal to] each of its children. If the parent nodes are greater than their children, heap is called a **Max-Heap**, and if the parent nodes are smalled than their child nodes, heap is called **Min-Heap**.

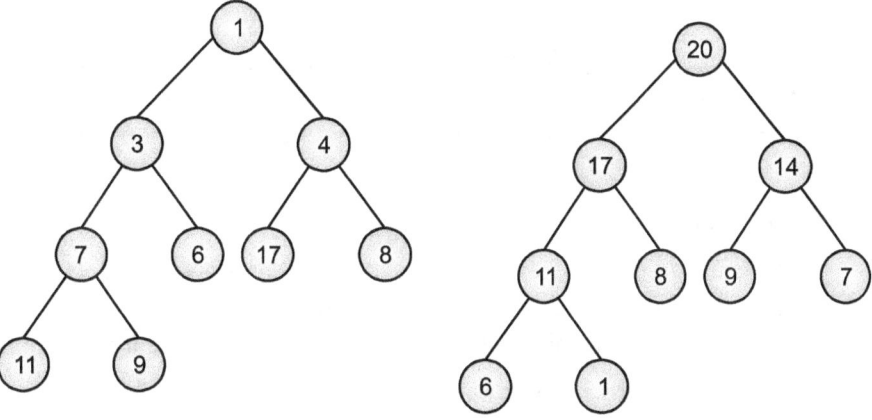

Fig. 5.37 : Min-Heap   **Fig. 5.38 : Max-Heap**

In min-heap, first element is the smallest. So when we want to sort a list in ascending order, we create a min-heap from that list, and picks the first element, as it is the smallest, then we repeat the process with remaining elements.

In max-heap, the first element is the largest, hence it is used when we need to sort a list in descending order.

How Heap Sort Works :

Initially on receiving an unsorted list, the first step in heap sort is to create a Heap data structure(Max-Heap or Min-Heap). Once heap is built, the first element of the Heap is either largest or smallest(depending upon Max-Heap or Min-Heap), so we put the first element of the heap in our array. Then we again make heap using the remaining elements, to again pick the first element of the heap and put it into the array. We keep on doing the same repeatedly untill we have the complete sorted list in our array.

Heap Sort is one of the best sorting methods being in-place and with no quadratic worst-case scenarios. Heap sort algorithm is divided into two basic parts :

*   Creating a Heap of the unsorted list.

*   Then a sorted array is created by repeatedly removing the largest/smallest element from the heap, and inserting it into the array. The heap is reconstructed after each removal.

5.4.1 Heap Sort

Heap sort is a comparison based sorting technique based on Binary Heap data structure. It is similar to selection sort where we first find the maximum element and place the maximum element at the end. We repeat the same process for remaining element.

What is Binary Heap?

Let us first define a Complete Binary Tree. A complete binary tree is a binary tree in which every level, except possibly the last, is completely filled, and all nodes are as far left as possible.

A Binary Heap is a Complete Binary Tree where items are stored in a special order such that value in a parent node is greater(or smaller) than the values in its two children nodes. The former is called as max heap and the latter is called min heap. The heap can be represented by binary tree or array.

Why array based representation for Binary Heap?

Since a Binary Heap is a Complete Binary Tree, it can be easily represented as array and array based representation is space efficient. If the parent node is stored at index I, the left child can be calculated by 2 * I + 1 and right child by 2 * I + 2 (assuming the indexing starts at 0).

Heap Sort Algorithm for Sorting in Increasing Order :

*   Build a max heap from the input data.

*   At this point, the largest item is stored at the root of the heap. Replace it with the last item of the heap followed by reducing the size of heap by 1. Finally, heapify the root of tree.

*   Repeat above steps until size of heap is greater than 1.

How to Build the Heap?

Heapify procedure can be applied to a node only if its children nodes are heapified. So the heapification must be performed in the bottom up order.

Lets understand with the help of an example :

Input data : 4, 10, 3, 5, 1

```
        4(0)
        / \
    10(1)  3(2)
        / \
     5(3)  1(4)
```

The numbers in bracket represent the indices in the array representation of data.

Applying heapify procedure to index 1 :

```
        4(0)
        / \
    10(1)  3(2)
        / \
     5(3)  1(4)
```

Applying heapify procedure to index 0 :

```
       10(0)
        / \
     5(1)  3(2)
        / \
     4(3)  1(4)
```

The heapify procedure calls itself recursively to build heap in top down manner.

```cpp
// C++ program for implementation of Heap Sort
#include <iostream>
usingnamespacestd;


// To heapify a subtree rooted with node i which is
// an index in arr[]. n is size of heap
voidheapify(intarr[], intn, inti)
{
    intlargest = i;  // Initialize largest as root
    intl = 2*i + 1;  // left = 2*i + 1
    intr = 2*i + 2;  // right = 2*i + 2


    // If left child is larger than root
    if(l < n &&arr[l] >arr[largest])
        largest = l;


    // If right child is larger than largest so far
    if(r < n &&arr[r] >arr[largest])
```

```
        largest = r;


    // If largest is not root
    if(largest != i)
    {
        swap(arr[i], arr[largest]);


        // Recursively heapify the affected sub-tree
        heapify(arr, n, largest);
    }
}


// main function to do heap sort
voidheapSort(intarr[], intn)
{
    // Build heap (rearrange array)
    for(inti = n / 2 - 1; i>= 0; i--)
        heapify(arr, n, i);


    // One by one extract an element from heap
    for(inti=n-1; i>=0; i--)
    {
        // Move current root to end
        swap(arr[0], arr[i]);


        // call max heapify on the reduced heap
        heapify(arr, i, 0);
    }
}


/* A utility function to print array of size n */
```

```
voidprintArray(intarr[], intn)
{
    for(inti=0; i<n; ++i)
        cout<<arr[i] << " ";
    cout<< "\n";
}


// Driver program
intmain()
{
    intarr[] = {12, 11, 13, 5, 6, 7};
    intn = sizeof(arr)/sizeof(arr[0]);


    heapSort(arr, n);


    cout<< "Sorted array is \n";
    printArray(arr, n);
}
```

Output :

Sorted array is

5 6 7 11 12 13

Notes :

Heap sort is an in-place algorithm. Its typical implementation is not stable, but can be made stable

Time Complexity : Time complexity of heapify is O(Logn). Time complexity of createAndBuildHeap() is O(n) and overall time complexity of Heap Sort is O(nLogn).

5.4.2 Min Max Heap

A binary heap is a heap data structure created using a binary tree.

Binary tree has two rules :

- Binary Heap has to be complete binary tree at all levels except the last level. This is called **shape property**.

- All nodes are either greater than equal to (**Max-Heap**) or less than equal to (**Min-Heap**) to each of its child nodes. This is called **heap property**.

Implementation :

- Use array to store the data.
- Start storing from index 1, not 0.
- For any given node at position i :
- Its **Left Child** is at **[2*i]** if available.
- Its **Right Child** is at **[2*i+1]** if available.
- Its **Parent Node** is at **[i/2]** if available.

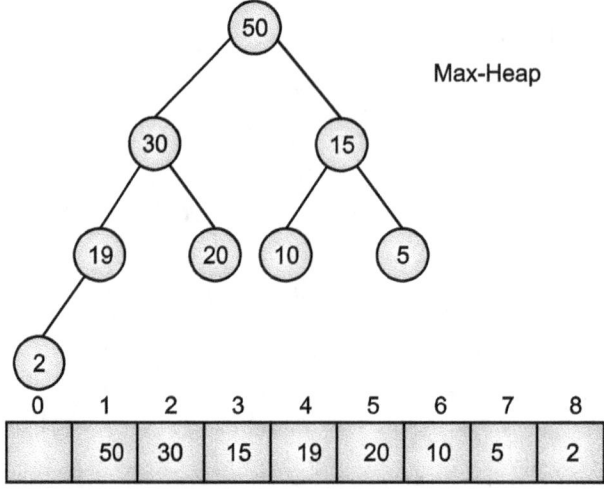

0	1	2	3	4	5	6	7	8
	50	30	15	19	20	10	5	2

For node at i : Left child will be 2i right child will be at 2i + 1 and parent node will be at [i/2].

Fig. 5.39 : Max-Heap

0	1	2	3	4	5	6	7	8
	1	2	3	6	9	5	10	14

For node at i : Left child will be 2i right child will be at 2i + 1 and parent node will be at [i/2].

Fig. 5.40 : Min-Heap

Heap Majorly has 3 operations :
- Insert Operation
- Delete Operation
- Extract-Min (OR Extract-Max)

(a) Insert Operation :
- Add the element at the bottom leaf of the Heap.
- Perform the Bubble-Up operation.
- All Insert Operations must perform the **bubble-up** operation(**it is also called as up-heap, percolate-up, sift-up, trickle-up, heapify-up, or cascade-up**)

Bubble-up Operation :
- If inserted element is smaller than its parent node in case of Min-Heap OR greater than its parent node in case of Max-Heap, swap the element with its parent.
- Keep repeating the above step, if node reaches its correct position, STOP.

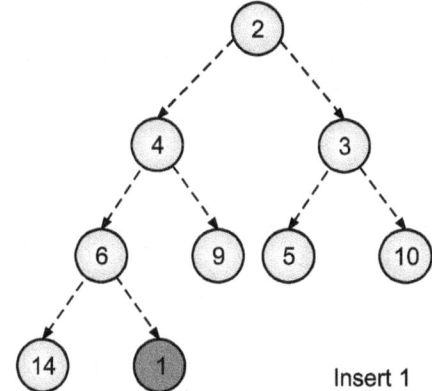

Fig. 5.41 : Insert() — Bubble-up Min-Heap

(b) Extract-Min OR Extract-Max Operation :
- Take out the element from the root.(it will be minimum in case of Min-Heap and maximum in case of Max-Heap).
- Take out the last element from the last level from the heap and replace the root with the element.
- Perform **Sink-Down**
- All delete operation must perform Sink-Down Operation (also known as bubble-down, percolate-down, sift-down, trickle down, heapify-down, cascade-down).

Sink-Down Operation :
- If replaced element is greater than any of its child node in case of Min-Heap OR smaller than any if its child node in case of Max-Heap, swap the element with its smallest child(Min-Heap) or with its greatest child(Max-Heap).
- Keep repeating the above step, if node reaches its correct position, STOP.

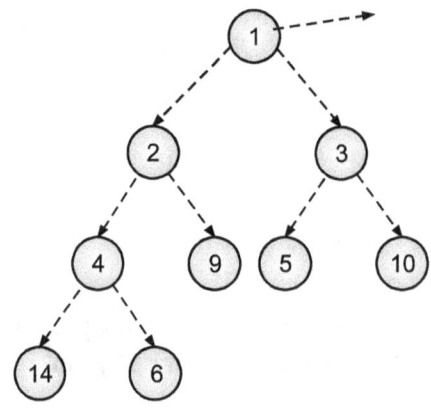

Fig. 5.42 : Delete or extract min from heap

(c) Delete Operation :

- Find the index for the element to be deleted.

- Take out the last element from the last level from the heap and replace the index with this element .

- Perform **Sink-Down**

Time and Space Complexity :

Space	O(n)
Search	O(n)
Insert	O(log n)
Delete	O(log n)

5.4.3 Applications of Heap

- Heap Data Structure is generally taught with Heapsort. Heapsort algorithm has limited uses because Quicksort is better in practice. Nevertheless, the Heap data structure itself is enormously used. Following are some uses other than Heapsort.

- Priority Queues : Priority queues can be efficiently implemented using Binary Heap because it supports insert(), delete() and extractmax(), decreaseKey() operations in O(logn) time. Binomoial Heap and Fibonacci Heap are variations of Binary Heap. These variations perform union also in O(logn) time which is a O(n) operation in Binary Heap. Heap Implemented priority queues are used in Graph algorithms like Prim's Algorithm and Dijkstra's algorithm.

- Order statistics : The Heap data structure can be used to efficiently find the kth smallest (or largest) element in an array.

SUMMARY

- The process of creating index is called indexing and the person who does it is called an indexer.

- A simple index is simply an array of (key, reference) pairs.

- Multi way search tree is generalized binary tree that can have more than two children's.

- B-tree is a self-balancing tree data structure that keeps data sorted and allows searches, sequential access, insertions, and deletions.

- A trie is a tree data structure that allows string with similar character prefixes to use the same prefix data and to store only the tails as separate data.

- AA tree is a variation of red black tree and a form of BST.

- A red–black tree is a kind of self-balancing binary search tree. Each node of the binary tree has an extra bit, and that bit is often interpreted as the color (red or black) of the node. These color bits are used to ensure the tree remains approximately balanced during insertions and deletions.

- In B+ tree, ach node of the tree contains an ordered list of keys and pointers to lower level nodes in the tree.

- Splay tree is a self balancing data structure where the last accessed key is always at root.

- ADT is a collection of data. The data can be Booleans, numbers, characters or other data structures.

EXERCISE

1. Insert the following keys to a 5-way B-tree :3, 7, 9, 23, 45, 1, 5, 14, 25, 24, 13, 11, 8, 19, 4, 31, 35, 56.

2. Explain indexing and indexing techniques

3. Explain B tree with example.

4. Explain insertion and deletion in B tree.

5. Explain splay tree rotations.

6. Explain the properties of red black tree.

7. Write a short note on :

   (a) K- Dimensional tree

   (b) AA tree

   (c) Trie tree

8. Explain set ADT operations.

9. What is heap? Explain heap sort.

10. Explain Applications of heap.

FILE ORGANIZATION

6.1 INTRODUCTION TO FILES

A file is a collection of records where each record consists of one or more fields. Files provide a mechanism for long term data storage in the computer. Hard disk, CD's, DVD's are generally used to store the files. All the data in the computer is stored in the form of files.

File organization can be defined as the method of storing data records in a file. The primary objective of file organization is to provide means for record retrieval and update.

The factors involved in selecting a particular file organization for uses are :

*   Economy of storage,
*   Ease of retrieval,
*   Convenience of update,
*   Reliability,
*   Security,
*   Integrity, and
*   Volume of transaction.

File management is one of the most visible services of an operating system. The operating system abstracts from physical properties of its storage devices to define a logical storage unit, the file. File is a collection of related information defined by its creator.

Following are the commonly used file types :

*   **Sequential Files :** In these files data records are stored in a specific sequence. Records are physically ordered according to ordering key or they can be stored in order of their arrival.
*   **Indexed Sequential Files :** An index is added to a sequential file to provide random access.
*   **Direct Access File :** This file is popularly known as a hashed file.
*   **Relative File :** Each record is stored at a fixed place in the file. Each record is associated with an integer key value, which is mapped to a fixed slot in a file.
*   **Index File :** Data records need not be sequenced. An index is maintained to improve access.

Many real life problems handle large volumes of data and in such situations we need to store this data on pen drive, hard disk etc. A file is a collection of related data, stored in a particular area on the disk. Programs can be designed to perform the read and write operations on these files. We prefer hard disk pen drives, CD's and DVD's (in short secondary memory devices) to store files because there are certain limitations of the main memory, which are given below.

Limitations of Main Memory :

- Limited in size
- Usually volatile.
- Convenient only for small amount of data but not feasible where large amount of data which is stored permanently and is in repeated use and repeated modifications.

Thus, we need a storage that is non-volatile and is unlimited, as secondary memory.

For example, Magnetic tape floppy disk, Hard disk etc. Hence, when we organize data in 'files' data structure, the data is permanent (non-volatile), which means data is residing on storage after execution of program is over.

6.2 PRIMITIVE FILE STREAM OPERATIONS AND IMPLEMEN-TATIONS IN C++

The I/O system of C++ contains a set of classes (such as fstream, ifstream and ofstream) that define the file handling methods. These classes are derived from fstreambase and from corresponding iostream class. These classes are designed to manage the disk files and are declared in fstream and therefore we must include this file in any program that uses file.

Input and output is initiated using the functions of the base classes istream and ostream.

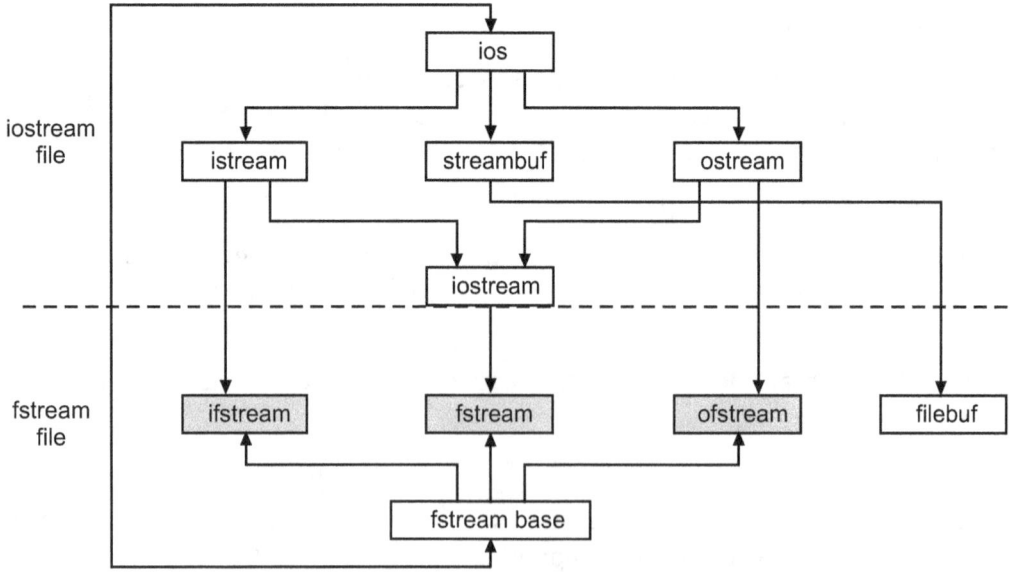

Fig. 6.1 : Stream classes for file operations

Class	Use	Contains Functions
fstreambase	Serves as base for fstream, ifstream and ofstream class.	Contains open() and close() functions
ifstream	Provides input (read) operations.	Contains open() with default input mode. Inherits get(), getline(), read(), seekg() and tellg() functions from istream.
ofstream	Provides output (write) operations.	Contains open() with default output mode. Inherits put(), seekp(), tellp() and write() functions from ostream.
fstream	Provides support for simultaneous input and output operations.	Contains open() with default input mode. Inherits all functions from istream and ostream classes through iostream.

6.3 PRIMITIVE FUNCTIONS IN C++ FOR FILES

1. **File Creation**
   - Basically three classes are used for file creation.
     - fstream class (used for reading as well as writing the data into the file).
     - ifstream class (used for reading the data from the file).
     - ofstream class (used for writing the data into the file).
   - Observe the following code snippets
     - Open the file for reading
       ```
       ifstream f_in;
       f_in.open("myfile.txt");
       ```
     - Open the file for writing
       ```
       ofstream f_out;
       f_out.open("myfile.txt");
       ```

The most important thing while creating the file is the mode in which we are opening the file.

File mode parameters are

Mode	Meaning
ios : :app	Append data at the end of file
ios : :ate	Go to end of file after opening
ios : :binary	Open file in Binary mode
ios : :in	Open file for reading
ios : :nocreate	Open fails if file does not exist
ios : :out	Open file for writing
ios : :trunk	Truncates file to zero length.

Opening Files Using open()

The function open() can be used to open the file. In such cases, we may need to create a stream object and use it to open the file. This is done as follows :

file-stream-class stream-object;

stream-object.open("filename", mode);

The second argument which is called as mode, specifies the purpose for which the file opened. Above table gives information about various modes in which we can open the file.

Example :

ofstream outfile;

outfile.open("data.txt",ios : :out);

. . . .

. . . .

ifstream infile;

infile.open("data1.txt",ios : :in);

// for closing the opened files use following syntaxes

outfile.close();

infile.close();

Detecting end-of-file

Detection of end-of-file condition is necessary for preventing any further attempt to read data from the file. This is illustrated using the following statement.

    while(f_in)

an ifstream object, such as f_in, returns a value of 0 if any error occurs in the file operation including end-of-file condition. Thus, while loop terminates when file returns a value zero on reaching the end-of-file condition.

There is one more approach to detect end-of-file condition, this approach we have used in the following program.

while(!f_in.eof())

{

//Read the file content

}

eof() is a function of ios class. It returns non-zero value if end-of-file condition is encountered and a zero otherwise.

Reading from a File :

```
#include<iostream.h>
#include<fstream.h>
#include<conio.h>
void main()
{
    ifstream f_in;
    char str[10];

    f_in.open("myfile.txt",ios : :in);
    while(!f_in.eof())
    {
        f_in>>str;
        cout<<"\n"<<str;
    }
    f_in.close();
    getch();
}
```

Writing into a File :

```
#include<iostream.h>
#include<fstream.h>
#include<conio.h>
void main()
{
    ofstream f_out;
    char str[10]="awaneesh";
    f_out.open("myfile.txt",ios : :out);
    f_out<<str;
    f_out.close();
    getch();
}
```

Reading and Writing into a File :

```
#include<iostream.h>
#include<fstream.h>
#include<conio.h>

void main()
{
    fstream f;
    char str[10]="awaneesh",str1[20];

    f.open("myfile.txt",ios : :in|ios : :out);
    f<<str;

    f.seekg(0,ios : :beg);

    f>>str1;
    cout<<str1;

    f.close();
    getch();
}
```

Sample File Program in C++ :

```
#include<iostream.h>
#include<stdio.h>
#include<stdlib.h>
#include<fstream.h>
#include<string.h>

// class for storing passenger record
class passenger
```

```
{
    char f_name[15],l_name[15];
   int age;
 public :
   void get_data();
   void put_data();
};

class PassengerFile
{
  private :
    char fname[12];
  public :
    void getfile();
  void create();
  void displayall();
};

// Function for getting passenger data

void passenger : : get_data()
{
    cout<<endl<<"Enter First name   : ";
    cin>>f_name;
    cout<<endl<<"Enter Last name    : ";
    cin>>l_name;
    cout<<endl<<"age : ";
    cin>>age;
}
// Function for displaying passenger data
```

```cpp
void passenger : : put_data()
{
    cout<<endl << " \t" << f_name << "\t" << l_name  << "\t" << age;
}


void PassengerFile : :getfile()
{
    cout << "\n Enter filename : " ;
    cin >> fname;
}
void PassengerFile : :create()
{
    fstream file;
    passenger p;

    int n,i;
    file.open(fname,ios : :out|ios : :binary );
    cout<<"\nHow many records do you want to enter ?";
    cin>>n;
    for(i=0;i<n;i++)
    {
        p.get_data();
        file.write((char *) & p,sizeof(p));
        flushall();
    }
    file.close();
}


void PassengerFile : :displayall()
{
```

```
    passenger p;                                          // object for passenger
    fstream file;
    file.open(fname, ios : :in );
    if(file.bad())
        cout<<"\nOpening error .....";
    else
    {
        cout << "\nid   Fname   Lname  Age \n";
        while(!file.eof())
        {
            file.read((char *) &p,sizeof (p));
            if (!file.eof())
            {
                        p.put_data();
            }
        }
        file.close();
        }


}

void main()
{
    class PassengerFile pfile;
    pfile.getfile();
    pfile.create();
    pfile.displayall();
}
```

Error Handling Functions :

1. eof() : returns true if end-of-file is encountered while reading the file, otherwise it returns false.
2. fail() : returns true when the input or output operation has failed.

Functions for Manipulation of File Pointers :

There are various functions that can be used to move the file pointer to the desired position. The file stream classes uses the following functions :

Function Name	Used for
seekg()	Moves get pointer (input) to the specific location.
seekp()	Moves put pointer (output) to the specific location.
tellg()	Gives the current position of the get pointer
tellp()	Gives the current position of the put pointer

For Example :

> infile.seekg(20);

moves the file pointer to byte no. 20. Remember the bytes in the file are numbered from zero. Therefore file pointer will actually point to byte no. 21.

Consider the following statements :

ofstream fileout;

fileout.open("awaneesh",ios : :app);

int p=fileout.tellp();

On execution of these statements, the output pointer is moved to the end of file "awaneesh" and the value of p will represent the no. of bytes present in the file.

Specifying the offsets :

seekg() and seekp() functions can be used with two arguments as follows :

seekg(offset, refposition);

seekp(offset, refposition);

The parameter *offset* represents the number of bytes the file pointer is to be moved from the location specified by parameter *refposition*. The *refposition* takes one of the following three constants defined in **ios** class :

1. ios : :beg   start of the file

2. ios : :cur   current position of the pointer

3. ios : :end   end of the file

seekg() function moves the associated file's 'get' pointer while the seekp() function moves the associated files 'put' pointer.

6.4 COMPARISON BETWEEN TEXT FILE AND BINARY FILE

Text File	Binary File
• The text file contains the data in the form of ASCII characters.	• The binary file consists of the data in binary form.
• The text file cannot store the graphical data. It can store only text.	• The binary file can store the data such as text, graphics, image, and sound.
• Text files can directly read and interpreted easily through editors.	• The binary files cannot be read directly. With the help of some tools the binary file can be read.
• Integer or real number requires more storage area when stored in text format.	• Binary file is more compact and takes less storage area.

6.5 SEQUENTIAL FILE ORGANIZATION

The sequential file is organized by appending record to the file in the order, as they were entered.

Thus the record found in the first position is the 'oldest' record and the last record in the file is the one most recently added.

• Records in the files are read or written sequentially.

• Records are of fixed length.

• Searching time is more because records are accessed sequentially from beginning.

• If we want to add a record, it can be always added at end of the file.

• Position of each field in the record and length of the field is fixed.

Drawbacks of Sequential File Organization :

• Insertion and deletion of records in between requires moving a large amount of data to create space for the new record.

• Accessing any record requires going through all the preceding records sequentially, which is time consuming operation. Therefore searching a record takes more time.

• Needs to reorganize the file time to time whenever record is added or deleted.

Advantages of Sequential File over Unordered Files :

• Reading of records in order of ordering key is extremely efficient.

• Finding the next record in order of the ordering key usually does not require additional block access. Next record may be found in the same block.

Sequential File Operations :

1. Creation
2. Insert record
3. Display record
4. Delete record
5. Update record
6. Searching of a record
7. Packing.

The structure used to store data in the file is given below :

```
struct student
{
    int roll;
    char name[20];
};
```

The Class Used to Hold Various Functions of Sequential File.

```
class database
{
    struct student st;
    public :
        void insert_data();
        void read_data();
        void search_data();
        void update_data();
        void delete_data();
        void sort_data();
};
```

1. **File Creation and Inserting a Record in it**
   - Open the binary file in app mode (if file does not exists, it is created). Append mode will preserve the old content of the file and will help to write new content at the end of the file.
     ```
     ofstream file;
     file.open("database.txt",ios : :binary| ios : :out| ios : :app);
     ```

- Accept the new record from the user.

    cout<<"Enter the roll and name of the student";

    cin>>st.roll>>st.name;

- Write the record in the file.

    file.write((char*)&st,sizeof(struct student));

- Close the file after writing the record.

    file.close();

Function for Writing Data into the File :

```
void database : :insert_data()
{

    ofstream file;
    file.open("database.txt",ios : :binary|ios : :out|ios : :app);


    cout<<"Enter the roll and name of the student";
    cin>>st.roll>>st.name;


    file.write((char*)&st,sizeof(struct student));
    file.close();

}
```

2. **Displaying file content**
   - Open the binary file in read mode.

       ```
       ifstream file;
       file.open("database.txt",ios : :binary|ios : :in);
       ```
   - Start reading the content of the file till file end encounters.

       ```
       file.read((char*)&st,sizeof(st));
       ```

```
while(!file.eof())
    {
    cout<<"\n"<<st.roll<<"\t"<<st.name;
    file.read((char*)&st,sizeof(st));
}
    file.close();
```

Function for Displaying File :

```
void database : :read_data()
{
    struct student st;

    ifstream file;
    file.open("database.txt",ios : :binary|ios : :in);

    file.read((char*)&st,sizeof(st));
    while(!file.eof())
    {
        cout<<"\n"<<st.roll<<"\t"<<st.name;
        file.read((char*)&st,sizeof(st));
    }
    file.close();
}
```

3. **Deleting Record from the File**
   - Accept the roll number of the student whose record you want to delete.

     ```
     cout<<"\nEnter the roll no. of the record that you want to delete :";
     cin>>roll_number;
     ```
   - Open "database.txt" file in read mode and "db1.txt" file in write mode.

     ```
     file.open("database.txt",ios : :binary| ios : :in);

     ofile.open("db1.txt",ios : :binary| ios : :out| ios : :trunc);
     ```
   - Read the content from database.txt, if the roll number of the record is not matching with the roll number of that record which we want to delete, then copy the record into db1.txt, otherwise do not copy the record into db1.txt.
   - So at the end db1.txt will hold all the record except the record that we want to delete.
   - Now delete database.txt file.

     ```
     remove("database.txt");
     ```
   - Rename db1.txt into database.txt.

     ```
     rename("db1.txt","database.txt");
     ```
   - Now the new database.txt file will not contain the record that we want to delete.

Function for Deleting Record from the File.

```
void database : :delete_data()
{
    struct student st;
    int roll_number,flag=0,flag1=0;
    ifstream file;
    ofstream ofile;

    cout<<"\nEnter the roll no. of the record that you want to delete :";
    cin>>roll_number;

    file.open("database.txt",ios : :binary|ios : :in);
    ofile.open("db1.txt",ios : :binary|ios : :out|ios : :trunc);

    file.read((char*)&st,sizeof(st));

    while(!file.eof())
    {
        if(roll_number==st.roll)
        {
            cout<<"\nRECORD FOUND!!!";
            flag=1;flag1=1;
        }
        if(flag==0)
        {
            ofile.write((char*)&st,sizeof(st));
        }
        flag=0;
        file.read((char*)&st,sizeof(st));
    }
```

```
    if(flag1==0)
    {
        cout<<"\nRECORD NOT FOUND!!!\n";
    }
    cout<<"\n";
    remove("database.txt");
    rename("db1.txt","database.txt");


    file.close();
}
```

4. **Searching Record from the File**
   - Accept the roll number of the student whose record you want to delete.
     ```
     cout<<"\nEnter the roll no. of the record that you want to delete :";
     cin>>roll_number;
     ```
   - Open database.txt file. Read the content from the file sequentially. Compare the accepted roll number with the roll number of the record read from the file. It match found, record exists, then stop. If file end encounters then print "record not found".

Function for Searching Record

```
void database : :search_data()
{
    struct student st;
    int roll_number,flag=0;
    ifstream file;


    cout<<"\nEnter the roll no. of the record that you want to search :";
    cin>>roll_number;


    file.open("database.txt",ios : :binary|ios : :in);
    file.read((char*)&st,sizeof(st));


    while(!file.eof())
    {
```

```
        if(roll_number==st.roll)
        {
            cout<<"\nRECORD FOUND!!!";
            cout<<"\n"<<st.roll<<"\t"<<st.name;
            flag=1;
            break;
        }
        file.read((char*)&st,sizeof(st));
    }
    if(flag==0)
    {
        cout<<"\nRECORD NOT FOUND!!!\n";
    }
    file.close();
}
```

5. **Updating Record from the File**
   - Record updation process is nearly same as that of the process of record deletion except one thing, whenever the record is found in the file, the new values for that record are taken from the user and then the record is written into db1.txt file.
   - Accept the roll number of the student whose record you want to modify/update.

     ```
     cout<<"\nEnter the roll no. of the record that you want to delete :";
     cin>>roll_number;
     ```
   - Open "database.txt" file in read mode and "db1.txt" file in write mode.

     ```
     file.open("database.txt",ios : :binary|ios : :in);

     ofile.open("db1.txt",ios : :binary|ios : :out|ios : :trunc);
     ```
   - Read the content from database.txt, if the roll number of the record is not matching with the roll number of that record which we want to modify, then copy the record into db1.txt, otherwise accept the new values for that record and then copy the new record into db1.txt.
   - At the end db1.txt will hold all the record as it is with the record which we want to modify with the modified values.
   - Now delete database.txt file.

     ```
     remove("database.txt");
     ```
   - Rename db1.txt into database.txt.

     ```
     rename("db1.txt","database.txt");
     ```

- Now the new database.txt file will not contain the record that we want to delete.

```
void database : :update_data()
{
    struct student st;
    int roll_number,flag=0,flag1=0;
    ifstream file;
    ofstream ofile;

    cout<<"\nEnter the roll no. of the record that you want to search :";
    cin>>roll_number;
    file.open("database.txt",ios : :binary|ios : :in);
    ofile.open("db1.txt",ios : :binary|ios : :out|ios : :trunc);

    file.read((char*)&st,sizeof(st));
    while(!file.eof())
    {
        if(roll_number==st.roll)
        {
            cout<<"\nRECORD FOUND!!!";
            cout<<"\nEnter new name of the student";
            cin>>st.name;
            ofile.write((char*)&st,sizeof(st));
            flag=1;flag1=1;
        }
        if(flag==0)
        {
            ofile.write((char*)&st,sizeof(st));
        }
        flag=0;
        file.read((char*)&st,sizeof(st));
```

```
    }
    if(flag1==0)
    {
        cout<<"\nRECORD NOT FOUND!!!\n";
    }
    remove("database.txt");
    rename("db1.txt","database.txt");
    file.close();
}
```

/* Program of Sequential File in C++ */

```cpp
#include<iostream.h>
#include<stdio.h>
#include<conio.h>
#include<fstream.h>
#include<process.h>

struct student
{
    int roll;
    char name[20];
};

class database
{
    struct student st;
    public :
        void insert_data();
        void read_data();
        void search_data();
        void update_data();
```

```
        void delete_data();
        void sort_data();
};
void database : :sort_data()
{

    ifstream file;
    ofstream out;
    struct student st[50],temp;
    int i=0,n,j;


    file.open("database.txt",ios : :binary|ios : :in);
    file.read((char*)&st[i],sizeof(st[i]));          //Important


    while(!file.eof())
    {
        i++;
        file.read((char*)&st[i],sizeof(st[i]));
    }
    file.close();


    n=i;


    for(i=0;i<=n;i++)
    {
        for(j=i+1;j<=n;j++)
        {
            if(st[i].roll>st[j].roll)
            {
                        temp=st[i];
                        st[i]=st[j];
```

```
                        st[j]=temp;
            }
        }
    }
    out.open("database.txt",ios : :binary|ios : :trunc|ios : :out);
    for(i=0;i<n;i++)
    {
        out.write((char*)&st[i],sizeof(struct student));
    }
    out.close();

}

void database : :read_data()
{
    struct student st;
    ifstream file;

    file.open("database.txt",ios : :binary|ios : :in);

    file.read((char*)&st,sizeof(st));    //Important

    while(!file.eof())
    {
        cout<<"\n"<<st.roll<<"\t"<<st.name;
        file.read((char*)&st,sizeof(st));
    }

    cout<<"\n";
```

```
        file.close();
}

void database : :update_data()
{
    struct student st;
    int roll_number,flag=0,flag1=0;
    ifstream file;
    ofstream ofile;

    cout<<"\nEnter the roll no. of the record that you want to search :";
    cin>>roll_number;

    file.open("database.txt",ios : :binary|ios : :in);
    ofile.open("db1.txt",ios : :binary|ios : :out|ios : :trunc);

    file.read((char*)&st,sizeof(st));    //Important

    while(!file.eof())
    {
        if(roll_number==st.roll)
        {
            cout<<"\nRECORD FOUND!!!";
            cout<<"\nEnter new name of the student";
            cin>>st.name;
            ofile.write((char*)&st,sizeof(st));
            flag=1;flag1=1;
        }
        if(flag==0)
        {
```

```
            ofile.write((char*)&st,sizeof(st));
        }
        flag=0;
        file.read((char*)&st,sizeof(st));
    }
    if(flag1==0)
    {
        cout<<"\nRECORD NOT FOUND!!!\n";
    }
    cout<<"\n";
    remove("database.txt");
    rename("db1.txt","database.txt");

    file.close();
}

void database : :delete_data()
{
    struct student st;
    int roll_number,flag=0,flag1=0;
    ifstream file;
    ofstream ofile;

    cout<<"\nEnter the roll no. of the record that you want to search :";
    cin>>roll_number;

    file.open("database.txt",ios : :binary|ios : :in);
    ofile.open("db1.txt",ios : :binary|ios : :out|ios : :trunc);

    file.read((char*)&st,sizeof(st));    //Important
```

```cpp
    while(!file.eof())
    {
        if(roll_number==st.roll)
        {
            cout<<"\nRECORD FOUND!!!";
            flag=1;flag1=1;
        }
        if(flag==0)
        {
            ofile.write((char*)&st,sizeof(st));
        }
        flag=0;
        file.read((char*)&st,sizeof(st));
    }
    if(flag1==0)
    {
        cout<<"\nRECORD NOT FOUND!!!\n";
    }
    cout<<"\n";
    remove("database.txt");
    rename("db1.txt","database.txt");

    file.close();
}

void database : :search_data()
{
    struct student st;
    int roll_number,flag=0;
```

```cpp
ifstream file;

cout<<"\nEnter the roll no. of the record that you want to search :";
cin>>roll_number;

file.open("database.txt",ios : :binary|ios : :in);

file.read((char*)&st,sizeof(st));    //Important

while(!file.eof())
{
    if(roll_number==st.roll)
    {
        cout<<"\nRECORD FOUND!!!";
        cout<<"\n"<<st.roll<<"\t"<<st.name;
        flag=1;
        break;
    }
    file.read((char*)&st,sizeof(st));
}
if(flag==0)
{
    cout<<"\nRECORD NOT FOUND!!!\n";
}

cout<<"\n";

file.close();
}
```

```
void database : :insert_data()
{
    ofstream file;

    file.open("database.txt",ios : :binary|ios : :out|ios : :app);

    cout<<"Enter the roll and name of the student";
    cin>>st.roll>>st.name;


    file.write((char*)&st,sizeof(struct student));
    file.close();
}

void main()
{
    database obj;
    int choice;

    clrscr();

    while(1)
    {
        cout<<"\n1.Insert Record";
        cout<<"\n2.Search Record";
        cout<<"\n3.Update Record";
        cout<<"\n4.Delete Record";
        cout<<"\n5.Sort Records";
        cout<<"\n6.Display Records";
        cout<<"\n7.Quit";
```

```cpp
            cout<<"\nEnter your choice ";
            cin>>choice;
            switch(choice)
            {
                case 1 :
                        obj.insert_data();
                                break;
                case 2 :
                        obj.search_data();
                                break;
                case 3 :
                        obj.update_data();
                                break;
                case 4 :
                        obj.delete_data();
                                break;
                case 5 :
                        obj.sort_data();
                                break;
                case 6 :
                        obj.read_data();
                                break;
                case 7 :
                                exit(0);
            }
        }

    getch();
}
```

6.6 DIRECT ACCESS FILE ORGANIZATION

A direct access file allows arbitrary blocks to be read or written. Thus we may read block 14, then block 53, and then we can write block 7. There is no restriction on the order of reading or writing for a direct access file.

Direct access files are of great use for immediate access to large amounts of information. They are often used in accessing large databases. When a query concerning a particular subject arrives, we compute which block contains the answer and then read that block directly to provide the desired information.

Random access file is a file in which records are accessed directly by referring to address where it is placed in a file.

Hash function is used in direct access file for accessing the record directly.

Hash function generates a natural address (whose range lies between 1 to file size) from the primary key of the record.

> Example, MOD (Primary key MOD N)

A good hashing function must minimize creation of synonyms. Synonym is defined as key which generates same address as address generated by another different key.

Primitive Operations :

The primitive operations for the direct access file are.

- **Open :** It opens the file and set currency pointer to immediately before the first record.
- **Read-next :** Returns the next record to user. If no records present, then EOF (end of file) condition will be set.
- **Read-Direct :** Set currency pointer to specific position and gets the record for the user. If the slot is empty or out of range then it gives error.
- **Write-Direct :** Currency pointer is set to specific position and write the record to file at that position. If the slot is out of range then it gives error.
- **Update :** Current record is written at the same position with updated values.
- **Close :** This will terminates the access of the file.
- **EOF :** If end of file condition occurs it returns true otherwise it returns false.

Program of Direct Access File Using C++

```
#include<iostream.h>
#include<string.h>
#include<conio.h>
#include<fstream.h>
```

```
#include<process.h>
#include<math.h>
#define MAX 15
class employee
{
    public :
            char name[MAX];
            int empid;
            int chain;
            int delflag ;
};


class hashfile
{
    fstream hfile;
    public :
        hashfile();
        int hash(int x) { return x %  10 ; }
        void insert();
        void search();
        void display();
};


// function to initialize empty file
hashfile : :hashfile()
{
     int i;
        employee rec2;
        fstream iofile;
        iofile.open("hfile.dat",ios : :out|ios : :binary);
```

```
        strcpy(rec2.name,"\0");
        rec2.chain=-1;
        rec2.delflag=0;


        for(i=0;i<10;i++)
        {
            rec2.empid=0;
            iofile.write((char*)&rec2,sizeof(rec2));
        }


        iofile.close();
}


// function to insert a record in hash file
void hashfile : :insert()
{
        int i,flag=0,pos,cnt=0;
        long temp,start,size;
        fstream iofile;
        employee insertrec,rec3,rec;

        cout<<"Enter name";
        cin>>insertrec.name;

        cout<<"Enter no of empid";
        cin>>insertrec.empid;

        insertrec.chain=-1;
        insertrec.delflag=0;
```

```
size=sizeof(insertrec);
pos=hash(insertrec.empid);

iofile.open("hfile.dat",ios : : in | ios : : out | ios : : binary);
iofile.seekg(0);

temp=pos*sizeof(insertrec);
iofile.seekg(temp);              // move to position given by hash function

flag=0;
iofile.read((char*) &rec3,sizeof(rec3));

if(rec3.empid==0)             // slot is empty
{
    flag=1;
    temp=pos*sizeof(rec3);
    iofile.seekp(temp);   // move to position given by hash function
    iofile.write ((char*) &insertrec,sizeof(insertrec));
    return;
}
else                                              // slot is not empty
{
    if (hash(rec3.empid)==hash(insertrec.empid))
    {
        while (rec3.chain!=-1)
                        {
                          iofile.seekg(rec3.chain * sizeof (rec3));
                          pos=rec3.chain;
                          iofile.read((char*) &rec3,sizeof(rec3));
                        }
```

```
                              flag = 2;
         }


         int nextpos=pos;
         trec=rec3;


         while(iofile.read((char*) &rec3,sizeof(rec3)))
                                                  // find next empty position
         {
                 if(rec3.empid==0)                              // empty slot
                         {
                                 iofile.seekp((nextpos+1) * sizeof(rec3));
                 // move to postion given by hash function
                                 iofile.write ((char*) &insertrec,sizeof(insertrec));
                                 if (flag==2)
                                   {
                                       iofile.seekp(pos * sizeof (rec3));
                                       trec.chain=nextpos+1;
                                       iofile.write ((char*) &trec,sizeof(trec));
                                   }
                                 flag = 1;
                                 break;
                         }
             nextpos++;
         }
}

if(flag!=1)
{
    cout<<"Error this rec was not inserted";
```

```
        cout<<"The file is full after this index";


         getch();
        return;

    }


    getch();
    iofile.close();
}  // end if insert


// function to search a record of hash file

void hashfile : :search()
{
    int pos=0,t_empid;
    fstream iofile;
    employee rec1;

    cout<< "Enter the empid of the book to be searched.";
    cin>>t_empid;

    pos=hash(t_empid);  // get the position of search record

    iofile.open("hfile.dat",ios : :in|ios : :binary);
    iofile.seekg(0);
    iofile.seekg(pos*sizeof(rec1));

    while(iofile.read((char *)&rec1,sizeof(rec1)))              // read record at position
    {
        if(rec1.empid==t_empid)                                // found
```

```
        {
            cout<< " NAME "<<rec1.name<<" EMP. ID."<<rec1.empid;
            getch();
            iofile.close();
            return;
        }
        else
            if(hash(rec1.empid)==pos)   // if record is stored at position
            {
                    iofile.seekg(0);
                    if (rec1.chain!=-1)
                iofile.seekg(rec1.chain*sizeof(rec1)); // jump at position of chain
            }
    }

    cout<<" Error no such rec exist ";
    getch();
    iofile.close();
}

void hashfile : :display()
{
    int i=0;
    employee rec2;
    fstream iofile;

    cout<<"\n\nSERIAL\tEMPID\tNAME\tchain";
    iofile.open("hfile.dat",ios : : in | ios : : binary);

    while(iofile.read((char *)&rec2,sizeof(rec2)))
```

```
    {
        cout<<"\n\n"<<i++;
        cout<<"\t"<<rec2.empid;
        cout<<"\t"<<rec2.name;
        cout<<"\t"<<rec2.chain;
    }

    getch();
    iofile.close();
}

void main()
{
    int ch,pos;
    float flag=1.1;
    hashfile file1;

    do
    {
        cout<<" \n 1. Insert a rec ";
        cout<<" \n 2. Disp all rec ";
        cout<<" \n 3. Search a rec ";
        cout<<" \n 4. Exit ";
        cout<< "\n Enter choice : ";
        cin>>ch;

        switch(ch)
        {
            case 1 :
```

```
                                        file1.insert();
                                        break;
             case 2 :

                                        file1.display();
                                        break;
             case 3 :

                                        file1.search();
                                        break;
             case 4 :

                                        exit(0);

        }
    }while(ch!=4);
}
```

OUTPUT :

   1. Insert a rec

   2. Disp all rec

   3. Search a rec

   4. Exit

   Enter choice : 1

   Enter name : Mita

   Enter no of empid : 11

   1. Insert a rec

   2. Disp all rec

   3. Search a rec

   4. Exit

   Enter choice : 1

   Enter name : Ritesh

Enter no of empid : 22

1. Insert a rec
2. Disp all rec
3. Search a rec
4. Exit
Enter choice : 1
Enter name : Nilima
Enter no of empid : 33

1. Insert a rec
2. Disp all rec
3. Search a rec
4. Exit
Enter choice : 2

Serial	Id	Name	chain
0	0		-1
1	11	Mita	-1
2	22	Ritesh	-1
3	33	Nilima	-1
4	0		-1
5	0		-1
6	0		-1
7	0		-1
8	0		-1
9	0		-1

1. Insert a rec
2. Disp all rec
3. Search a rec

4. Exit

Enter choice : 1

Enter name : Adi

Enter no of empid : 41

1. Insert a rec

2. Disp all rec

3. Search a rec

4. Exit

Enter choice : 2

Serial	Id	Name	chain
0	0		-1
1	11	Mita	4
2	22	Ritesh	-1
3	33	Nilima	-1
4	41	Adi	-1
5	0		-1
6	0		-1
7	0		-1
8	0		-1
9	0		-1

1. Insert a rec

2. Disp all rec

3. Search a rec

4. Exit

Enter choice : 1

Enter name : Ekta

Enter no of empid : 44

1. Insert a rec

2. Disp all rec

3. Search a rec

4. Exit

Enter choice : 2

Serial	Id	Name	chain
0	0		-1
1	11	Mita	4
2	22	Ritesh	-1
3	33	Nilima	-1
4	41	Adi	-1
5	44	Ekta	-1
6	0		-1
7	0		-1
8	0		-1
9	0		-1

1. Insert a rec

2. Disp all rec

3. Search a rec

4. Exit

Enter choice : 3

Enter the empid of the book to be searched : 44

NAME Ekta EMP. ID.44

1. Insert a rec

2. Disp all rec

3. Search a rec

4. Exit

Enter choice : 3

Enter the empid of the book to be searched : 41

NAME Adi EMP. ID.41

1. Insert a rec

2. Disp all rec

3. Search a rec

4. Exit

Enter choice : 4

6.7 INDEX SEQUENTIAL FILE ORGANIZATION

What is Index?

Index is a data structure that allows locating a particular record in a file more quickly. e.g. Index in a book.

Indexing is used to speed up retrieval of records. Each record in the index file consists of two fields e.g. a key field and a pointer to the main file. To find a specific record for a given key value, index is searching for the given key value. Binary search can be used to search in index file. After getting the address of record from index file, the record in main file can be retrieved easily.

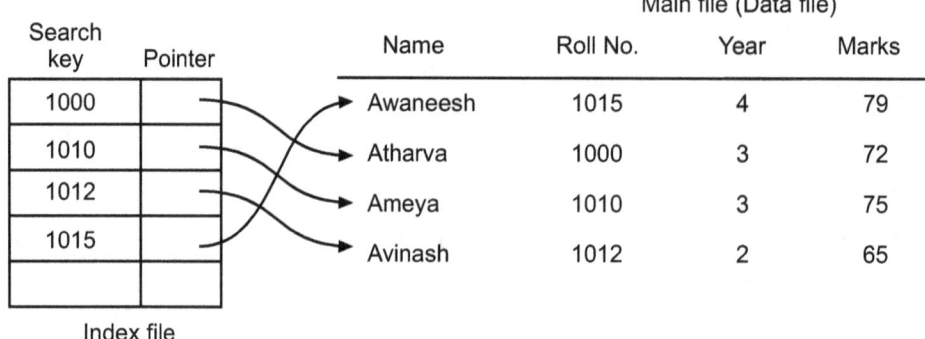

Fig. 6.2 : Index file

Types of Indexes :

1. Primary indexes

2. Secondary indexes

3. Clustering Indexes

6.7.1 Primary Indexes (Indexed Sequential File)

- Indexed sequential file is ordered as well as indexed. Records are organized by using primary key. For supporting random access to the records, an index is used.
- Index sequential file always maintain two major files : 1.Data file and 2.Index file. Number of records in the index file is always equal to number of blocks in the data file.
  (Note that one block may contain multiple records). See the following Example carefully to understand the concept of data file and index file.
- For creating primary index on the ordered file we can use emp_no as primary key.
- Every entry in the in the index file has two fields : emp_no and block pointer. Block pointer holds the address of the block. The total number of entries in the index is same as that of the blocks in the data file. Index file requires very few blocks as compared to the blocks of data file. Binary search on the index file require very few block accesses.

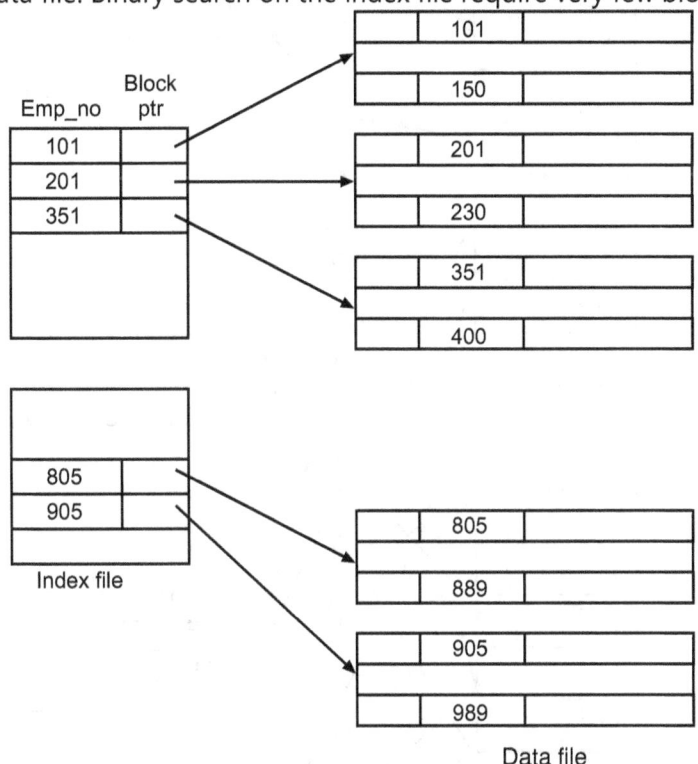

Fig. 6.3 : Primary index on ordering key field emp_no

6.7.2 Secondary Indexes (Simple Index File)

Sequential and indexed sequential files are not suitable for operations involving a search on a field other than ordering or hashed key.

If searching is required on various keys, secondary indexes on these files must be maintained.

A secondary index is an ordered file which contains following two fields :

- A block pointer
- Some non-ordering field of the data file.

The drawback of secondary index is, it requires more storage space and longer search time than that of primary index. There could be several secondary indexes for the same file. In secondary index file there is an entry for every record in the data file.

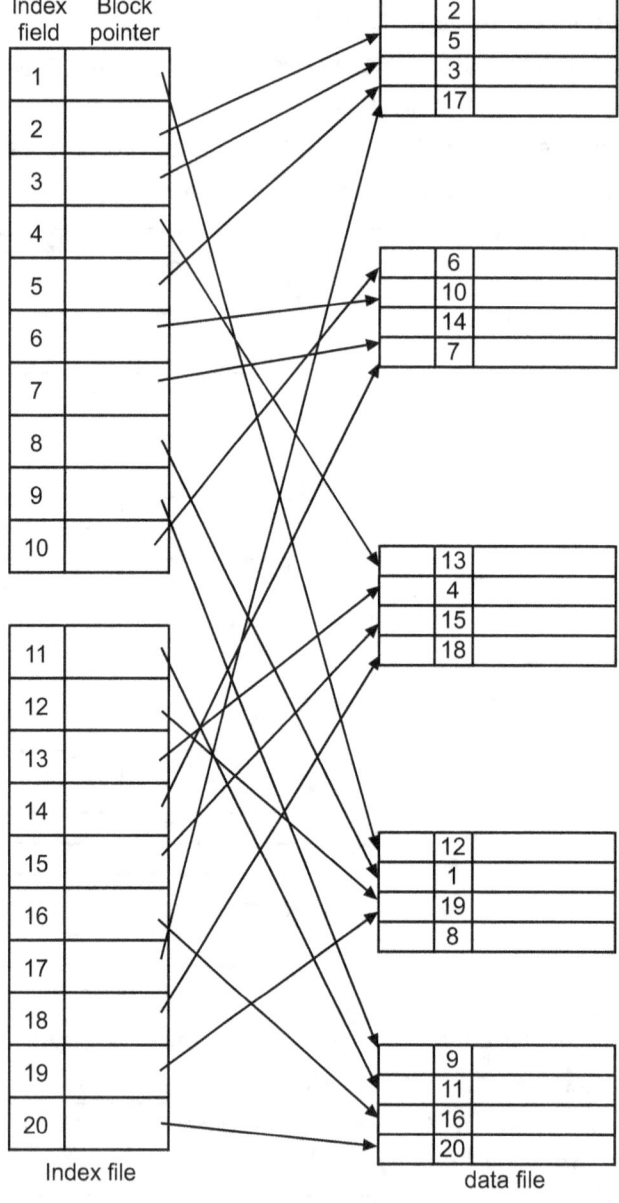

Fig. 6.4

Operations on Simple Index File :

```c
#include<stdio.h>
#include<conio.h>

struct itemrec
{
    int itemcode;
    char itemname[20];
    float cost;
};

struct indexrec
{
    int itemcode;
    int position;
    int flag;
};

void displayindexfile()
{
    FILE *indexfile;
    struct indexrec index;

    indexfile=fopen("index.dat","r");

    printf("\n Index file is ");
    printf("\n Itemcode \t Position \t Del Flag");

    while (!feof(indexfile))
    {
```

```
        fread(&index,sizeof(index),1,indexfile);
        if (feof(indexfile))
            break;
        if (index.flag==1)


            printf("\n\t%d\t\t%d\t\t%d ",index.itemcode,index.position,index.flag);
        else


    printf("\n\t%d\t\t%d\t\t%d?Deleted,index.itemcode,index.position,index.flag");
    }
}

insertrecord()
{
    struct itemrec item;
    struct indexrec index;
    FILE *indexfile, *itemfile;
    long position;

    printf("\n Enter itemcode : ");
    scanf("%d",&item.itemcode);
    printf("\n Enter itemname : ");
    scanf("%s",item.itemname);
    printf("\n Enter cost : ");
    scanf("%f",&item.cost);

    itemfile=fopen("item.dat","r");
    fseek(itemfile,0,SEEK_END);
    position=ftell(itemfile)/sizeof(item);
    fclose(itemfile);
```

```
    itemfile =fopen("item.dat","a");
    fwrite(&item,sizeof(item),1,itemfile);
    fclose(itemfile);


    indexfile=fopen("index.dat","a");
    index.itemcode = item.itemcode;
    index.position= position;
    index.flag = 1;
    fwrite(&index,sizeof(index),1,indexfile);
    fclose(indexfile);
}

void search()
{
    int searchitcode;
    struct itemrec item;
    struct indexrec index;
    FILE *indexfile, *itemfile;
    long position,found=0;

    printf("\n Enter itemcode to be searched ");
    scanf ("%d",&searchitcode);

    indexfile=fopen("index.dat","r");
    while (!feof(indexfile))
    {
        fread(&index,sizeof(index),1,indexfile);

        if (index.itemcode==searchitcode&&index.flag==1)
        {
```

```
                found = 1;
                break;
            }
        }

    if (found==1)
    {
        itemfile=fopen("item.dat","r");
        fseek(itemfile,(index.position)*sizeof(item),0);
        fread(&item,sizeof(item),1,itemfile);

        printf("\n Item Record is ");
        printf("\nItemcode \t  Item name \t  Cost");
        printf("\n\t%d\t\t%s\t\t%f",item.itemcode,item.itemname,item.cost);
        fclose(itemfile);
    }
    else
        printf("\n Record not found ");

        fclose(indexfile);
}

void deleterecord()
{
    int searchitcode;
    struct indexrec index;
    FILE *indexfile;
    long position,found=0,c;

    printf("\n Enter itemcode to be deleted : ");
```

```
    scanf ("%d",&searchitcode);

  indexfile=fopen("index.dat","r+");
  c=0;
  while (!feof(indexfile))
  {
      fread(&index,sizeof(index),1,indexfile);
      if (index.itemcode==searchitcode&&index.flag==1)
      {
          found = 1;
          break;
      }
      c++;
  }

  if (found==1)
  {
      fseek(indexfile,c*sizeof(index),0);
      index.flag=0;              // Make a delete flag 0
      fwrite(&index,sizeof(index),1,indexfile);
  }
  else
      printf("\n Record not found");

  fclose(indexfile);
}

void main()
{
  int choice;
```

```
do
 {
    printf("\n 1. Insert \n 2. Search \n 3. Delete a record");
    printf("\n 4. Display Index file \n 5. Exit");
    printf("\n Enter choice : ");
    scanf("%d",&choice);
    switch(choice)
    {
      case 1 :
                    insertrecord();
                        break;
      case 2 :
                    search();
                        break;
      case 3 :
                    deleterecord();
                        break;
      case 4 :
                displayindexfile();
    }
 }
   while (choice<5);
}
```

6.7.3 Clustering Indexes

A data file can associate with at most one primary index plus several secondary indexes.

In this organization key searches are improved. The single-level indexing structure is the simplest one where a file, whose records are pairs, contains a key and pointer. This *pointer* is the position in the data file of the record with the given key.

This is how a key search is performed : The search key is compared with the index keys to find the highest index key coming in front of the search key, while a linear search is performed from the record that the index key points to, until the search key is matched or until the record pointed to by the next index entry is reached.

Hardware for Index-Sequential Organization is usually Disk-based, rather than tape. Records are physically ordered by primary key. And the index gives the physical location of each record. Records can be accessed sequentially or directly, via. the index. The index is stored in a file and read into memory at the point when the file is opened. Also, indexes must be maintained.

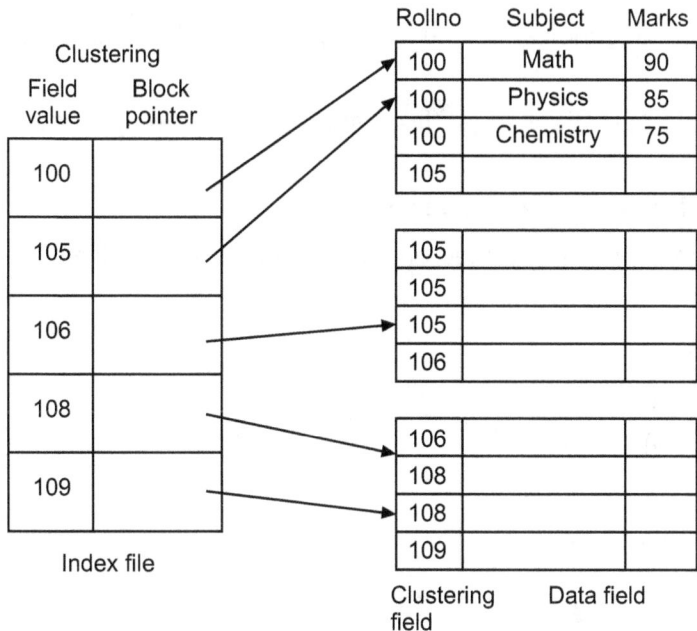

Fig. 6.5

Indexed Sequential Characteristics :

- Records are stored sequentially but the index file is prepared for accessing the record directly.
- Records can be accessed randomly.
- File has records and also the index.
- Magnetic tape is not suitable for index sequential storage.
- Index is address of physical storage of a record.
- When randomly very few records are required to be accessed then index sequential is better.
- Faster access method.
- Additional overhead is to maintain index.
- Index sequential files are popularly used in many applications like digital library.

Advantages :

- Accessing any record is more efficient than sequential file organization.

- Large amount of data can be stored using this type of file organization.

- It can handle variable length records.

- A key can be quickly searched in the index file using binary search.

Disadvantages :

- Often more than one indices are needed for the records which occupies large storage area.

- Insert and delete operations are difficult and time consuming as data records needs to be shifted.

Operations on an Indexed Sequential File :

Following operations can be performed on the indexed sequential file.

1. Create File
2. Delete Record
3. Search Record
4. Display Record/Records
5. Modify Record
6. Insert Record
7. Packing

A block is assumed to contain five records.

Index file is named as "index.dat".

Data file is named as "data.dat".

Program of Indexed Sequential File :

```
#include<iostream.h>
#include<conio.h>
#include<string.h>
#include<stdio.h>
#include<process.h>
#include<fstream.h>


struct student
{
```

```
    int rollno;
    char name[20];
    int status;
};

struct index
{
    int rollno,record_no;
};

class index_sequential
{
    char data1[30];
    char index1[30];

    fstream data, index;

    public :
    index_sequential(char*str1,char*str2)
    {
        strcpy(data1,str1);
        strcpy(index1,str2);
        data.open(data1,ios : :binary|ios : :in);
        index.open(index1,ios : :binary|ios : :in);
        if(data.fail())
            data.open(data1,ios : :binary|ios : :out);
        if(index.fail())
            index.open(index1,ios : :binary|ios : :out);
        data.close();
        index.close();
```

```
    }

    void display(int record_no)
    {
        student rec1;
        data.open(data1,ios : :binary|ios : :in|ios : :nocreate);
        data.seekg(record_no*sizeof(student),ios : :beg);
        data.read((char*)&rec1,sizeof(student));
        cout<<"\n"<<rec1.rollno<<" "<<rec1.name;
        data.close();
    }

    void create();
    void read();
    void readi();
    void insert(student rec1);
    void pack();
    void reindex();
    void update();
    int Delete(int rollno);
    int search(int rollno);
};
void main()
{

    class index_sequential object("master.dat","index.dat");
    int ch,rollno,recno;
    student rec1;
    clrscr();
```

```
while(1)
{
    cout<<"\n1.Print Record";
    cout<<"\n2.Insert Record";
    cout<<"\n3.Delete Record";
    cout<<"\n4.Update Record";
    cout<<"\n5.Search Record";
    cout<<"\n6.Pack";
    cout<<"\n7.Exit";
    cout<<"\nEnter ur choice : ";
    flushall();
    cin>>ch;

    switch(ch)
    {
        case 1 :
                    object.read();
                    object.readi();
                        break;
        case 2 :
                    cout<<"\nEnter the record to be inserted (roll and name)";
                    cin>>rec1.rollno>>rec1.name;
                object.insert(rec1);
                        break;
        case 3 :
                    cout<<"\nEnter roll no ";
                    cin>>rollno;
                    object.Delete(rollno);
                    break;
        case 4 :
```

```
                              object.update();
                              break;
              case 5 :
                              cout<<"\nEnter a roll no ";
                              cin>>rollno;
              recno=object.search(rollno);
                              if(recno>=0)
                                      {
                                        cout<<"\nRecord No : "<<recno;
                                        object.display(recno);
                                      }
                                  else
                                      {
                                        cout<<"\nRecord not found ";

                                      }
                              break;
              case 6 :
                              object.pack();
                              break;
              case 7 :
                                      exit(0);
          }


      }
}


void index_sequential : :read()
{
```

```
        student rec;

        int i=1,n;


        cout<<"\n-----------Content of DATA.DAT-----------------";

        data.open(data1,ios : :binary|ios : :in|ios : :nocreate);

        data.seekg(0,ios : :end);

        n=data.tellg()/sizeof(student);

        data.seekg(0,ios : :beg);


        for(i=1;i<=n;i++)

        {

            data.read((char*)&rec,sizeof(student));


            if(rec.status==0)

            cout<<"\n"<<i<<rec.rollno<<" "<<rec.name;

            else

            cout<<"-----Deleted..-----";

        }


        data.close();

}


void index_sequential : :readi()

{

    class index rec;

    int i=1,n;


    cout<<"\n-----------Content of INDEX.DAT-----------------";
```

```
    index.open(index1,ios : :binary|ios : :in|ios : :nocreate);

    index.seekg(0,ios : :end);

    n=index.tellg()/sizeof(index);

    index.seekg(0,ios : :beg);


    for(i=1;i<=n;i++)

    {

        index.read((char*)&rec,sizeof(index));

        cout<<"\n"<<i<<rec.rollno<<" "<<rec.record_no;

    }

    getch();

}


void index_sequential : :insert(student rec1)

{

    student crec;


    int n,i,k;


    data.open(data1,ios : :binary|ios : :in|ios : :nocreate|ios : :out);

    rec1.status=0;

    data.seekg(0,ios : :end);

    n=data.tellg()/sizeof(student);


    if(n==0)

    {

        data.write((char*)&rec1,sizeof(student));

        data.close();
```

```
        return;
}


/*shift records till the point of insertion*/
i=n-1;
while(i>=0)
{
    data.seekg(i*sizeof(student),ios : :beg);
    data.read((char*)&crec,sizeof(student));

    if(crec.rollno>rec1.rollno)
    {
        data.seekp((i+1)*sizeof(student),ios : :beg);
        data.write((char*)&crec,sizeof(student));
    }
    else
    break;

    i--;
}
/*insert record at (i+1)th position*/
i++;

data.seekp(i*sizeof(student),ios : :beg);
data.write((char*)&rec1,sizeof(student));
data.close();
reindex();
}
```

```
int index_sequential : :Delete(int rollno)
{
    student crec;
    int i,recno,n;

    recno=search(rollno);
    if(recno>=0)
    {
        cout<<"\nRecord is found ="<<recno;
        data.open(data1,ios : :binary|ios : :in|ios : :nocreate|ios : :out);
        data.seekg(recno*sizeof(student),ios : :beg);
        data.read((char*)&crec,sizeof(student));
        crec.status=1;
        data.seekp(recno*sizeof(student),ios : :beg);
        data.write((char*)&crec,sizeof(student));
        data.close();
    }
    else
    {
        cout<<"\nRecord not found...";
        return 0;
    }
    reindex();
    return 1;

}
```

```
int index_sequential : :search(int rollno)
{
    class index indexes[50];
    student rec1;
    class index crec;
    int i,n,recno;

    index.open(index1,ios : :binary|ios : :in|ios : :nocreate);
    index.seekg(0,ios : :end);
    n=index.tellg()/sizeof(index);
    index.seekg(0,ios : :beg);
    index.read((char*)indexes,n*sizeof(index));
    index.close();

    if(n==0||rollno<indexes[0].rollno)
    return -1;

    for(i=1;i<n&&rollno>=indexes[i].rollno;i++)
    recno=indexes[i-1].record_no;

    data.open(data1,ios : :binary|ios : :in);
    data.seekg(recno*sizeof(student),ios : :beg);

    for(i=1;i<=5&&!data.eof();i++,recno++)
    {
        data.read((char*)&rec1,sizeof(student));
        if(rec1.rollno==rollno&&rec1.status==0)
        {
```

```
            data.close();

            return(recno);

        }

    }

    data.close();

    return(-1);


}


void index_sequential : :pack()

{

    fstream temp;

    student crec;

    int i,n;


    data.open(data1,ios : :binary|ios : :in);

    temp.open("temp.txt",ios : :out|ios : :trunc|ios : :binary);

    data.seekg(0,ios : :end);

    n=data.tellg()/sizeof(student);

    data.seekg(0,ios : :beg);


    for(i=0;i<n;i++)

    {

        data.read((char*)&crec,sizeof(student));

        if(crec.status==0)

        temp.write((char*)&crec,sizeof(student));

    }

    data.close();
```

```
        temp.close();

        temp.open("temp.txt",ios : :binary|ios : :in);
        data.open(data1,ios : :binary|ios : :out|ios : :trunc);
        temp.seekg(0,ios : :end);
        n=temp.tellg()/sizeof(student);
        temp.seekg(0,ios : :beg);

        for(i=0;i<n;i++)
        {
            temp.read((char*)&crec,sizeof(student));
            data.write((char*)&crec,sizeof(student));
        }
        data.close();
        temp.close();
        reindex();

}

void index_sequential : :update()
{
    int rollno,n,i;
    student crec;

    cout<<"\nEnter the rollno of the record to be updated ";
    cin>>rollno;

    cout<<"\nEnter a new record (roll no and name) ";
```

```
    cin>>crec.rollno>>crec.name;

    if(Delete(rollno))
    insert(crec);

    else
    {
        cout<<"\nRecord not found ";
        return;
    }

    reindex();
}

void index_sequential : :reindex()
{
    int rollno,n,i;
    student crec;

    class index rec1;

    index.open(index1,ios : :binary|ios : :out|ios : :trunc);
    data.open(data1,ios : :binary|ios : :in);
    data.seekg(0,ios : :end);

    n=data.tellg()/sizeof(student);
```

```
data.seekg(0,ios : :beg);


for(i=0;i<n;i=i+5)
{
    data.seekg(i*sizeof(student),ios : :beg);
    data.read((char*)&crec,sizeof(student));
    rec1.rollno=crec.rollno;
    rec1.record_no=i;
    index.write((char*)&rec1,sizeof(index));
}
data.close();
index.close();
}
```

6.8 DIFFERENCE BETWEEN SEQUENTIAL FILE ORGANIZATION AND DIRECT ACCESS FILE

Sr. No.	Sequential File Organization	Direct Access File
1.	A sequential file access one record at a time, from first to last, in order.	A direct file access the records in any order by record number.
2.	Each record can be of varying length.	Each record must be of identical length.
3.	A sequential file might look like this, with records separated by commans bear, skunk, moose, fish, alligator.	A direct file with same data would look this bear_skunk_moose_fish_alligator.
4.	Sequential file access is similar to the tape drives where the files are accessed in a sequential manner.	Random access is similar to the one in hard disk and optical drives.
5.	No overhead of hash function.	Hash function needs to be calculated for direct access.

6.9 DIFFERENCE BETWEEN SEQUENTIAL FILE AND INDEX SEQUENTIAL FILE

S. No.	Sequential File	Index Sequential File
1.	It can be searched effectively on ordering key.	Search for a record on the basis of some other attribute.
2.	It usually takes more storage space.	An index file usually requires less storage space.
3.	Require movement of records, while inserting.	Records can be added at the end of the main file.
4.	Updation of sequential file requires more block access.	Upadation of index file requires fewer block accesses.
5.	When all records are to be processed sequential files are suitable.	When random records are to be accessed index sequential files are used.
6.	Slower access.	Faster access.

6.10 INDEXING AND HASHING COMPARISON

Hashing is often considered as a fastest method for accessing records. The speed of operation depends on number of block access.

In hashed files collision is a major problem.

If the number of records exceeds in number, the length of the linked list constituting the bucket will also increase. This will slow down the operation speed in hashed files.

Same thing can also be happen in case of indexed files as the number of records gets exceed.

Initial storage requirement for hashed file is very high. Indexing has no such initial requirement, as file grows blocks are acquired.

Batch processing of queries in database application is extremely difficult in hashed files.

Compared to hashed files indexed files or sequential files perform better in batch processing of queries.

6.11 LINKED ORGANIZATION OF A FILE

Logical sequence of records is different from physical sequence.

Next logical record is obtained by following a link from the present record. (Like a linked list)

Linking of records with ascending value of primary key makes insertion and deletion easier.

When there is no index available it becomes difficult to search a record of the given primary key. As index is unavailable the only method one can use for searching is a linear search.

To facilitate searching on the primary key as well as secondary key it is necessary to maintain several indexes, one for each key.

We can set up indexes for each key. Each index entry contains key values pointer to list and the length of the associated list.

6.11.1 Multi-List Files

In a multi-lists file organization, indexes are defined on the multiple fields and multiple fields are also used to search the record. It is also called as multi-index linked file organization. A linked file organization is a logical organization where physical ordering of records is not of any concern. In this, the series of records is connected by the links that verify the next record in series. Linking of records can be unordered. If we use unordered linking then the cost of searching is more. So for the betterment of deletion and insertion algorithms, linking of records should be done in increasing order. Consider following example where linking is unordered.

Table 6.1 : Sample Data for Employee File

Record Number	Empid	Name	Job	Qualification	City	Salary
A	800	Suraj	Software Engineer	B.E.	New Delhi	15,000/-
B	500	Abhi	Software Manager	B. Tech.	New Delhi	18,000/-
C	900	Ashish	Software Manager	M.E	Mumbai	16,000/-
D	700	Sayali	Software Engineer	B. Tech.	Mumbai	12,000/-
E	600	Jueeli	Software Manager	MCA	Mumbai	13,000/-

For the above employee file, the linked order of records should be defined as B (500), E (600), D (700), A (800), C (900). Though, as the file size will grow the search performance of the file would decreased. Please note that in this file the records are in the logical series and tied together using links and not physical placement.

Coral Rings :

The coral ring structure is an adaptation of the doubly linked multilist structure. Coral ring is a linked file organization in which circular doubly linked list is maintained for linking multiple records together. Coral ring contains forward circular list and backward circular list.

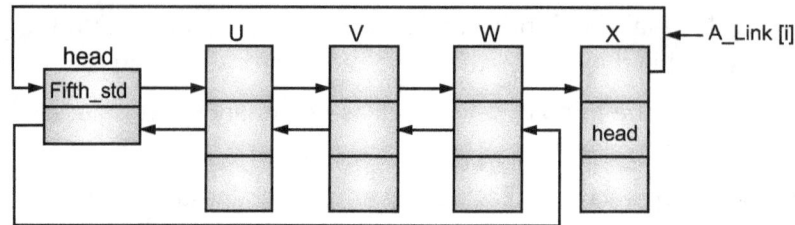

The forward circular list contains nodes U, V, W, X.
The reverse circular list contains nodes head W, V, U.

Fig. 6.6 : Coral ring

6.12 INVERTED FILE ORGANIZATION   [Dec. 05, 09, 10, May 07]

These files are similar to multilists. In this file only index structure is important. Record can be stored in any way.

Maintenance of index is complex than that of multilist.

Inverted files may also result in space saving compared with other file structures when record retrieval does not require retrieval of key fields. In this case key fields may be deleted from the records. In the case of multilist structures, this deletion of key fields is possible only with significant loss in system retrieval performance.

Insertion and deletion of records requires only the ability to insert and delete within indexes.

E # index

510	
620	
750	
800	
950	

Index file

Occupation index

Analyst	B, C
Programmer	A, D, E

Sex index

Female	B, C, D
Male	A, E

9,000	E
10,000	A
12,000	C, D
15,000	B

Fig. 6.7 : Indexes for fully inverted file

6.13 CELLULAR PARTITIONS

It is used in order to reduce file search times, where storage media may be divided into cells.

A cell may be an entire disk pack or it may simply be a cylinder.

Lists are localized to lie within a cell.

All records in the same cell may be accessed without moving the read/write heads.

In case if cell is a disk pack then using cellular partitions it is possible to search different cells in parallel.

6.14 EXTERNAL SORTING

External sorting is a type of sorting technique which is applied when the data to be sorted is too big to reside in primary memory.

Characteristics of External Sorting

- During the sort, the data will be stored in the external memory (tape, disk etc).
- The cost of accessing data is greater than comparison costs.
- There can be constraint on accessing files. For example, if tape is used, items must be accessed sequentially.

6.14.1 Consequential Processing

Consequential processing is a coordinated processing done on two or more sequential files to produce single output file. The output may result in merging or union, matching or intersection or combination of matching and merging.

6.14.2 Matching Names in Two Lists

Given two lists, we want to output the common names from the lists shown below. This operation can be called as match or intersection.

Let Item (1) be the current item from list 1 and Item (2) be the current item from list 2.

- If Item (1) < Item (2), get the next item from list 1.
- If Item (1) > Item (2), get the next item from list 2.
- If Item (1) = Item (2), output the item and get the next items from the two lists.

Pseudo Code for Matching :

```
int Match( char *L1, char *L2, char *Output)
{
int Remain;   // true if items remaining in both the lists
// Initialize both the lists.
initL1 (1, L1);      initL2 (1, L2);
Remain= getL1nextItem (1) && getL2nextItem (2);
While (Remain) // loop until no item remain in both the lists.
{
If (item (1) < item (2))
Remain= getL1nextItem (1);
Else if (item (1) == item (2)) //items matched
```

```
{
OutputItem (1);
Remain= getL1nextItem (1) && getL2nextItem (2);
}
Else Remain= getL2nextItem (2);
}
return 1;
}
```

Example :

Input Lists	
List 1	**List 2**
Abhijeet	Abhijeet
Amruta	Prasad
Suraj	Suraj
Satyam	Satyam
Kalpesh	Kalpesh
Mayur	Rahul

Output List
Abhijeet
Suraj
Satyam
Kalpesh

6.14.3 Merging Two Lists

Merging is the combining of two lists to produce single merged list. The difference between matching and merging is that in merging we have to read completely through each of the lists. Pseudo code for merging two lists without duplicate values :

```
int Match( char *L1, char *L2, char *Output)
{
int Remain1 , Remain2;   // true if items remaining in the list.
```

```
// Initialize both the lists and output list.
initL1 (1, L1);
 initL2 (1, L2);
InitOutput (Output);

Remain1= getL1nextItem (1);
Remain2= getL2nextItem (2);

While (Remain1 || Remain2) // if any of the list has items remaining
{
if (item (1) < item (2))
{
OutputItem (1);
Remain= getL1nextItem (1);
}
else if (item (1) == item (2))
{
OutputItem (1);
Remain1= getL1nextItem (1);
Remain2= getL2nextItem (2);
}
else
{
OutputItem (2);
Remain= getL2nextItem (2);
}
}
return 1;
}
```

Example :

Input Lists	
List 1	**List 2**
Abhijeet	Abhijeet
Amruta	Prasad
Suraj	Suraj
Satyam	Satyam
Kalpesh	Kalpesh
Mayur	Rahul

Output List
Abhijeet
Amruta
Prasad
Suraj
Satyam
Kalpesh
Mayur
Rahul

6.14.4 Multiway Merging- a K Way Merge Algorithm

Two list's Merge and Match functions are limited for two lists. To merge more than two lists, an algorithm is developed named as a K-way merge algorithm. Here, we want to merge K inputs and generate a single sequentially ordered output list.

Function for a K-way merge algorithm :

Ascending order by name : (makes no allowances for duplicates or out-of-sequence records)

```
while (more_names)
out_name = min (name1, name2, name3, ... namek )
write (outfile, out_name)
if (name1 == out_name) then
   read( file1, name1 )
if (name2 == out_name) then
```

```
  read( file2, name2 )
if (name3 == out_name) then
  read( file3, name3 )
.

.

.

if (namek == out_name) then
   read( filek, namek )
endwhile
```

Example :

Input :

A = 3, B = 4

array [][] = { {1, 3, 5, 7},
                {2, 4, 6, 8},
                {0, 9, 10, 11}} ;

Output :

0 1 2 3 4 5 6 7 8 9 10 11

SUMMARY

- In indexed sequential files, an index is added to a sequential file to provide random access.

- A direct access file accesses the records in any order, by record number.

- In sequential file, each record can be of varying length but in direct access file, each record must be of identical length.

- Index sequential file takes less storage space than sequential file.

- Index sequential file has faster access than sequential file.

- Multi list files are also called as multi- index linked file organization.

- A linked file organization is a logical organization where physical ordering of records is not of any concern.

- In inverted file organization, records can be stored in any way but the index is important.

- External sorting is a type of sorting technique which is applied when the data to be sorted is too big to reside in primary memory.

- Consequential file is a coordinated processing done on two or more sequential files to produce single output file.

EXERCISE

1. Give any three points of comparison between Text files and Binary files.

2. What are indices? What are different characteristics of the index file organization?

3. (i) What is a sequential file ?

   (ii) Give any two advantages of sequential files over unordered files.

   (iii) Explain any-three operations on sequential files in brief?

4. What are the differences between sequential and index sequential files?

5. Write brief notes on :

   (i) Linked organization of a file.

   (ii) Inverted file organization.

6. Explain Primitive operations of direct access file.

7. Explain Primitive operations of sequential file organization.

8. Explain Multi list files & coral rings.

9. Explain cellular partitions.

10. What is external sort? Write pseudo code for merging two lists.

11. Explain Multiway merging.

12. Explain K- way merge algorithm.

End Sem. Theory Examination

Time : 2 Hours   **Max. Marks : 50**

Instructions to the candidates :

(i) Answer four questions.

(ii) Neat diagrams must be drawn wherever necessary.

(iii) Figures to the right indicate full marks.

(iv) Assume suitable data if necessary.

1. **(a)** Construct Binary tree if following traversals are given.   **[5]**

    Inorder : D, F, E, G, A, H, I, C

    Postorder : D, F, G, E, B, I, H, C, A

   (b) What is minimum spanning tree? Find minimum spanning tree of the following graph using Kruskal's algorithm.   **[5]**

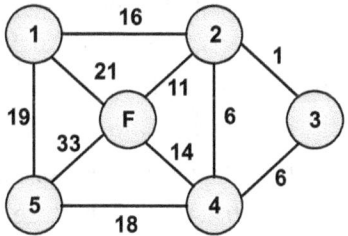

Fig. 1 : Graph

OR

2. **(a)** Write a recursive function to count and print leaf nodes of binary tree.   **[5]**

   (b) Define DFS and BFS for graph. Show DFS and BFS for the graph given below: **[5]**

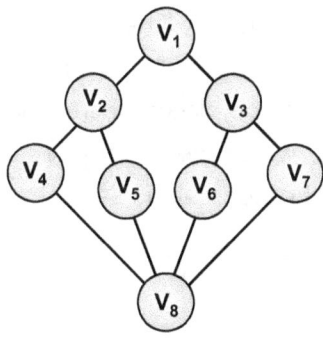

Fig. 2

3. **(a)** The keys 12, 18, 13, 2, 3, 23, 5 and 15 are inserted into an initially empty hash table of length 10 using open addressing with hash function $h(k) = k \bmod 10$ and linear probing. What is the resultant hash table?

Index	Value
0	
1	
2	2
3	23
4	
5	15
6	
7	
8	18
9	

Index	Value
0	
1	
2	12
3	13
4	
5	5
6	
7	
8	18
9	

Index	Value
0	
1	
2	12
3	13
4	2
5	3
6	23
7	5
8	18
9	15

Index	Value
0	
1	
2	12, 2
3	13, 3, 23
4	
5	5, 15
6	
7	
8	18
9	

(b) Add a SEARCH () function to the sample algorithm in order to enable the user to search for a certain key in the constructed optimal binary search tree. If the key is found, increase its corresponding frequency 'p'; otherwise, if the search ends unsuccessfully, increase the corresponding 'q' value. Note that after the search, certain modifications may appear in the tree. Compute the matrices W, C and R again, in order to make sure the structure of the tree is correct. **[5]**

OR

4. (a) Explain various techniques of Open Hashing. **[5]**

(b) Suppose that we are designing a program to simulate the storage and search in a dictionary. Words appear with different frequencies, however, and it may be the case that a frequently used word such as "the" appears far from the root while a rarely used word such as "conscientiousness" appears near the root. We want words that occur frequently in the text to be placed nearer to the root. Moreover, there may be words in the dictionary for which there is no definition. Organize an optimal binary search tree that simulates the storage and search of words in a dictionary. **[5]**

5. (a) Define top down multi way search tree. Create it using following elements of order 5:

20 65 72 15 90 85 10 70

5 77 87 17 88 11 75 30 **[5]**

(b) Insert keys 382, 518, 508 in the following B-tree of order 5.

Also delete the key 493 **[5]**

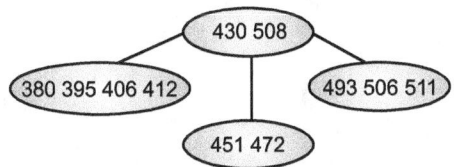

Fig. 3

(c) Explain Heap Sort technique with suitable example.   **[5]**

OR

6. **(a)** Insert the keys 43, 120, 58, 70 in the following B-tree of order 5.   **[5]**

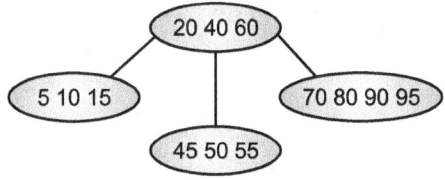

Fig. 4

(b) What do mean by thread in binary search tree? Also state the significance of the same and draw the threads for the following tree   **[5]**

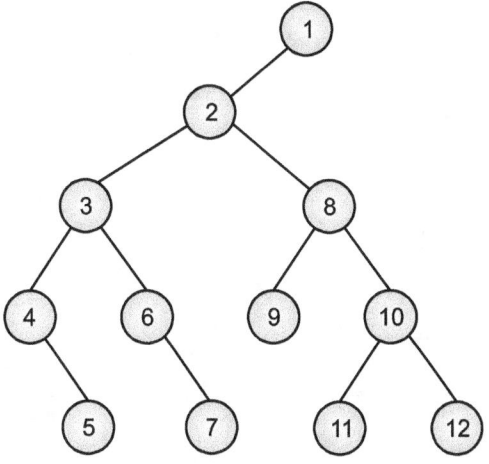

Fig. 5

(c) Explain various techniques for indexing with suitable example.   **[5]**

7. **(a)** Explain different file organization in brief   **[5]**

(b) Explain the concept of index sequential file along with its structure   **[5]**

(c) Write short note on following   **[5]**

1. Coral rings

2. Inverted files

3. Cellular Partitions

OR

8. **(a)** Give difference between sequential and random access file structure **[5]**

   (b) Explain the concept of direct access file and also state its primitive operations **[5]**

   (c) What do you mean by multi list files? Explain with suitable example. **[5]**